"Nash—"

He shushed her with a finger over her lips. "You have the most beautiful mouth I've ever seen on a woman. When I'm alone in this room with you, and the rest of the world is some distant nightmare outside that door, all I can think about is that kiss we shared yesterday."

"You were delirious with fever. You probably aren't remembering it accurately."

At last those firm lips crooked up with a dangerous grin. "How's my temperature now, Nurse Rodriguez?"

"Normal. Your fever hasn't come back." Was that hushed quiver of anticipation really coming from her throat?

Nash brushed the calloused pad of his thumb across her bottom lip, sparking a dozen different nerve endings. "My eyes are focused? My thoughts are sane? No delusions?"

Her mouth was parched with anticipation. "As far as I can tell, you're...healthy."

"Good. I just wanted to make sure we're clear on this." Then he leaned in, replacing his thumb with his mouth.

CROSSFIRE
CHRISTMAS

BY
JULIE MILLER

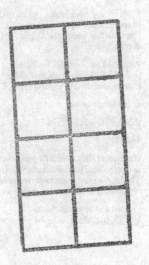

Published in Great Britain 2014
by Mills & Boon, an imprint of Harlequin (UK) Limited,
Eton House, 18-24 Paradise Road, Richmond, Surrey, TW9 1SR

© 2014 Julie Miller

ISBN: 978-0-263-91376-7

46-1114

Printed and bound in Spain
by CPI, Barcelona

USA TODAY bestselling author **Julie Miller** attributes her passion for writing romance to all those books she read growing up. When shyness and asthma kept her from becoming the action-adventure heroine she longed to be, Julie created stories in her head to keep herself entertained. Encouragement from her family to write down the feelings and ideas she couldn't express became a love for the written word. She gets continued support from her fellow members of the Prairieland Romance Writers, where this teacher serves as the resident "grammar goddess." Inspired by the likes of Agatha Christie and Encyclopedia Brown, Julie believes the only thing better than a good mystery is a good romance.

Born and raised in Missouri, this award-winning author now lives in Nebraska with her husband, son and an assortment of spoiled pets. To contact Julie or to learn more about her books, write to PO Box 5162, Grand Island, NE 68802-5162, USA or check out her website and monthly newsletter at www.juliemiller.org.

For the cast and crew of Grand Island Little Theater's production of *Twelve Angry Men*.

I don't think I've ever been prouder of a show I've directed.

With particular thanks to Jeremy Johnson and Liz Boyle for the title idea for this book!

Chapter One

"You're a dead man, Nash!"

DEA agent Charlie Nash slammed his back against the metal shelves that had blocked the spray of bullets and saved his life. One step slower and he'd be bleeding out on the floor like the young man lying in the open aisle beside Thug One.

"Kid?" He wasn't really expecting a response.

He didn't get one. Check one more black mark in the loss column of his soul.

Yet there was no time for guilt or regret or even grief. He'd spotted the trap the moment he'd pulled into the parking garage and would have backed out then, evading the threat that had trailed him seven hundred miles from Texas to Kansas City, Missouri. But with the rookie handler climbing out of his car without a clue, Nash had been left with no choice but to stay put and warn the young agent back into his vehicle.

Revealing himself to the three goons lying in wait hadn't made a damn bit of difference.

The kid was still dead.

And he was still the Graciela cartel's most wanted man.

The cop who'd put together the plan to stop them.

Nash pulled a bandanna from the back pocket of his

jeans and tied it around his left thigh, trying to slow down the blood seeping from the wound there. As he tightened the makeshift bandage, he listened to the clomp of running feet, pinpointing the locations of the two remaining assailants as they tried to flank him. He ignored the throbbing burn in his leg and fought to calm his labored breathing so the clouds of stress and exertion in the open warehouse's wintry air wouldn't give his position away. He figured he had about two minutes—three if he was lucky—to find a way out of this mess.

The desk agent who'd met him in this run-down auto-parts warehouse near the Missouri River to try to help him reestablish his undercover persona hadn't been so lucky. He'd wager most of the car parts in this place weren't legal, and that Tommy Delvecchio had never been in the middle of a real firefight before. Stupid kid must not have been wearing his flak vest, judging by the size of that puddle of blood pooling beneath him.

If Delvecchio had been one of Nash's operatives, he'd have trained him better than that. Hell. If he'd been one of Nash's undercover operatives, he'd probably still be dead. Just like the other embedded agents whose covers had been blown.

Glancing over at the still figure crumpled on the floor between storage racks, Nash felt his gut twist with anger and remorse. "Damn it, Tommy. Told you I didn't need backup." All he'd asked for was cash and a new ID to be sent to a PO box. He hadn't needed a personal delivery. He hadn't wanted the kid to come all the way to K.C. "You should have stayed at the office."

You can't risk hiding out for more than forty-eight hours, boss. And you said you can't trust anyone in the field. You need someone who isn't part of the Graciela-Vargas turf war to do this for you. Nash could imagine

Agent Delvecchio rising to attention beside his computer, eager to get on the next flight to KCI and prove himself. *I'm not a field agent. They don't know me. I can help.*

Smart kid. Good logic. Still dead. Just like Torres and Richter back in Harlingen and Houston. Nash's team was another man down, he had no ID on the traitor who'd marked them as cops, and he was on his own in this nightmare.

Pushing aside the distracting emotions that could get him killed, too, Nash quickly evaluated his options. The stinging smell of sulfur in the air told him the three shooters—down to two now—had used up a lot of their bullets coming after him and Delvecchio. But that didn't give him the advantage it should have.

He kicked out the magazine from his Smith & Wesson and checked his own ammo supply before reloading the clip. Three bullets left. The rest of the ammunition and backup weaponry he needed were in the go bag lying on the floor beside Delvecchio. The only chance of a get-away was his truck, parked a good thirty yards from his position. And as far as he could tell, there were still two of Berto Graciela's thugs in the warehouse with him.

Unless these were Santiago Vargas's men. Vargas had been loyal to Berto's older brother, Diego. Ever since Diego's death two years earlier, the two had been vying for power within the organization. What did a few cops mean to either of them? Just collateral damage in a war to control a drug-trafficking pipeline that funneled cocaine, pot and an assortment of designer concoctions across the border—or straight into the U.S. at import traffic hubs like Houston, K.C. and Chicago.

But Nash's team had been making progress. They'd fed the DEA precious intel, helping the agency shut down some key distribution centers. Now Nash and his men were dying.

How had they found him here in Kansas City? Who had found him? He was over ten hours away from his last encounter with Graciela's men in Houston. Had they followed the kid? If so, how had they connected computer geek Thomas Delvecchio to him? Was there a hidden tracking device on his Ford F-250 he'd missed? Unlikely. He'd gone over the thing with a fine-tooth comb at a truck stop in Tulsa, Oklahoma, the last time he'd checked in with his captain in the Houston office and made the arrangements with Delvecchio.

There had to be a leak somewhere in the system. One of the DEA's confidential informants wasn't keeping things so confidential. Torres or Richter had let something slip in the wrong place at the wrong time. Or worst-case scenario? One of Graciela's or Vargas's men had infiltrated the Houston office and Nash's men were at the mercy of a double agent.

That had to be the answer. A team didn't lose three agents in a week unless someone was leaking inside information.

"You're outnumbered, Señor Nash!" one of the thugs taunted, his accent rolling his *R*s and making the gibe sound like a joke instead of a promise of death. "You are the mouse and we are the *gatos*. When you come out of your hole, we'll be waiting to pounce."

So at least one man had taken up position near the open garage door.

Time to stop speculating about who had betrayed him and deal with the threat at hand. Nash craned his neck to peer through a stack of sports car bumpers to gauge the distance and amount of open ground he'd have to cover before reaching his truck.

On a good day, he could do it in a matter of seconds. But this was far from a good day. And he didn't have a location on the second shooter.

Time to go old school.

After slipping off the black felt Stetson that the years had shaped so perfectly to his head, he kissed the crown and set it on the shelf beside him, nudging it into clear view near the end of the row. Then he pushed to his feet and pulled down the pile of bumpers, creating a noisy diversion while he ducked into the next aisle and ran for his truck.

Boom. His hat flew off the shelf, giving him a twenty on Thug Three. The angle of that last shot told Nash the man was running parallel through the stacks with him.

Well, *running* was a relative term. Thug Three was an overweight man who moved with the grace of a lumbering buffalo, while Nash was hobbled by the wound on his leg.

But Nash was still faster.

Sorry, kid. I owe you one. He scooped up the heavy nylon go bag from the floor beside Delvecchio and limped toward the open garage area with a galloping gait. Twenty yards. Fifteen. He could feel the blood running down his leg and filling his left boot. Thank God the shot hadn't taken out his knee or ankle.

Ten yards.

The damp wind and flakes of blowing snow pelted his face as he broke into the open garage area.

Ah, hell.

Thug Two stepped out from behind a rolling toolbox and shot at him. Either the guy had piss-poor aim or Nash was lurching on his gimpy leg more than he thought. One bullet smacked into the side of the truck bed, punching a hole through the black metal. The second shot went wide and shattered the driver's-side window.

Nash raised his gun and squeezed the trigger.

Thug Two didn't get off a third shot.

Nash swore when Thug Three stumbled out from shelves near the dead body by the garage door. Couldn't a guy catch a break? Nash swept the broken glass off his seat, tossed the bag into the truck and climbed in behind the wheel. The big man silhouetted against the sunny glare of the snow outside was panting hard. But he wasn't relying on perfect aim to stop Nash. He pulled out a second handgun and fired both in a smoky barrage of sparks and firepower.

Nash started the engine and stuck his left hand out the broken window. Bracing his wrist on the mirror to steady his aim, he pulled the trigger. With a flurry of Spanish curses, Thug Three dropped one of his weapons and shook his fingers. Lucky shot. Nash must have hit the gun and stung his hand.

But two shots and he was done. No way could he reach his bag on the floorboards across the truck and reload in time. Dropping the gun into his lap, Nash shifted the truck into Drive. He'd only irritated Thug Three. The big man clasped both hands around his remaining weapon and fired.

Nash stomped on the accelerator. A bullet smacked the windshield on the passenger side, splintering the glass into a web of cracks. The wheels spun until they found traction on the smooth concrete. A second bullet took out his side mirror. The truck lurched forward and barreled toward the exit. A third bullet found the open window and ripped through his left shoulder, spinning downward through the muscle, oblivious to the protective vest he wore.

The explosion of pain in his shoulder and back was instant and intense. Damn lucky shot robbed him of breath and jerked his grip on the wheel, sending the truck into a sideways skid. Squeezing his elbow to his side, Nash collapsed into the steering wheel, hugging his right arm around it—regaining control of the truck and making himself a smaller target. He was close enough to see the yellowed teeth of Thug Three's smile as the man steadied the gun and took aim at Nash's head.

But what good ol' Texas boy didn't know how to play chicken?

"For Tommy," Nash wheezed, stomping on the accelerator. Before Thug Three could pull off the kill shot or dive out of the way, Nash plowed into him.

With a sickening double jolt, the truck bounced over the body and burst into the sunshine of the clear December afternoon. Nash raced away from the warehouse, clipping a couple of junker cars and jumping the curb out of the back alley before pulling onto the street.

"Brilliant plan, Nash," he muttered through gritted teeth as he slowed to merge with a line of cars. His entire left side was on fire and the pain doubled every time he tried to catch a deep breath. No way to tell yet if the bullet had gone through or had clipped a lung and was bouncing around inside him. But he knew from the light-headed haze he had to shake off that he was losing a lot of blood. Delvecchio was dead and, like him, any hope that Nash had escaped to Kansas City undetected had literally been shot to hell. He was no closer to finding out the identity of the traitor who had exposed his men as undercover cops and marked them, and now him, for death.

Worse, he was on his own. He'd better report in to Captain Puente and tell him he was going off the grid until further notice. No more help from the remnants of his team. No more deaths on his conscience. He wasn't putting any more of his people in the line of fire until he could figure this thing out.

Nash slowed to a stop at a traffic light and unsnapped the cell phone on his belt. After wiping away the clammy sweat that dotted his forehead, he searched the screen for Jesse Puente's office line, punched it in and tucked the phone between his ear and shoulder so he could twist around and untie the blood-soaked bandanna on his thigh.

The light turned green before the number picked up.

"Captain?" Nash dropped the bandanna in his lap and gripped the wheel again as he pressed on the accelerator. The responding silence raised every suspicious hackle Nash possessed. Puente liked the sound of his own voice too much for him not to start talking. "Who's this?"

"Agent Cruz Moreno, Drug Enforcement Agency, Houston office." Like Nash, the officer spoke with a hint of suspicion coloring his tone. "Who is this? How did you get this number?"

A quick grunt of relief clouded the cold air leaching in through the truck's shattered window. Cruz Moreno was the newest man Puente had recruited. He'd transferred over from the San Antonio office and was being trained to replace the slain officers working in the Graciela organization. Thank God Nash had convinced Captain Puente to hold off sending Moreno into the field. Although not as green as Tommy had been, he wasn't up to speed yet on the intricacies of their long-term investigation. "This is Nash. Put the captain on."

"Puente isn't here right now." Urgency replaced the caution in Moreno's tone. "Where are you, man? The captain booked it out of here as soon as we lost contact with Delvecchio's phone. Tommy missed his call-in time. Did you two meet up?"

Nash pulsed his grip on the wheel, his body feeling hot and chilled at the same time. And it wasn't just his injuries messing with his ability to focus right now. "Tommy's dead."

"Dead? I knew that kid couldn't—" Moreno's bilingual curses pretty much summed up the grief and rage Nash felt. "I'm calling Puente on the other line. You need backup? An extraction?"

"No. I need to disappear. I need time to find this guy before he finds me. I'm gonna put a stop to this." Nash released the steering wheel at the next stop and wadded up the bandanna to stuff it beneath his vest to stanch the wound. Pain knifed through him at the added pressure and he swore. "Tell Puente he can claim Tommy's body in Kansas City."

"Is that where you are?"

The agonizing jolt cleared his head for a split second, and Nash got the feeling he'd already said too much. Someone had leaked his name, along with Torres's, Richter's and Delvecchio's, to Graciela's or Vargas's men. That someone could be listening in on the line right now. And even though Cruz wore the same badge Nash did, trusting anyone—even a fellow agent—just wasn't going to happen. "Not anymore, Moreno. I'm halfway to Chicago," Nash lied, wondering how far away he could get before another thug or the hole in his chest stopped him. "I'll call again when it's safe. Until then, I'm going off the grid."

"What about backup?"

No. Solo was the only way to go until he knew who was killing his team. "If I'm as good at this job as I hope I am, I won't need it."

Bold words for a man whose left hand was going numb

inside his glove and whose sheer will was keeping him upright.

"We've got no idea who's behind this yet, so watch your back, Nash."

"You, too."

He could hear Captain Puente's voice in the background, grousing on the other line as Moreno gave him a brief sit rep. Then Cruz was back, no doubt relaying a message. "Is this phone clean?"

"What?"

"Are you using the burner phone Tommy brought you? If Graciela's men could track Tommy, then chances are they can locate you, too."

Nash cursed. *Rookie mistake.* "I'm done."

"Wait. The captain wants to know where in Chicago—?"

But Nash had already disconnected the call. He raised his aching leg to guide the wheel on the straight stretch of road, freeing his good hand to turn off the phone and raise it to his teeth to pry open the back. He pulled out the battery and GPS chip and spit them out on the seat beside him, going dark on any kind of satellite trace. Unfortunately, though, that meant he had no means of communication on him, either, until he could find a spot to stop where a bleeding man in a broken truck wouldn't draw attention, and he could unpack the new phone in his go bag.

And since he was clearly off his game, Nash had driven into the heart of downtown instead of catching one of the highways and had the dumb luck to be caught in the heart of rush-hour traffic. Until he could get his bearings, until he could think this whole mess through and decide where he needed to go, he'd just keep driving.

He'd come to K.C. to hook up with an old friend, Jake

Lonergan, a former agent who'd gotten out of the business. He'd hoped for a spare bed or sofa to bunk on for a night or two until he could make some inquiries and form a new plan of action. But Jake had a family now, complete with a wife and little girl, and another baby on the way. Nash seriously doubted his old friend would appreciate him bringing a drug war to his front doorstep.

He'd met a couple of guys at KCPD a little over a year ago, working on another case. But they weren't the kind of buddies a desperate man called on for off-the-record help. He'd trusted every man on his team—would have called Torres or Richter in a heartbeat. But now they were gone. Besides, he didn't want to be responsible for the deaths of any more cops. Whether the Graciela-Vargas war had extended its reach to Kansas City or they'd come here just for him, he could imagine they wouldn't take too kindly to interference from anyone else who wore a badge.

Nash slowed his truck and followed the flow of traffic through a fancy shopping district decorated with more lights than he could count and window displays for the upcoming holiday. He hadn't even thought about Christmas. Besides the fact his parents were gone and he had no siblings and was married to his work, he'd been too busy trying to stop the drugs and save his team these past few months. Celebrating the holidays was for men with families and kids who still believed in the kind of magic and hope he'd stopped believing in long ago.

Right now he just had to live long enough to ID a traitor and exact a little revenge on the man who'd sentenced his agent brothers to death. Legally, if he could. But a bullet to the head would be justice enough if he couldn't find any other way to finish this.

Maybe he'd see Christmas next week. If he was lucky,

he'd see New Year's. He glanced down at the blood seeping through the hole in his leather coat.

Or maybe, if he didn't clear his head and think of some options fast, he wouldn't even live to see tomorrow.

"FINALLY. HERE'S THE horse I've been looking for."

Teresa Rodriguez watched Laila Alvarez sag into her wheelchair, dropping the scissors and magazine she held into her lap. Despite the little girl's brave smile and never-ending chatter, Teresa could tell that thirty minutes of making ornaments in the playroom of the Truman Medical Center's children's wing had taxed the eight-year-old's energy.

Knowing her patients better than they sometimes knew themselves, Teresa slipped her hand over the glue stick on the table and dropped it into the pocket of her cartoon-print scrub jacket before Laila noticed. She nodded toward the image of a team of brown-and-white horses. "Those are Clydesdales. They grow big and strong and pull heavy wagons. They'll be a nice addition to your stable."

"Are they bigger than you?"

At five foot three, Teresa found that a lot of things, except her patients, were taller than her. "Bigger than you and me both." She leaned in with a smile and gently took the magazine and scissors from her young friend. "How about I set the Clydesdale aside, and we can cut him out and put him on a new ornament tomorrow."

Laila closed her fingers in a halfhearted grab. "But I want to finish decorating the tree." She gazed longingly over at the Christmas tree in front of the bank of windows. An Appaloosa, a buckskin, a pinto, a palomino and a Lipizzaner stallion already hung from yarn bows in the branches, along with ornaments other children had made. "And I want one to hang in my room."

"I said we could work until we ran out of supplies, remember?" Teresa gestured to the tabletop. "We're out of glue. I'll have to get some more on my way home. But we'll finish them later. I promise."

Despite the wistful expression in her cocoa-brown eyes, Laila nodded. She moved her small fingers to the picture of a barn and hay bales that she'd already glued to a piece of cardboard for Teresa to cut out and string a loop of yarn through. "I need a cowboy to watch the horses for me when I'm not here."

"After I get the glue, I'll go by a bookstore and find a magazine with lots of cowboys in it to bring to the hospital."

"You're the best nurse ever, Teresa," Laila gushed on little more than a whisper.

Teresa smoothed her hand over the knit cap that covered the girl's bald head. "You're the best patient, sweetie." With a quick glance at her watch, Teresa rose and turned Laila's chair toward the hallway. "Come on. Let's get you back to your room. It's time for your medication, and I think maybe you can use a nap."

"But I—"

"You want to be fresh and smiling when your mom and dad come in after work, don't you?"

Laila nodded. "Can we show them the ornaments I hung up?"

"Absolutely." Teresa parked her friend at the central desk to chat with an aide and a receptionist while she went into the dispensary and unlocked the prescribed medication. Then she wheeled her patient through the wide door to her room and locked the chair beside the bed before helping the determined girl stand and climb beneath the covers herself.

Teresa handed Laila the stuffed horse from her bedside table and the little girl hugged the well-loved toy to her chest while she chewed her tablets. After giving her charge a sip of water and tucking her in, Teresa checked the girl's vitals and recorded the details and medication on her computer tablet. Laila was asleep before she was done.

"Oh, sweetie." With a smile that was part admiration and part heartache, Teresa caught her long ponytail behind her neck and leaned over to kiss the girl's pale cheek. Then she closed the blinds, unlocked the wheelchair and headed back into the hallway.

Returning to the playroom, Teresa quickly cleaned up their mess and pulled over an ottoman to set Laila's artwork safely out of the way on the top shelf of the supply cabinet. As she climbed down to return the glue stick to a lower shelf, she made a mental list of other craft supplies they were running low on that she could pick up to keep the children who visited siblings or were patients here entertained. She suspected that Laila and a few of the other long-term care patients would be here over Christmas next week. Maybe she'd add some small gifts for them to her shopping list, too. Plan a party. Bring decorations from home to add more holiday color to their sterile environment. She had a couple of days off she could spend shopping, decorating and wrapping gifts. She glanced toward the waning sun and white flakes floating past the windows and grinned. If she cleared it with the doctors, maybe she could even bring the ingredients to help the children make snow ice cream.

No one should have to be alone on Christmas Day, denied the family and fun of the blessed celebration. No one should have to be sick or injured and in the hospital, either.

Humming a tune at the plan that was coming together in her head, Teresa locked things up and headed back to the nurse's station to update her end-of-day reports. Although it had nothing to do with physical care, putting together a holiday party for the patients in the children's wing would do wonders to raise their spirits. That was probably why she'd become a nurse instead of the artist she'd originally intended to be in college. Teresa was hardwired to help anyone in need. She needed to make a difference in other people's lives.

Even if all she could do was make a little girl with a brain tumor forget her surgeries for a few minutes and bring a smile to her face at Christmastime, she was going to do it.

"There you are."

Teresa looked up from her laptop to see a petite woman with dark brown hair and cheekbones that matched her own waddling up to the counter.

"Emilia." She quickly stood to greet her oldest sister. The white coat and shadows beneath her eyes told Teresa that Dr. Emilia Rodriguez-Grant had just finished a long shift in the E.R.—if she wasn't still on duty. "What brings you to the third floor?"

"Have you looked out the windows?" Emilia pointed to the bank of glass in the playroom before bringing her hands back to rub at her pregnant belly and the small of her back. "We're supposed to get three to five more inches of snow on top of what's already on the ground tonight."

Here we go again.

Teresa inhaled a steadying breath but couldn't keep

the sarcasm out of her voice. "It's December in Missouri? Snow happens."

"Don't get smart with me." Emilia tugged a lock of her recently bobbed hair behind her ear, practically clucking like a mother hen. "It'll be dark soon. But the sun was bright enough today to melt some of the snow. You know when the temperatures drop, it will refreeze into ice. Driving will be very dangerous."

Although she would've liked to blame this overprotective streak on Emilia's pregnancy and the fact their mother had passed away just over a year ago, Teresa was far too familiar with her older sibling's smothering concerns. It was both a blessing and a curse to be part of such a tight-knit, loving family. While she knew she was loved and would never lack for someone to care about her, she was the baby of the family, and asserting her independence was a challenge she'd been working on for most of her twenty-nine years.

"Thanks for the weather report. But I've been driving since I was sixteen—in worse conditions than this. I'll be fine."

"You know we promised Mama we'd look out for you." Why hadn't that dictate been given regarding any of her older sisters and brother? Maybe their father's murder when she was a baby or the fact she'd been mugged her first summer out of high school or having a veteran cop for a big brother made them all unusually cautious about protecting their own. Still, it would be nice if one day her brother and sisters would see her as an equal adult and not that fatherless baby or traumatized teen. "I want you to head for home as soon as your shift is done," Emilia cautioned.

Teresa risked a little nudge toward independence. "I

need to pick up some groceries. And I was planning to do a little Christmas shopping."

"Teresa—"

"Then I'm going straight to my apartment to bake cookies for Laila and the other pediatric patients to decorate. What kind of trouble can I get into buying baking goods and Christmas gifts?"

Emilia arched a dark brow. *"Gamberro—"* aka Troublemaker "—is your middle name, Teresa." She tempered her skepticism with a smile and a hug. "Just remember you can call any of us if you have a problem with your car or the roads. I don't want you stranded out in the cold."

Were any of her older siblings getting the same lecture? Of course, they all had spouses and children at home expecting their arrival, who'd worry if they didn't show up at a certain place at a certain time. Teresa didn't even have a cat waiting for her at her apartment. She should be more appreciative of their concern.

"I won't be. But just in case, I've got an emergency kit in my trunk, complete with blankets and flares, and I'll keep my cell phone in my pocket." Teresa tightened her arms briefly around her sister, then pulled back to touch Emilia's distended belly. "Now you go home and get off your feet. Hug Justin and my nephew and get yourself and this little one some rest."

The tension in her sister's face eased as she placed her hand beside Teresa's. "I think this one is going to be like her *tía* Teresa."

"Pretty and smart?"

Emilia laughed. "A handful. I swear this one tosses and turns twenty-four hours a day. Not at all like when I was pregnant with her big brother."

Teresa sobered with concerns of her own. "Do you

need me to drive you home? Is your blood pressure spiking again?"

"No, no." Really? Her family wouldn't even let her do this little thing? "Justin is coming by the hospital to get me after he picks up Joey from day care. I'm fine. You just take care of yourself. Unless you want Justin to drive you home, too?"

Teresa bit down on her frustration and summoned a smile for her sister. "No, thanks. I'll be fine."

Emilia cupped Teresa's cheek before turning away. "Have you decided what you're doing for the holiday yet?"

"I'm planning a Christmas party for the children here the afternoon of the twenty-fifth."

"I mean Christmas morning. It would be fun for all of us to help with your party later in the day. We could make extra food and bring gifts. Joey and our nieces and nephews would have fun playing with the boys and girls here." Teresa knew that look—the one that said *I love you* and *You'll need our help* at the same time. "But you'll be joining us all at AJ and Claire's to unwrap presents and eat brunch, right?"

Teresa understood mixed emotions all too well. Just as much as she loved her family, she wanted them to respect her skills and maturity and desire to be who she needed to be. But that battle was for another time. Not the holidays.

Her answer was sincere. "I wouldn't miss it for the world."

Chapter Two

Nash couldn't remember how long he'd been driving, and he had no clue where the highway was taking him.

Shaking off the fogginess in his head, he pulled off the next exit ramp and drove through some cookie-cutter neighborhood mecca. The front yards were dotted with wire reindeer and giant inflatable lawn ornaments. The snow and suburbia were as foreign to him as the need to find an ally who could help him.

He blinked away the frost forming on his eyelashes as his brain skipped from one random thought to the next. It was freaking cold here in Missouri; he had no driver's-side window to roll up and he'd lost his hat. He loved that hat. It was a sentimental homage to the boys ranch where he'd lived and worked and gone to school after his parents' deaths at the hands of a pair of drugged-up teenagers who'd invaded their home. Nash had grown up and taken a job with the DEA to combat the flow of drugs into Texas and other parts of the U.S., to stop another tragedy like his parents' murders, to help troubled kids like he'd been find a healthier way to deal with the crap life threw at them.

He usually oversaw or handled undercover operations where an agent infiltrated a gang or cartel or independent meth lab to gather information to stop the drugs being made, trafficked or sold. But two of his agents had been exposed as cops and killed. So he'd gone undercover himself to find out how and why and who and had ended up with too many suspects and too little concrete evidence.

Somehow, Berto Graciela had found out he was a cop, too.

He was driving in circles.

Tommy Delvecchio was dead.

"Ah, hell." A moment of painful clarity put the brakes on Nash's rambling thoughts.

He'd come to Kansas City with one desperate plan in mind. Without knowing who'd betrayed him in Houston, he'd gone elsewhere to find a sanctuary where he could lie low long enough to safely figure out his next move.

He reconsidered calling Jake Lonergan, who'd left the DEA due to a nearly fatal head injury that had robbed him of his memory. Jake probably didn't want any part of the violence chasing Nash to enter his happily-ever-after life. But, sitting in a pool of his own blood and panting for nearly every breath, Nash knew his luck was running out. It might cost him a friendship, but Jake was all he had left.

Taking his hand off the reloaded gun at his side, Nash brushed the snow off his lap at the next stoplight and reached inside the bag Tommy had brought him to pull out the untraceable phone. Even that subtle shift in his seat renewed the pain like a stab in the back. Thug One had winged him in the leg, creating a discomfort he could simply throw a bandage over. But Thug Three had got him good. He still couldn't tell if the bullet had gone through or if it was lodged inside him somewhere. All he knew was that he was hurt. He was bleeding. And he wasn't going to get any better on his own.

The light changed. A horn honked behind him before

Nash stepped on the accelerator and moved along with the traffic past a busy shopping mall and a modern hospital. He debated whether or not to turn off into the hospital's E.R. But if the men after him were smart—and clearly they were or they wouldn't have tracked him to K.C.— they'd be checking E.R.s across the city looking for him. Besides, a gunshot victim showing up in a hospital was an automatic call to the local police and a subsequent alert to the DEA office in Houston. That was the kind of publicity he didn't need. Until he knew who had set him up, trusting anyone, even a cop, wasn't a good idea.

When he reached the next crossroads, Nash spotted a narrow two-lane road leading away from the suburbs and turned. He needed to get someplace without all these cars and people—someplace where he could put the first-aid kit in his bag to good use without anyone trying to help him or ask any questions. He needed a place where he could pull off and make sense of the dancing letters and numerals on his phone as he tried to recall Jake Lonergan's number, which had been programmed into the phone he didn't want to reactivate.

The truck wheels spun on a patch of snow-packed road and he dropped his phone to grab the wheel and keep the big Ford from skidding across the asphalt. Coming from Houston, he wasn't used to driving in weather like this. Of course, if the world outside his cracked windshield hadn't been such a blur, and he hadn't been shivering from the icy wind blowing in through his busted window, he might have been able to handle the treacherous stretch of winding road he'd pulled off onto.

But he was hurt. He was bleeding. He was cold.

When he crested the hill and hit the next patch of black ice, Mother Nature finally did what a half dozen thugs in two different cities hadn't been able to do.

She took him out.

Nash's truck sailed off the shoulder of the road and plowed into the ditch. It careened up the other side and slammed into a tree. A wave of snow flew over the truck as he banged his head against something hard and blacked out.

TERESA DRUMMED HER gloved fingers against the steering wheel and hummed along with the Christmas music on the radio while she waited at the stoplight.

She tilted her gaze up to the big flakes of snow drifting from the charcoal sky into the light from the streetlamps. "See, Emilia?" She taunted the invisible big sister she felt arching a warning eyebrow over her shoulder. "Shopping's done. Traffic's fine and I'm on my way home with nary a problem whatsoever. And I did it all by my little lonesome."

Not like a couple hours of defiant refusal to heed Emilia's warning and go straight home in the nasty weather could really quell the nagging, indulgent voices of her siblings in her head.

You're so good with children, but if you want any of your own, you'll have to get serious about a man first. I'd already had Olivia and Maria by the time I was your age. A girl can't wait forever.

But she could wait for the right one.

My husband has a friend I want to introduce you to. He has a good job at the college business office and he's stable.

Dullsville. Sounded like another overprotective trap in the making.

You should move closer to us. They're building new condos across the street. And it's a better neighborhood.

She liked her apartment—had it decorated just the

way she wanted. The neighborhood might not be prime real estate, but there were some good people living in her building. Besides, big brother AJ had taught each of his sisters, wife and nieces the basics of self-defense and personal safety. She could take care of herself.

I don't want you driving without an emergency kit in your car, especially in winter. Flashlight? Jumper cables? Kitty litter? Make an appointment to get the tires rotated, too.

Done, done and done. Even before AJ, Emilia, Luisa or Ana had all mentioned reminders about winter driving safety to her.

Just because she longed for her family's respect for her choices and a little bit of independence in her life, didn't mean she was a naive fool. An optimist, yes. A resourceful go-getter. A hopeless holiday lover. But not a fool.

"Why can't they see that?"

The light turned green, and Teresa cranked up the radio, turning her thoughts to something more pleasant. Like sugar cookies. And wrapping gifts.

She drove through the intersection after the cars ahead of her turned off toward the highway, and she continued on to the back-road shortcut to her neighborhood. The busy roads and businesses open late for holiday shopping gave way to country homes on hilly acreages. Then civilization thinned out to a recycling center and a shooting range. Finally, she was winding through woods and farmland. She'd pass through about two miles of bare trees reaching up like dark, gnarled fingers in the foggy twilight and pretty hillsides of undisturbed snow.

Although the twisting road was more dangerous than the straight lanes of bypasses and city streets, she loved this drive, especially in the winter. When the stars were out and the moon was full, it could be as bright as all the holiday lights on the Plaza. And on cold, damp evenings like this, with big flakes of snow swirling in and out of the shadows, it conjured up images of gothic romance, with mysterious heroes, hidden castles and storm-swept moors.

Teresa was imagining a castle hidden behind the frosted branches of the trees when she crested the hill and saw the tire tracks cutting through the snow at the side of the road. Automatically, she pumped her brakes and slowed, peering over the edge of the blacktop.

"Oh, my God."

A silent alarm tightened her grip around the steering wheel. She braked again and pulled onto the shoulder for a closer look, angling her headlights toward the trees.

The tracks ran down into the ditch and up the next incline, leading to a black pickup truck that had finally been stopped short by the trunk of an old pine.

The truck's lights were on. The plume of exhaust making a black spot in the churned-up snow meant the engine was still running. The accident was recent. Or else the driver wasn't able to turn off the motor....

Gamberro is your middle name. Despite her sister's teasing, Teresa didn't believe she caused that much difficulty or misfortune. But she wasn't about to walk away from trouble like this when there was something she could do to help.

Teresa clicked on her hazard lights and pulled her cell phone from her pocket. She glanced ahead at the dark road. She checked the pavement behind her in her mirrors—equally dark. A curtain of falling snow seemed to mask her and the accident below from the rest of the world.

Had the driver called for help yet? Was he or she even able to call?

Taking a deep breath, Teresa pulled the hood of her
parka up over her dark hair and unbuckled her seat belt.
She pulled out the flashlight AJ had insisted she keep in
her glove compartment and braced herself for the blast of
winter outside. Deciding to leave the engine and heater
running in case the driver was able to move and needed
a warm place to sit and wait for a tow truck, she climbed
out and circled to the front of her car.

Dots of blowing snow melted on her cheeks and nose
and obscured her vision as she huddled inside her coat.

"Hello?" Her shout was swallowed up by the cold,
damp air. Her flashlight was too small to pierce the
gloom at this distance. "Is anyone in the truck?"

Her sigh formed a puffy cloud in the air. The snow
was knee-deep for a woman who was only five-three.
And even though she'd changed from her work clogs to
wool-lined ankle boots, she knew they wouldn't be tall
enough to get her past that first drift where the road crew
had piled snow when they'd scraped the road.

"What's a little wet and cold, anyway?" she dared herself, tightening her scarf against the biting wind.

She punched in 911, put the phone to her ear and
plunged into the shallowest part of the drift. By the third
step, she was sinking in up to her thighs, and the snow
quickly chilled her through the scrubs and long underwear she wore. When she lifted each foot, she scooped
the icy crystals into her boots, where they melted, wet-
ting her socks and freezing her skin.

The dispatch operator answered. "This is 911. What
is the nature of your emergency?"

"I need to report a vehicle off in the ditch by... Oh,
heck." Teresa glanced back up the hill. Since she'd been
daydreaming, she had no idea how far she'd come or how
close she was to reaching the nearest subdivision. "I'm

somewhere along old Lee's Summit Road—between the medical center and 40 Highway. On the east side."

"Are you in the vehicle?"

"No, I just drove up on the accident." She broke through the snow at the bottom of the ditch and stepped into ankle-deep slush that soaked her to the skin in icy water. Her teeth chattered through the dispatcher's next question. "I'm sorry, what?"

"Is there anyone inside the truck?"

Teresa's wet feet left her shivering as she climbed out of the ditch. "Just a minute. Let me check."

She tilted her flashlight up to inspect the damaged vehicle. The driver's-side window was down—no, it was missing. It must have shattered with the impact of the crash, leaving tiny blunt shards along its bottom edge. Still, with the coming night and no light on inside the cab, she couldn't make out any driver or passenger. Not for the first time in her life, she silently cursed her diminutive height. When she reached the door of the jacked-up truck, she was too short to see in.

"Hello?" she called again. She reached up and tried the handle, but it was locked. She knocked on the door panel. "Is anyone in there?"

No response.

"Just a sec," she warned the dispatcher. Finding a safe spot to grasp the edge of the open window, she tucked the flashlight into her pocket, stepped onto the running board and pulled herself up. *"Madre de Dios."*

There was a man inside, slumped over the steering wheel. His dark blond hair was frosty with moisture. There was blood oozing from a knot on his forehead, and his skin was far too pale.

"Sir?" The ice cubes of her toes and the woman on the phone were forgotten as alarm, compassion and her years of training kicked in. "Sir?" She stuck the tip of her wool glove into her mouth and pulled it off with her teeth. She slipped two fingers beneath the collar of his padded leather jacket and pressed them to the side of his neck. Even with the thick jacket and the heater running, his skin was cold to the touch. But she could feel a pulse. It was faint and erratic, but it was there. "You're alive." She spat out the glove and raised her voice for the dispatcher to hear. "He's alive."

Pushing up onto her frozen toes, she gently leaned him back against the seat. With a groan, his head lolled toward his shoulder. A quick glance across the cab revealed a heavy nylon duffel bag but no other passenger to worry about.

"One victim," she reported. Hooking her arm inside the door to free her hands, she reached across his lap to turn off the ignition and saw more blood staining the front of his coat and the left leg of his jeans. "How fast were you going?" she mused out loud, wondering at the extent of his injuries. The wreck hadn't looked that bad from the road. Plus, he was still wearing his seat belt.

An answering moan silenced the random thoughts, and she moved her chilled fingers to his face, willing him to open his eyes. "Sir? Hey. I'm a nurse. I'm here to help." She pushed aside the damp spikes of straw-colored hair on his forehead to inspect the gash there. It might need a bandage, but no way could it account for all this blood. She pushed open one eyelid, then the other. Honey-brown irises looked back at her, trying to focus. She smiled. Good. Probably no concussion, then. "I need you to talk to me. I'm Teresa. What's your name?"

His pale lips drew together. "Don't need a candy striper, kid. Run along."

His speech was slurred. But it could be from the cold.

Kid? A little defensive fire crept into her veins before common sense reminded her to ignore the dig. The man was in trouble and needed her assistance. "I'm a registered nurse, and you're badly hurt. You want me to hike back to the road to get my hospital ID or do you want me to help?"

"Bossy little thing," he muttered. His eyes blinked open again, long enough to assess her face. "You… nurse?"

"What's your name?" she repeated.

He inhaled a quick breath, gritted his teeth, then squeezed the words out. "Charles. I'm Charles."

"Like Charlie? Or Mr. Charles? No, don't close your eyes." She cupped her palm against the sandy beard stubble on his jaw. "Keep looking at me. Can you tell me where you're hurt?"

He pulled his left hand from his lap and grabbed the steering wheel. By sheer will, his vision seemed to sharpen and his gaze dropped to the phone tucked to her ear. "Is that 911?"

"Yes." When he reached for it, she handed it over. "Good idea. You can tell them exactly what hap— What are you doing? Give me my—"

"No cops." He disconnected the call and tossed her phone onto the dashboard. With a jerky shift of his broad shoulders, he pulled his right hand from beneath the duffel bag.

"¡Oh, mi Dios!"

He had a gun.

Teresa instinctively recoiled, but before she could jump off the running board, a big gloved hand anchored her arm to the door with surprising strength. "Let go!"

His fingers tightened around her wrist, trapping her

beside him as he pounded her phone with the butt of the wicked-looking pistol, smashing it into pieces.

"Hey!"

And then he turned the barrel of the gun on her. Bleeding Charles tilted his eyes up to the shoulder of the road. His voice was raspy, deep. "That your car, kid?"

Teresa's answer was a frozen gasp in the cold air. "Yes."

The gun barely wavered as he pushed open the door, forcing her into the snow. She landed on her butt and slid down the hill a few inches, but her bare hand, numb toes and panic slowed her efforts to scramble back onto her feet. He swung one long leg out, then the other, his black cowboy boots sinking into the snow, his breath hitching when his feet hit solid ground. Leaning against the cab for support, he pulled the duffel bag across the seat and tossed it at her. It hit her square in the stomach, knocking her onto her bottom again.

Judging by its weight and rattle, whatever was inside was heavy and metal and… "Son of a…" More guns.

Teresa shoved the bag away and climbed onto her knees, letting gravity pull her down into the ditch, farther away from the bleeding man, until she could find solid ground and bolt away.

She'd come to the aid of some drug dealer or gunrunner or mass murderer.

She was the one in trouble.

"I'd stop if I were you."

The ominous double click of a bullet sliding into the chamber of his automatic weapon rang clear in the crisp, frigid air, spurring her to her feet.

"I said stop!"

The deafening report of a gunshot froze her in her tracks. Teresa pushed her hood away from her face and turned her head, lifting her gaze to the tall, pale man with the narrowed eyes and bloody coat.

The mysterious Charles-slash-Mr. Charles was still leaning against the truck to hold himself up. But the gun he'd fired into the tree behind him was steaming in the cold air. The smell of sulfur filled her nose as he pulled the weapon down to aim it right at her. "Don't get any idea that you're going to run from me." His raspy, low-pitched threat was a whispery cloud in the night air. "Now you're going to pick up that bag and get me the hell out of here."

Chapter Three

Please don't make me scare you any worse than I have to, darlin', Nash silently begged. *Just do what I say. Take me where I want to go. And then you never have to deal with my sorry butt again.*

But those dark brown eyes tilting up to his were wide and frightened and telling him exactly what he didn't want to see—she was about to run.

"Ah, hell."

He was already sliding the gun into his holster when she spun around to leap across the bottom of the ditch. He was in no shape to chase anyone down, but she wasn't leaving him many options.

She landed on her hands and knees, a tangle of turquoise coat and pink scarf in the snow. But before she could find her footing, Nash ignored the protest jolting through his stiff leg and dove after her, using his six feet three inches of height to full advantage. He wasn't fast, but he was big enough to catch her around the thighs and tackle her. He landed across her legs and bottom, crushing her into the snow beneath him. Pain radiated through his shoulder as he hit the ground beside her, and he groaned.

But she didn't leave him any time to clench his teeth through the blinding agony or even to catch his breath.

With a feral roar, she rolled onto her back beneath him, spitting snow in his eyes and clawing at his neck and face.

"Get off me!"

Nash deflected the first blow. The second caught him square in the nose and made his eyes water. Hobbled by cold and pain and utter fatigue, he was about to be out-maneuvered by the thrashing woman unless he resorted to doing her some serious harm. And since he was still a hairbreadth away from that kind of desperation, he crawled on top of her and let his weight pin her down until the night stopped reeling about him.

She screamed in his ear and shoved a palmful of snow against his cheek.

"Stop struggling." The icy cold on his skin was like a reviving slap across the face. But when the empty fist arced toward him a second time, his temper flared. He caught her wrist with his good hand and pinned it on the ground above her head. "I said stop!"

For one surprising moment, she went still beneath him. Through the rapid puffs of breath that clouded the air between them, he took in the quick dart of her tongue across her full bottom lip and the halo of long coffee-brown hair fanning over the snow beneath her head. The defensive anger that had spiked inside him gave way to a flash of something wildly inappropriate for a wanted man fighting to survive for a few more days.

He was still processing those quick impressions of curves and heat and spirited beauty when she offered up a husky whisper. "What are you going to do with me?"

Keep your head in the game, Nash. Don't let the pretty girl distract you.

"Not a damn thing. Look, I don't want to be a part of your life any longer than you want to be a part of mine." Running on fumes, he summoned what little energy he had left and went the tough-guy route again. "You can either drive me where I want to go or I can take your keys. But I don't especially want to leave you abandoned out here on a night like this."

"Don't worry about me." He saw the spark in her eyes a split second before he felt her leg sliding beneath his and sensed her target.

Of all the... Nash pulled his knee between her thighs, beating her to the intimate contact. With a startled gasp, she went still again—long enough for him to release her wrists and unholster his gun. "I wouldn't if I were you."

"Those injuries aren't from any car wreck." Although her rosy cheeks indicated she was as aware of their intimate position as he was, it seemed nothing could silence that smart mouth. She brought her hands to the uninjured side of his chest, and he let her shove a few inches of breathing room between them. "And that's body armor. Who are you, Mr. Charles? What did you do?"

"The less you know about me, the better." Good. He hadn't slipped and given her his name in his groggy state in the truck. That meant it wasn't out there on the wire or in cyberspace, flagging his location to the cartel or the inside man who'd set him up.

Nash raised his head and glanced around him, suddenly wary that he'd already spent too long out in the open. That gunshot he'd used to intimidate her when he realized he couldn't stop her from running might have alerted a nearby farmer or some other fool who was out here in the middle of nowhere on this wintry night. And even though he'd severed her call, the authorities were almost certainly already on their way.

He assessed the subdued flight risk in her warm chocolate eyes before easing his hips off hers and gingerly pushing himself up on one knee in the snow. "I don't have much time. I can't afford to let the police get here before I'm gone—and you're my only way out of here, Peewee. I need you to grab my bag and get me to your car, then take me someplace where you can patch me up."

"Peewee?" She sat up as soon as she was free. A second later she was scooting away, climbing to her feet and brushing the snow off the clinging wet cotton of her pink pant legs. "I should just leave you here to freeze to death."

"Can you outrun a bullet?" If she tried, he'd have to let her go. But he was hoping he still had that big-and-mean-and-on-his-last-nerve look going for him to convince her to cooperate.

Apparently, he did.

Although that defiant spark never left her dark eyes, she lifted her gaze from the gun up to his, nodding her acquiescence. "Now that you've conveniently gotten us both soaked to the skin, we're at risk for hypothermia if we stay out here much longer. And I'm not dying for the likes of you."

She stumbled down the hill, kicking her way through knee-deep snow with every step. Man, she was a little spitfire. Maybe not as afraid of him as she should be, and definitely not the teenager he'd first thought her to be. She stood over his go bag, breathing deeply, rubbing her bare hand inside her gloved one, no doubt feeling the cold and damp, especially after that tumble in the snow.

Or maybe she was contemplating another avenue of escape.

Nash shifted the angle of the gun toward her. "Pick it up and don't try to run again," he warned. With an answering glare, she hoisted the heavy bag onto her shoulder. It was almost as big as she was. But other than a Spanish curse beneath her breath, she trudged up the hill without further protest or complaint.

Nash, however, struggled to find his footing. His leg ached but felt solid enough. It was more a case of finding his balance and catching his breath. He lurched to his feet, swaying with the first step. White spots swam before his eyes, but it was more than the snow swirling past.

The nurse was several steps ahead of him when she dropped the bag into a drift at the shoulder of the road and turned.

Nash willed the light-headedness to go away and raised the gun toward her. But his left arm hung at his side and his right was getting weaker. "I said—"

"I don't think I can carry you both," she groused, marching back down the hill.

He almost laughed at the idea of this little bundle of sass thinking she was going to carry him. But she moved to his right side, wound her arm behind his waist and urged him to put his arm around her shoulders. "Lean on me," she ordered.

Nash hesitated. She fit right beneath his arm, the perfect height for the crutch he apparently needed. And yeah, it put the crown of that silky dark hair that had fallen out of its ponytail and gotten dotted with snow right beneath his chin. He tightened his grip around the gun that rested on her shoulder when she grabbed his wrist and butted her hip up against his. Was this cozying-up tactic some kind of trick to get the weapon away from him?

"Come on, tough guy." She latched her fingers around his belt and tugged. "You can get fresh with me in the snow and threaten me with a gun all you want. But if you really want my help, you'll put your weight on me and move your feet." She flashed her dark eyes up to him before urging him forward with a jerk at his waist and a grunt of effort. "In about two minutes, my extremities are going to be so numb I won't be able to do anything for either of us—even if you do shoot. So move."

He couldn't have been rescued by some meek, mousy thing who'd do what he said without the attitude? He tapped the butt of the gun against her shoulder. "That's pretty bold talk for a woman who's got no advantage."

"Uh-huh. I'm not the one bleeding to death. Your color's awful. Your skin is cold to the touch. I don't want your dead body on my conscience." She tugged again, forcing him to take a step. "How long have you been losing blood?"

"The leg's just a graze," he informed her, bracing more of his weight on her shoulders to limp another step up the hill. "I stanched the hole in my chest," he ground out as his right boot slipped and he came down hard on his injured leg.

"Nice dodge," she chided. "That means longer than you want to admit." She yanked back on his belt to keep him from falling. "So if you won't tell me about your injuries, then tell me what the other guy looks like."

The exertion of climbing the hill and keeping his wits about him left Nash gasping for breath. But he kept moving. "You don't want to know."

Three steps. Four. They'd reached the tracks in the snow where he'd plowed through the drift on the shoulder of the road. "Is he kidnapping some poor unlucky Good Samaritan, too?"

"Nope. They aren't doing anything right now."

"They?" She was breathing as hard as he was when she stopped beside the car and tipped her face up to his. "Wait a minute. Are they...? Did you...?"

"Yeah, darlin'. I killed all three of them."

"Killed—?"

"I preferred them in the morgue instead of me."

Her cheeks blanched as she opened the passenger door. "You murdered three men?"

No jury would call what he'd done anything but self-defense. But she didn't have to know that those hired guns had come to the warehouse to murder *him*. And Tommy. Remembering the young man dead on the warehouse floor created a different kind of pain in Nash's chest. He should have dragged the body to his truck, made sure Agent Delvecchio got the proper burial he deserved, instead of letting him lie alongside his own killers on a cold concrete floor. Losing Tommy had been like losing a kid brother. One by one, Graciela and his thugs were taking out the closest thing he had to family. There had to be justice. They had to pay.

Nah. He wouldn't feel remorse about taking advantage of this woman's nursing skills or scaring her into the no-questions-asked cooperation he needed. Even if he wound up dead at the end of all this, he was going to make sure the traitor was exposed and no one else on his team died.

"You gonna stop giving me trouble now, Peewee?" He looked down at her and saw the bravado or anger or whatever had fueled her defiance these past few minutes disappear. Now she was finally truly afraid of him. Ignoring a deep stab of guilt and reminding himself of the necessity for haste and maintaining anonymity—for her sake as well as his—he lowered himself into the seat of her midsize car. He pointed the gun over the crest of the hill. "Now the bag. Put it in the back."

With a nod, she hurried to obey his orders. Fisting the gun in his lap, Nash risked tipping his head back against the headrest and closing his eyes for a few seconds. The heat inside the car was a drugging mix of pain and relief. The thawing nerve endings around his wounds and frozen toes stung like hundreds of needles piercing his skin. Yet drawing warm air into his lungs after so many hours exposed to the elements seemed to ease the constriction in his chest. Maybe it was the influx of oxygen into his system, or maybe these were the last moments of his life seeping away, and all he wanted to do was sleep.

This was humiliating, to be so helpless, so dependent on a frightened woman for survival. And while he might be more comfortable giving orders to his men or smack-talking his way with the bad guys, he'd sweet-talked a woman or two in his day. But that required a degree of thought and patience, and minding the words that came out of his mouth, that he didn't possess the energy to stay on top of this evening. So he'd resorted to the bull-in-a-china-shop approach to gaining her cooperation.

Once he was in better shape, he'd let her go. She could report him to the local police after she'd gotten him off this exposed stretch of road, stitched him up and bought him a few hours of rest. Of course, by the time he released her and any cops got wind of his presence here in Kansas City, he intended to be long gone.

The car door slammed behind him, startling him from a dozing state, reminding him that he probably needed a good twelve hours of rest and recovery time before he could let his reluctant rescuer contact anyone. That meant he had to stay alert and he had to stay mean to maintain the upper hand and keep her from asking any questions or turning him in. If she never found out who he was or who was after him, the cartel wouldn't be able to tie him to her. He needed her to believe he was a threat, but Nash intended to walk away without doing more than inconveniencing her for one night. Berto Graciela and Santiago Vargas and their selfish greed were real dangers he wouldn't risk her life on by making her any kind of witness or information source.

When she opened the driver's door and got in, the blast of cold air revived him further. "Let's go."

Instead of obeying, she cranked the heat, peeled off her remaining glove and rubbed her fingers in front of the heating vent. He could see her visibly shaking now, but he wondered how much of that was the cold and how much was fear. "What's going to happen to me?"

"Nothing, if you do what I tell you."

She slid him a sideways glance before focusing on bringing warmth back to her fingers again. "You owe me a new phone."

The corner of his mouth wanted to crook with amusement at the woman's refusal to say die. Ignoring his growing admiration for her spirit, though, he reached over and turned the heat back down to low—partly to keep his head clear and partly to remind her who was in charge. "Drive."

"I'd like to wait until I can feel my toes first."

He shifted the gun in his lap. "It wasn't a request."

She tucked a long strand of tangled hair behind her ear, peeking at him around her hand. Her gaze dropped to the Smith & Wesson pointed at her before she buckled herself in and shifted the car into gear. "You're a bully, you know that?"

"I know," he answered, surprised she hadn't called him worse. Nash checked the mirrors right along with her, ensuring the road was clear in both directions before she pulled out. "Did you give 911 my license plate number?"

"No. I was more worried about your safety. Stupid me, huh?"

Good. That should buy them a few minutes. A police officer, ambulance and fire engine were most likely already en route to the scene. But if she hadn't reported his truck, then the authorities wouldn't be able to track him or put his name over the wires until they arrived on site. And he intended to be long gone by then.

She tapped on the brake, slowing their speed as they neared the bottom of the hill. "What are you, a hit man? Drug dealer? Is that what's in that bag? Your payoff? Drugs and guns? Is there some innocent man somewhere I should have stopped to help instead of you?"

"Less talking, more driving."

She nudged on the accelerator as they followed the dark ribbon of road up the next hill. "The moisture in the air is freezing on the pavement, so I don't trust myself to turn around here. I'll have to drive up to the next intersection or driveway to turn around and get you back to the med center."

"We're not going to the hospital."

"Then where…?" She stomped on the brakes and they started to skid.

His instinctive reaction to reach for the wheel burned through his shoulder like a fresh gunshot. Nash swore as the edge of the road zoomed up to his window.

But she jerked the wheels into the skid, jerked them the other way. Leaving dirt and drift on the blacktop behind them, she steered them back to the middle of the road.

"Easy, Peewee." Nash gritted his teeth as new waves of pain shot through him. "We need to get there in one piece."

She slowed their speed and guided them back into the right lane. "Enough with the nicknames, okay?"

He nudged back the front of his jacket and pulled the blood-soaked bandanna from beneath his vest. His time was already limited—he didn't need a panicked driver cutting it any shorter. "I thought you were a kid when you first walked up to my truck. What are you? Five foot nothin'?"

"I'm five-three. I'm not even the shortest one in my family, and I'm not going to have any personal conversation with you." She glanced over at the bandanna dripping on his pant leg. "Here." She released her death grip on the steering wheel to untie the pink scarf from her neck and pull it free. She tossed it across the seat into his lap. "Pack that against the wound. The cold temps have probably slowed the bleeding enough for you to survive this long. You need to see a doctor."

"I've got a nurse."

"A pediatric nurse," she reminded him.

Bit by bit, he stuffed the scarf beneath his vest. "Can you stitch up a wound?"

"Yes, but you need antibiotics. Maybe even surgery. At the very least, you need an X-ray to find out what damage that bullet's done inside you."

"I'm not going to any damn hospital."

"Then where am I taking you? The nearest cemetery?"

"That's a sweet bedside manner you've got there, darlin'." She reached over and shut off the heat. "Turn it back on. You're shivering."

"Like you care." She shook her head. "The cold's better for you. That's probably the only reason why you haven't bled to death yet."

"You're a smart girl."

"I'm not a *girl*." She said the word as if it left a sour taste in her mouth.

"No, you're not." Her cute little curvy shape and endless backbone proved that. Her grown-up strength was also giving him an idea for plan B or C or whatever letter of the alphabet he was on now with this mess of an assignment. He could see the glow of lights in the distance now, a neighborhood or highway interchange, he guessed. But there was still no oncoming traffic or vehicles on the road behind them. The site of his crash had been swallowed up by hills and darkness. So the ambulance and cops must be coming from the south—not the direction they were headed. He'd have to play the kidnapper for a day or so longer, but he could make this work. "You married?"

"No."

"Got a boyfriend? Kids? Roommate?"

She smiled, but there was no humor in her tone. "I've got a big brother who's a cop. A fugitive like you is probably already on his radar."

Good. "So no boyfriend, either."

"I didn't say—"

"Eyes on the road," he warned when she glared at him again. "You don't play the big-brother card unless you've got no other man in your life to stick up for you. You live alone."

Her fists tightened around the steering wheel. "My personal life is none of your business."

This plan was going to work. The woman lived alone and no one was expecting her. She had the skills he needed—if he could just keep her in line. "A pretty little thing like you with that sassy mouth and no husband or boyfriend? Are you a widow or a workaholic?"

"Am I a...?" He met her glare this time, and she quickly glanced away. "It's...complicated."

As intriguing as that answer might be to follow up on, Nash had the information he needed. She lived alone. No one was expecting her for a date. No one would worry if she didn't check in for the next few hours. Steer clear of the cop big brother—if he wasn't just a story she'd made up to try to intimidate him—and this plan could work. "Trust me. I understand complicated."

"I bet you do." They passed a sign indicating a state highway up ahead. She pointed to the traffic lights in the distance. "Am I taking you to your place? Just tell me where to turn. I'm bad with street names. I promise if I see the address, I'll erase it right out of my head."

"I'm not from here."

"Are we going to your hideout?"

"Hideout?" Amusement threatened a smile again. "Isn't that a little Sam Spade-ish?"

"Whatever you call it. To meet up with your friends? Will they take care of you? Or are they the three men who did that to you?"

"They were from…" Ah, hell. He was saying too much. He didn't want to give her any names or places she might share later. "I don't have friends in K.C."

"Why doesn't that surprise me?" She adjusted her lights down from bright as a car coming from the opposite direction appeared over the next hill. "Why *are* you here?"

"You ask an awful lot of questions, darlin'."

"Darlin'? I think I prefer Peewee."

Nash considered her answer. He could give a little as long as she was cooperating. "What's your name again?"

"Teresa." She rolled her *R* with a musical lilt.

"Take me home, Teresa."

"You said you weren't from here." Her gaze darted down to the dashboard, and her posture straightened a tiny bit, putting him on guard. "Oh. I wondered where the twang of yours was from. How far south are we going? I'll need to stop for gas if we're driving any distance. There are a couple of gas stations up on 40 Highway."

Really? She thought she could outfox him and stop in

a public place where she could call for help? His momentary lapse into nice-guy territory had just ended. "Don't get too smart, Teresa." He nodded toward the needle on her dash before raising his gun in his lap. "Your tank is practically full. Very responsible for this kind of weather. Nice try, though. I'm guessing our destination isn't that far or you wouldn't be on this backwater stretch of road. You're taking me to *your* place."

Chapter Four

How had this happened to her?

How had she gone off on such a wrong turn from proving herself to be a smart, self-sufficient adult? She'd been taken hostage by a bleeding stranger, and now she was helping him limp up the steps into her apartment building—sneaking a fugitive into her own home! Although he carried her bag of groceries in the hand at the end of his injured arm, and they walked hip to hip as if they enjoyed holding on to each other, there was nothing normal about this stroll from the parking lot.

Teresa felt the barrel of Mr. Charles's gun nudge her side through the blanket she'd draped around his shoulders to mask his weapon and injuries from anyone who might see them stumbling across the scraped and salted concrete. "Remember," he warned in that deep-pitched drawl of his, "if anyone asks, we just took a tumble in the snow. You say anything to anyone that gives me away, and this bullet will go right through that pretty hide of yours."

Maybe *Gamberro was* her middle name, and her older brother and sisters were right to worry about her.

"I get it. You have a gun. I'll do what you say." She hiked that mysterious black bag of his higher onto her shoulder, freeing her arm to unlock the outer door. She had to release her grip on the back of his belt to hold it open for him.

But there was no thought of closing the door behind him and running away. The man was like a wounded bear. Even without the gun, her captor was mean and unpredictable and all sinewy brawn. Although he said he wanted to draw as little attention to himself as possible, she had no doubt he'd shoot right through the glass or wrestle her to the ground again if she didn't do his bidding.

"This is crazy," she whispered, sliding her arm behind his back again, steadying his uneven gait. "You're going to die. And I don't want a dead man in my apartment."

"Then don't let me die."

There were two more stairs inside before they reached the carpeted lobby and elevators. The fist of fear squeezing her gut tightened with every step. What would he do if she couldn't make him well enough to travel? Who was he running from? Were there other armed men in the city looking for him? What if she was still his prisoner when they found him? The sooner she could send him on his way and call her brother, AJ, to report him, the better. "We should have gone to the hospital."

"Not an option."

"You'd rather die than be turned over to the police?" Teresa pushed the call button and the doors opened. "What if I can't fix you? I don't exactly have a fully equipped E.R. in my apartment."

He limped in beside her and rested his backside against the railing, easing some of his weight off her shoulders. "A smart girl like you will figure it out. What floor?"

"I'm in 417." Teresa pushed the number 4. "What if you die? Is there someone worse than you out there who's going to blame me?"

"No one cares if I die. Only if I live."

Teresa swung her gaze up to the haggard shadows darkening his eyes. "I don't care what you've done—that's a horrible thing to say."

As the doors started to close, a familiar quavering voice called out from the lobby. "Hold the door, please. My arms are full."

"Don't you dare, dar—"

But Teresa had already pushed the door-open button. She wasn't sure if it was ingrained politeness or some latent survival instinct kicking in that made her ignore his warning and invite company into the elevator with them. Florence Walker, with her snow-white hair pulled up in a bun on top of her head, toddled into the elevator car with a basket of neatly folded clothes perched on her hip. "Good evening, Teresa. I'm trying to be healthy and use the stairs to do my laundry, especially since I can't get out and walk now. But my knee only made it up one flight from the basement before I decided exercise is for the birds."

"Good evening, Mrs. Walker. This cold weather will aggravate your arthritis."

Those same light brown eyes that had been matter-of-factly devoid of emotion a moment earlier drilled her with a silent warning. He straightened beside her, keeping his long thigh—and the gun—in contact with her body.

But the woman who lived in the apartment beneath Teresa's seemed completely unaware of any tension inside the elevator. She glanced up at the man wearing a blanket draped around him like a serape and smiled at Teresa. "Am I interrupting something? A date?"

A date? Florence thought *this* was the kind of man Teresa wanted in her life?

The elevator bobbed once before it slowly began to

rise. The motion rocked Teresa into her captor's side. He slid his arm behind her and let the icy steel of his gun rest on the curve of her bottom. She flinched at another round of full-body contact with his tall, hard frame.

And flinched again when she realized she hadn't immediately pushed some space between them. How sick. Why would she even notice the shape of his body? Was her skin tingling with awareness at being pressed against him? No, it had to be the numbing cold wearing off now that they were inside. She should not—could not—think that there was anything to like about this dangerous bully of a man.

Trouble. Trouble. Trouble.

"Have I embarrassed you, dear? Your cheeks are red."

Teresa tore herself from her humiliating thoughts to look into the concerned blue eyes behind Florence's wire-rimmed glasses. "No. Of course not. I… It's the cold."

Flattening her palm against the worn wool of the blanket, she tried to put some distance between them. If anything, he moved closer, pushing his rib cage against her hand and wedging her firmly against the gun at her back. She needed to get away from this man. Now. But how? Running hadn't worked. Neither had arguing or begging.

Her gaze fell to the drops of blood on her captor's round-toed boot. *Look, Mrs. Walker. Be suspicious. Help me.* Teresa lifted her gaze to Florence, willing the older woman to notice the danger she was in, silently asking her to go to her apartment and dial 911. "Mr., um…" *See? If this was a date, wouldn't I know his name?* Teresa made sure her smile looked forced. "This, um, man I just met is feeling a little under the weather." She glanced down at the tiny bloodstains again. *Look.* "He—"

"I took a nasty fall and got hurt." Florence might not

be noticing the clues Teresa was giving her, but her captor certainly had. "Might have dislocated my shoulder."

"Oh, I'm sorry to hear that." Florence clucked her tongue against her teeth. "You really have to watch that ice."

Really? This sweet, clueless woman was sympathizing with the ratty, pale stranger instead of the neighbor who lived in the apartment above her and shared tea on the fire escape when the weather was nice? Teresa bit down on her frustration and tried communicating a silent cry for help one more time. "I offered to drive him to the hospital, but—"

"She's taking real good care of me, ma'am." He grinned and lifted the bag of groceries he held a few shaky inches. "She's going to fix me a nice hot meal."

Florence turned her full attention up to Mr. Charles. No way would she notice the blood now. "I imagine our Teresa would make any patient of hers feel better. She's the sweetest young lady in our whole building."

"I bet you give her a run for her money." Was he flirting with the older woman?

Mrs. Walker laughed. "Now, aren't you a dear." She winked at Teresa, without noticing one bit of distress. "This one's a keeper. Not only is he tall and good-looking in that scruffy cowboy kind of way, but he's a charmer."

A keeper? Charming? *Do you see me smiling?* "I'm just his nurse. He's a patient."

"If that's what you want to call it." The elevator dinged for Mrs. Walker's floor and slowed its ascent. Florence winked at Teresa and smiled. "Don't you worry. I may be old, but I read books. I know what codespeak is. I won't tell your family that you had a young man over tonight."

That was what she thought all the pleading signals had been about? Hiding a lover from her family?

The elevator doors opened, and Florence headed down the hallway.

"Mrs. Walker? Would you—?" But a poke of steel against Teresa's hip stopped her from calling back her white-haired neighbor.

The older woman turned. "Yes, dear?"

Her captor dropped his head, his breath a warm tickle against her ear. "Give me away and I'll shoot *her*."

Teresa tilted her head back to read the deadly promise in his honey-brown eyes.

Somehow, she remembered how to smile when she spoke to Florence Walker again. "Thanks for keeping my secret."

"Of course, dear. You two have fun playing doctor."

Mr. Charles reached behind Teresa to tap the door-close button with the end of his gun. "Good night, ma'am."

"Good night."

The moment the doors drifted shut, Teresa pushed him away, hating that little sting of guilt she felt when he grunted with the effort to keep himself on his feet. "Really? You'd shoot that sweet old grandmother?"

"Whatever it takes to survive." He sagged back against the railing, his jaw clenched in a tight cord of pain. "You don't have to like me, Peewee. You just have to do what I tell you."

"I hate you," she muttered into the corner.

"That's the idea." Whatever injuries he'd sustained, his hearing was just fine. The elevator had barely started to move before the bell dinged again. "We're here. Fourth floor, right?"

For a split second, Teresa considered bolting out of the elevator and letting the doors trap the slow-moving man behind her. But the last thing she wanted was for Mrs.

Walker or any of the other innocent residents to stumble onto a collapsed gunman in the elevator, think they were doing the right thing by stopping to help him and end up his prisoner. At least she had some understanding of how the criminal mind worked. With a murdered father, a brother who was a cop and a sister who worked in the E.R., she stood a better chance of getting out of this unscathed than any of the elderly residents or young families who lived in the apartment building with her.

"Come on." She braced her wet boot against the door when it started to slide shut and reached for the wounded man. "Let's get you inside before you threaten any other neighbors."

He tossed his right arm around her shoulders, leaning on her a little more heavily than before as he stepped out beside her. "You always this mouthy, Peewee?"

"Pretty much."

The chuckle that rumbled in his throat became a groan of pain. He was in bad shape, probably even worse than he'd let on. As much as she normally admired that kind of determination to survive in a patient, a part of her wished he'd go ahead and pass out so that she could take his gun and escape to call AJ and the police. She had to lean him against the wall beside her door and drop the deadly black bag so she could fish out her keys from her purse. By the time she had the knob and dead bolt open, he'd dropped the sack of groceries to the floor beside his boot. The blanket he wore had gaped open to reveal the bloody shoulder of his jacket and the gun down at his side. His face was pale and his eyes had drifted shut.

"Don't you die here," she warned, as concern mixed with anger, fear and the impulse to run from the dangerous man.

"Not yet, darlin'. Not yet." Those golden-brown eyes

opened, looking straight down at her. He shifted the gun to his weak hand and swiped the ring of keys from her fingers before pushing his way inside the door ahead of her. "Grab the food and my bag."

Damn it. She hated feeling any kind of compassion for this man even more than she hated being forced to help him. She should have run when she'd had the chance.

Dropping his belongings on the tiled entryway without any regard for the bag's noisy contents was the only protest she made when he locked the door behind her. He slipped her keys into the pocket of his jeans while she took off her wet coat and draped it over the back of a dining-room chair, then carried the smushed groceries to the kitchen peninsula.

"What is this? Santa's workshop?"

Teresa turned and eyed the rolls of wrapping paper, ribbon and sacks of yet-to-be-wrapped presents strewn across the top of the table. "I have a big family with lots of nieces and nephews. Don't bad guys celebrate Christmas, too?"

"Not this year." She caught his gaze across the entryway and thought she detected something more like longing in his weary gaze, rather than the sarcasm she'd imagined in his tone.

But when his eyes focused and met her curious perusal, his expression hardened like ice. He limped up beside her at the kitchen peninsula, reaching over to the phone above the counter and pulling out the line that connected it to the wall jack. "Hey!"

"My rules, darlin'." That cord ended up in the pocket with her keys as he scanned the main rooms of her apartment, no doubt looking for any other means of communication to disable. When his gaze landed on her again, the bully who gave the orders was back. "Pull that table over in front of the door."

"You have the gun, remember? I'm not running."

"Forgive me if I don't trust you."

With a huff, Teresa scooted the chair aside and lifted the edge of the oak table she'd inherited from her mother.

"Wait." Before she'd dragged it a foot, he was waving her away from the table with the gun and pointing into the living room. "Try the sofa." Again, as soon as she started sliding it across the carpet, he stopped her. He nodded to the armoire against the wall where her television and sound system were stored. "Can you move that?"

A tad breathless, Teresa straightened, shoving her long, damp hair off her face. "Not unless I empty it out first."

"Good."

"What are you...?" As she curled her cold toes inside her boots to curb the urge to stop him, he put his good shoulder to the thick oak wood and pushed it in front of the door, effectively barricading the exit.

"Like I said, I don't...trust..." He was bent over, breathing heavily, the fist with the gun braced on one knee, by the time he was finished. The man was running on fumes and sheer determination. But even that massive stubborn streak wouldn't sustain him much longer.

"You really have a death wish, don't you. You'd better sit before you keel over." She picked up the blanket that had fallen to the floor and hooked her hand beneath his elbow, guiding him over to a stool at the kitchen peninsula. She draped the blanket over his head and shoulders, futilely trying to ignore the way, even when he was sitting down, that he was still a head taller than she was. It was equally hard not to notice how his chest and shoulders were broad and muscled and seriously imposing up close like this. She didn't need the gun in his lap or the nothing-to-lose expression in his eyes to know she was completely at his mercy. She tucked the tattered edges of the blanket together and quietly pulled away. "Try to stay warm while I get my things."

Instead of obeying even that most practical suggestion, he sloughed the blanket to the floor and stumbled after her into the bathroom, where she fetched her first-aid kit. His ragged breathing stirred the crown of her hair as he trailed her to the linen closet, too, where she pulled out her sewing kit and a stack of towels and washcloths.

But when she would have returned to the kitchen, he raised the gun and forced her on into the bedroom at the end of the hall. He spotted the phone on her bedside table and disconnected its cord just as he had the one in the kitchen. "You can work in here."

"In my bedroom?" What kind of sick twist was he adding to this abduction-and-intimidation game now? "Look, I don't know what else you think you can threaten me with, but I won't let you touch—"

"Don't flatter yourself, Peewee. In another lifetime, I might be tempted by all those curves. But tonight I only need you to be my nur...se." He swore at the strain of shoving her bed in front of the window and the snow-packed fire escape outside. He collapsed onto the edge of the mattress, cradling his wounded arm in his lap. His rugged face was pale as a ghost, his lips quivering and nostrils flaring as he struggled to catch his breath. With another vicious curse, he tugged his ruined jacket off his shoulder, slowly uncovering the flak vest and her blood-soaked scarf sticking out from the neck and armhole. "The only other point of entry to your apartment is in here. And you'll have to get past me to get out."

If it hadn't been for the gun clutched in his fist, she'd

have banked on him passing out and would have climbed right over him without batting an eye to open that window and hurry down to Mrs. Walker's to use her phone. But the one thing on the man that didn't seem to be affected by his injuries was his grip on that gun. And, as intent as he was on ripping open the vest's Velcro straps beneath each arm, she believed his assertion that using her bed as an examination table was only about keeping her prisoner, nothing more. So she set her supplies on the bed beside him, pulled on a pair of sterile gloves from the first-aid kit and went to work.

"Here, Mr. Charles. Let me." She took over getting the jacket and protective vest off him, dumping both on the rug at her feet. She touched his right arm, pushing his hand up to the scarf, avoiding the gun while asking for his help. "Keep pressure on the wound."

"It's just Charles," he answered, pressing the wool against his shoulder. "Charlie, to some."

She pulled a pair of scissors from her sewing basket. "Do you have a last name, Charles?"

"Be careful with those." She was keenly aware of his eyes following her every move as she cut away the left side of his black knit shirt and T-shirt. "You get any idea about stabbing me and I'll—"

"So no last name?" She carefully peeled away the bloodied layers of cotton, exposing a landscape of corded muscle, dark bruises and faint white scars dotting his skin. "*Madre de Dios.* What happened to you?"

"Had a disagreement with three guys who wanted to kill me, wrecked my truck, tussled with a petite brunette in the snow."

"Stop it." Compassion fisted in her gut as she touched her gloved fingertip to the oldest and palest mark branding his biceps, tracing the puckered ring, raising goose bumps across his ashy skin. "This is from an old gun-shot wound. My brother has a scar like this. The kind of work you do must take a terrible toll on your body. And yet you keep going back for more punishment. Who did this to you? Who's after you?"

"You feeling sorry for me, Peewee?" He turned his face to hers, the low rumble of his voice whispering across her skin like a warm breeze.

"You've been hurt so many…" Her voice trailed away when she realized how close she was standing to him. Her fingers still rested against his arm. Her thighs were touching his. And if she angled her head a fraction to the left, her cheek would slide against the raspy stubble of his jaw. Her heart rate kicked up a notch, thundering in her ears. Those firm male lips were just a hair-breadth away from the apple of her cheek. Seriously? She couldn't catch her breath? She was turned on by this brute? Surprise and shame poured through her blood, and she pulled her hand away, retreating a step from his disturbing masculine heat.

What was happening to her? She must be suffering from some form of Stockholm syndrome already, feeling this perverted connection to her captor. She hated this man for threatening her life, for endangering Florence Walker and the rest of her neighbors simply by being here. He'd taken advantage of her desire to help some-one in need and made her feel like a fool for doing so. He'd made her angry and afraid. She couldn't feel sorry for the terrible harm that had been done to him over the years, and she certainly wasn't attracted to him.

Yes, the men her sisters usually set her up with were safe and boring. None of the men she'd dated had ever made her heart thump against her ribs with an irrational awareness like this. This reaction to Charles No-Name

Mystery Man was just fear talking. Adrenaline. These unwanted feelings of compassion and attraction to the hard planes of his body and the soft color of his eyes didn't mean she had a death wish to get involved with anyone as dangerous and controlling as this creep.

She picked up a washcloth. "No. You made the choice to do what you do. If you want to lead a life of violence, I suppose it makes sense that you'd bear the marks of that decision."

But when she turned around to walk to the bathroom sink to wet the cloth, Charles clamped a hand around her wrist like a vise, pulling her back between his knees. "You don't have to understand me at all, Teresa." Her gaze dropped to the gun on the quilt beside him, and he quickly released her to snatch it up before she could even think about making a lunge for it. "I'm not going to tell you my last name, because the less you know about me, the better. You may not believe this, but I'm trying to protect you."

She retreated beyond his reach, rubbing at the traitorous warmth that lingered on her skin where he'd touched her. "Hence the threats and the kidnapping."

"Does that mouth ever get you into trouble? Or is all the tough talk just a defense mechanism for you?" He nodded, as if something in her posture or expression had answered his question. "Try not to be too afraid. If you do everything I say, you'll be safe."

Teresa was too wet and cold and exhausted to stifle her sarcasm. "Well, guess what, Charlie. I don't trust you, either."

The corner of his mouth crooked up with half a grin at her expense. "No wonder you don't have a boyfriend. You're prickly when you get worried or riled up."

"I'm not worried about you," she lied.

The grin faded as he tugged at the scarf, now sticky with his blood, exposing the ragged wound at the front of his shoulder. "The people who tried to kill me this morning will try again. They've already tracked me to Kansas City. I have no doubt they'll send someone else to find me and finish the job. I don't want you caught in the crossfire. Enough innocent lives have already been lost."

"What do you care about innocent lives?"

"Even men like me have a code of honor they live by. Rules about what's right and wrong." There was no trace of humor anywhere in his expression now. With the flecks of gold-and-brown beard dotting his neck and jaw, he looked even more like the wounded bear she'd imagined him to be earlier. He dropped the scarf onto the other soiled garments on the floor and raised his gaze to hers. "Rule One? I need to live. For a few days longer, at least. To do that, I need your help. That makes you an asset to me. Rule Two is protect your assets. So no last name. No warm fuzzies between us. I don't need you to get close or to give a damn about me. Just do your job."

"In a few days, it'll be Christmas," she pointed out. "Is there really a rule on that list of yours that says you're going to let me go once I take out that bullet?" He arched a wheat-colored brow in a silent question. She moved around his knees and pointed to the bump in the skin beside his scapula. "I can see it protruding through the skin near your shoulder blade. Your protective vest must have worked in reverse. Instead of keeping the bullet out, it prevented the projectile from exiting your body. You need a surgeon, not a pediatric nurse."

He shook his head. "I've got you. That's all I need."

"You're lucky it's not buried inside by a lung or other vital organ. And there's no way to tell what muscle or bone damage there is without an X-ray." She didn't bother reminding him again that a hospital was where they should be right now.

He tipped that grizzled bear of a face up to hers. "Can you cut it out and stitch up the wound?"

Did he not understand the enormity of what he was asking of her? "Yes, but that's only a superficial fix. A muscle tear will probably heal on its own. But if there's a bone chip inside or a nicked blood vessel or nerve damage—"

"Do it."

"I need a few minutes to boil water and sterilize everything."

"No boiling water." He slipped his long arm behind her waist, pulling her close again. "You think I'm going to trust you with a potential weapon like that?"

Ignoring the heavy weight of the weapon resting against her hip, Teresa jerked away. "You may have no problem hurting people, but it's not my job or my nature to intentionally inflict any harm."

"Oh, yeah? Who was going to knee me a half hour ago?"

Guilty. She silently thanked him for the reminder she needed to clear her head of her confusing feelings. "I've got isopropyl alcohol in the bathroom." She thumbed over her shoulder to the hallway. "Is it all right if I go and get that?"

Charles the Bully simply nodded.

She returned with a bowl of soapy water and a bottle of rubbing alcohol and went to work cleaning and sterilizing as much of the wound, needle, thread and paring knife she'd brought from the kitchen as she could. At his bidding, she'd turned her dresser mirror so that he could watch her work with the knife behind him. It was the reflection of jaded suspicion she spoke to now. "This isn't standard procedure. And these conditions are far from sterile. What if I make it worse?"

His gaze met hers in the mirror. "Trust me, darlin', I'm as tough as I look. You can't make me hurt any worse than I already do."

"The sooner you're fixed up, the sooner you're out of my life, right? Even though I know your name and can describe your face, I'll be a free woman again? You won't hurt anyone else?"

Those golden eyes, seemingly lit from within, offered her an unexpected reassurance. "You're not who I'm after, darlin'. You're not the one who needs to worry about me."

So who was he after? Who should be worried about the toughness and the single-minded determination and all the guns she suspected were in that bag? Charles was big, strong, wounded, armed and serious as a heart attack. Whoever he was after *should* be afraid. She'd been a fool for not minding her tongue and risking his anger, for thinking for even one minute that she could run away or leave him behind or talk him into letting her go before he was done with her.

Shivering again, though with something more unsettling than the cold of her damp clothes, Teresa dropped her gaze to the broad expanse of his back. She opened the antiseptic spray and doused the injured shoulder. "This is only a topical anesthetic. When I cut through the skin, it's going to hurt. If you cry out, the neighbors will hear. I don't want anyone calling 911 and getting caught in the middle of another shoot-out with you."

"I won't cry out."

She didn't know whether to admire or fear a man with that kind of control. In the end, she reminded herself that what she felt didn't matter. As a nurse, she simply did her job and took care of the patient, no matter what it might cost her emotionally.

Teresa patched him up the best she could. She cleaned and bandaged the wound on his left thigh, as well. An hour later, she had an exhausted man, dressed in little more than gauze and tape and the fresh jeans he'd pulled from that bag, sitting on the edge of her bed. He was flexing the fingers of his left hand. Although it still pained him to raise his arm, he was getting some feeling and use back in the hand, making him twice as dangerous as the one-armed thug had been. Per his instructions, she dumped the ruined clothing and medical supplies into a trash bag and picked it up to carry it out to the kitchen to dispose of later.

"You got any duct tape, Peewee?" he asked, slowly pushing to his feet. He towered over her, even in his bare feet, reminding her who was in charge. Teresa meekly nodded. "Bring it when you come back. Once you've cleaned up and put on some dry clothes, I'm tying you up in case you get any idea about escaping while I catch a few hours of sleep."

Forget *meek*. Hadn't she been cooperating? She tilted her face up to his. "You don't have to restrain me. I promise I won't try to go anywhere but the kitchen and bathroom."

"Either I tie you up or you're sleeping in this bed with me tonight."

The bald statement shocked her, and maybe not entirely in the way it should have. So what if he was the most manly thing she'd ever had in her apartment? He was the enemy. Her captor. Compassion for his injuries and this rudimentary attraction didn't matter. "You said you'd let me go."

"When I'm done with you, I will. I figure I need six to

eight hours of solid sleep to get my energy back before I can get out of your life. I can't risk you calling the cops or giving me away to anyone before I'm ready to leave. Until then, I'm tying you up." As if testing the newfound strength in his left hand, he closed his fingers around her chin and tipped it up, forcing her to look at him. "Do we understand each other?"

Teresa pulled away from his gentle yet firm, callused touch, nodding. "I'll get the tape."

Chapter Five

Nash turned his face away from the ribbon of sunlight that squeezed between the wall and curtains and hit him in the eyes.

He rolled over onto his back, moaning at the stiffness that made every joint ache. He raised his forearm to shield his eyes from the blinding glare of sunlight off the snow outside. Yeah, there was a chill on the bare skin of his torso. And yeah, he was pretty beat up. He could tell from the throbbing in his shoulder that he was far from 100 percent.

But he must have slept through the night. As consciousness pushed away the dregs of sleep, he was able to remember the echoes of his nightmares—familiar faces, doors closing all around him, locking him out, keeping him from reaching Axel Torres and Jim Richter and Tommy Delvecchio. And blood. Way too much blood. At least, that was how he interpreted the wispy clouds of scarlet hanging around him like warm breath in the wintry air of his dreams.

Despite the disturbing images that clung to the fringes of his thoughts, he felt a little more rested, a little more like a normal person. As normal as the last surviving member of a team marked for death could feel, at any rate.

That sobering thought raised him to another level of consciousness. He blinked his eyes beneath his arm, slowly taking stock of his surroundings. Sore thigh. Shoulder that felt as if it had been through a meat grinder. Soft quilt beneath his back. Softer pillow beneath his head. The subtle scents of alcohol and soap and…garlic? teased his nose. His stomach grumbled in a visceral response to the enticing aroma. Right. Food hadn't exactly been a priority for him these past two days. And whatever was cooking smelled mighty good.

Whatever was cooking?

No longer dreaming, no longer speculating, but wide-awake and suddenly aware of the keen gaze watching him, Nash opened his eyes and curled his fingers around the gun at his side before lowering his arm. He turned his head slightly to the right and saw that it was too late to go on the offensive.

"Ah, hell."

Teresa Rodriguez, that sweet little bundle of curves and sass, sat in the kitchen chair beside the bed, where he'd left her bound and gagged last night.

Except the tape he'd stuck loosely over her mouth was gone.

Not only was she free of her bindings, but she'd changed her clothes and held his badge and a magazine of bullets in either fist. "Good morning, Agent Nash."

Nash swung his legs off the side of the bed and sat up. Maybe a little too fast because her dark eyes and blue sweater swirled around in his vision. He shook off the dizziness, tossed aside the blanket she'd covered him with and spared the time to check his Smith & Wesson to confirm that the magazine she held came from his weapon. He was empty. At a distinct disadvantage. The captor was now the captive.

She bombarded him with questions before he could decide on his next plan of action. "Why did you make me afraid of you? Why did you kidnap me? Why didn't you just tell me the truth?"

That clever little minx. She'd cut herself loose from the duct tape he'd bound her wrists and ankles with last night. And while he couldn't stop the grin of admiration from hooking the corner of his mouth, he wasn't about to get her more involved with the mess that was his life right now than she already was. "It's complicated."

"Oh, I understand complicated. Why didn't you tell me you were a cop?" She leaned with him to keep them face-to-face when he tucked his empty weapon into the back of his jeans. "I would have helped you. I wouldn't have put up such a fuss. I thought you were a fugitive from the law—a drug dealer or a hit man. I was thinking of ways I could disable you long enough for me to get away. I almost sewed up a dirty wad of gauze in your wound to create a sepsis. If the pain and discomfort didn't slow you down, the resulting blood infection would eventually kill you."

She had plans to sabotage his injury? "Did you do that?"

"No. I took an oath to help people, not hurt them." So she had the brains to think like a survivalist, but she lacked the killer instinct to ensure her freedom by whatever means were available to her. That still gave him a slight edge over her because she had a heart and a conscience that restricted her actions, while he was willing to do whatever was necessary to complete his mission. "You should have told me the truth instead of bullying me. I grew up with cops. I understand the dangers they face. My brother's a cop. My sister Emilia is married to one."

He'd snatch that magazine of bullets right now if he

didn't think the room would start spinning again at the sudden movement. Nash didn't like feeling weak like this. He didn't like having his secrets exposed. And as much as he appreciated her resourcefulness, he didn't like that his hostage had turned the tables on him. He blinked her chocolate-brown eyes into clearer focus and let his gaze sweep down the clingy lines of her sweater and jeans. Nice. He'd been aware of those breasts and hips from the moment he'd pinned her body beneath his in the snow. But the rosy pink lips, adorned with nothing but accusation and shine, made him hungry for something more than food.

Priorities, Nash. He corrected the errant thought that warmed his blood. A man in survival mode didn't have time for fantasies like wondering what a woman would taste like beneath his kiss. At least she hadn't taken his gun or stolen another one from his go bag to aim at him. And he'd just have to take her word that she hadn't booby-trapped his wound to hasten his death. "What are you, a pickpocket?"

"I've developed certain skills over the years," she explained. "I'm the youngest of five children. I never could outmuscle AJ or outsmart Emilia and my sisters. So I developed a knack for being sneaky. I'd pocket a piece of a jigsaw puzzle or steal a couple of Mama's cookies so I could make sure I had my share of whatever they were doing before they were done."

Nash tapped his left front pocket, still trying to get his brain up to speed on the shifting situation. The cell phone was still there, nestled right next to the promised land. Could he have slept through her taking it off him? Had she already called 911 or turned him in to the brother or brother-in-law at KCPD she kept throwing at him? "How long have you been loose?"

"I waited a couple of hours until I was sure you were in a deep sleep. Then I crawled to the bathroom, got the scissors out of my sewing kit and cut myself free." She lifted her hand to the tiny pink welts and bruising that dotted her cheek. "I didn't realize how bad it would hurt to pull tape off my skin. The rest were easier."

"I tried to tape it to your clothes, not your skin." Feeling a pang of remorse for her getting hurt interfering with his annoyance, Nash instinctively reached out to touch his fingertips to the spot. A muscle quivered beneath the brush of his fingers, and her cool skin warmed. "I'm sorry."

"I wasn't exactly cooperating when you were restraining me."

"It's my fault, Peewee. Don't apologize or make excuses." What was it about good people getting hurt when he was around? Snatching his hand away, Nash pushed to his feet. And wobbled. Teresa immediately stood up to help him. He savored a moment of her steadying strength tucked to his side, then took advantage of her switching the badge and bullets to one hand by grabbing the magazine from her loose grip.

"Hey!"

He stepped away and pulled the gun from his belt, reloading it. Reclaiming a little more advantage. "I need my bag."

But turning around to survey the room forced him to grab the nearest bedpost as everything swayed.

"What am I going to do with you? Sometimes you really piss me off. Sometimes I feel sorry for you, and sometimes I even kind of like you. I don't understand you."

She'd get over it. "Where's my bag?"

Despite a sotto voce curse, her hand was at his elbow

again. "The dizziness is probably from blood loss and the fact that you haven't eaten anything for at least fourteen hours. I heated up some soup. It's my mama's chicken soup recipe—the best thing you can put in your stomach when you're not feeling a hundred percent."

"You made soup?" Now the smell of herbs and garlic made sense. His mouth watered at the deliciously homey aroma drifting through the apartment. Embarrassed by the answering grumble in his stomach when he was trying to be the tough guy and throw a little intimidation around, he searched the room for a clock. "How long have I been out?"

"About twelve hours." He pushed away her helping hand and staggered toward his bag near her dresser. "If you sit back down or come to the kitchen, I'll fix you a bowl."

"I need to get dressed."

She hurried past him and planted herself between him and the go bag. "You're running a low-grade fever. It may be your body's reaction to the hypothermia and trauma you went through yesterday. But it could also mean there's an infection setting in."

"I thought you said you didn't tamper with my wound."

"I didn't." She tipped her face up to his, her eyes flashing with temper. "You're managing that side effect all by yourself."

"I'm not going to any hospital." He watched her open those bow-shaped lips to argue. The desire to bend his head and silence that sassy mouth with his hit him like a punch to the gut. He must have a fever to forget for one moment the urgency of his mission. Instead of listening to his body, Nash snatched his badge from her hand and ignored both her arguments and that sirenlike pull she had on him. He tucked the wallet with his badge into the pocket beside his phone and reached down to pick up the bag.

But the moment he gritted his teeth and struggled to sling its heavy weight onto his shoulder, Teresa was there to help. She plucked the straps from his hand and carried it to the bed, where she set it on the rumpled blanket and unzipped it.

Nash had to slowly switch course to follow her. "Did you call anyone?"

She scooted away when he stepped up beside her to pull out a white T-shirt. Her arms were crossed in front of her and she was keeping her distance as he retrieved a snap-front Western shirt and gingerly started to dress in the clean clothes.

"You need a winter coat if you're going out," she groused, turning her head when he dropped his pants to pull on a fresh pair of briefs.

"I'm not staying here."

Nash pulled out his socks and sat on the edge of the bed. "Did you call anyone?" he repeated. He needed to know exactly how much lead time, if any, he had before this place would be swarming with KCPD officers or something worse.

"You conveniently destroyed all my phones, remember?" Her gaze lifted from the cord sticking out of the pocket of the jeans he wore, where he'd stashed the burner phone. "And I didn't want to get that close to you."

"You didn't call 911 on me? Didn't call big brother?" Bending over made him dizzy. Pulling his knee up to his chest to tug on one stupid sock nearly wore him out. Talk about being a sitting duck.

"No, Charlie. Charles? Agent Nash? What should I call you? Let me." With a noisy sigh, she dropped to her knees in front of him to help him push up his pant legs and put on his socks.

Hell. In addition to escaping and cooking and going through his things, she'd washed and dried her long hair. The long ponytail that fell down the middle of her back was dark and shiny like a bay horse's well-brushed coat. Double hell. He should be worried about the fact he hadn't heard the water running in the next room or awakened when she'd pulled those jeans and that figure-hugging sweater from a drawer or closet in here—not wondering if her hair was as soft to the touch as her skin had been.

And he damn sure shouldn't be wondering if she'd bumped those compact yet decadent curves against him when she'd been robbing him of his ammunition. Even though she'd drawn the line at rummaging through his pockets, she had to have practically lain on top of him to reach over him to get the gun his fingers had been touching all night. At least, he thought he'd kept his weapon beside him. But he was quickly learning there was little he could predict about this woman.

Again he wondered why he couldn't have stuck himself with a meeker, more amenable captive to stitch him up and hide him for a few hours. Stupid luck. Nurse Teresa wasn't like any woman he'd been involved with before. A man in his position should have minded his misfortune a little more than he did.

"Nash. Everybody calls me Nash." He pointed to the end of the bed, reminding them both who had the upper hand—and the loaded gun—now. "Boots."

"You're in no shape to walk out of here. And you don't have a car." She picked up his Justin boots and helped him pull them onto his feet. But she stopped in the middle of tugging his jeans over the shaft of his left boot.

"Unless you plan to steal mine?" She tilted her face to his, her cheeks flooding with heat. "You're stealing my car?" Then she was standing up, backing away. "I *am* reporting you. I was dumb to think you needed a second chance. I unloaded the electronics from my armoire, so I can go anytime I want to. I think I can outrun you in the shape you're in."

"Wait." She spun toward the door, but Nash grabbed her by the arm and pulled her back. She landed on his lap.

"Let go of me." He grunted when she put her hand against his bandaged thigh and tried to push away. "Sorry."

But his pain didn't stop her from scrambling to get away. She just changed tactics, swatting a fist at his good shoulder but avoiding doing the damage she should have by going after his injuries and freeing herself. Still, she was enough of a handful that Nash caught her flailing arms at her sides and pulled her against his chest. Anchoring her in place sapped his strength, but he refused to let her go. If she got away from him and made it to Mrs. Walker's apartment or some other neighbor's phone and brought the local cops down on him…

"Please, darlin', I need you to stop."

Please? Now who was lacking the killer instinct? Now her boots were aiming for his shins and the side of her hip kept brushing against his groin. *You don't have time for this. Tie her up again. Make her cooperate. You owe it to Tommy and Richter and Torres.* "How much is your car worth?"

"What?" Curiosity made the twisting stop. She settled on top of his thighs and looked up at him as if this was some kind of embrace instead of a snare. "I don't know. My brother's the car nut. I bought it for a few thousand dollars when I graduated from nursing school and he put a new engine in it for me. I don't know what he paid. It was a gift."

Risking another bolt to the door, Nash released his grip on her waist to reach inside his bag and pull out his flash wad of rolled-up bills. Her eyes widened as he counted out ten hundreds and pushed the cash into her hand. "Is this enough to borrow it for twenty-four hours?"

Teresa jumped to her feet, tossing the money back at him as if it burned her fingers. "Oh, my God. You're a dirty cop? How much money do you have in there?"

The sanctimonious accusation stung more than it should have. He retrieved the scattered bills and set them in a neat pile on her bed. "You ought to know. My badge was in the same pocket."

"I was looking for another phone. I didn't even touch the other pistol or shotgun or boxes of ammunition in there. Once I found your badge and that little black book…"

His contact book?

Any truce between them had just ended. He dove back into the bag. It wasn't there. "Teresa?"

She realized her mistake a moment too late and darted toward the bedroom door. Nash was on his feet in an instant, lurching forward as the room tilted. Damn it. She *could* outrun him.

But even in his condition, she couldn't outmuscle him. He looped his arm around the waist, lifting her off the floor. Yet he was too off balance still to simply hold her against him, so he let his momentum back her into the wall and trapped her there with his body. She braced her hands against his chest, defiantly tipping her chin. "Stop grabbing me, you big bully."

But the contact book was nonnegotiable. "Uh-uh, darlin'. You're not going anywhere. Where is it?"

"Stop doing that."

He felt her up, patted her down, checked every pocket until he found the book tucked in the rear of her jeans and he pulled it out. He waved the leather book in her face. "Who did you call?"

"No one. You trashed all my phones and the cords were in your pants.

He wasn't buying it. If she'd looked through the pages of names and notes and numbers, then she already knew too much. Cartel names. Notes about his team's murders. A list of potential suspects masquerading as coworkers. Any one of whom might want him dead. The idea that she might already know too much made him sick to his stomach. "Some of the people who want me dead are in here. Who did you call?"

The tone of his voice changed from a threat to a very real concern. Her fingers curled into the front of his shirt, pleading with him, and the struggles stopped. He hoped. Something was stirring behind his zipper, and it wasn't the instinct to defend himself. He still held her suspended above the floor, his hips wedged into the cradle of hers. As he regained control of his fears, he realized his fingers had tunneled into the velvety length of her ponytail. Yes, it was as soft and thick as he'd imagined, it smelled cleaner than any horse he knew, and he was a fool to let this crazy heat she ignited in him distract him for even one moment.

"Teresa." He let her toes slide to the floor but didn't release her. "Whose name did you pull out of this book?"

Her fingertips pulsed against his chest. Was she afraid of him? Perhaps soothing the wounded beast? Was this the nurse trying to take care of him again? Or was she as vividly aware of each ragged exhale pushing their bodies against each other as he was? Was she just as baffled by the electricity arcing between them?

"Technically, I didn't call anyone."

"But...?"

She tilted her dark eyes up to his. "My internet comes through the cable line. I sent an email to the name with the star at the front of your book. Jesse Puente. I searched for his name online and it said he worked at the DEA like you do. So I emailed him."

Nash dropped his forehead to hers and swore a blue streak. Then he pulled away from the grasp of her hands, arming himself, getting ready to leave. She clung to the wall beside the bedroom door but watched his every move. "He said you were a good cop. I'm an idiot for trusting him, aren't I? I wanted to justify you kidnapping me, so I believed him. I took him at his word because I needed to make sense of everything my gut is telling me about you."

Nash fastened his belt and holstered his gun. "What nonsense is your gut telling you?"

"That you're not really a bad guy. Even if you're a bad cop, there has to be a good reason why you've made whatever choices you've made and why you have all that cash." She pushed away from the wall and blocked his path again. "If you were really a criminal without a conscience, you'd have shot at me instead of that tree behind your truck last night. You wouldn't have cared if the duct tape pulled my skin or stuck to my clothes. I think there's good in you. Or believe me, I'd have been long gone before you woke up this morning."

Chapter Six

I think there's good in you.

Well, if that didn't sound a lot like the counselors at the Texas boys ranch where Nash had grown up. He'd been so angry after his parents' murders, resentful that he'd been stuck in some remote patch of sandy grassland filled with hard work and horse manure. He'd started and finished his share of fights and wrestled with his own vengeful tendencies enough that it was easy to draw on the experience of his youth whenever he needed to assume a less-than-savory undercover identity. The men and women who worked the land, ran the school and counseled the troubled boys and teens there had worked a miracle on him, inspiring him to get his act together to get through school and become a cop.

But every now and then—when his closest friends were being murdered, when innocent lives were being destroyed and he couldn't do a damn thing about it, when the woman he loved said she couldn't handle his life and walked away—those masochistic demons would reappear.

He'd need some time to process Teresa's opinion of him. Seeing him as anything positive, as someone she might trust, was just wishful thinking on her part. He was on a mission to find out the truth about the traitor who'd gotten his team killed—or he was going to die trying. It was whatever he needed, when he needed it. His life was all about survival and hard choices right now—not sexual attraction or guilty consciences or idealistic guts that had the wrong impression about him. Nash was afraid there'd be more casualties like Tommy Delvecchio before he got to the truth. But as long as he got the job done, he didn't care.

There wasn't anything good about that.

He clipped his badge back on his belt where it belonged. "What did Puente say?"

Teresa recoiled half a step, hugging her arms around her waist when he dismissed her overture of trust and support. "He thanked me for contacting him. I thought I was helping. Did I get you into trouble?"

A little bit, darlin'. "Where's your computer?"

"In the living room."

"I need to see it."

It hurt to do it, but Nash lifted the bag onto his uninjured shoulder and stalked down the hallway after her. The main rooms smelled like Christmas with the fragrant pine needles on her tree and the scents of home cooking filling the apartment. Taking stock of his surroundings in daylight, Nash shook his head. Teresa had not only emptied out the armoire, but she'd shoved it back into place, away from the door. He'd been a sitting duck for several hours, plenty of time for the mole in his department to find that email to Captain Puente and track it back to its source.

While she sat at the computer desk behind her couch to turn on the machine, Nash pushed aside the hodgepodge of toys and other gifts, wrapping paper and ribbons on the dining room table and set his bag down. He checked the front window and peephole of the door. Everything was still locked down, and nobody appeared to be showing more interest in her fourth-floor apartment than they should be. Reassured there wasn't a pending home invasion, at least, he crossed to stand behind her chair.

"Show me the messages," he ordered.

Teresa pulled up her email account. Nash leaned over her shoulder to read her message to the captain.

Dear Mr. Puente—I have a man here with ID that says his name is Charles Nash. He's badly wounded, but I've taken care of his injuries. I don't have a picture to send, but he's about 6'3", muscular, has dark blond/light brown hair and needs a shave. He has scarring on his left arm and back. To be honest, they look like knife cuts and a bullet wound. Is he really a DEA agent? Is he working a case for you here in Kansas City? He's warned me several times not to contact the police, but I found your name in his bag and took a chance that you could help me.

He hasn't hurt me yet, but there have been plenty of threats. Please advise before I turn him over to the authorities here. He asked me not to, which makes me wonder if he's telling me the truth.

He doesn't know I'm writing you. I don't know how long I have before he wakes up, so I'd appreciate a quick reply. Sorry to contact you this way, but I don't have access to a phone.

Thank you.
Teresa Rodriguez, R.N.

After he nodded to her, she clicked on Captain Puente's alleged reply.

Dear Ms. Rodriguez,
Sounds like the Charlie Nash I know. You say he's in-

jured—have you taken him to a hospital for proper care?
I'd like to follow up on his condition because yes, he's
working an important case for me, and if he's out of
commission, I need to replace him on the investigation.

Rest assured, you are safe with him. He's a good man,
if a bit of a loose cannon sometimes.

As soon as you can reach a phone, please call me at
this number to verify your identity and confirm Nash's
badge number. Thank you.

Captain Jesse Puente
Houston Office
DEA

Nash read the phone number at the bottom of the
email. Puente's direct line. Was that significant? Why
not simply request a reply to his email? Why not instruct
Teresa to call the general office to get whoever was on
duty, or notify the local cops to request backup for an
injured officer?

While sorting out possibilities, Nash rubbed his jaw,
massaging the stubble there. He needed a shave. He
needed some food. He checked the clock on the computer
and the time stamp of the two emails. Almost three hours
old. Plenty of time to catch a flight to K.C. He needed
to get out of here. But things had just gotten more complicated. He needed to come up with a plan F or G now.

"Have you made any other contact with the captain?"
Nash asked.

Teresa shook her head. "I heard you moving in the
bedroom. You must have been having a nightmare. But
I didn't want to risk you waking up and catching me
out here. So I shut the computer down and went back to
watch you sleep."

The nightmare was the same whether he was asleep or awake. Nash pushed away from the chair. "There's no proof that it was Puente who got the message. Anyone could have answered that."

She followed him across the living room, rubbing her arms as though she was cold. "He made me think I could trust you. Should I have emailed my brother instead?"

"If it was me, I would have run out that door." He nodded toward the television and sound equipment on the floor. "Your survival instincts are on the fritz. You had the means to escape. To turn me in. Why didn't you?"

"If you didn't have me, you might take Mrs. Walker or someone else in the building hostage. I can deal with you better than an old woman or a young family can."

"Deal?"

"Yes." She moved into the kitchen to stir the soup. "If Mrs. Walker knew about the guns in your bag and all the blood you were hiding under that blanket, she'd probably have a heart attack. If you're a good guy and need help, I have connections no one else in this building has. If it turns out you're a bad cop, I can put up a better fight than anyone else. So you're stuck with me."

Nash stopped at the kitchen peninsula, breathing in the fragrant meal simmering on the stove. "You're a lot of trouble, you know that, Teresa Rodriguez?"

"I know." Her agreeable response surprised him. She covered the pot and held up her hands, showing she had no hot liquid or dangerous utensils on her as she circled the counter to join him. "That's my nickname. *Gamberro.*" The Spanish word for *troublemaker.* "I've been called that my entire life."

So his wasn't the only life she'd turned sideways? He settled onto the nearest stool, bringing his height closer to hers. "Who calls you that?"

"My older brother and sisters. My mother, when she was alive. I'm too impulsive. I have a temper. I lead with my heart."

"You get yourself into trouble before you figure out a way to get out of it." *Like stopping to help a stranded motorist on a wintry night.*

Nash felt a little of that same chill that had her rubbing her arms for warmth again. "They make me feel like a child. But I'm twenty-nine years old. I have skills and talents I need to use. I can do more with my life than be taken care of. I've dealt with some horrible things as I've grown up. I don't need to be protected from everything."

"Yeah, you do." Although he wondered how her idea of "horrible things" stacked up against his murdered parents and violent youth, he didn't have time for curiosity or compassion. "The moment Captain Puente or whoever's impersonating him opened that email in Houston, a clock started ticking."

"What does that mean?"

He might as well spell it out since, as far as he was concerned, they were in this together now. "I'm an undercover agent, Peewee. I supervise a team of agents who've infiltrated a drug war. Only my cover's been blown. So were theirs. By a crooked cop or someone else on the take in the Houston office."

Her eyes widened in shock. "The men who tried to kill you were cops?"

"I doubt the three goons who came after me yesterday were actual cops, but they're definitely working with one. No one except for the people in my office knew I was heading for Kansas City. Yet the cartel thugs who shot me up and murdered a friend didn't just track me to my location. They were waiting for me."

Her soft gasp barely registered. "You lost a friend yesterday?"

"A rookie agent. He was trying to help me." Nash's wry laugh elicited a frown. "Maybe I should have you contact your brother—see if KCPD has had a report of four dead bodies at a chop-shop near the river. They could at least get Tommy back to his family in Houston." Any urge to laugh, even with that raw sarcasm, was crushed beneath the load of guilt he carried. "I didn't even hold his hand or check to see if he was killed instantly. I just… There were too many bullets flying. I had to leave him behind."

And now her hand was on his arm—comforting him? Seeing an opportunity to finagle her own rescue? "I can do that. If you give me back the cords to connect my phones, I'll gladly call AJ and find out if he knows anything about your friend."

Nash shook his head. "Just kidding, Peewee. No cops."

She pulled her hand away. "I don't understand. Clearly you're upset. AJ can help. If I ask—"

"No." Even if her brother had good intentions, it'd be too big a risk to take. "Someone at Houston HQ is funneling sensitive information to the Graciela cartel. I'm the only survivor of three different hits. Until I can identify the mole in our office, I'm off the grid. At least, I was until someone in Houston read your email. There are warring factions within the cartel, and both sides want me dead—I get that. But knowing someone I trusted leaked our names and locations? I intend to live long enough to find out who betrayed my men."

"And you. He betrayed you, too." Man, she was still feeling sorry for him.

He'd get her over that real quick. "Now your name is

on that hit list, too. Every bad thing you think about me? Those cartel thugs are worse."

"What did I do?"

He pointed to the computer. "You sent an email that can lead the traitor straight to Kansas City. Straight to this apartment. Straight—"

"To me." She sank onto the stool beside him, her skin turning pale beneath its warm olive tone. "You think they'll come after me to find you?"

"Yep."

"Can't you just call this Captain Puente to see if he's the one who got the email?"

"What if he's the traitor?" Nash had been proud to get assigned to Captain Puente's team, had always considered the older officer a straight shooter. But then, he'd thought the best of every man on their undercover unit… until his friends had died, and the only explanation that made sense was a mole on the inside who'd leaked their names to the cartels.

Teresa's knuckles turned white where she gripped the counter. "There isn't anyone you can trust?"

"I'm flying solo on this. At least, I was until you picked me up." Knowing he was wasting precious time and energy caring about her distress, he slid his hand across the counter to rest it over both of hers anyway. There was only so much guilt a man could bear. "That's why I didn't want you to call the local cops or your big brother. That's why I didn't want to go to the hospital. They're all red flags to where I'm hiding out that I'm not ready to put up yet."

Her grip on the counter relaxed, but she didn't pull away. "You need to get better before you deal with those horrible men."

"I don't have that luxury. But I do need to stay ahead

of these guys. I need to get some leads and pinpoint who set us up before they strike again. If I die, they'll get away with murdering my men. I'm the only one who knows the leak came from our office. That's why they're looking for me. Once I'm gone, the bastard who gave up my team can go right on selling information to the cartels." She shook her head and started to pull away, but Nash curled his fingers around hers, apologizing, reassuring, warning her of the danger. "And since they're going to be looking for you now, too…"

"You're not going to let me go, are you?"

"Nope. Rule Two, remember? Protect your assets." He threaded the fingers of his left hand through the velvety strands of coffee-colored hair that had fallen over her shoulder. "I thought I could use you to patch me up enough to keep me going a few days longer. If I kept you from asking questions, if I kept things anonymous, you'd stay an innocent bystander and I could leave without making you a target. None of the people after me would even know of your existence. But that's all changed now. You're part of my team now. I'm not going to lose anybody else to these bastards. Especially a sweet thing like you." Her chin tipped up with a jerk at the offhand compliment. Barely noticing the twinge in his shoulder, he pulled his fingers down through the length of her hair before letting her go and nodding to the kitchen. "You got a thermos or something you can pack up some soup in? Get an overnight bag with whatever you need for a few days."

She gathered her ponytail and flipped it behind her back as she pushed to her feet. "I have a job. I have plans for Christmas. I can't go with you."

"Right now mine's the only plan you have to worry about. You're going to need my protection."

"That sounds like a really desperate pickup line."

"The only thing desperate is the situation. I can't let you go until I find this guy, but I won't let you get hurt. I give you my word."

"Your word?" She went into the kitchen and turned off the burner beneath the soup. "Forgive me if I don't jump at the chance to go on the lam with you."

"There isn't anybody who can vouch for me right now. But when I make a promise, I keep it. I know it's a huge leap of faith, considering how I've treated you. But I will keep you safe. What does your heart tell you about me?"

Her eyes locked on to his for an endless moment. Yeah, he'd been listening when she said she led with her heart instead of listening to common sense. And yes, he would play on that weakness of hers to ensure her cooperation. "This…mole would really come after me?"

"You're his best lead to finding me."

Teresa nodded slowly, as if evaluating her options. "And you'd probably die of infection or pop those stitches and bleed out without me to take care of you."

Possibly.

"Would I be your partner or your captive?"

"Depends on how well you cooperate, *Gamberro*."

"Don't call me that. Peewee is bad enough." And then the energy in the room shifted. She squatted down and disappeared while he heard her rummaging through a cabinet. "I actually only have one day I'm scheduled between now and Christmas because I'm working the holiday. But Christmas Day is nonnegotiable. I'm planning a party for the patients who'll be hospitalized over the holiday. I have presents and cookies and decorations. I could only help you through Christmas Eve."

"Teresa, this isn't a negotiation. I can't leave you—"

"I won't disappoint those children. I suppose I could

call someone to take my shift tomorrow and clear the trade with my supervisor." The cabinet door closed and a thermos appeared before she popped up to face him over the counter. "If I had a phone."

Nash tapped his cell in his pocket, wondering how many other saps had succumbed to that sweetly innocent smile of hers, which he suspected wasn't so innocent at all. Yet he was actually toying with giving the phone to her. "I suppose I could trust you enough for one call. But only with me listening in."

"Partner or captive?" she pressed.

A knock on her apartment door startled them both. "Teresa, are you in there?"

She set down the thermos at the man's deep, slightly accented voice. "AJ?"

Nash pulled his weapon and stood. "Big brother the cop, AJ?"

She'd tricked him again.

Chapter Seven

Nash grabbed Teresa by the arm to keep her from hurrying past him to the door. His voice was a furious whisper. "I thought you said you didn't contact anybody else."

"I didn't."

Screw that innocent act. Why had he not seen this coming? "You set me up. All this chitchat was a stall until he could get here."

"No. I swear." She splayed her hand against his chest, her eyes wide, her voice hushed. "Put your gun away. Please. I don't know why AJ's here, but he can help us. We'll just tell him the truth. He can give you protection. Put you in a safe house."

Nash's voice was equally toneless and urgent. "If I had a little sister that some desperate man had kidnapped, I don't think I'd be willing to listen to any explanations before I slapped the cuffs on him and threw his butt in a jail cell." He leaned down to whisper against her ear. "Where I'd be easy pickings for Graciela's and Vargas's hit squads, by the way."

"Hit squads?"

He raised his head enough for her to see he was dead serious. "If they think you know anything about me—about my investigation or where I'm hiding—they won't be nice about how they get the information out of you.

And if I'm in a holding cell or even an interview room, I won't be able to protect you."

The color blanched from her cheeks before she turned her head to another knock on the door. "I swear I didn't contact him."

"Tía Teresa, I have some visitors for you." AJ Rodriguez sounded patient, cajoling, not at all like a big brother bent on smashing the man who'd endangered his sister.

"Tía Teresa," a child's voice called. "Did Santa come to your house?" Someone even younger laughed.

"My nephews." Teresa's fingertips pinched the skin beneath Nash's shirt as she held on tighter. "Please, put the gun away. AJ will be armed, too, and I don't want my family to get hurt. I'll get rid of them."

Nash's thumb rubbed tiny circles in the wool of her sleeve as he evaluated her sincerity.

Another knock, and the tenor of AJ's voice had changed. "Teresa, are you in there? Is everything all right?"

"I'm fine," she shouted, the volume of her voice jarring to Nash's ears. "I just need a minute." She dropped her voice to a whisper again. "If you expect me to trust everything you've told me, then you'll have to trust me first."

Big brother knocking at the door wasn't leaving Nash much choice. "Teresa?" AJ called.

"One wrong word," Nash warned, "and this could get ugly fast."

"I won't give you away. I promise."

With a curt nod and a refusal to holster his weapon, Nash pried her hand from his shirt and ducked behind the armoire, where he could peek through the back to watch the door open without being seen. Smoothing her sweater back into place and taking a deep breath, Teresa opened the door. "What? Is the building on fire? I said I was coming. *Buenos días,* AJ."

She beamed a smile and traded a hug and a kiss with the stocky dark-haired man. That compact size must run in the family. AJ might be only five-nine or so, but he was built like a fighter. His badge flashed from a chain around his neck in the opening of his padded leather jacket. And despite the small hand clutched in his, the detective was carrying at least one sidearm. Nash lowered his gun to his side, pointing it away from their visitors but keeping himself ready to move if he needed to.

"Claire." Teresa exchanged a hug with a beautiful blonde who carried a mini Michelin Man on her hip. "And my two favorite boys. Tony and little Adam." There were noisy kisses for the toddler stuffed into a snowsuit and the older boy, who held on to his father's hand. "What brings you here this morning?"

Nash didn't get another look before Teresa scooted them all out into the hall and pulled the door behind her, leaving it ajar just enough that he could hear the entire conversation.

"You're not inviting us in?" AJ asked.

The woman called Claire, AJ's wife, Nash assumed, answered in an oddly toned yet articulate voice. "I told you we should have called first. Maybe she has a guest."

"No guests," Teresa assured them. Then she lowered her voice to a fake whisper. "But plenty of secrets. Santa stopped by for an early visit this week and asked me to wrap up some goodies for him and hold them until he's back to pick them up on Christmas Eve. I can't let you into Santa's workshop, now, can I?"

"I told you Tía Teresa was helping Santa." The little boy named Tony sounded quite certain of his holiday rules. "We can't peek, Daddy, or Santa will know, and he won't bring the presents to our house. We have to go."

Although he could imagine the little boy tugging on his father's hand, the prolonged silence made Nash wonder if AJ was doubting Teresa's whimsical story of aiding and abetting the bearded little elf in the red suit. Nash wished he had eyes on the scene, to make sure there were no coded messages being exchanged.

"You're wrapping presents?" AJ finally asked. The doubtful inflection in his tone made Nash think no SOS signals had gone up.

"I am. I've even got one for you, big brother. And you're hard to surprise, so no coming in." Nash saw Teresa's hand reach for the doorknob behind her to keep the view into her apartment blocked. "Not that I don't love seeing all of you, but why are you here?"

"We were just a few blocks away," her brother explained. "Tony had a basketball game this morning. We thought you'd like to join us for lunch."

"Normally, I would, but…" she slurred her voice through clenched teeth "…there is a lot of work to do." Then she was speaking normally again. "Did you win your game?"

"No." Tony's pout was audible. "But I did make a basket."

"That's great," Teresa cheered. "And you'll get them next—"

Claire interrupted. "Tony's game was all the way out in Oak Grove." Nash was beginning to think the woman might be hearing impaired, from the unique quality of her voice. But that didn't stop her from being an active part of the conversation. "What your brother really wanted was to see with his own eyes that you're all right."

"All right?" Teresa feigned innocence very well. "Why wouldn't I be all right?"

"KCPD got a report on a truck shot up on Lee's Summit Road last night." AJ Rodriguez was definitely a cop. Nash recognized the direct, no-nonsense demeanor. "I know you take that route home from work, even though I've told you to use a safer, well-lit route when it's late. Especially in this weather. You know the city doesn't clear that road as often as the main routes."

"I did take that road home after I did some shopping last night," Teresa confessed. She was smart, mixing in enough of the truth to make her lies sound plausible. "There were a couple of slick spots, but the snow wasn't an issue for me."

"Did you see anything?" AJ asked. "Dispatch got a call from a woman about the truck. She never identified herself. They got disconnected before the dispatcher could get an ID."

Nash held his breath, waiting to hear her answer.

"So of course you assume it was me." Nash recognized the defensive bristle in Teresa's voice. "Like no other drivers would be on that road?"

Nash hadn't seen much traffic except for her sedan. He'd been lucky she'd stopped.

"I tried calling you this morning and there was no answer."

"I lost my cell."

AJ wasn't giving up on this. "I called the landline, too."

"I had a late night. I unplugged the phones so I could sleep in. I knew one of my siblings would be checking up on me this morning."

AJ remained coolly unruffled, despite the growing tension in his baby sister's tone. "You didn't see anything? I got a look at that truck this morning. There was nothing in it except for blood on the seat. There were tracks from more than one vehicle at the side of the road, and multiple footprints in the snow."

Nash could count the seconds of silence as Teresa hesitated. This was it. He wondered how good she was at lying to her family—or if this was the moment when she tossed him over to the enemy. "Well, I did see a black truck in the ditch and thought I could help, but…it was already empty when I got there. The driver must have hitched a ride."

"You went up to a stranger's truck? Alone?" Nash heard a low-pitched curse in Spanish. "Teresa, there's a BOLO out for the owner of that truck."

Be on the lookout for the driver in question. *Him.* Nash clenched his teeth to stifle his own curse. The mole in Houston must have listed him nationwide as some kind of fugitive.

"Why?" Teresa asked.

"Usually, when there's that much blood, we look for a body to go with it."

"Antonio." Claire chided her husband, probably not wanting their children to hear details like that.

"I saw an accident on the side of the road, AJ," Teresa insisted. "I'm a nurse. I'm expected to help if someone's injured."

"At the hospital." So Teresa's independent streak could get under her big brother's skin, as well. "No one expects you to risk your life on a dangerous road in the middle of the night."

"*I* expect it of me." Her temper was brewing. "I'm okay. I didn't see…" Nash tensed. *Don't hesitate, darlin'. He'll know you're lying.* "There was no one in the truck. I'm all in one piece. See for yourself. Claire, a little help here? I'm sorry I have to turn down the lunch invitation, but I have things I need to take care of today."

"There was a *lot* of blood, Teresa. The truck had out-of-state plates and, did I mention, bullet holes?" Nash held his breath while AJ pushed Teresa for the truth. "You take foolish—"

"Antonio. *Amo*," Claire interrupted in a quiet voice. "Your sister is fine. She's also grown-up. She has a job to do, just like you and me. We need to go and give her her space. Come on, boys, tell your aunt goodbye."

"Bye-bye," the little one chirped.

"Bye, Tía Teresa," Tony echoed.

There was a rustle of hugs and goodbyes.

And one last warning from her brother. "If you run into something like that again, you call me before you take matters into your own hands. *¿Comprendes?*"

"*Entiendo.*" Yes, she understood.

"I'm trying to take care of you," AJ insisted.

"And I was trying to take care of the injured driver."

"I know, little one. But you could have run into a dangerous man. You give me cause to worry, yes?" There was a momentary pause, then, "I love you."

Judging by her muffled voice, there was another hug. "I love you, too."

And then the door was closing and Teresa threw the dead bolt.

Nash crept out of his hiding place to find her leaning against the door with her eyes shut. "You okay?" he asked.

Her eyes popped open to meet his gaze. "I got rid of them, like you said. Endured the lecture, lied to my family. It's all good," she added, her sarcasm evident in her tone.

"I get the idea your brother knows you're lying."

"Well, it's the first time I've harbored a fugitive, so I wasn't quite sure what to say."

"Teresa…" Maybe she was partner material after all. Nash holstered his gun, surprised at how well she'd covered for him. But it might not be enough. The tiny dots of bruising beside her mouth were a clear indication to even a bad detective that something wasn't quite right in Teresa's world. "There are other reasons why law enforcement might issue a BOLO besides looking for a criminal. Maybe someone in Houston filed a missing-person report on me."

Her gaze flashed up to his. "Do you think that's what happened?"

Honestly? Nash shook his head, wishing he had a better reassurance to give her. "Your brother sounded too worried about you."

"AJ always worries." Teresa tapped her thumb against her chest. "*Trouble,* remember?"

He hated that she joked about herself. Ignoring the urgency of the situation and the instincts that warned him her brother was a hard man to fool, Nash stroked his fingertips across the injury again. "I'm sorry. I wish I didn't need you to do this for me."

"I wish I could believe you." Her dark lashes fluttered against her cheeks at his touch. Man, he was taking liberties he had no right to. He didn't have time to care about anything except finishing this job and avenging the deaths of his men. But this woman who was full of surprises stunned him again when she turned her face into the cup of his hand, turning his comfort into a caress. "I've seen your injuries. If nothing else, I do believe you need me."

Nash let his fingertips slide into the edge of her hair.

"What you did for me last night was a brave thing. You knew you could help, and you did."

She smiled up at him, easing a little of his guilt before pulling away and leaving his palm tingling with the imprint of her cool skin pressed against his. She headed for the kitchen. "You didn't give me a choice."

"Take the compliment, darlin'. You didn't have to stop on that empty stretch of road. And I'm still alive, so you must be doing something right."

"Thank you for saying that." She pulled a ladle from a crock beside the stove and pointed it at him. "This is all going to turn out right in the end, isn't it?"

Nash was done lying to her. "I can't make that kind of guarantee."

She held his gaze for several seconds longer before her eyes shuttered and she went to work.

While she packed them some food, Nash sorted through his go bag, taking stock of his gear and prepping another magazine of bullets. "You're protecting AJ and his family, too. Remember that. I'm sure lying to your family sucks, but the fewer people who know about me, the better for both of us."

"I know. I'll pack some medical supplies, too. And you still need a winter coat."

"We'll buy one somewhere along the way. And a hat." A real Stetson to replace the one he'd sacrificed would take too much of his cash. But Kansas City had been a stockyard town back in the day—there had to be some knockoff cowboy hats for sale somewhere.

"There's a Chiefs stocking cap in the front closet you can borrow," she offered. "It's not too girly."

Nash went to the closet and pulled out her coat and the stocking cap he found in a basket on the top shelf. The red and gold clashed with his Texans football spirit, but sporting the local team's colors would certainly help him blend in in K.C. He pulled the knit cap over his head. "This'll do for now."

"Is that what your money's for? Coats and hats?"

"It's for whatever we need. I always keep a stash when I'm undercover so I don't have to use credit cards or ATMs that can be traced." He got out his phone and met her at the sink. If they were going to be a team, with her following his orders to the letter, then he was going to show her a little of that trust she'd asked for. He pulled her hand away from the dish towel she held and placed the cell in her palm, curling her fingers around it and holding on. "Call your supervisor and someone to cover your shift. Do everything I say, and I promise I will keep you alive. And I'll do my damnedest to solve this case and have you home to your family and that hospital party by Christmas."

She nodded, accepting the deal. He hoped. She pulled away, crossing to the dismantled wall phone to open the thick directory beneath it. "What about your family, Nash? Are they safe from the men who are after you? Do you need to warn them?"

"Ain't nobody at home to call, Peewee. It's one of the hazards of the job. No parents. No siblings. No girlfriend…" *Phone calls.* A nagging suspicion, one that should have registered sooner, finally worked its way through the pain and guilt and low-grade fever. He followed her to the phone book. "Why didn't your brother mention your cell phone? You said you lost it, but I trashed it and left it on the floor of my truck. If he saw the blood in the seat, he would have seen that, too."

Teresa shrugged. "AJ said there was nothing inside."

Nash processed all the possible explanations, not liking a one of them. "So who cleaned up after we left?"

"The police?"

"AJ's the police. If they found your cell, they could get your number from the computer chip inside. He'd know it was yours."

She nodded, understanding his concern. "And if he knew that was my phone, especially in pieces like that, he'd have been on my case even more. Especially if he found it in a truck belonging to someone the police are looking for."

"Someone else beat the cops to it." And that someone could already be en route to Teresa's apartment.

With a renewed urgency pumping through his blood, Nash crossed the living room to peek outside through the blinds again. He'd checked earlier for anything that seemed suspicious, but he was noting the details now. There was some slow-moving traffic, but the block was too long and there were too many trees along the winding road to know if anyone was circling around for a closer look. There were two parking lot entrances to Teresa's place. Seventeen cars parked there and at the curb in front. More in the lot for the apartments across the street.

"Is something wrong?" Teresa's voice at his shoulder startled him. "You're scaring me a little bit."

A bundled-up man was sweeping snow off the sidewalk across the street, showing no interest in anything except his task. Nash looked for occupied vehicles. A van in the parking lot had a mom strapping a child into a car seat in the back. The wind shifted, blowing the exhaust away from a black SUV parked across the street, revealing a dark-haired man behind the wheel, talking on his cell.

Nash didn't startle when Teresa touched his arm, although his pulse still kicked into a higher gear. "What is it?"

He pulled her off to the side of the window, keeping her out of sight as he pointed out the black vehicle. "Is that your brother?"

She peeked through the blinds. "No. I don't know who that is. AJ drives a Trans Am. Or Claire's red Escalade when they have the kids."

Taking her hand, Nash pulled her into step behind him. "Come on. We need to go." He tossed Teresa her coat and hoisted his bag onto his good shoulder. "Is there a back entrance we can use to get to the parking lot?"

"Sure." She slipped into her coat, pulled a backpack from the closet and loaded it with the thermos and food. Nash picked up her purse and dropped the whole thing into the knapsack's main compartment when she started to pull out certain items, hurrying her along. "Do you think that man is here to kill you?"

"I'm not waiting around to find out. Let's go."

She stopped tying the backpack and snapped her fingers. "The first-aid kit."

When she dashed past him, he grabbed her hand again and turned her toward the door. "We don't have time. Vargas's and Graciela's thugs travel in packs."

"Packs?" Her fingers shook as she unlocked the door.

"If that's a cartel man, I don't know where his partner is. He might already be in the building." Nash entered the hallway first, scanning both directions to make sure they were alone while she locked her door behind him. The elevator at the front of the building hummed to life as the gears in the shaft engaged. Not good. "Someone's on their way up."

Teresa nodded toward the opposite end of the hall. "The back stairs are down there."

When she started to walk, Nash pressed his hand to the small of her back and hurried her into a jog. "Move it, darlin'." The elevator might not be coming to the fourth floor, but no sense taking any chances on being seen. "Rule Three—avoiding a confrontation beats fighting your way out of one. I won't get caught in the middle of a shoot-out with you here."

"I'm okay with that rule."

They were cutting this too close. "No wonder your brother didn't ask you any questions about my truck."

"What do you mean?" She reached the stairwell door and shoved it open.

He scooted in right after her. "KCPD would have run the Texas plates and ID'd that truck as mine. An alert would have gone over the wire. Headquarters in Houston should have answered the alert by identifying me as an agent, one in need of assistance with that blood on the scene."

"AJ didn't ask me any questions about the accident. If he'd suspected a fellow cop was in danger, he'd have asked me for details about what I'd seen. He wouldn't have gone ballistic about me trying to help. He didn't know your truck belonged to a cop." The woman was smart. Thankfully, she was also sharp enough to check over the railing before heading down the stairs. "The mole in your office must have gotten that alert. And labeled you a fugitive."

"Or buried it without a response." Nash waited to peer through the closing crack of the door as the elevator opened. The dark-haired man he'd spotted out front stepped out. That bulge beneath his coat wasn't his cell phone. The guy was armed. Despite the bandaged graze in Nash's thigh, his legs felt solid as he raced down the stairs behind Teresa. "The cartels already have someone else here."

"That guy out front?"

"The guy knocking on your apartment door right now."

"My…?" When she stopped at the first-floor exit and spun around, he nearly plowed into her. "My email must have… What did I—?"

"Forget it." The fear or apology or whatever had widened those beautiful dark eyes was too much. He palmed the back of her neck, tipped her face up and pressed a quick kiss to her mouth. "None of this is your fault." When her lips softened beneath his, he lifted her onto her toes and leaned in to kiss her again. "None of it."

The second kiss was almost as quick. But firmer. More satisfying. Less like an apology and more like a man testing his welcome with a woman he cared about.

And she wasn't pushing him away.

He heard her soft catch of breath, felt her palm bracing against the thump of his heart, read the question in her upturned gaze and realized the import of what he'd just done. "What rule is that?" she whispered.

"Sorry." Why didn't she slap his face? Why had she responded to his kiss? Why couldn't he keep his priorities straight around this woman? But those were all questions to be answered later.

Nash lowered her heels to the floor, released her and reached over her shoulder to push open the door. The blast of cold air that swept in instantly chilled his skin and cooled his roiling emotions. He nudged Teresa out the door, taking her hand and moving in front of her to lead her down the sidewalk to the corner of the building, where he paused to peek around and ensure their path was safe. He made certain there were no other unwanted visitors watching the parking lot or searching outside the building before he pulled her into a quick pace beside him. Her short legs had to do double time to keep up with his long strides, but she didn't complain. She clicked the car's remote start and had the doors unlocked when they got there.

"You drive." Although he trusted his skills behind the wheel more than hers, she knew the city. Plus, she was 100 percent while his stamina and reflexes were still iffy. Nash swung open the back door and tossed his bag on the seat, pulling out the scraper to brush snow off the windows while she hurried around and climbed inside. "Get the car warmed up and drive out of here nice and normal so we don't draw any attention to ourselves. We'll make your calls on the road and pick up whatever supplies we need later."

She had a blanket waiting for him when he got in beside her, then backed out of the parking space and shifted into Drive. "Where are we going?"

Breathing hard enough to make his shoulder ache, he pulled the cover up to his chin, partly to mask his face and the gun he set in his lap and partly to reclaim the body heat he'd lost outside. "Turn right. Not too fast. I want to get a look at that car."

Nash pushed the seat all the way back and hunkered down as they passed the parked SUV. He didn't see anyone else inside the vehicle. Possibly, they'd split up to pursue different leads to find him or Teresa. Or the man they'd spotted had been calling in backup and was scouting ahead.

"Do you see him?" she asked, catching him looking into the sideview mirror.

"Just getting the license plate."

"Texas?"

"Local rental."

He heard a throaty gasp, this one far different from

that dreamy little sound she'd made after he'd kissed her. "Nash? Behind us."

She'd turned her head to the mirror on her side of the car. Nash glanced back over the seat and sat up straight. He saw it, too. A second black SUV, pulling out of the parking lot across the street and picking up speed. Closing the gap between them.

Forget stealth. "Get us out of here."

He pushed the blanket aside and loaded a bullet into the firing chamber of his gun. Teresa's sedan picked up a little speed, heading down the winding residential street toward some lake or creek at the bottom of the hill. The driver was talking on his cell. That meant he was reporting to… Nash glanced back to the right to see the first man burst through the front door of Teresa's building and charge straight through the snow toward their position on the street.

The man swapped out his phone for his gun and opened fire.

Thunk. The sedan lurched. "Oh, my God! Is he shooting at us?"

"Faster, Peewee." Nash spared a moment to make sure she hadn't been hit as he rolled down his window. The guy popped off two more shots, which pinged off a parked car as they whizzed past and took out one of her taillights.

Nash stuck his arm out the window and fired a pair of warning shots, forcing the man to dive into the snow. He pushed himself halfway out the window and twisted back to take aim at the SUV speeding up behind them. But there were too many civilian targets to risk a shot. The man with the broom. Kids building a snowman. Parked cars and too many trees messed with his line of sight.

But the other driver had no such compunction. He

pointed a weapon out the driver's-side door and fired wildly at Teresa's car. A lucky shot clipped the trunk, and Teresa screamed. Her car zigzagged through a patch of slush, and chips of ice flew up, biting into Nash's face. He recoiled from the stinging assault, wrenching his shoulder.

His luck was going from bad to worse. A block behind him, the other SUV whipped out of its parking spot and spun in a U-turn to join the chase. Nash dropped back into his seat, swearing in pain and frustration.

They weren't going fast enough. "Floor it!"

He stretched his long leg out and stomped on Teresa's foot, pushing the accelerator to go faster. They hit a bump in the road and sailed into the air for a split second before coming down hard and scraping the undercarriage against the pavement.

"What are you doing?" Teresa bounced against the binding of her seat belt. They were passing newer houses now, fewer trees and cars. The road widened, making them easier targets.

"Turn!"

"At this speed?"

Nash grabbed the wheel and jerked it to the right, keeping his foot on the gas when her instinct was to slow down. "Where's the nearest highway?"

"Not close."

They bounced across a bridge over a frozen lake and hit a roundabout intersection. Ah, hell. They were circling back toward the oncoming SUV! Teresa cursed when she saw the gun leveled at them. But the driver hit the same bump they had and lost his grip on the gun. He quickly pulled both hands back to regain control of his vehicle. But as he slowed, the second SUV picked up speed and passed him.

Nash reached for the steering wheel again. "Get us out of this neighborhood!"

"I've got it." Teresa smacked his hand away and stepped on the accelerator. "I've got it!"

She gripped the wheel in both fists and hunched forward. The car careened away from the roundabout, plowing through a drift and careening off the curb as she sped past a stop sign. "I know where we can lose them."

With oncoming cars pulling to the side and the SUVs in hot pursuit, Nash rebuckled his seat belt and braced his hand against the door as Teresa drove through a neighborhood gate and wheeled the car in a sharp right, then sped up the hill to the north. She honked the horn and flew around a slower vehicle. The two SUVs lost a little more distance when she cut through a corner convenience store lot and came out on a four-lane highway heading east, merging with heavier traffic.

One SUV followed the same path but got stuck a few cars back. The driver darted from lane to lane, trying to get around the cars between them. The second SUV was nowhere to be seen. And by the time they'd doubled back through a massive shopping center parking lot near the intersection of two highways, they'd lost both cars following them.

A few minutes later, they were cruising up and down the snow-covered hills of 40 Highway, matching the flow of traffic. With no sinister pursuers reflected in any mirror, Nash holstered his Smith & Wesson and leaned back against the headrest, taking note of his aching shoulder and the slightly winded cadence of his breathing. That encounter had been too close. He was clearly off his game. Yes, they'd gotten away—for now. But they'd have to ditch this damaged car that the cartel thugs could identify as Teresa's now.

But he'd wait and give her that bit of news after she relaxed the death grip she still had on the wheel. "That's some sweet driving, Peewee."

"Thanks. That was exciting." She glanced across the seat at him. "No. It was terrifying. My heart's still racing. Who were those men?"

Cradling his left arm against his side, Nash reached over the center console to capture a velvety strand of coffee-colored hair that had worked free from her ponytail and smoothed it behind her ear. "Try to stay in the moment, Teresa." He stroked his fingers along the line of her jaw, anxious to soothe the tension there. "Don't worry about the future or the past. Allow yourself a minute to just breathe. The crisis is over. We're safe for now. You did great."

He knew she was finally coming out of fight-or-flight mode when she pulled his hand from her face and gave it a quick squeeze. "You're favoring your shoulder again. Did you pull the stitches?" She waited until he sank back into his seat to crank up the heat. "You're the one who should be relaxing. Pull the blanket over you."

"I think that was just a little too soon for that kind of exercise." He winced at the effort of picking up the blanket from the floorboard. She wanted answers as to why her life was being turned upside down, and he needed to talk this through before fatigue turned his brain to mush. "I'm guessing with bullets flying and a high-speed chase that we're definitely on KCPD's radar now."

"Of course we are. Someone is bound to have gotten a plate number or description of the drivers. They'll report it."

"They'll have your license plate number, too. And somebody we drove past might have even recognized Teresa Rodriguez."

Her lips buzzed with a weary sigh. "I'm going to need a new car, aren't I?"

Nash laughed. "I was going to wait and spring that one on you a little later."

She slowed to turn onto a road that would take them to the interstate. "So what do we do next?" Teresa tapped the console between them when he asked for a pen to write down Thug One's license plate number in his log book. "How are you going to find out who's after you if you're hiding? You're not calling your boss in Houston again, are you?"

Not directly, at any rate. Yesterday he hadn't wanted to call in any favors. But today, with Teresa's life as well as his own on the line, he had no choice. "Do you know a place called the Shamrock Bar?"

She nodded. Her eyes were as glued to the mirrors as his had been, still looking for any signs of the SUVs returning. "It's a cop bar downtown. I've been there several times. But you shouldn't drink alcohol in your condition. And a drink is the last thing I want right now. Especially if I have to drive like that again."

"I'm not thirsty, darlin'. I just need to see the bartender there."

Chapter Eight

Shivering, Teresa paused at the neon shamrock in the front window of the Shamrock Bar and gazed through the glass. Inside, the window was framed with a shiny green garland and the corners had been dusted with that fake white spray snow. She'd been here before for a couple of family gatherings, a few outings with her friends and even on a pleasant-enough date with a detective who worked with AJ. But she'd never gone in specifically looking for a man to invite out to a secret rendezvous in the parking lot.

When she heard a car driving past on the street behind her, she peeked over her shoulder to see if one of the black SUVs from this morning had followed her. But as the blue car bounced over the ruts of grated, packed and melted snow on the pavement, she exhaled a puffy cloud of determination and pushed open the front door.

Jake Lonergan was easy enough to spot. There were only a few customers sipping a beer at the polished walnut bar or eating a sandwich for an early dinner at one of the tables.

Nash's description had been simple. *He'll be the biggest thing in there.*

Teresa pulled off her gloves as the bell above the door chimed behind her. Nash was tall and carried plenty of muscle on his lanky frame. From her petite perspective, he was big. But the man setting a stack of crated glasses behind the bar was built like a Mack truck. The silver hair he wore cropped close to his scalp highlighted the scars of a tragic encounter that Nash said had cost the man a good chunk of his memory. If Nash was a wounded bear, then Jake Lonergan was a T. rex with a toothache. Even the green apron and wedding ring he wore did little to soften his beastly appearance.

Definitely the biggest thing in the room. His unsmiling bulk made him the quintessential bouncer who commanded respect and looked as though he could easily handle any customer who dared to step out of line.

And Nash said he was a friend?

Teresa shuddered in nervous anticipation rather than with the cold this time. Her heart rate hadn't been normal since those two men had chased them from her apartment and shot up her car. She needed a nap to ease the stress. She needed to talk with one of her sisters about this emotional pull she felt toward Nash and tell AJ the truth about the man she'd saved, endangered and made a desperate deal with. She needed a chance to rethink some of the choices she'd made in the past twenty-four hours.

Her chance to walk away from Charles Nash and the nightmarish drama he'd brought to her frustratingly sheltered life was staring her right in the face. A public pay phone hung on the recessed wall between the two bathroom doors.

While Nash pulled the tags off the sheepskin-lined coat and gloves they'd bought at a thrift shop and bundled up in the car, she could walk right over there and call 911 or AJ and tell them she'd been kidnapped by an armed stranger. That she'd hidden him in her apartment. That she'd helped him escape from the men pursuing him. That her apartment had probably been ransacked and that two men who worked for a drug cartel had tried to kill her.

They'd tell her to stay put. They'd drop everything and run to her rescue. AJ would put a twenty out on her car and have this place swarming with cops in a matter of minutes. He'd tell the entire department that Nash was armed and dangerous—that he might have harmed his baby sister. There wasn't a cop in the city who would stand by while the family of one of their own was in danger.

Nash would be arrested.

She'd be free of this nightmare.

He'd be taken to a holding cell until he was turned over to a DEA agent who might betray him…or a hit squad found him and finished the job they'd started the day before.

Charles Nash had sworn her life was in as much danger as his.

He'd promised protection in exchange for keeping his secrets and tending his wounds.

He'd kissed her.

Teresa's tongue darted out to touch the rim of her lips. She could still feel him there. The ticklish rasp of his day-old beard against her skin. The firm pressure and unexpected warmth of his slightly crooked mouth molded against hers.

Could she really be feeling something for Nash after knowing him for so short a time? Was this dangerous attraction a lusty response to being forced into the most thrilling adventure of her life? Or was she just as foolish as her brother and sisters claimed because she was so eager to be treated as a useful adult that she mistook Nash's need for her medical assistance and knowledge of the area as some kind of emotional connection?

Should she do this favor for Nash? Or walk over to that phone and call her family? Did she do what she thought was the right thing? Or did she do the safe thing?

"Can I help you, ma'am?" The muscle man behind the bar was talking to her.

Teresa snapped her attention away from her thoughts and focused on the icy-blue eyes watching her. Decision made. She inhaled a steadying breath. She was Nash's partner, not his captive. She didn't need to escape. She didn't want to leave him to face his enemies on his own. She didn't have to understand what she was feeling right now, either. She just had to do what was necessary to keep them both alive.

Her family was going to lock her away in a tower and throw away the key. But not yet.

Teresa threw back her hood, unzipped the top of her coat and crossed the bar to carry out her mission.

"Mr. Lonergan?" She stepped up on the brass railing beneath the bar stools to erase a fraction of the difference between their heights and thrust her arm over the top of the bar. "I'm Teresa Rodriguez."

Jake eyed her hand but didn't immediately take it. "Ms. Rodriguez. I've seen you around. You any relation to Detective AJ Rodriguez?"

"He's my brother."

He nodded as if the familial connection made her presence acceptable and finally shook her hand. "How's he doin'? I don't see him in here much now that he's got those boys to raise."

"AJ's fine. I just saw my nephews this morning. The whole family is well. I'm actually here to talk to you about another friend of yours." She glanced at the lush sitting closest to her, his chin propped in his hand, his leering stare indicating he would have liked to make her acquaintance, too.

But a sharp look from Jake, and the young man turned his curiosity up to the television hanging over the end of the bar.

Jake pulled a towel from his apron and a glass from the top crate to dry it. "I don't have that many friends."

"This one's an old friend from Houston." Jake set the glass on a shelf below the bar and reached for another one, his expression revealing nothing but polite patience. She hurried to recount the message Nash had given her. "He said to tell you that he's the only man from your past who cares that you don't remember him."

That earned her a chuckle. "Charlie Nash."

"You *do* know him." She smiled with relief that he understood the coded message. "He said to tell you he knows you're not in the business anymore, but he's working something big and needs to call in a favor from you."

"Nash is here in K.C.?" She shushed him when the man watching television glanced their way again. Jake dropped his gruff voice to almost a whisper. "How'd you hook up with him?"

"You want to hook up with me, sweetheart?" came a slurred offer from beside her. "I'll buy you a drink."

Another silent warning from Jake and the dark-haired man pulled a ten-dollar bill from his shirt pocket and slapped it on the bar beside his empty glass. "I guess that's a no. I'll be leaving now, Miss Teresa Rodriguez. Merry Christmas."

The man trilled all the *r*s in Teresa's name and the greeting as if the sound amused him before staggering to his feet. He made an effort to straighten his tie before picking up the long wool coat he'd draped over the stool beside him.

"You need me to call you a cab, mister?" Jake offered.

"I'm good." The tipsy man shrugged into his coat and started slipping his buttons into the wrong holes. He pointed to Jake and winked at Teresa. "Not as good as you're doing, pal. But I'm good."

Wondering if this unsettled feeling would plague her anytime a man with dark brown hair showed too much interest in her now, Teresa waited for the drunk to stumble out the door and turn his collar up against the Arctic blast. He was huddled against the front window, punching in a number on his cell phone, when she faced Jake again.

"That was weird." She tried to laugh off the awkward discomfort she felt. "Sober, that guy might be halfway attractive if you go for the preppy type. Drunk, he's just creepy."

"I thought I knew everybody who came into this place," Jake groused, indicating the nosy flirt was as much a stranger to him as he was to her. "I hope he's calling for a ride out there." He stowed the glass and dragged his attention back to Teresa. "Where is Nash?"

"In my car. He doesn't want anyone to know he's in Kansas City. Well, someone does know who shouldn't, but…" She silenced her nervous rambling and matched Jake's direct approach. "Will you come talk to him?"

Jake nodded, understanding this was a serious, as well as secretive, request. "Let me get Robbie in here to cover for me. I'll be right back."

Once Jake exited through the swinging door behind the bar, Teresa perched on a green vinyl stool and glanced furtively around her, wondering if any of the other patrons were paying as much attention to her as that man with the long coat had. The two women in the booth across the way didn't seem to notice her. They were more interested in the two hotties shooting pool nearby. Once

Teresa saw the badge hanging from a chain around one of their necks, she realized they were probably both cops.

Oh, great. Even if they weren't on duty, they might still have been given a description of Nash or even her and her car. Turning her attention back to the door where Jake had gone, she pulled the hood of her coat around her neck and tucked her chin to her chest, hoping none of them knew AJ well enough to recognize her. When the bell over the door rang behind her, indicating more customers, possibly more cops, she hunched down even farther, willing Jake to hurry back out and help her.

She heard a low-pitched drawl behind her instead. "It's me, Peewee. Don't jump."

She startled anyway at the arm that slid behind her back. She spun on her seat to face Nash as he settled on the stool beside her. "What are you doing here?" she whispered in a mild panic. "I thought you were hiding in the car where no one could see you." At least he'd had the sense to turn up the collar of his bulky coat. She reached up to pull the red-and-gold knit cap he wore farther down over his forehead. "You shouldn't be here. Those men at the pool table are cops. What if there's a description out and they recognize you?"

He captured her hand against his warm cheek to mask his face. "You were taking too long. I got worried."

"That drunk was bothering me. But Jake sent him on his way."

"What drunk?" Nash raised his head, scanning the bar, his posture instantly on alert.

But Teresa quickly framed his jaw with both hands and pulled his focus back to her before he drew any-one's attention. "That man by the front window with the misbuttoned coat..." When she glanced over at the shamrock sign and Christmas decorations, she saw nothing through the glass except for a few cars driving past. "Where did he go?"

"I didn't see anyone out front." Nash straightened, concern lining his features.

"Just look at me, okay?" She pulled his chin back to her again. "I don't want anyone to see you."

He leaned in and they touched foreheads, his golden eyes looking right down into hers. "Not a hardship for me, darlin'."

In fact, he spread his knees and moved closer, resting a foot on either side of her stool and sliding a possessive hand along her thigh, turning her efforts to hide him into what probably looked like a lovers' embrace to any curious eyes that might be watching.

It certainly felt like an embrace. She wasn't sure if it was the compliment that warmed her, his protective posture or the levity he used to try to lessen her worry that made her actually feel like smiling. "Maybe the drunk who hit on me caught a cab. I guess he freaked me out a little bit because of those other two men shooting at us."

"Hit on you?" Nash's eyes narrowed above hers. He pulled away a fraction of an inch. "Was something off about this guy? Did he scare you?"

"All he did was offer to buy me a drink. Said my name in a funny way. Like I said, Jake got rid of him." She pushed Nash's stocking cap back from his temple to finger his short thick hair. "I guess I'm only going to be able to trust blonds and redheads now."

"Let's make it just one blond in particular for the next day or so, okay?"

Teresa heard the faintly possessive admonition but was frowning as she felt the dampness in his hair. There was more warmth to his skin than the pseudo embrace could account for, too. "Your fever's getting worse. How are you feeling?"

Before he could evade her question, the door behind the bar swung open. Jake Lonergan entered, followed by an older man with curly black hair and a bushy beard.

"Charlie Nash." Instead of putting on the coat he'd brought with him, Jake reached across the bar to her patient. "You look like hell."

"I'm still better lookin' than you," Nash teased, standing up to shake hands with Jake.

Teresa rose, too, pressing the back of her knuckles against his ashy skin to gauge the warmth there. "He needs to go to the hospital, but he won't listen to me."

Apparently, none of these men were going to. Jake introduced them both to the bar's owner, Robbie Nichols, a robust man who spoke with a lilting Irish brogue. "You go with your friends, Jake. I'll take care of things here."

Really? She wasn't here just to look pretty and be taken care of. Hadn't she put her life on the line, too? Hadn't she lied to her family and taken a huge risk on a man she barely knew? These men might have a few survival skills she lacked, but she had knowledge and training neither one possessed. She tugged at the sleeve of Nash's jacket and insisted he look at her. "You need to listen to me."

"Later. We need to get out of sight first." Nash covered her hand with his and nodded, at least acknowledging her concern before turning his attention to Jake. "You got a place we can talk?"

Robbie was the one who nodded and pointed to the door behind him. "Use my office. No one will bother you there."

"Thanks, Robbie. This way." Jake went to the end of the bar and lifted the hinged gate for them to pass through as the owner picked up a towel to dry the glasses Jake had brought out earlier.

Fine. There was more than one way to handle a recalcitrant patient. If Nash wouldn't listen to reason, then she could do the bullying thing herself. Teresa asked the older man for a lemon-lime soda with lots of ice before Nash scooted her into the back hallway. Jake locked the office door behind them and offered them guest chairs. Nash sat in the closest one, his strength clearly flagging. While the two men talked about Agent Nash's desperate situation, Teresa opened her backpack on the corner of the desk and dug out a bottle of aspirin.

She recognized the small black notebook Nash pulled from inside his coat. She'd gotten herself into hot water that morning by reading through his secret names and cryptic notes and had possibly made it necessary for them to go on the run. Whatever the names and numbers in there meant, clearly it was of vital importance.

"This is everything I've been able to put together on this case." Nash held up the notebook. "Three days ago in Houston, I must have asked the wrong question of the wrong person. Next thing I know, my apartment's been trashed, my confidential informant inside the Graciela cartel says their chief, Berto Graciela, knows I'm a cop and he's put a hit out on me. I had two other agents, Axel Torres and Jim Richter—you don't remember them, but we've all worked together in the past—inside different arms of the organization, as well. They were both exposed as undercover agents and murdered last week."

Teresa's stomach twisted into a knot at the revelation of such tragic events. Nash had lost men he worked with—friends, most likely—to the senseless violence of the drug trade. He must have been aching with grief and guilt, and yet the two men talked as if conducting a business meeting.

"How can I help?" Jake asked, thumbing through the notebook Nash handed him. "You know these names don't mean anything to me anymore. My amnesia wiped the slate clean—until I dealt with that hit man the Gracielas sent after me."

"Yeah, you did a good job of disrupting business there for a while when you took out old Diego Graciela." Nash grinned, although his humor never reached his eyes. "We were having pretty good luck working inside the organization and taking advantage of the power struggle between Berto and Diego's lieutenant, Santiago Vargas. It's easy to funnel intelligence in and out when one side doesn't know or trust what the other's doing. That all ended last week when my men started dying."

Jake tapped one of the pages in the notebook. "And these starred names are your suspects as to who leaked your identities to the cartel?"

"Oh, my God." Teresa felt the blood drain from her head to her toes. She sank onto the corner of the desk beside her bag. "I thought the stars meant those people were important to you. That they were the good guys. I'm so sorry."

"It's okay." He reached over to squeeze her hand. "You didn't know. I'd have tried the same thing if I'd been in your shoes. Maybe if I'd told you the truth instead of tying you up, you wouldn't have contacted Puente."

Jake arched a silvery eyebrow at that last exchange. "Umm...?"

Nash released Teresa and waved aside any curious questions about the rocky start to his partnership with her. "Let's just say we've had some trust issues."

"So what's the deal with you two?" Jake asked, leaning his hip against a credenza in front of the frosted-glass window. "Teresa's no agent. And it's not like you to get someone involved who isn't trained for the job."

"No, it's not," Nash agreed. "But I need her." He unsnapped the top buttons of his shirt and pushed it back to reveal the bandage covering the wound on his shoulder. "I figure a hospital is the first place the DEA and the cartel will look for me."

Teresa saw a small dot of red seeping through the gauze. "I should change that dressing."

"Later."

"Later you'll be dead if you don't let me do my job." She peeled back the tape to look at his injury.

He smoothed the bandage back into place. "Peewee?"

She propped her fists at her hips. "Nash?"

Jake interrupted the dueling wills. "I heard about the shoot-out at the chop shop on the news. The reporter said it was gang related."

Nash snapped the front of his shirt, effectively brushing aside her usefulness. "Not any local gang. They were cartel men. And there are at least two more in town still after me." He glanced up at Teresa. At least he had the good grace to stamp an apology on his chiseled features. "After both of us." He returned to his conversation with Jake. "That reminds me. Can you get your hands on a local police report? See if there was a break-in reported at Teresa's apartment? Find out if anything was damaged or taken." His gaze ping-ponged back to her. "I want to buy you a new phone, get your car fixed for you and repay you for any damages to your home."

"You're the only thing damaged in my life. Here. Take these and drink all this. Your body needs the electrolytes." She held out two aspirin and the lemon-lime soda. When he shifted in his chair to continue his conversation with Jake, Teresa shifted, too. "Now, Nash. You asked me to take care of your injuries and keep you alive. I can't do that if you won't let me help."

Jake chuckled behind her. "Now I get it. She's tough enough to go toe-to-toe with you. Sounds like a lady I'd listen to." Teresa turned and nodded her appreciation for his support once Nash had swallowed the pills and taken a few sips of the drink. "So she keeps you alive. What do you need from me?"

"Information. I don't know who to trust back in Houston, so I can't call for backup. I need you to run a couple of local license plate numbers—see if the rental agreement gives me a name I can run down."

Jake nodded. "I've got a connection I trust at KCPD. He knows how to be discreet. I'll give him a call."

"I know I'm asking a lot. I've already lost three men on my team."

"I used to be on your team before this." Jake pointed to the scar at his temple. "You were the only one who ever bothered to try and find me when everyone else gave me up for dead. You helped me fill in the blanks of my memory so I was free to marry Beth and make a life here in K.C. I owe you."

Brushing aside his friend's avowal of loyalty and gratitude, Nash picked up a notepad off the desk and started copying down some names and numbers from his black book. "I know you don't remember Captain Puente—the guy we reported to at the Houston office—"

"I've heard you mention his name. He was our boss on undercover ops. You want me to try and reach him?"

"I wouldn't," Teresa cautioned, regretting the mistake she'd made that morning.

But Nash seemed to have it all figured out. He tore off the top sheet of paper and handed it to Jake. "I want you to call every name on that list, not just the captain. Even though we'll be alerting the mole, it should also alert anybody else who's on our side. Maybe you'll get a feel for whoever is hiding something." He snatched the paper back and wrote another name. "I want you to ask about Tommy Delvecchio, too."

"The agent who got killed here in K.C.?"

Nash nodded. "Let me know that his body got back to Houston okay. And any funeral arrangements if they got 'em. The number for my disposable cell is at the bottom. I don't know if he was seeing anyone, but his parents are both alive. I want his family to know that he died doing his job."

Jake folded up the paper and pocketed it in his jeans. "It'll take me some time to make the calls to get the information you need. You got a place to stay? My home is on an acreage. It's pretty remote—"

"No." Using the armrest to brace himself, Nash stood. "I saw a nondescript place that won't ask too many questions when we were picking up supplies. We can crash there for a few nights. We'll be fine. You've got a little girl and a baby on the way. These guys have had pretty good luck tracking me. I'm not going to bring a gun battle to your home."

Was that twist on Jake's mouth a smile? "Wouldn't be the first time."

She'd probably just imagined his morbid idea of humor. The scars that both men bore indicated a sad familiarity with violence. Yet, like her brother, it hadn't stopped them from standing up to the bad guys and protecting what they believed in—their city, their homes, the people they cared about.

Teresa packed her bag and zipped her coat, feeling woefully inadequate to be a part of their quest for justice

for their fallen friends. At the very least, she would not
be a burden to their investigation. And she would not be
the source of any more trouble. "I'm ready to go whenever you are, Nash."

His golden-brown gaze dropped down to hers. "I know
you are." He reached for her hand and laced their fingers
together, pulling her to his side as he faced Jake. "This
one's ready for anything. I wouldn't be here without her."

Had he read her mind? Had he sensed her second-
guessing her place in this partnership? Whatever the reason for his words of praise and tactile show of support,
the simple gesture warmed her, reassured her. It felt good
to be needed. It felt better to hear Nash admit how much
he needed her. *Her.* As though she could handle the job.
As though she was enough.

She could do this. They could do this. Together.

"What about wheels?" Jake asked, his presence reminding her that her relationship with Nash was all about
protection and medical treatment and finding out the
truth. It wasn't about the way Nash forced her to be stronger, smarter, more stubborn—the capable adult she'd always known she could be. He hadn't babied her. Not once.

No wonder she kept thinking she was falling for him.
He treated her the way she wished her family would treat
her. Like a grown woman. She'd never had anyone like
that in her life before. If she wasn't careful, she really
would fall in love with Charlie Nash.

Nash's fingers reached for hers when she pulled away,
but she wisely pulled her gloves from her pockets and
kept both hands busy putting them on. If Nash noticed
her sudden withdrawal, he didn't let on.

Neither did Jake. "You're going to need a vehicle that
can't be tied to either one of you. Here." He pulled a key
from his wallet and tossed it to Nash. "Take my truck.

It's the silver pickup behind the bar. There's a gun in the glove compartment, if you need it."

Nash thanked him. "I've got a go bag. We'll be fine."

After checking to make sure the hallway was clear, Jake shrugged into his coat and escorted them down the hallway to the bar's rear exit. "I'll find out what I can and call you tonight on the burner phone." Hunching his big shoulders against the evening chill that dampened the air and hinted at another dusting of snow later on, he led them out to the silver pickup truck parked near the Dumpster. "The gas tank is full. I'll get a ride from Beth after work."

The two men retrieved Nash's bag from her car and stowed it in the back of the extended truck cab. They exchanged a few more private words before shaking hands one more time. "Thanks, Jake. Call as soon as you know something."

"I will." And then the big man nodded to Teresa. "Ma'am. You take care of this guy. He's the oldest friend I can remember. Take care of yourself, too."

"I will. Thank you."

After Jake strode back inside the bar, Nash opened the driver's-side door and handed her the key. "You'd better drive."

He made sure she was settled behind the wheel of the big four-wheel-drive truck before he circled around and climbed into the passenger seat beside her.

Once more, she and Nash were outside in the cold, alone again.

Chapter Nine

The Seaside Motel wasn't much of a tropical oasis in the wintry urban sprawl of Kansas City, Missouri. The "sea" was a cracked concrete pool filled with drifts of snow and two plastic palm trees chained to a peeling wrought-iron fence. The "motel" included two single-story buildings arranged in a U shape with the office around the empty pool. Twelve chipped and dented steel doors faced their own parking spaces.

The old man at the front desk who checked them in had a flask behind the counter, a reality show on his portable TV and not so much as a curiously raised eyebrow for Nash when he registered as Mr. and Mrs. John Smith and paid an extra twenty dollars in cash.

He had to give the owner credit for trying to upgrade the place by lining the porchlike overhang with colored Christmas lights. Some blinked, some didn't. And every so often along the way, a bulb was burned out, broken or missing. Each door was draped with tattered fake greenery studded with red plastic berries. Teresa fingered one of the sprigs of plastic holly as Nash unlocked the door to 6A.

"Festive, huh?" he teased before pushing open the door and turning on the lights.

The musty smell of disuse greeted them inside. Teresa

dropped her backpack on one bouncy mattress and his go bag on the other while he locked the door and pocketed the key. Then she pulled back the velour bedspread and sniffed one of the pillows. "At least the sheets are clean. They've been bleached."

Great, so no bedbugs. Still, it wasn't the kind of place he'd ever want to take a woman like Teresa. In this kind of weather, he pictured them in a cozy lodge with big throw pillows and a thick wool blanket on the floor in front of a stone hearth. Sipping cold beers, warming themselves by the fire, getting better acquainted. Him exploring those curves. Her putting those soft, firm hands on him. The two of them getting *very* well acquainted.

Nash swallowed hard, scratching his parched throat, quickly burying wherever that fantasy had been headed. Teresa had shed her coat and was already running water in the sink and checking out the bathroom when he apologized. "Sorry it's not the Ritz."

"It's not like we have much choice," she answered through the door. "Your friend Jake said those men went through my apartment."

He'd already gotten the first of what he hoped to be several informative reports from Jake Lonergan. Unfortunately, learning her place had been broken into and searched wasn't exactly the positive news he'd been hoping for. "Yeah. Sorry about that, too. I don't think we left anything behind that could tell them where we are, but they know we're together, they know I'm alive, and they won't stop hunting for us."

"Thank you for letting me call AJ to tell him I'm all right. I'm sure he'd still prefer to see me in person to tell him that, but—"

"That's not going to happen. It's hard enough to stay

hidden from Graciela's men. I can't have half of KCPD looking for us, too."

"I know." The toilet flushed and she reappeared. "I told him I'm staying with a friend for a few days. That'll just have to hold him until we're done with your mission."

"A friend?" He hardly qualified. Maybe she was getting a little too good at telling lies.

"Don't worry. I have a lot of friends. Even if he does check up on me, it'll take him a while to contact all of them." She stuck her fingers under the tap to wash her hands. "I'm mostly mad that those men damaged some of the presents I'd gotten for my nephews and the kids at the hospital. I'll have to replace those before the twenty-fifth."

"I'll replace them," Nash insisted, hoping the traitor in his office would be exposed and he'd be alive to celebrate Christmas. As fatigued as he was, he was determined to stand tall on his own two feet and show her he could protect her. "It's my fault your place was violated by those scum. You send me a bill for whatever replacing the lock and door costs, and let me know how much I need to reimburse you for your patients' gifts or anything else they ruined."

She shut off the water and reached for a thin white towel. When she was done drying her hands, she turned and chucked the towel at his head. "You're doing it again, Nash. All this talk about tabulating expenses and reimbursing me makes me feel like the hired help. That's not the mutual partnership I agreed to."

"I'm not used to needing anyone but the men I work with, Peewee." Nash caught the towel and tossed it onto the bed. "I'm not quite sure how I'm supposed to deal with you."

"How did you deal with the team you worked with in

Houston?" She walked straight across the room to him and started unbuttoning his coat. Despite the professional efficiency of her fingers, having her undress him felt a little too intimate for his waning self-control around her.

"Not like this." When she started to push his coat off his shoulders, Nash caught her by the wrists and pulled her hands away. But he wasn't strong enough to let her go, and with a surrendering sigh, he pulled her right up to his chest, winding his arms behind her back and tucking his chin atop the crown of her hair. "I want to take care of you, but you don't want to be taken care of."

She snuggled inside the opening of his coat, her fingers clinging to the front of his shirt. "Did you try to 'take care' of your men? Or did you let them do the job they were trained to do?"

"Both," he answered honestly. "Richter, Torres and Delvecchio were like little brothers to me. On one hand, I knew they were good agents—I trained Jim and Axel myself. On the other hand, they were my responsibility." His arms convulsed around her, and he dipped his head to bury his nose in the fragrant softness of her hair, clinging to the present as the grief and guilt of the past few days surged through him. "I did a real whiz-bang job of taking care of them."

"Charlie, don't."

"Charlie, hmm?" He shouldn't have liked her calling him by the given name nobody used as much as he did.

"None of this is your fault. That's what you told me, right?" Her arms snuck around his waist beneath his coat, and she turned her cheek into his shoulder. "None of it." She found where his spine met his belt with her fingertips and dug them in, pulling herself into his embrace. Her breasts pillowed against his chest. Her hips rubbed against his. Her cheek rested over the thump of his heart. "Does this hurt?"

He knew she was talking about the bruising, stitches and bullet hole in his shoulder. But all he noticed was the way her warmth and energy seemed to wrap around him and seep into every cell of his body, easing some of the emotional pain and making even those most beat-up parts of him hum with an awareness of her feminine strength. "Not a bit."

"It's like I tell my patients when they have to go in for another treatment or operation. Don't judge the future by your past. Yes, horrible things happen." Her fingers drummed a nervous pattern against his back before linking together and tightening her hold around his waist. "My father was murdered when I was little—I barely remember him. My mother died of cancer early last year. I got mugged walking home from my first job after high school. The guy gave me a black eye and stole my purse and probably sentenced me to forever being the Rodriguez that everyone else has to look out for."

Nash rubbed slow circles up and down her back, surprised to learn that she'd had to endure such tragedies. "If you're trying to make me feel better, I have to tell you that all you're doing is pissing me off. I hate that you had to go through all that." He slipped one hand up to the nape of her neck, tunneling his fingers beneath her thick ponytail and massaging the tension he found there. "And now I've gotten you involved with this mess? I'm the one who's trouble."

She laughed at his grousing, sending warm vibrations through his body. She turned her lips to his chest and pressed a kiss to the swell of his pectoral through his cotton shirts before snuggling in again. "But good things happen, too. There are more patients who get well than who never make it out of the hospital. AJ finally arrested the man responsible for my father's death. I miss my mama, Sofia, but I have so many wonderful memories of her." She loosened her grip at his back and leaned back against his arms, tilting her face up to his. "You'll get this guy. We'll stay two or three steps ahead of those gorillas he works with, and you'll get him. I know you will."

The spicy scent of Teresa's skin and hair filled his head with every breath. As much as he loved the feel of her diminutive curves clinging to the length of his body, he loved her spirit even more.

Nash lifted a strand of coffee-colored hair that had fallen across her cheek and rolled the soft silk between his thumb and forefinger. "You just don't know how to quit, do you?"

"Nope."

He unwound the hair behind her ear. He smoothed aside another strand and tucked it behind the other ear. He stood head and shoulders above her, framing her face between his hands, looking down at those dark eyes and that beautiful mouth.

Then she pushed up onto her toes, and he lowered his head and they were kissing. Not that sweetly tentative introduction they'd shared at her apartment building. This was twenty-four hours of pent-up desire and battling wills and raw desperation breaking free in a meeting of mouths and tongues and gaspy moans.

Teresa's lips parted in welcome, giving him a taste of her utter softness and fiery warmth. Her hands braced at his waist. His fingers slid into her beautiful hair, tangling, sifting, holding on as her tongue danced with his. He traced a path along the smooth line of her jaw with his lips, then worked his way back, dropping a dozen little nibbles along the way. He nipped at the decadent curve of her bottom lip, and she murmured his name in a sound that was heady pleasure to his ears. He touched his tongue to the spot and felt her lips tugging at his, urging him to deepen the kiss again.

When Nash obliged, she skimmed her hands up the planes of his chest, caught his rough face between her hands and rubbed her palms against his beard stubble, creating a passionate friction. And then her arms were snaking around his neck, her hands were in his hair.

He fell back against the door, and she came with him, her toes leaving the floor as he palmed her butt and took her weight against his chest. His pulse thundered in his ears. His body burned. Her nipples beaded beneath her sweater, poking him like delectable hot brands. He wanted his hands on her breasts. He wanted his mouth there.

This was all kinds of crazy. All kinds of stupid. All kinds of right.

Her thigh wedged between his, her arms tightened around him, and she sort of crawled up his body, her eager gasps and clinging hands tempting him to forget everything except the perfect storm of this moment. But even as anticipation leaped behind his zipper, Nash's energy short-circuited. He was crashing.

Of all the lousy luck.

He wanted this sexy little spitfire in ways beyond what his body was craving. But if he was going to make love to this woman, he damn sure wanted to do it right. He wanted to make sure he could follow through and give her everything she wanted. Everything she deserved.

And she deserved a lot better than the one-night stand in this seedy dump of a motel that he could offer her. She deserved her family and Christmas and a guarantee that being with him wouldn't get her killed.

Nash tore his mouth from hers and nuzzled the softness of her hair, dragging in ragged breaths beside her ear. "Darlin', I'm sorry."

Her breath gusted across his cheek. "What's wrong?" Her lips scudded across the same spot. "I'm not complaining. This pull that I feel toward you doesn't make any sense, but I wanted you to really kiss me. I wanted..." She stiffened in his arms. She pushed his chin away from her ear and leaned back to read his face. "Nash?"

The hand squeezing her bottom and the one palming the bare skin of her back tried to hold on when she began to slide back down his body. "I'm so sorry."

She braced her hands against his chest and pushed to free herself. Nash flinched at the stab of pressure against his bum shoulder. His left hand popped open and he dropped her.

As soon as her feet hit the floor, she was at his side, sliding beneath his right arm and walking him to the closest bed. "You're white as a ghost. I'm such an idiot."

"No." He squeezed her shoulder, glad that she didn't have to carry his weight like the night before but appreciating the balance she offered. "The mind is willing, but the body just isn't up to doing this tonight."

He sank onto the edge of the bed, and she immediately felt for his temperature. "I'm the one who's sorry." She reached around him to help him remove his heavy coat without lifting his left arm. "I got carried away by my hormones and the stress of the past couple of days. I wasn't even thinking."

"That makes two of us."

She tossed his coat onto the chair beside hers and went to work on the snaps of his shirt to get to the wound. "But I should know better."

That stung worse than the blow his male ego was already dealing with. He grabbed her wrists and stopped her halfway down the placket. "And I'm such a lowlife taking advantage of the woman I kidnapped that I don't?"

Her mouth was still pink and swollen from the passion they'd shared. But the argument for trust remained. "I thought we were beyond that, Nash."

He liked *Charlie* better coming from her, but going back to trading barbs with Teresa was the splash of reality he needed. He released her and let her tend to him. "Right. We're partners. But trust me, none of my team ever tempted me to forget a mission the way you do."

She paused with her hands at the hem of his T-shirt. "I'm on a mission, too." Her sure hands weren't quite so efficient as she peeled off his T and inspected the entry and exit wounds she'd stitched up. Then she retrieved her backpack and set out the medical supplies they'd purchased. She put on a pair of disposable sterile gloves, unwrapped a gauze pad and soaked it with distilled water. "You need me to be a nurse. I'm determined to do my job and do it well. I'm so tired of not being allowed to do the things I'm capable of, of not being trusted to make good decisions. And then when I sabotage myself—"

"By making out with a randy cowboy cop from Texas?"

A soft smile finally relaxed her mouth. "My brother and sisters would call for an intervention if I told them that."

"They don't picture you with a bad boy like me, huh?"

"On some days, I don't think they picture me with anybody. Unless he's staid, boring and unlikely to ever put his hands on me." He gritted his teeth as she gently cleansed his mending skin. Yeah, that keeping his hands to himself would definitely cut him from the family approval list. "They don't trust me to make the best choice in men or where I live or—" she shook her head "—who I stop to help along the side of the road."

Nash turned so she could clean and dry the stitches in his back. "I think I understand where your family is coming from. You're lucky that someone cares enough to worry about your safety and happiness."

"Your team was like that for you, weren't they," she deduced. "They were your family, and you guys cared about each other—like brothers, you said. No wonder you're so determined to get the man responsible for their deaths."

He nodded and faced her again while she opened a tube of antibiotic ointment. She didn't have anything in that bag that could fix the wounds inside his head and heart. But there was something about the woman herself that seemed to find those hurting places inside him. She exposed them—probed deeper into a few, gently tended others and, somehow, made him feel a little better.

No wonder he was so drawn to her. He really did need her. Maybe more than he'd ever needed anyone his whole life. If she thought for one moment that he didn't know just how lucky he was to have her with him in this night-mare, then he needed to make that right.

"Teresa…" He reached out to pull down the hem of her sweater, which his groping hands had bunched up around her waist. "I'm trying to do the right thing here. Not just by my men but by you, too. I may not be the smoothest guy on the planet. But I do know how to treat a lady right. I can't tell you how much I want you. But this is the wrong time, wrong place—I may even be the wrong man." Her hands stilled their work and rested on his shoulder. "I can't offer you much of a future. I may not even be able to offer you next week. You deserve better than that."

She nudged aside his knee and stepped between his legs, winding her arms around his neck in a hug. "So do you, Nash."

His arms encircled her waist, and he rubbed his cheek against hers. "Yeah, well, I just want you to know that I'm grateful you're here with me."

They held each other like that for several endless moments, her legs butting against the bed, her chest pressed to his, her strong, tender arms holding him close as she gently rocked him in her embrace. The sting of tears made his eyes feel gritty, but he refused to shed them. Grief, guilt and regret tore through him just as violently as those two bullets had. He'd been in survival mode for far too long. This ornery, petite, strong, irresistible woman had forced him into human mode. It hurt to care about the people he'd lost. It scared him to think about everything he could still lose.

He buried his face against her neck and held on to her healing compassion for just as long as she'd let him.

A BING CROSBY holiday tune played softly through the static of the AM station Teresa had found on the radio. Other than the twenty-four-hour Christmas music playing in the background, it was silent as Nash polished off a sandwich and two cups of Teresa's chicken noodle soup while they sat on the edges of their respective beds, facing each other.

Part of his current aversion to conversation was savoring just how filling and delicious her food tasted, even under these crude conditions. Part of it was the nagging feeling that he really was growing weaker by the minute and wouldn't be able to keep watch over her the way he'd promised. And part of it was his wayward thoughts, which kept reliving that kiss and imagining where it would have ended up if he was a whole man—imagining where this deep, unexpected bond he had with this woman could lead if he didn't have a crooked cop and at least two cartel thugs breathing down his neck.

Not even the late hour or the flyaway strands of dark hair that had pulled loose from her ponytail throughout the day could diminish her beautiful Latin vitality. Realizing he'd been staring, he blinked and looked away.

But she had his number and was on her feet in an instant. "You look like you're about to fall asleep."

She took his empty cup and paper napkin in one hand and pressed the other to his forehead and cheek. He was sorry that touching him made her frown like that. He was sorrier when she moved away, taking her homey kitchen scent and her soft, firm touches with her. She set the trash on the table beside the thermos and reached into her bag. "I'm going to give you another aspirin, and then I'm putting you to bed. Sleep is what your body needs most right now." She spun around and snapped her fingers. "And an ice pack."

She took a sharp turn from the trash can to grab her coat and headed for the door.

"Wait." Nash pushed to his feet and caught her by the arm before she reached the door. "You can't leave. It's dark out there. You won't be able to see if anyone's following you."

"I'm just going down to the office to get some ice. If I'd thought of it sooner, I'd have gone when we first arrived." She nudged him, encouraging him to sit back down. When he refused to move, she patted his arm. "There are lights on each of the buildings and streetlamps out front. I'll be there and back before you even miss me. Unless you'd rather go to the hospital?"

"Nicely played, Peewee." Nash covered her hand with

his. "Okay. I'm not getting much better on my own. We'll risk the ice run."

While she zipped her coat and put on her gloves, Nash pulled his gun and went to the window. He peered out through the drapes. What was it, maybe twenty, thirty yards to the office door? When she stood beside him with the ice bucket, he looked through the peephole to make sure things were quiet in every direction before he turned out the interior lights and opened the door. "I'll watch you from here. Go straight down the sidewalk and back. Don't speak to anybody. If you're out of my sight for more than twenty seconds, I'm coming after you."

"You could be resting while I'm gone," she suggested.

"It's not a negotiation."

"What else is new? I'll be quick." She flattened her palm at the center of his chest, maybe thanking him for the little taste of freedom, maybe reassuring him that she'd be back, before she turned around and hurried away.

Nash grinned as she power walked those short legs beneath the glow of the Christmas lights hanging from the gutters. Lurking in the darkness of the doorway, with his gun down at his right thigh, hidden from view of anyone outside, he counted how many rooms at the motel were occupied and familiarized himself with the vehicles parked there. There were two pickups with ladders and gear boxes that probably belonged to construction workers or a road crew. There was a tank of an old sedan with some kind of medals hanging from ribbons on the rearview mirror. There was what he assumed was the manager's car parked in front of the office and a sporty little muscle car caked with ice and road grime that had come from Colorado.

But there were no black SUVs cruising past on the street. He saw no one peeking through a window blind to follow Teresa's movements or note him standing in the shadows beneath 6A's plastic garland.

He couldn't believe how good the brisk night air felt on his face and in his lungs—until he started to shiver with the chills. He knew he should go get his coat, but he wasn't about to leave his post. Still, the moment the office's glass door swung shut behind Teresa, Nash sagged against the doorjamb and exhaled a puffy cloud of breath in the frigid air.

Maybe he should let her call her brother again and have her request protection from the vaunted Detective AJ. Her family had to be going out of their minds with worry if they knew about the shoot-out near her apartment. If he felt this weak, this weary, he wasn't going to be any good to her, much less capable of going toe-to-toe with a traitor.

And if anything happened to Teresa because of his failing, he might as well be a dead man.

Nash's cell phone rang, and he straightened against the door frame again to pull it from his pocket. Since only one person had this number, he had no qualms about answering. "Hey, Jake. What do you got for me?"

Jake Lonergan might not have remembered his life as a DEA agent, but he sure remembered how to give a mission brief. "Made all your calls. Everyone in the Houston office knows you're alive and knows you're in the wind. Captain Puente says he and a Cruz Moreno have already booked a flight into KCI Airport tonight. They asked for your contact info. Both said it was vital that you get in touch with them if I hear from you again."

Nash trusted that Jake hadn't given him away. "Did they give you a hard time?"

"They both pumped me for info on your location and condition, but I wasn't in a talkative mood."

Stubborn cuss. The Jake he knew had never been much of a talker. "What else?"

"Puente confirmed that the Gracielas have men in the area."

"That's not news. Did he say how many?"

"He wasn't sure. He thinks even Berto Graciela himself is en route to find you. Sounds as if Santiago Vargas maligned Berto's name, saying he had no business leading the cartel if he didn't even know he had DEA agents working for him."

Nash checked the time and started counting down the seconds until Teresa needed to reappear at the office door. "Vargas has no room to talk. He didn't know, either. Not until Puente or Moreno or whoever it was sold us out."

"Captain Puente said Vargas hasn't been seen for a couple of days. There's no word of any hit on him going down, either."

"What are you saying?"

"What if Vargas is in K.C., too?"

"Both of them? Here?" He almost laughed. So who was back home running the drug-smuggling business?

"What better way to show the cartel who really gets the job done than by serving up your head on a silver platter?"

Nash swore under his breath. Didn't that just make a man's day? Knowing two ruthless drug-lord wannabes and a potential army of well-armed thugs had joined him here in Kansas City for a deadly reunion? "What did they say about Tommy Delvecchio?"

"No details yet. Apparently, there's some kind of holdup at the medical examiner's office with the bodies from the warehouse. Neither Puente nor Moreno could tell me what the problem was. I can ask Spencer to look into it."

A pulse of light bounced off the palm trees by the pool, drawing Nash's gaze. A car must have turned the corner and was coming down the street toward the motel. "Is that your friend at KCPD? Did you talk to him?"

"Yeah. Spencer Montgomery. That conversation went about as well as you thought it would."

"Tell me."

"He says that AJ Rodriguez is personally investigating the break-in at Teresa's apartment. I don't think he bought her story about staying with a friend for a few nights."

Just what he didn't need. A big brother with a beef and a badge. "Does he know if AJ has figured out anything?" he asked.

"Not yet." Jake's answer wasn't reassuring. "But Spencer said AJ worked several years on a drug task force, doing undercover work. He knows all the same tricks you do. If anyone is going to piece together what's going on, it's Rodriguez."

"Ah, hell." That wasn't just any car coming down the street. It was a black-and-white unit from KCPD. No lights flashing, no sirens blaring. But it was pulling into the Seaside's parking lot.

"Nash?"

He pulled back into the darkness of the room and closed the door, leaving just a few inches open to see out. His toes tapped anxiously inside his boots as the squad car pulled into the parking space right beside the manager's car. Nash's gaze shot over the two uniformed officers climbing out of the vehicle to the office door. *"Teresa?"*

"Talk to me," Jake urged, understanding that something had put Nash on alert.

"We may have company. Keep me posted. Talk to you later." Nash disconnected the call and jammed the cell into his pocket. The need to take action, to dash across the parking lot to get her out of there, jolted through his legs. "Come on, darlin'."

There she was. She appeared in the glass doorway, pushed it open. Nash's breath locked in his chest. But she never made it out the door. One of the officers said something to her and pointed back inside the office. Her gaze breezed past Nash's position before the officer's bulky frame blocked her from view.

Nash's pulse kicked up a notch. What the hell was going on? Had they been discovered? Had that slimy manager somehow recognized Teresa from a news story or description her brother had put over the wire and called it in for some kind of reward? While the first uniformed cop ushered Teresa back inside the office, the other pulled back the front of his coat and braced his hands on either side of the utility belt at his waist, scanning the motel and parking lot. Nash quietly closed the door and moved to the window to watch the office and cops through the drapes.

The second officer left his position at the black-and-white and walked toward building A. Nash glanced back at his go bag. What if these weren't cops at all? What if the mole had somehow gotten wind of the vehicle switch they'd made at the Shamrock Bar and reported Nash for auto theft and marked him as a fugitive? He could arm himself to the teeth and take both men out. But there'd be a lot of witnesses, maybe even a few innocent bystanders who'd get hurt.

Nah, if they'd come for him, he'd surrender peacefully. He'd take his chances in lockup. No way was he going to put Teresa's life in more danger than he already had.

The cop batted at some of the Christmas decorations when he stepped up to the first door. But as he strolled down the sidewalk, Nash could see there was nothing nonchalant about his purpose here. The older officer glanced at the license plates of the two construction trucks. When he stopped in front of Jake's silver pickup, Nash pulled back from the window and flattened his back against the wall, waiting for the knock at the door.

Thirty seconds, maybe a minute, passed before Nash heard the man's boots on the cold concrete. Once he was certain the cop was moving on, Nash returned to the window to see him walking on to building B. Was that a misdirection to get him to drop his guard and reveal himself? Or were the officers looking for someone else?

Wouldn't that just be his luck? Nash eased out a tense breath, beginning to suspect the latter, when the officer circled around the white Impala with the ribbons hanging from the mirror. Then he turned his mouth to his shoulder to report something on his radio—probably to his partner.

Raised voices and movement at the opposite end of the motel pulled Nash's gaze back to the office. The first blue suit was coming out of the office, holding Teresa and the manager both by the elbow. The young man released her and exchanged a few words. The complaints were coming from the gray-haired manager, whom the officer had handcuffed. "Come on, darlin', get out of there."

But Teresa stood there hugging the ice bucket and shivering in the cold while the cop put the old man in the backseat of the cruiser. Her gaze came straight to 6A, even paused at the window as if she could see him there—asking him what to do, perhaps warning him.

The young officer slammed the car door, startling her. When she whipped her head around, he said something to dismiss her and she scuttled out of the way. While she stepped onto the sidewalk, the young cop jogged straight across the parking lot.

He ran past Jake's truck as Nash heard pounding on another door. The first cop announced himself as KCPD and ordered the occupant to open up. In the midst of shouts and protests, Teresa approached their room. But to his surprise, she walked on past, not letting the uniformed officers know her destination, not giving him away.

She was well past 2B when the officers dragged two half-dressed teenagers out the door. They put them both into the Impala with some serious kind of lecture, because the lanky boy kept putting his hands up in the air instead of starting the car. Once the engine was running and the kid was nodding yes to everything the older cop was saying, the younger cop went back to their black-and-white. He picked up his partner and they followed the teens out of the parking lot.

As soon as the drama left the Seaside Motel parking lot, Teresa ran back to the room.

Nash was there to open the door before she could knock. He pulled her inside and locked it behind her. "What the hell?"

She set the bucket on the table beside the door and paced the length of the room and back. "Apparently, Mr. Moscatelli rented one of his rooms to a pair of minors. At first the officer said they were looking for a couple who hadn't registered under their real names. He asked me if I'd seen anyone."

Hence taking her back inside the office. "Did he threaten you in any way? Did he seem suspicious of you?"

"No. I don't think so." Man, she was pale beneath the cold red apples on her cheeks. Whatever had happened had scared her. "The manager pointed to us in the registry, but then Officer Britt got a message from his partner about a license plate and he told me to get back to my room. I thought they were coming for you. For us."

Nash holstered his gun and stopped her when she turned to pace away again. "They were here to escort those teenagers home. The police probably got a call from a concerned parent."

Teresa nodded. "Officer Britt's partner said something about finding 'the boyfriend's' license plate number."

So they'd tracked the kid's car. "Did the officers recognize you?"

"I don't think so." She was visibly shaking as she unzipped her coat. "I didn't know either one of them."

"Did they ask for your name?"

"Yes. Teresa Smith. Right?"

Relief warred with pride. Nash palmed the back of her neck and kissed her, hard and quick, thanking her for being smart enough to think on her feet and protect them both from discovery. "Thank you, Mrs. Smith."

As quickly as she smiled at his praise, her forehead knotted with concern. "You didn't need another stressor like that. Get to bed before you fall over." She shushed him when he started to protest. "I need you healthy, okay?"

He nodded, feeling the clammy chills that had probably alarmed her. "Okay."

In five minutes flat, she'd given him another aspirin, removed his boots and pulled the blanket and bedspread over him. She made an ice pack out of one of the hand towels and placed it on his forehead.

As warmth and fatigue rushed up to claim him, he pulled away the ice pack and sat up. "You don't open that door for anybody, understand? Don't answer the phone if it rings. Don't call anyone. Don't give anybody any reason to know that we're here."

"Yes, sir." She nudged him back down to the pillow and put the towel back in place.

"I'm trying to protect you. I'm about to pass out for a few hours. I need to know you'll do exactly what I tell you so I know you'll be safe."

She pulled the bedspread off her bed and tucked the extra layer of warmth around his shivering form. "I will. Is it all right if I keep the radio playing until I fall asleep?"

He nodded, wondering if she'd slipped him some kind of sleeping pill or if he really was too exhausted to stay tough with her. He hadn't listened to any Christmas music this season, hadn't thought much at all about the holidays until he was hiding in this dump with this woman who was starting to mean a lot more to him than a nursemaid should.

He pushed himself up on one elbow before sleep could claim him. He reached for the Smith & Wesson on the shelf between the beds. "Do you know how to fire a gun?"

"Yes." She pushed his hand away from the gun and covered him up again. "AJ showed me. He's taken me to the firing range a couple of times. He wanted us all to understand gun safety since he kept one in the house. But I don't like using them. I've dealt with more than one gunshot victim in the children's ward."

"Still, if it's a choice between dying and shooting someone, I want you to—"

"I'll wake you up."

He nodded, surprised at her trust. He sank back into the pillow, praying he could live up to that trust. "Don't leave me, Peewee."

"I won't."

"Don't be all clever and brave...." Man, his eyelids were heavy. "It's not safe out there."

"I'm here to take care of you, remember?"

Yeah. She'd promised to stay. He wouldn't lose her. He wouldn't lose anyone else. "Good night, Peewee."

"Good night, Nash."

She was still watching over him when he drifted off to sleep.

Chapter Ten

"Nash." Teresa tugged the covers tangling around his long, writhing legs and leaned over him to touch his burning face. "Nash, wake up. We're going to the hospital."

When she'd awakened to the sounds of his heartbreaking moans and the bed rattling against the wall, Teresa hadn't been sure if Nash was caught in the throes of a nightmare or delirious from fever. Probably some combination of both. But if he kept twisting around in the bed like this, he'd rip his stitches. And then she'd have a whole new possibility for infection to worry about.

Fear sharpened her decision and made her reactions quick. She'd already fished the keys from his coat pocket, loaded his bag in the truck and started the engine to warm up the cab. There was no negotiating this particular difference of opinion anymore, either.

She gave his cheek a firmer pat. "Come on, cowboy. Wake up."

"Teresa?" She barely got a glimpse of golden-brown eyes before he grabbed her by the shoulders and pulled her down onto the bed beside him. He pushed the hood off her head and ran his fingers over her hair, dropping kisses onto her forehead, her nose, her mouth before he wrapped her up in a suffocating hug. "I couldn't get to you. They had you and I couldn't get to you."

Teresa held on for a few precious seconds, then wedged her elbows between them to push away. "It was a bad dream. I'm right here. I'm real. I'm fine."

"I don't want to lose you."

When he reached for her again, she rolled away off the far side of the bed. "You can't get rid of me now, partner."

The focus in his eyes was still half-blurred with sleep when he sat up. "You should have just told them what they wanted to know."

"Told who?" She pulled his legs over the edge of the bed and knelt in front of him to tug on his boots.

"Berto Graciela and his men. They had you and…" He caught her face between his hands and tipped it up to see the agony lining his. "Don't let them hurt you. I'm not worth it."

A surge of anger fired through her blood that he'd think that. She grabbed his wrists and stood. Even if he was a tad delirious, she still argued with him. "Don't you ever say that, Charlie Nash. Your men are counting on you. I'm counting on you. We're going to get through this." As her words sank in, he slowly nodded. "Now get on your feet. You're coming with me."

While he tucked his shirttails into his jeans, she picked up his gun from the bedside shelf, checked the safety and opened up her backpack. But a big hand closed over hers and the gun before she could place it inside. Nash rose unsteadily beside her, taking the weapon from her grasp. "Not your job."

He holstered the gun at his belt. She fetched his coat and helped him into it. She stretched up on tiptoe to pull the red-and-gold stocking cap over his head. And then they stumbled out the door into the dim morning light.

After loading him into the passenger seat of the truck, Teresa paused for a moment, looking for any signs of activity or curious eyes around them. But the sun was barely an orange glow peeking over the horizon. It didn't look as though anyone else was up yet. Besides the blinking Christmas lights, the only glimmer of any kind of movement besides them was the strobing effect of the television someone was watching in the office, although the different car parked near the door made her think someone else had come to finish out Mr. Moscatelli's shift.

Convinced their departure remained undetected, Teresa climbed into the truck and buckled up. She spared a few moments to rub her fingers together in front of the heat vent to get some feeling back into them.

"I'm okay, Peewee."

"No, you're not."

"I know. I'm in a bad way." He reached over and folded his hand around hers, offering a warmth and reassurance that were in short supply this morning. "I mean, I was having a nightmare before. I couldn't shake some of the images. But I'm not losing it. I promise."

She shifted her grip to lace their fingers together and squeeze his hand before pulling away. "Good. You're hard enough to handle when you do make sense." That earned her an echo of that crooked grin. She checked her mirrors and shifted the truck into Reverse. "I'm still taking you to the hospital."

As she pulled into the street, he leaned back into his seat. "If anything happens, I want you to—"

"Nothing's going to happen." She watched the cars pulling in behind her, as much to see if she recognized any black SUVs as to note the beginnings of rush-hour traffic filling up the streets. Once she was on the six lanes of interstate heading south, she pushed her speed, knowing she had to get across the city to one hospital in particular. "I know people I can call in favors from, too. I've got a way to sneak you in."

"I'll make a fugitive out of you yet."

Teresa glanced over to smile at the teasing remark. But his eyes were closed and his handsome mouth was pressed into a tight line of pain. She moved her seat forward another half an inch and put more pressure on the accelerator.

Dr. Emilia Rodriguez-Grant got very quiet when her temper was brewing. Instead of giving Teresa the order, she nodded to her sister to inject the syringe of antibiotics into Nash's exposed hip. His answering grunt was the loudest noise for the past five minutes in the silent E.R. bay at the Truman Medical Center.

"You actually did a good job with the stitches," Emilia announced, her tone nothing but that of one medical professional to another. "And the wound track looks clean."

Teresa disposed of the syringe in the sharps receptacle while Nash pulled up his shorts and refastened his jeans. Emilia picked up the gauze and tape from the rolling supply tray beside the examination table and re-covered Nash's wounds, carefully avoiding jostling the IV needle and tube attached to the back of his hand.

"I can do that," Teresa offered, knowing a trauma nurse usually took over for the E.R. doctor at this point anyway.

But Emilia was focused solely on Nash, completely unintimidated by his towering height or the fact she had to stand on a step stool beside the exam table to address his injuries. She met his probing gaze while she worked, chatting with him as though he was any other patient who'd come into her emergency room—instead of one who'd bypassed most of the check-in paperwork and been sequestered immediately inside a curtained-off trauma bay.

"I replaced the cotton stitches beneath the skin with degradable sutures," Emilia explained. "The biggest part of your discomfort is from the muscle tear in your shoulder. But that should heal itself with time if you let it rest and don't strain it with repetitive motion. The X-ray doesn't show any bone fragments besides the tiny one I removed. That should ease any of the sharp pain you had in your shoulder. You're lucky that bullet didn't ricochet in the other direction and nick your lung or your heart. Or else even my resourceful baby sister here wouldn't have been able to save you."

"Yes, ma'am. Real lucky." Her dark eyes narrowed, as if judging the sincerity of his humble agreement. Teresa's gaze bounced from one to the other, trying to figure out to what degree her sister resented doing this favor for her—and what retribution it would require to make up for it.

"I've ordered you a prescription for antibiotics." Emilia was back in efficient work mode again. "That spike in temperature could be attributed to a combination of dehydration and blood loss. The IV fluids seem to be bringing it down. I don't detect any signs of infection, but the pills are precautionary when you have a foreign object like that rip through your body. Do you want painkillers, too?" Nash's silent glare was answer enough. "No, I don't suppose a man like you would."

She set the remains of the tape onto the tray, then turned atop the step stool, rubbing both her back and belly simultaneously, indicating the toll this eighth month of pregnancy and demanding workload was taking on her body. When she leaned over to brace her hand on the bed to step down, Nash's hand was there. For a moment, Teresa thought her sister might stubbornly refuse the offer to help.

But she took Nash's hand, accepting his support only long enough to get both feet on the floor before quickly pulling away. "Thank you."

"Thank you, Dr. Grant."

Emilia nodded, accepting some kind of détente with him. But she wasn't quite ready to deal with her sister yet.

"Emilia—"

"We finish with the patient first." Emilia peeled off her sterile gloves, nodding to Teresa as she walked past. "Then you and I need to talk."

Fine. While her sister tossed her gloves into the trash and jotted something onto Nash's chart, Teresa climbed up on the same step stool to pull the hospital gown hanging at the crook of his elbows back over his shoulders before tying it loosely around his neck. "I sent your shirts up to your room. You can re-dress as soon as the IV is done and we take it out. I told the orderly to move you to room 3010. Standard procedure is to keep someone with an injury like yours overnight for observation."

"I can't do that, Peewee. We can't stay in one place that long. Especially a location as public as this."

"For a few hours, at least."

Emilia lifted her observant gaze from the clasped fingers between Teresa and Nash. "Thirty ten is in the children's ward."

Teresa let go and stepped down. "I know that part of the hospital better than any other. I'll recognize if anyone or anything is out of place there. I can watch over him and *I* won't look out of place."

She tucked the stool back into the closet cabinet where it had come from while Nash eased to his feet. "I still vote for getting out of here."

Teresa was holding firm on her original plan. "You promised me a few hours here. You have to stay until that IV is finished. And what if you need a blood transfusion? Or more fluids? I snuck you into this place once. If you have a relapse, I don't think I'll be able to do it again without raising even more suspicion."

There was a soft knock at the open door beyond the curtain. Teresa peeked through the drape before pulling it aside and letting the bald orderly pushing a wheelchair enter. "The patient's ready. Would you take Mr. Smith up to 3010."

The dark-skinned man arched a nonexistent eyebrow. "The children's ward?"

She walked Nash to the wheelchair, rolling the IV stand along with him, dismissing the orderly's confusion with a smooth lie. "He wants to be near his daughter."

Nash halted beside her, dipping his head to her ear before sitting. "Do you know him?"

Teresa smiled, helping him into the chair and covering him with a heated blanket. "I can vouch for Chester. He's worked here longer than I have. I went to high school with his daughter." She squeezed Nash's hand and sent him on his way. "I'll be right up." She gave directions to the orderly that weren't on the chart. "It's a private room, Chester. I don't want him startling any of the kids up there, so close the door."

"Will do." Chester unlocked the wheels, hooked the chart over the back of the chair and rolled him toward the door. "Okay, sir. I'll make this ride as smooth as I can."

"Teresa—"

"I know." She stopped Nash's warning by pulling the blanket up past his chin to mask his face a little. "If I'm not up there soon, you'll come looking for me."

He nodded, then pulled down the blanket and shifted his gaze to Emilia. "Don't blame her."

"I don't." Emilia was waiting for an explanation after Teresa closed the door and pulled the curtain. "Really? Sneaking a wounded agent into my E.R.? Is he why someone broke into your apartment and trashed it? Justin said there were reports of gunfire in your neighborhood. Did he have something to do with that, too?" Teresa didn't have to answer the barrage of accusations. Emilia was already shaking her head, turning away. *"Madre de Dios."*

"You can't tell AJ."

"You may have become a pretty little liar over the past few days, but I haven't." Emilia rolled the tray over to the counter and sorted items into trash and what could be stored away for use. "You know the hospital is mandated to report gunshot and stabbing victims to the police."

"Couldn't you lose his paperwork for a day or two?"

"Teresa." Emilia pulled out a metal stool and sank onto it, already tired on a shift that was only a few hours old. "Has he brainwashed you? Now he's got you thinking like one of them."

"One of *them?*" Teresa's shoulders stiffened at the insult. "He's not a criminal."

"He's not John Smith, either. Are you sure his badge is real?"

"Yes. Try not to stress any more than you have to. I'm worried about your blood pressure." Teresa advised her sister to stay put and took over cleaning up the supplies for her. "I told you, Nash is an undercover DEA agent. The man who set him up to be murdered is a fellow cop. He didn't have anyone he could trust. He asked for my help. What would you do?"

"I'd call Justin." Her husband the cop. "Or AJ."

"But Nash thinks the agent who betrayed him in Houston is covering up the fact that he's a cop so that KCPD will treat him like a fugitive from the law." She stowed the last of the supplies before facing her sister. "The cartel has far-reaching influence, Emilia. Nash said that if he goes to jail, there'll be someone there to kill him."

"How do you know you can trust him? Do you believe everything he says?" Emilia's eyes narrowed, then widened as if she'd just discovered something in Teresa's expressions. Maybe something more than the utter trust she had for Charles Nash. "Oh, *Gamberro,* no. You don't think you're in love with him, do you?"

Was that what this feeling was? This gut-wrenching fear that she could lose him that clouded every decision? The fiery desire that made the passion she'd felt for any other man pale by comparison? That curious instinct that made her believe she knew Charles Nash better in three short days than she knew any other man?

"I don't think it," she finally answered.

Emilia shook her head. "And he's put you in that kind of danger?"

"He's protected me at every turn."

"And what kind of future does he promise you?"

"He doesn't." The sorrow that gripped Teresa's heart at that notion proved the depth of her feelings for the man. "I imagine that once he finds out who set him up and has that man arrested, he'll go back to Houston. To his job, to his life there. But right now he needs me, Emilia. Like no one has ever needed me before." Teresa circled the room, finally making sense of why Charles Nash meant so much to her. "He needs me to be strong and capable. He lets me do things. He lets me argue with him. I don't feel like the baby of the family when I'm with him. I just… I feel like…me. He lets me be me."

Emilia reached for her hand across the stainless-steel

counter, perhaps understanding more than Teresa had given her credit for. "When I first met Justin, I thought he was a criminal. When I found out he was an undercover cop, he was still just as dangerous. It's not an easy life."

Teresa squeezed her sister's hand, unused to hearing this cautionary tale about her marriage. "But you looked past the danger. You got to know the man he was underneath that bad-guy persona. Justin is a good man. You love him."

"With all my heart." Emilia's serene smile warmed with the love she was used to seeing there. "Justin saved my life."

"I remember the bomb threats around the city that year. He saved me, too."

"He's a wonderful husband and a good father. And now we're having our second child together." Emilia released her hand to cradle her swollen belly in a maternal hug. "I'll keep your secret. I'll list the patient as John Smith and send the bill to you—with the promise that he pays you for it, like he said."

Tears stung her eyes as Teresa smiled her gratitude. "He will. Nash is a stickler for repaying a debt and keeping his promises."

Emilia stood, slipping back into doctor mode for a moment. "He'll need his dressings changed once a day for a couple of days. After that, he'll need air to get to the wounds for them to heal properly. If there's any green or yellow discharge, he'll need to come back and see me."

"I know the drill." Teresa pulled her sister into a hug. "Thank you. For taking care of Nash—and for giving me the chance to take care of him."

"Don't make me regret this." When Emilia pulled away, her eyes were a little bright, as well. "If anything goes wrong…if you get hurt—"

"I know a good doctor."

"I don't just mean physically. If you care for him, and he—"

"I know a good friend, too." She hugged her again before gathering up their coats and her bag and heading out the door. "I love you."

"I love you, too." Teresa was halfway to the elevators when she heard her sister groan. "What are we going to tell AJ?"

THE HOSPITAL WAS swarming with cops.

Okay, so maybe *swarming* was a bit of an overstatement. But the black-haired man with the graying temples and wrinkled suit striding down the hallway carried himself with an air of authority like law enforcement. The uniformed KCPD officer walking beside him confirmed it.

Teresa ducked back into the hospital gift shop, hugging the bag of clothes she'd just bought for herself and Nash. She pretended a rapt interest in a display of Kansas City postcards as the two men entered the gift shop and crossed to the clerk at the counter to introduce themselves.

The dark-haired man pulled out his badge and clipped it onto the pocket of his suit jacket. "Good afternoon, ma'am. I'm Jesse Puente, an agent with the Drug Enforcement Administration. This is Officer Reynaldo from your local police. We're looking for someone."

That man was Nash's supervising officer? The captain she'd inadvertently alerted to Nash's location when she'd sent him that frightened email? Panic jumbled her thoughts for a moment. What should she do? Nash was only two floors above them. How had Puente and the other officer tracked him here to the hospital?

Go. Run. No. Don't draw attention to yourself. Just mosey on out of here, then beat it upstairs to warn Nash.

The conversation faded as Teresa shifted the package in her arms and headed into the hallway. But the glass door hadn't closed behind her before Captain Puente called out to her. "Teresa? Teresa Rodriguez?"

She kept walking. She wasn't in scrubs today, wasn't wearing her name badge or classification pin since she was off the clock. For all anyone knew, she was a guest here to visit a sick friend.

"Ms. Rodriguez?"

When he asked the clerk for confirmation of her name, Teresa knew she had no choice but to stop and face the two officers hurrying down the hall behind her. "Yes?"

The older man was all smiles as he slowed his pace and approached. "Hi, I'm Captain Puente. We exchanged emails?"

"Ma'am." Officer Reynaldo looked bored with introductions and more interested in watching everyone who entered the hospital's main lobby and came down this corridor to the gift shop or visitor elevators at the end of the hall.

She shook the captain's hand when he offered it. "Nice to meet you."

If he noticed any reticence in her greeting, he didn't respond to it. "In your email to me, you mentioned you were a nurse. But you didn't mention where you worked. Some of my men from Houston and your local PD are checking out area hospitals, searching for Agent Nash. It's lucky I ran into you."

"Yes." She moved her sack behind her back, hiding the men's shirt and underwear she'd just purchased. "Lucky coincidence."

"Do you mind if I ask you a few questions?"

Teresa shook her head. She minded like crazy, but if she could keep the cops occupied down here on the first floor and maybe even send them on their way, then they wouldn't find Nash upstairs.

"This is where you work?" he asked, probably confused by her sweater and jeans. "You're out of uniform."

"Yes. I'm off duty today. Doing a little Christmas shopping. We get a discount here."

"I'm glad that Agent Nash has released you. He's no longer holding you against your will?" So much for pleasantries.

Something down the hallway caught Officer Reynaldo's attention and he circled around behind her. Teresa clenched her toes inside her boots to keep from bolting. Even though they'd effectively blocked her escape in either direction, he still didn't seem that interested in her, so she tilted her gaze back to the older man and concentrated on Puente. If Nash wasn't sure he could trust him, then neither was she. "No. As you can see, I'm a free woman. I was never in any real danger. It was just a…miscommunication."

Puente pulled back the edges of his jacket, giving her a clear look at the gun he carried as he rested his hands at his waist. "I was hoping you'd call me so I could reach Nash. I've lost three agents already. I don't want to lose another one."

His paternally indulgent tone made her suspicious instead of putting her at ease as he'd most likely intended. "Some men broke into my apartment. Looking for Mr. Nash, I expect."

"You weren't hurt in the break-in, were you?"

She was getting too good at this twisting-the-truth-into-a-lie thing. "I wasn't there at the time, but I haven't wanted to go back to check my computer or anything else on the premises. And I didn't have your number."

He arched a black eyebrow. "You can't check your email from another location?"

"I've been very busy."

"Excuse me, sir." Officer Reynaldo came up behind Teresa, and she stiffened. But the brief whiff of the tacos or burritos he'd had for lunch quickly receded as he backed away again. "There's a good view of the parking lot across from the elevators. I thought I'd go take a look."

Puente nodded, dismissing him. "I'll be back in a few minutes. You can show me around the rest of the hospital then."

The rest of the hospital?

A nervous suspicion shimmied down her spine. "How many of your officers did you say were here, Captain?"

"I didn't." He folded his hand around Teresa's arm and pulled her aside, ostensibly to clear a path for the balloons-and-wheelchair entourage coming down the hallway with a new mother and baby. But he didn't release her. "I get the idea you don't trust me, Ms. Rodriguez. I want to help you. I want to help Nash. But I need information. Where is he? How is he? Look, I get that he's threatened you to keep his secrets."

Teresa twisted her elbow from his grasp. "He hasn't threatened me. I'm not afraid of him."

"He's probably told you, then, that if we can connect you to him, then the Graciela cartel can, too." He braced a hand against the wall and leaned toward her. "Graciela's men are here in Kansas City. They want Agent Nash. I suspect they're the ones who broke into your apartment. They'll use you to get to him. I've seen the Gracielas' torture victims. Most of them would rather be dead."

She tightened her grip around her backpack and the

sack. "Stop trying to scare me. Nash explained how dangerous the men after him are. Why do you think I'm avoiding my apartment?"

Puente grinned, dropping his hand and pulling away. "So at least I know he's alive. And nearby, I'm guessing."

"All I did was patch him up. I haven't seen him recently." At least that, technically, wasn't a lie. She'd been hunting down clean clothes that would fit him for the past half hour. "He was injured in the shoot-out where your Agent Delvecchio got killed."

His dark eyes narrowed. "What do you know about Tommy?"

"Only what Nash—Agent Nash—mentioned when I was helping him. He said Agent Delvecchio was like a kid brother to him." She glimpsed movement behind her from the corner of her eye. Officer Reynaldo. Had there really been anything to look at outside? Or were the two men cornering her into a trap? Teresa's breath stuttered in her chest. "Maybe you all felt that way. I'm sorry for your loss."

He shrugged. "We're still looking into Delvecchio's disappearance. Thank you."

"Wait." Something wasn't right. "You said disappearance?"

For a moment, Jesse Puente looked grim. But just as quickly, that pleasant professional facade reappeared. "Apparently, the M.E.'s office here in Kansas City isn't releasing the bodies from the warehouse to us, pending identification."

"Sir?" She startled at Reynaldo's voice beside her. "I just got a call that the main office has the E.R. record for the past few days you were asking for."

"Good." Captain Puente pulled out his wallet and handed her his card. "If you see Nash again, have him call me. He may not trust anyone right now, but I can help him. But not if the cartel finds him first. If he needs backup, tell him I'm closer than he thinks."

Teresa accepted the card, a little surprised to see Puente already retreating down the hall after Officer Reynaldo. "You're letting me go?"

He paused. "This is just a friendly conversation, Ms. Rodriguez. I'm not detaining you in any way. This is a big city. And I'm not that familiar with it. It's hard to find someone under those conditions. Especially when he doesn't want to be found."

And yet Puente had found her.

"It's my job to follow up on any leads. And you're the best one I've had so far. But as you said, you've had no further contact with Nash. So I have no reason to take up any more of your time. *Gracias.*"

Teresa didn't realize she'd been holding her breath until the captain caught up with Officer Reynaldo, and the two men fell into step and crossed the lobby toward the business offices.

Then her lungs emptied with such a rush of relief that it left her light-headed. She swayed against the wall for support. But only for a few seconds.

The moment Puente and Reynaldo disappeared around a corner, Teresa spun around and hurried toward the elevators. But five steps and she stopped.

She glanced back over her shoulder to see if either officer or anyone else was watching her. The hospital lobby was busy. The gift shop had the clerk and a handful of customers inside. Although Puente and Reynaldo hadn't reappeared, there were too many people to keep track of. She needed to make sure no one followed her up to the third floor.

Instead of heading for the elevators, she changed

course and opened the door to the first empty consultation room she passed. With one last peek over her shoulder for curious eyes, she closed the door and cut through the room's back exit into the hospital employee area. She hurried through a break room and came out in an inner hallway, away from anyone's watchful eyes. Once the coast was clear, she dashed over to the employee elevator and got in to go to the third floor to find Nash.

Chapter Eleven

"Nash?" Teresa pushed open the door to 3010 and darted inside.

"That was too long, Peewee."

She butted the door shut and tossed him the bag of clothing. Nash was sitting up on the edge of the bed and caught it with his good hand. He dumped the contents onto the bed and ripped open bags and tore off tags with an urgent sureness that made her think he was feeling stronger.

"I know. Sorry."

"Tell me what's happening." His dirty-gold hair stuck up in rumpled spikes on one side of his head, as though he'd just awakened from a nap. But he'd already pulled on those big scuffed boots and had his gun strapped to his belt. Shirtless and golden, bruised and bandaged, her wounded bear seemed to have found the energy for one more battle.

"Your captain is here. In the hospital." Teresa dropped Jesse Puente's card on the bed as she hurried past to open the tall slim cabinet that functioned as a closet. She pulled out their coats. "He wants you to call him. He said he could help you and offer backup if you need it."

"He showed you his badge? You're certain it was him?"

She nodded, stopping at the bed to stuff her own change of clothes into her backpack. "There was another man with him. He wore a local uniform, but he kind of gave me the willies. He wasn't paying attention to the conversation. He was just…lurking."

He pulled a T-shirt over his head. "Did you catch a name?"

"Officer Reynaldo. Does that mean anything to you? Is he in your little black book?" Nash squeezed her shoulder as he shook his head. "Puente said he had a whole team of officers and agents combing the city looking for you."

He pulled the IV from his hand and shucked into his shirt. "They're not going to find us. Let's go."

Grabbing their coats in one hand and her arm in the other, Nash peeked into the hallway before opening the door. "Which way?"

She pointed to the right. "Back stairs are down there."

Clinging close to the wall, keeping his head bowed but his gaze on a constant scan, he led her down the pristine white hallway. Three steps. Four. Five. She plowed into his back when Nash suddenly stopped and swore beneath his breath. "Moreno."

He snatched her hand and quickly reversed course.

"What is it?"

"Company."

She glanced back to see the two men at the counter of the ward's central desk. Although they had their backs to her, it was easy to recognize a uniformed police officer. But she guessed it was the man with the cowboy hat and curly black hair Nash wanted to avoid. "Do you know him?"

"Yeah." He ducked into the first room on the left, pulling Teresa in behind him. "*He's* in the book."

Her stomach knotted. A cartel man or the suspected mole. Right here. In her hospital. Not twenty feet from where Nash was peering through the slit he'd left open in the doorway. Teresa fisted her hand in the back of his shirt, willing him to put more distance between them and the people who wanted him dead.

Nash retreated, all right. But only to urge her to move. "Hide our stuff."

Teresa turned. Froze. She hadn't checked the room number. "Oh, no."

Laila Alvarez was propped up against the pillows in her bed, playing with her stuffed horse. She smiled. "Hey, Mr. Nash."

"Hello again."

"Again? Mr. Nash?" She couldn't stop him from brushing past her and pulling aside the middle curtain to make sure the second bed in the room was empty. "You two know each other?"

He closed the curtain and opened the closet, pausing for a moment to assess its size. "We've met. Hide our gear."

"Hey, sweetie." She spared a reassuring smile for Laila before following him to the cabinet closet, where he was pulling out hangers and tossing them into a drawer. "We can't stay here and endanger a patient."

"We can't go out there."

"But—"

"Every person in this hospital could be in danger if one of Graciela's men decides to take a shot at me." He grabbed their coats and stuffed them into the drawers, too. "If we get out of here, the danger comes with us. Now hide."

"I hate this. How do you two know each other?" She opened another drawer and set her backpack inside.

"I took a walk as soon as Chester left me in the room. I needed a better idea of exits and who belonged here and who didn't." He winked at the girl in the bed. "We talked about Texas for a couple of minutes."

"You were supposed to be resting—"

Nash pressed his finger over her mouth and shushed her. "Moreno's coming this way. Get in."

"There's no room for both of us, you big beanpole." She heard the men's voices approaching, too. "Bend your legs. That's it."

"Teresa—"

She pushed him into the closet and shut the door. She nervously patted her chest to make sure she wasn't wearing any identifying pins or nametags, then pulled up a stool beside the bed. This wasn't much of a plan, but it was the only one she could come up with on a split second's notice. "Laila, I need you to be very brave. Don't tell anyone anything about Mr. Nash. It's like hide-and-seek, and we have to win."

"Okay." Her favorite patient looked small and fragile with her pink knit cap on her bald head and the oxygen clip on her finger.

But her dark eyes lit up with anticipation as Teresa asked for her help. "We're going to play a pretend game now, okay? You be a patient, and I'll be your friend who's come to visit you."

"That's not much of a game."

"You can't call me Teresa. You have to make up a name."

The little girl laughed. "Okay, Laila."

Teresa squeezed the girl's hand as she heard men's voices outside the room. She picked up one of the Marguerite Henry stories stacked beside the bed. "Shall we read a book?"

"You go down that side. I'll check over here." A man's voice preceded the soft knock at the door. It opened without invitation, and the curly-haired cop from Texas strolled in. He stopped when he saw Teresa and pulled back the front of his jacket, flashing both his badge and his holstered gun. "Excuse me, ma'am. Good afternoon. I'm Agent Cruz Moreno, DEA. We're following up on a lead and conducting a search of the hospital."

"What do you think you'll find in this little girl's room?"

He smiled, probably used to charming his way into getting what he wanted. "Mind if I take a quick look around?"

"As a matter of fact, I do. She needs her rest."

Agent Moreno took a couple more steps into the room. "I just need a quick look at that bed behind you, ma'am."

Before Teresa could stand and block his path at the foot of the bed, Laila piped up with one of her curious questions. "Are you a cowboy?"

"Huh?" Cruz Moreno stopped, looking almost startled to hear the patient speak.

"You're wearing cowboy boots and a hat. You're supposed to take it off inside. Do you have a horse?"

"No, kid. I'm a cop." He dismissed Laila and directed his explanation to Teresa. There was no charm to his words or smile now. "I'm looking for a man. Taller than me. Light hair. He may be injured."

Teresa shrugged. "This is a pediatrics ward. We don't have any adult patients here."

"This is my friend Laila," the little girl interjected.

Agent Moreno ignored the introduction and moved toward Teresa. The man wasn't that tall, but he was huskily built, and she got the idea that he was willing to throw some of that weight around. "He might not be a patient.

He might be masquerading as one of the staff or acting like a fugitive."

"What's that?" Laila sat up from her pillows, determined to be heard.

"A criminal. Someone who doesn't want the police to catch him. Seen anyone like that, kid?"

Sensing his irritation, Teresa drew his attention back to her. "I haven't seen anyone like that. Are we safe here?"

"Depends on how desperate he gets. Don't worry, ma'am. We'll find him." His shoulder brushed against Teresa's and she flinched away as he reached around her to pull open the curtain. He chuckled when he saw the empty bed. "I thought maybe you were hiding something from me, Laila."

Teresa held his suspicious dark-eyed gaze, keeping his focus on her and not the closet. But before she could think of the dismissive words that would chase him from the room, the real Laila started talking. "You have an accent. Are you from Mexico? They have horses there. They speak Spanish and Andalusians are Spanish. From Spain. They're horses."

"What?" Agent Moreno shook his head. Laila's questions seemed to confound him. And distract him from his purpose.

"Do you have an Andalusian horse?" she asked.

"No, kid." He tipped his hat to Teresa and slipped past her to the door. "Sorry to have bothered you, ma'am." Teresa's feet stayed rooted into place until the door closed and she heard Moreno talking to the other officer outside. "Without any better leads than what we've got, this is like searching for a needle in a haystack. Let's call this floor clear and start looking where the grown-ups are."

Teresa hurried to the door and peeked through a small

opening just as Nash had, waiting for Moreno and the other officer to get on the elevator at the end of the hall. She looked the other direction, too, seeing no one but a couple of staff members she recognized.

"They're gone," she announced, dashing back into the room. She opened the closet door and crossed over to Laila to give her a gentle hug. "Sweetie, you were wonderful."

"Did we win?"

"You bet we did," Nash answered, sliding out of the cramped space.

Laila was still sitting up straight in the middle of the bed, her dark eyes eagerly following Nash's every move. "I don't like him. He wears fancy cowboy boots. Not real ones you can work in, like yours. His were too shiny." Nash handed Teresa her bag and coat. "I like you. You listen when I talk. Even when I'm boring."

He flashed the girl a crooked grin that had captured Teresa's heart, as well. "I like you, too, darlin'. And somehow I doubt you could ever be boring. I owe you one for helping me out." He slipped into his coat before helping Laila get situated back under her covers. Teresa's breath did funny things in her chest when he leaned over to kiss the girl's cheek. "I won't forget."

Teresa had a kiss for her, too. "Bye, sweetie. You do whatever the doctors tell you, okay? I'll be back for Christmas."

Laila held on to both their hands. "Are you coming to the Christmas party, too, Mr. Nash?"

Golden-brown eyes locked on to Teresa's over the girl's bed. She read the message there. Christmas, even just a few days away, was too far in the future for him to even consider. To even hope for.

Before Teresa could plead with him to move beyond

that fatalistic outlook, he released Laila and started for the door.

"We'll see, darlin'." He clasped Teresa's hand instead, pulling her into step behind him. "Let's get out of here. I assume you know a back way?"

Teresa nodded and moved into the hallway ahead of him. "Follow me. The emergency wing is closest to the garage where we parked."

A nod or a smile to the coworkers they passed was enough to discourage any conversation. Although she imagined there'd be plenty of questions about the tall, tough-looking man following her down the hallway when she came back to work on the twenty-fifth.

Provided she'd be alive and able to report back to work.

The possibility that she might not, that she might lose Charlie Nash even if she did survive, sharpened her gaze and hurried her steps.

No one met them coming or going down the back stairs. They didn't even run into anyone as they jogged through the employees' inner hallway.

But when she opened the door into the busy waiting area down by the E.R., she saw the one thing that could stand in the way of their escape. A cop.

Teresa pulled up and hung back in the stairwell. "Nash, look. With Emilia."

He peeked over her shoulder to watch Emilia and the uniformed officer walking down to the E.R. bays where they'd been that morning. "Do you think she's telling him about me being here?"

"No. She promised."

"Wait a minute. Ah, hell." He tensed behind her. His fingers bit almost painfully into her shoulders. "That gun isn't regulation."

"What difference does that…?" The shiny silver pistol that stuck up out of the officer's holster had meant nothing to her. But when the man chatting with Emilia turned, glancing up and down the hallway, his gaze moving right past the shadowed doorway where they hid, Teresa's knees wobbled, and she leaned back into Nash's grasp. "That's the man who was at my apartment. Why is he dressed like a cop?"

Nash swapped positions with Teresa. He pulled back the front of his coat, checking his own sidearm. "Why do you think?"

"Captain Puente," she groaned. "He called me by name. He knows I work at this hospital."

Nash swore as the fake cop held open one of the swinging doors and followed Emilia inside. "Then he knows your sister does, too. Stay put."

"He won't hurt her, will he?" Nash's answer was to dart across the hall, flattening his back against the wall there. "Where are you—?"

But he was already stealing down the hall and slipping into the E.R. entrance next to the door through which Emilia and the man had disappeared.

Worried now for both Nash and her sister, Teresa followed. She copied the slim profile Nash had used and sidled along the wall until she reached the E.R. doors. Although there were four separate sets of swinging doors along the way, the workstations inside were sectioned off into several more bays divided by privacy curtains. The configuration of the rooms made it easier to change the layout to meet patient needs. Unfortunately, the interior curtains also made it nearly impossible to know where her sister and the cartel thug had gone or where Nash might be. But when she heard the fake cop's thickly accented voice challenging something Emilia had said, Teresa went straight to the doors where their conversation was escalating into an argument.

"Where is your sister and her boyfriend?" the creep demanded.

Teresa peeked through the window. When she saw the curtain was drawn, she pushed the silent door open and sneaked inside to do whatever she could to protect Emilia.

Although the curtain blocked her view, Teresa could hear Emilia moving about the work area with the cool efficiency of the doctor she was. "I have no idea what you're talking about. I told you the E.R. was empty. Now get out of here. You're contaminating this room."

"You don't know how to reach your own sister?"

"She's on vacation from work. It's the holidays."

"You lie."

Teresa dropped to her knees at Emilia's startled yelp. Her blood ran cold when she peeked beneath the curtain to see the man point his gun at her sister's belly. Emilia backed against the stainless-steel counter, shielding the baby with her arms.

What should she do? Cry out? Show herself? Tell that vile, gutless bully that she was the one who could lead him to Nash, not her sister?

The man was screwing a silencer onto the end of his gun. "Don't think I won't do this. According to my sources, she was in the hospital this morning with an injured man. The man I've been paid to find. You choose. Your sister or your baby. Where—?"

Teresa shot to her feet when he aimed the gun again.

But her shout was muffled by the rolling tray table that came flying through the side curtain and smashed into the would-be assassin, knocking him off his feet and crushing him against the storage counter. Nash!

Before the fake cop could get to his feet, Nash's fist

crunched against the man's jaw, driving him back onto the table. But the man kicked out, forcing Nash back. He swung his gun around, but Nash charged his midsection and lifted him off his feet. Teresa ran in to pull Emilia aside as the two men tumbled over the edge of the table and hit the floor. Hard. The gun slid beneath the table. She heard Nash's grunt of pain, cringed at the thud of fist against bone.

She had to help. Nash had had a bullet in him just three days ago. His strength wouldn't last. It wasn't a fair fight.

The men flipped, rolled, knocked over a stool. Emilia dodged their twisting legs while Teresa spotted the medicine dispensary and got an idea. She dashed around the table. "Emilia, what's the combination?"

Her sister rattled off the computer code and Teresa unlocked the cabinet. She grabbed a vial. Peeled open a syringe.

"Teresa!" Emilia warned.

She spun and saw the knife the thug had pulled out.

But Nash was on top again, his fist clamped over the other man's wrist. He banged the hand clutching the knife on the floor—once, twice—until the man released his grip and the weapon skittered away into the next bay.

And then he pressed his forearm against the other man's throat, pinning him to the floor, choking him.

"Who's Graciela's inside man?" he demanded on a wheezing breath. He increased the pressure on the man's throat. "Who told you where to find me?"

The black-haired man with the bloody lip laughed and spit at Nash. *"Son todos los muertos."*

You are all dead.

The moment Nash blinked and swiped the spittle from his face, the other man reared up with a roar. Teresa dropped to her knees and jabbed the loaded syringe into his thigh. The last-ditch rebellion was short-lived. Nash pushed him back to the floor, pinning him until the other man's muscles relaxed and he passed out.

"You don't threaten the pregnant lady, understand?"

Only then did Nash ease his grip and roll off onto the floor beside the unconscious man. With his chest heaving in deep, labored breaths, he pulled the gun from beneath the examination table and sat up.

He braced his elbows against his knees and grinned at her. "Good shootin', Peewee. But I thought I told you to stay put."

"He pointed a gun at my sister and future niece. I wasn't going to lose any of you." Teresa crawled over to him and started to tug at his jacket. "Are you all right? I need to check your stitches."

"Let me do that." Emilia picked up a stack of gauze pads to wipe the mess from Nash's jaw and dab at the bump on his cheek that was oozing blood.

"Sorry, ladies, but there's no time." Nash shrugged off both their efforts and tucked the oversize handgun into his belt. He got up on one knee and rolled the black-haired assailant from one side to the other, checking his pockets. He removed the would-be killer's wallet and opened it. "Angel Sanchez. All the way from Harlingen, Texas. I've heard of the Sanchez brothers. They do a lot of work for Graciela. First time I've met one in person."

Teresa could see there was no badge in his billfold or anywhere else on the unconscious man, either. Her stomach soured as she feared the worst. "Where do you think he got the uniform?"

"Hopefully, he got it from someone's locker. I don't see any bullet holes to indicate he took it off an actual cop. With his DEA badge, our mole could walk right into any KCPD building and help himself." Nash pocketed Sanchez's wallet and cell phone before he unhooked the handcuffs from his belt. "These look real enough."

He flipped Sanchez onto his stomach and pulled his hands behind his back to cuff him. "Peewee, I need you to go find his knife. Dr. Grant, is there anything in here I can gag and restrain this guy with?"

"Yes. And it's Emilia." She opened the storage cabinet and ripped open a packet of IV tubing to hand him. "Will this work?"

"Perfect."

Nash had hog-tied the hit man and righted the stool for Emilia to sit on by the time Teresa had picked up the knife. "Are you all right, Doctor?" he asked, winding a few strips of gauze through the man's mouth to keep him quiet when he regained consciousness.

"Emilia?" Teresa hurried to her sister's side. "You look pale."

"I'm fine." Emilia rubbed the side of her belly. "The baby is still reliving the excitement, however. Oh, this girl can kick." She nodded toward the man on the floor. "Is he the man who's after you?"

"One of them."

She reached for Teresa's hand and squeezed it tight. "So you're not safe yet?"

Nash eyed the sisterly clasp of hands and turned to the door with a blend of regret and alertness stamped on his bruised face. "There's another brother out there somewhere. We need to go. If he's here, there are more on the way. They travel in packs, remember?"

Teresa peered out the door, too, wondering if anyone in the lobby had heard the commotion. "We can't leave her here with him."

Emilia picked up the phone on the counter beside her. "You gave him a full dose of that sedative. He'll be out for a couple of hours. I'm calling security now. I'll be fine. Go."

"It's his friends I'm worried about," Teresa insisted.

Nash agreed. "Don't let security touch that guy." He put Angel Sanchez's wallet on the counter beside the phone. "Call your brother or husband to pick him up. I'm sure he's got a rap sheet a mile long. And there's plenty more they can charge him with today. Ask if they'll keep him in isolation for as long as possible so he can't get word out that he's found me."

Emilia nodded. "I can do that."

"And ask your husband or AJ to stay with you, in case one of Sanchez's buddies shows up to ask you some questions."

"I will."

"Thank you." To Teresa's surprise, Nash leaned down and kissed her sister's cheek. "I owe you and your family more than I can repay."

To her greater surprise, Emilia smiled up at him. "Thank you for protecting my child." Her smile included Teresa. "And my sister."

Nash nodded, dismissing her acceptance and returning to the door to keep watch. Teresa could tell he was antsy to be on their way. But she hated to leave her sister unprotected, despite knowing the man on the floor could no longer harm her. "I'm sorry I brought this danger into your world."

"I told you it wasn't an easy life." Emilia stood to offer one more piece of advice. "I know my sister is trying to prove she's invincible. But she's not. Neither are you, I suspect. Keep each other safe." She wrapped Teresa up in a tight hug. Then she released her and scooted her toward the door. "We have plans for Christmas, remember? You come home to us."

Nash reached for Teresa's hand and linked his fingers with hers. "She will."

Ten minutes later, Teresa drove the silver pickup out of the employee parking garage into the glare of the sun reflecting off the snow outside. With his shaggy beard growth, hat pulled low over his forehead and a pair of sunglasses they'd found in Jake's truck, Nash was practically unrecognizable as the man she'd first pulled out of that ditch. She, too, put on her sunglasses to help mask her face from all the searching eyes who seemed to be at Truman Medical Center today.

It felt weird, wrong, perhaps, to be donning disguises and leaving her family behind to go into hiding with Nash and continue to help in his quest. The fear she'd known when he'd first forced her to do his bidding at gunpoint was gone. But so was any sense of excitement or adventure. That urge to show herself as competent and capable had matured into a sense of duty, a commitment to a cause…or person she believed in.

As she pulled into a line of cars to wait for the traffic light at the parking lot exit to change, her gaze slid across the front seat to Nash. He was busy scrolling through the information on the perp's phone, seeking answers. Her blood warmed in her veins at the sight of his broad shoulders and bowed head. But she chilled again just as quickly.

Emilia was wrong. She wasn't trying to prove her invincibility. Teresa knew she was anything but. She'd fallen in love with Charles Nash. And if anything happened to him, if men like Angel Sanchez got to him before he uncovered the truth, then she could lose him.

And that would be a wound that even her talented sister wouldn't be able to fix.

"You're staring at me, Peewee." His golden-brown eyes tilted up to hers. "I'm not bleeding again, am I?"

"Are you sure Emilia will be safe in the E.R. with that man?" Teresa still felt uneasy about leaving her sister behind to deal with Sanchez's brother and friends.

"She had her husband on the phone before we left," he reminded her. He reached across the center console to squeeze her thigh. "You can call her when we get back to the Seaside Motel to make sure she's okay."

Teresa flashed him a weak smile. "Thanks." She glanced down at the phone in his hand. "Did you find anything?"

"No names. But our Señor Sanchez has a lot of incoming calls from the same number. Three within the past hour."

"Is the number in your black book?" She turned her attention back to traffic as the light changed.

"It's a Houston prefix. I'll check it when we get back to the motel. Maybe Jake's friend Detective Montgomery can run the number for me."

Teresa followed the car in front of her up to the road and turned right just as another car was pulling into the parking lot. What the…? She glanced in her sideview mirror, checked the rearview, too. There was something familiar about the dark-haired man behind the wheel. But he sped away before she could get a second look.

"What is it?"

Probably just her frazzled nerves working overtime, making her see ghosts. "Nothing. Just thinking of what a small world it is."

"Teresa, there are armed men in your hospital looking for us. They threatened your sister and tried to kill me. What did you see?"

Maybe she was smart to be more suspicious of the

people around her. "That car that just passed us. I swear the driver was that drunk who was hitting on me in the Shamrock Bar."

Chapter Twelve

Teresa had forgotten how good a shower could feel, even with bargain-brand soap and shampoo for her hair. She felt revived, refreshed, warm, clean, relatively normal.

Since the Seaside Motel's amenities didn't include a hair dryer, bathrobe or complimentary pajamas, she blotted her wet hair, then twisted it up on top of her head with a towel before dressing in her underwear and jeans. She opened the bathroom door to let the steam out before pulling on a camisole and stepping out to use the mirror to dab some lotion onto her cheeks. She squirted more lotion into her palms, and while she rubbed it into her arms and hands, she let her gaze slide to the mirror to study the man working in the room behind her.

Nash sat in the chair beside the rickety table, jotting notes in his little black book of clues and suspicions. He, too, had showered and was letting the stitching around his wounds air out and dry before he put on a warm shirt to sleep in. This was the first time she'd seen him clean shaven, too. It was a different look from the scruffy bear she was used to seeing. She wouldn't call him handsome, exactly—there were too many hard angles and bruises and bumps. Then there was that slightly crooked mouth that charmed like a little boy when he grinned and molded so perfectly to hers when they kissed.

Maybe not handsome, but masculine, compelling. Sexy.

The shave wasn't the only thing different about him tonight. There was more tan than pale to his skin now that he was feeling better. He seemed to have more energy, more focus.

He'd checked the security of the room and peeked outside several times, ensuring they'd drawn no undue attention from anyone. He'd made a couple of calls to Jake. Nash had given his friend the suspicious number to trace off Angel Sanchez's phone, hoping that would lead back to his contact within the DEA or even get a ping on his brother's location if he was here in Kansas City. He'd given Jake Teresa's description of the driver she'd seen. But a man in a suit with dark brown hair and dark eyes wasn't much to go on. Jake promised to run everything past his friend at KCPD and ask some questions around the bar, as well.

Nash had even trusted her, encouraged her, to make an important phone call of her own to her family. Emilia was home with Justin and their son, Joey, and AJ had Sanchez tied up at Fourth Precinct headquarters for all kinds of questioning related to both the assault at the hospital and the break-in at Teresa's apartment.

Not that AJ was pleased to learn the extent of her involvement with the Graciela cartel or just how much she'd been helping one agent in particular. But he understood undercover work and protecting his family. So he'd sit on Sanchez for now and save lecturing Teresa and strangling Nash for later.

This healthier, warier version of Nash felt different from the man she'd stitched up at her apartment. He was different from the man who'd held on to her last night and wept for the friends he'd lost.

This Nash was prowling, driven, self-sufficient—an intensified version of the man she'd fallen in love with.

And maybe he no longer needed her as much as she needed him.

Suddenly, she was aware of golden-brown eyes meeting hers in the mirror. "I can hear you thinking all the way across the room, Peewee."

Caught staring, caught musing, caught revealing far more of her feelings than a smart woman should, perhaps, Teresa quickly straightened the counter around the sink and headed into the main room. The hour had grown late. They'd eaten the last of the soup and split the last sandwich, and she'd given Nash his pill. "Thanks for cleaning up in here."

He grinned. "You've been cleaning up after me long enough. You okay?"

"I'm just worried about people. Worried about everything. Wishing I could do more." She walked past him to pick up the new Kansas City Chiefs sweatshirt she'd bought for herself at the hospital gift shop.

"I think risking your life to help me and your sister qualifies as more." He closed the black book and tucked it into the go bag on the floor beside him. "There's nothing else we can do until I hear from Jake about tracking down those phone numbers."

"Nothing?"

"Try to get a good night's sleep?" he suggested.

"You need one." Instead of putting on the heavy shirt and removing the damp towel, Teresa gathered up the first-aid supplies and brought them back to set on the table beside Nash. She gently poked at the stitches in his shoulder. They were dry. "I'll get this rebandaged so you can get dressed and go to bed. It'd be ridiculous if you caught a cold now, after everything you've been through."

But when she picked up the first gauze pad, Nash captured her wrist and stopped her. "That's not what I need, Peewee." He pulled her onto his lap. "I'm not cold."

He wasn't. The heat on his skin sizzled beneath the hand she'd braced against his uninjured shoulder. And it wasn't from any trace of fever. Teresa tried to make light of the hyperawareness she suddenly felt expanding every pore of her body. The goose bumps on her arms gave her the perfect excuse. "Well, one of us is cold."

He wound his arms around her, pulling her closer to all that bare skin on his chest. "Is that better?"

Yes, she was warmer. But that dusting of tawny hair across his chest was a prickly caress beneath her sensitive palms, and the sleek ripple of muscle that shifted beneath her hands each time he moved was even more distracting. She tried to remember that she was the nurse and he was the patient, that they'd known each other for only a matter of days, that extraordinarily difficult circumstances in close quarters had probably led to this shared feeling of intimacy. He was the injured man. She was the strong one, right? "What are you doing, Nash?"

He rubbed his hand up and down her arm, chasing away the goose bumps there. "There's something about being locked inside this little room with you that makes me crazy."

"Gee, thanks."

"Your scent is in every corner."

"The smell of soap and antiseptic?"

But as much as she tried to make a joke about the tension that drew them to each other, he wasn't laughing. There wasn't so much as a teasing chuckle in those warm golden eyes as he dipped his head to nuzzle her neck. He inhaled and exhaled softly against the indentation behind her ear, tickling the microscopic hairs there.

"You smell like goodness and home and—" he reached up to release the towel from her hair, sending the long, damp strands tumbling down her back "—all the things I may never get to have in my life."

Teresa turned in his lap. "Don't talk like that. You've gotten another lead with Sanchez's phone. Jake is helping. Justin and AJ are working on the case, too." The glimpse of despair she saw in his eyes touched something much deeper than the physical desire his encompassing warmth and gentle touches were stirring inside her. She brushed her fingertips across the line of his bruised cheekbone and cupped the side of his smooth jaw. "We'll get through this."

He sifted his fingers through her hair, smoothing the long layers over her right shoulder and breast, rolling the curling tips between his thumb and fingertips. "For days, all I've been able to think about is avenging Tommy's and Axel's and Jim's deaths. Exposing a traitor. Protecting all the agents who go up against the cartel. From the moment I drove into that Kansas City warehouse, I've fully expected that I'm going to die trying to get this job done."

"Nash—"

He shushed her with a finger over her lips. His gaze, which had been so fascinated with her hair a moment earlier, landed there. "You have the most beautiful mouth I've ever seen on a woman. When I'm alone in this room with you, and the rest of the world is some distant nightmare outside that door, all I can think about is that kiss we shared yesterday."

Her gaze instinctively zeroed in on his mouth. "You were delirious with fever. You probably aren't remembering it accurately."

At last those firm lips crooked up with a dangerous grin. "How's my temperature now, Nurse Rodriguez?"

"Normal. Your fever broke and hasn't come back since this morning." Was that hushed quiver of anticipation really coming from her throat?

Nash brushed the callused pad of his thumb across her bottom lip, sparking a dozen different nerve endings. His smile grew at her soft gasp. "My eyes are focused? My thoughts are sane? No delusions?"

Her mouth was parched with anticipation. "As far as I can tell, you're...healthy."

"Good. I just wanted to make sure we're clear on this." Then he leaned in, replacing his thumb with his mouth. He stroked his tongue across the curve of her lip. He kissed her gently, then drew the sensitive bow between his lips to suckle and tease. Teresa's breath stuttered in her throat, then rushed out to blend with his. He touched his tongue to hers, retreated, touched her again. With one hand palming her hip and the other buried in the weight of her hair at her nape, he held her in place against his mouth and thighs.

Her fingers dug into the warm skin of his chest. The tips of her breasts pearled into needy nubs at this leisurely seduction of her mouth. The liquid heaviness of growing need settled between her legs. She whimpered in her throat at the thoroughness with which he tasted, aroused, soothed. She squirmed in his lap to find a better angle to meet each kiss, threaded her fingers into his short hair to pull him closer, to increase the pressure, to deepen the kiss.

"Nash?"

"Me, too."

Suddenly, the atmosphere in the room changed. The kiss grew more impatient. Like a match lighting a fuse, Nash's right arm snaked around her waist and he stood. Her bare toes never touched the carpet. He hauled her up to his chest with his good arm and kissed her harder. "Hold on to me, darlin'. Unless you want me to stop."

Teresa willing obeyed, winding her arms around his neck and reconnecting the kiss. His left hand threaded into her hair and his right hand palmed her bottom, holding her body flush against his as he turned, sat on the edge of the bed and fell back with her on top of him.

"Watch your should—" He kissed her into silence. Other than a single grunt when they landed, the man didn't appear to be feeling any pain at all. Her thighs parted around his and he bent his knee slightly, rubbing its solid strength at the juncture there, stoking the pressure and leaving her gasping for release against the salty warmth of his neck.

With his knee trapping her against the flexing heat of his body, he rolled her to the bed beside him. While he kissed her cheeks, her chin, that sensitive bundle of nerves behind her ear, his hands went to work, too. He pushed the knit camisole up to her breasts, stroking his hand along her stomach, exposing her heated skin to the room's cool air. He skimmed the camisole off over her head. And then his hand was on one breast, squeezing, playing. His mouth was on the other, tonguing her to a feverish pitch through the wet satin of her bra.

Teresa bucked beneath the weight of his lower body pinning hers, wanting to be closer, needing to feel more. She laced her fingers through his hair and clutched at his scalp, holding his raspy tongue against the thrusting tip of her breast. There wasn't a cell in her body that wasn't on fire, and all that extra heat seemed to be building in the sensitized weight of her breasts and priming something bigger, hotter, deep inside the heart of her.

As he explored her body with his hands, she tried to take the same liberties with him. She found the stiff bead of a male nipple in the crisp curls on his chest. She discovered the quivering response of her fingertips brushing across the flat of his stomach, dipping beneath the snap of his jeans. She squeezed her legs around the wedge of his thigh and skimmed her palms up his strong arms and back.

When she accidentally brushed her fingers over the wound by his shoulder blade, there was just one little flinch of discomfort. Just one big reminder of what was happening here.

"Nash," she gasped. "We probably shouldn't. You're still on the mend." And though she couldn't quite seem to catch her breath, she braced her hands on the relatively neutral space of his chest and started to shift away. "Just because we—"

"Don't you dare." Nash pulled her right back. He brushed the hair away from her face, looked down into her eyes. "I've never felt as strong as I do when I'm with you. I need you more than I need the truth, more than I need my next breath." He threw one long leg over both of hers, letting her feel the bulge of his arousal at her hip. Very healthy indeed. "Please, Peewee." Although his chest heaved in and out with every deep, ragged breath, brushing against hers, he held himself back. "Will you?"

"Nash, I…" She tiptoed her fingers around his neck, looked up into his handsome, expectant eyes and knew her answer. "I want to call you Charlie. It feels more personal. Is that okay?"

His mouth slowly crooked into a grin. "That's very okay with me."

"And, Charlie?"

"Hmm?"

"No more Peewee, please. Not when we're close like this."

He slipped his hand between them, slowly unzipped her jeans and slid his fingers inside to torment her. "Close like this?"

She clenched her thighs against the pressure of his hand, barely able to speak as the pleasure built inside her. "Yes."

"I've never met anyone like you, Teresa Rodriguez. Strong and gentle, brave and full of fire." He pulled her panties aside, thrust a finger inside her, and she moaned against the fragrant warmth of his chest. "I've never wanted to be with anyone the way I want to be with you."

"Me, either."

"We make a great team, don't we?"

"Yes."

"I've been on assignment or focused on my work for so long that I can't remember the last time I wanted—"

"Charlie?" She pressed a kiss to his chest. Kissed his chin. Pulled his mouth close to hers.

"Yeah?"

"We only have until Christmas, remember? Less talking. More action."

He grinned. "Yes, ma'am."

For several needy, frustrating seconds, they pulled apart to remove the rest of their clothes, to dig a condom from his wallet, to fall back onto the bed together.

And then his mouth closed over hers. Her body melted beneath the beauty of his kiss and the weight of his body moving on top of her and sliding inside. "That's it, darlin'. Let it happen."

There were no more words. Only touches and kisses, moans of need and gasps of pleasure. The heat detonated inside her, and Teresa held on tight, riding the shock waves of pleasure. She held on tighter as Charlie's fingers tangled in her hair, and he groaned with the power of his own release.

Afterward, they drifted off to sleep, still cradled in each other's arms. Her dark hair and the warmth of Charlie's body draped possessively around hers were the only cover she needed.

SOMETIME LATER IN the night, Nash awoke to find a petite package of decadent curves spooned against his chest. When he stroked her long, soft hair down her back, Teresa shivered against him, stirring the interest of his body again.

When he looked down, he found her beautiful dark eyes open, watching him. "Are you okay?" she asked. "You were sleeping pretty hard."

"Always taking care of me, hmm?"

Her fingers drew tantalizing little designs across his chest. "That was the deal, right? I take care of you, and you live long enough to catch the bad guys?" Her gaze shuttered and dropped to the middle of his chest. Her hands stilled. "I think I'm in love with you, Charlie Nash."

His heart swelled at her softly spoken admission, spreading light into his dark world, filling him with a humility and hope he had no business feeling.

Similar words danced across his tongue. But he couldn't bring himself to say them. This woman was too good, too sweet, too important for him to make her any promises he couldn't keep.

Instead he captured her chin between his thumb and finger and tipped her face back up to his. "Teresa…"

Her mouth softened with a beautifully serene smile and she nodded, as if she understood the things he couldn't say. And then she stretched up against his eagerly attentive body and kissed him. This he could do. This he could give her.

Making love the second time was a little more urgent, a little more familiar, a little more poignant. When he buried himself inside her, the lights exploded behind his eyes, and her slick body collapsed on top of his, leaving Nash utterly exhausted. He felt completely happy and strangely bereft.

His life had never been this good, yet it had never been this complicated, either. The rational side of his brain told him that this connection he felt to Teresa was all an illusion, a cosmic lining up of a sexy woman, a dangerous situation, close quarters and a man who might not have many tomorrows.

But the woman in his bed was real. Her bravery and stubbornness and compassion were all real. In his heart, something was telling him that these feelings he had for her were just as real. But he couldn't bring himself to believe that this reality could last. He'd lost too much in his life—his parents, his friends, his faith that there would always be someone who had his back, the security of believing there would be a tomorrow.

But this woman made him believe. For now. For tonight.

If he died tomorrow, he'd die a happy man.

And if he survived this hell and lived to be a hundred, he'd never regret this one perfect night he'd spent with Teresa Rodriguez in his arms.

NASH WAS SNORING contentedly beneath the covers when Teresa stepped out of the bathroom fully dressed. Although her body was a little tired from the extra exercise and fewer hours of sleep she'd gotten last night, she suspected she still had more energy than a man who'd been shot twice less than a week ago.

Besides, she'd heard the empty grumblings in Nash's stomach while he slept. Her own tummy was hungry for breakfast. Making sure the patient ate regularly and kept up his strength was part of a nurse's job, too.

Besides, if she stayed cocooned in bed with Nash much longer, her foolish heart might begin to believe the passion and tenderness they'd shared could last beyond the terms of the partnership they'd made. Nash hadn't made her any promises. And though she had no doubt that the man truly cared for her on some level, she wasn't going to ask for any. There were any number of reasons why a relationship between them wouldn't work—the simplest being that they lived in two different cities, the most difficult being that a drug cartel wanted him dead.

So for now, she'd tuck her heart away and take care of the practicalities that had been her responsibility from the moment they'd met.

After bundling up in her coat and pulling her billfold from her bag, she crossed over to the bed and smiled down at the familiar tawny stubble shading Nash's jaw. She caught her ponytail behind her neck and leaned down to press a kiss to the crooked line of his mouth.

One golden eye popped open, then the other. He smiled. "Morning, darlin'."

"Good morning, Charlie."

The smile vanished and he sighed in disappointment. "You have all your clothes on."

Teresa laughed and dodged away when he reached for her. "I'm hungry and we're out of food. I'm going down to the office to see if there's anything breakfastlike in the vending machines there."

The sheet and blanket pooled around his hips as he

sat up. He gently stretched some of the stiffness from his left shoulder and nodded toward the window. Nakedness aside, he sternly reminded her of the safety precautions that had become ingrained in her during these past few days together. "Make sure you check the parking lot before you go out. Account for all the cars we saw last night. If there are any extras, you'll have to wait a few minutes for me to go with you."

Determined to allow him the rest he needed, Teresa pulled aside the dusty drape and peeked out. "The two work trucks are gone, and it looks like Mr. Moscatelli is back. Otherwise, they're the same."

Nash nodded his approval, but he wasn't ready to quit the protection job. He reached for his jeans and shorts at the foot of the bed. "All right. Straight there and straight back. If you're gone too long—"

"You'll come looking for me. I'll be back in a couple of minutes. Long enough for you to get dressed."

Teresa opened the door and stepped onto the sidewalk, quickly closing the door behind her. The air felt particularly brisk and damp this morning. Shivering almost at once, she pulled up her hood and stuffed her hands into her pockets. It was probably the shock of the cold after spending such a toasty night in bed that made the wintry morning feel particularly harsh. Another reason not to tarry any longer on her errand than necessary.

She hurried her steps in front of building A, checking windows the way she'd seen Nash do. But there was no movement to any of the curtains. No curious eyes on her. The traffic on the street looked like any other morning in the city. Drivers were focused on getting to work, not slowing down for a look at the Seaside's cheesy decor.

A blast of heat and the noisy chatter of the morning news on TV welcomed her into the motel office. Although there was no one sitting behind the counter at the desk, the television and flask were certain signs that Mr. Moscatelli had paid whatever fine or bail was asked of him, and the police had allowed him to return to work at the family business. The door to the laundry-and-storage room behind the counter stood slightly ajar. Maybe he was taking a break from his television shows and doing a load of laundry.

Breathing easier at the lack of company, Teresa pulled out her billfold and inspected the two vending machines set up in the nook beside the ice machine. Her choices were limited and the prices were steep, but she inserted her cash and got a couple of granola bars and bottles of orange juice for a relatively nutritious, if not necessarily filling, meal.

She was stuffing the bottles of OJ into her pockets when she heard the gravelly voice behind her. "That's her. She's the one in 6A."

She turned to see Mr. Moscatelli stepping out of the laundry room. A younger man, dressed in a suit and a long winter coat, slipped some cash into the old man's hand as he stepped out around him. Wariness turned to surprise, then confusion, then to guarded fear.

The man in the car yesterday, the obnoxious drunk from the Shamrock Bar, perfectly sober now, walked to the end of the counter.

Teresa eyed the distance to the door as the man approached. "You. Are you following me? Who are you?"

He paused at the counter to stuff his hands into his pockets. He pulled one back out but left the other in his slacks. His charming smile and delay in answering were altogether creepy. He flipped open a wallet she recognized, dark brown and narrow, like the one Nash carried. Like the ones Cruz Moreno and Jesse Puente had both shown her.

Oh, no.

His wallet held a badge he clipped onto the chest pocket of his coat. *The mole.* "Good morning, Mrs. Smith. Or should I say Miss Rodriguez? You've led me and my friends on quite the merry chase. But I believe you are the key to getting what I want."

What was in the other hand, a gun? She drifted toward the door. "How do you know my name?"

"Police reports. An introduction at the Shamrock. A chat with one of my associates at the hospital."

How long had she been gone? One minute? Two? Five? How long before Nash got worried and came storming in here to find her? How long before he walked straight into a trap? She had to warn him.

"I forget my manners. Allow me to introduce myself." He tapped his badge and took a step forward. "I work for the Drug Enforcement Administration out of Houston, Texas. I'm Agent Tommy Delvecchio."

Nash's dead friend?

The young man he'd wept for?

He was the traitor?

"You're dead."

Agent Delvecchio grinned. "A bladder of blood and enough crossfire to keep Nash from checking my vital signs? Not so much. Of course, this whole week would have been much easier if the men who hired me had just done their job and killed him in the first place."

It would destroy Nash to learn who had betrayed him and his men. One of his own team. Part of his family.

But she wouldn't let him die.

She was inches from the door now. Closer to escape than to the man advancing on her.

And then she heard the squealing of tires on the pavement and glanced out to see a black SUV jumping the curb and speeding into the motel parking lot.

Tommy Delvecchio pulled his left hand from his pocket, showing her the cell phone he'd used to send one of his cartel buddies a text.

"Six-A," Tommy deadpanned.

Teresa hurled the two bottles at his head, forcing him to duck. She shoved open the door as a second SUV veered around the corner into the driveway. She ran across the slick asphalt, praying, hoping.

"Nash! Nash!"

THE HAIRS ON the back of Nash's neck stood on end. Teresa had been gone too long. He fastened the buckle on his belt, securing the Smith & Wesson at his side, and reached for his shirt. If she wasn't back here before he got his coat on, then he was marching down to the office, throwing her over his shoulder and hauling her back to the secure confines—

The sound of speeding tires screaming for traction on the snowy asphalt turned his blood to ice.

He was already running to his bag for backup when he heard Teresa shouting his name. "Nash! Nash!"

He whipped aside the drapes and swore. Teresa was charging across the parking lot. A black SUV was barreling toward the building from the other direction.

Nash jammed the shells into his shotgun and threw open the door. He braced the butt of the gun against his good shoulder and took aim. "Get down!"

Boom! The recoil jolted through him, but he'd hit the front tire.

"Nash!"

He saw a blur of turquoise coat in his side vision as he

aimed at the fishtailing car and pulled the second trigger. "Stay back!"

With the vehicle disabled, the driver shot to hell and the passenger clinging to whatever he could grab, the big SUV flipped, crashing into the fence around the pool and knocking over a palm tree. Nash dropped the shotgun and drew his sidearm, cradling the pistol between his hands and advancing out the door as a second SUV braked to a stop in front of the office.

"Teresa?"

"Charlie?"

Her strangled gulp squeezed his heart in an iron fist. He turned and saw the impossible.

His aim went instinctively toward the movement at the corner of the building. A man's arm, cinched around Teresa's neck. A gun pointed to her head.

For a split second, his brain refused to work. He lowered his gun from the shield Teresa created, raised it again to the man who held her captive. "Tommy?"

The eager young agent who'd been so pleased with his idea for helping a field veteran like him was still looking pretty pleased with himself. But he didn't look young or naive as he pushed the barrel of his Glock against Teresa's temple and backed up with his prisoner to the second SUV. "You and I will talk later, Nash."

Nash followed them a step, glanced down at the trusting hope in Teresa's dark eyes and stopped. An unaccustomed fear sucker punched him, and anger raised bile in his throat. "Let her go."

"Somehow I don't think you'll come quietly if I do." The driver of the SUV pushed the door open behind Tommy. Teresa tugged at his arm around her neck, but neither it nor the gun was budging. "You're the one Berto wants. You've been so much trouble that he's here in town to finish the job himself."

Nash didn't know if he was that good a shot with one bum arm to trust that he could take out that rat bastard without hitting Teresa. "If you hurt her—"

The wail of sirens sounded in the distance. Someone must have called in the speeding cars and gunfire.

Tommy had reached the car with Teresa. Nash's gaze darted down to Teresa. *I love you, Peewee.* "I will protect you," he vowed.

"That's what I'm counting on." Tommy laughed and shoved her inside, climbing in behind her. "Gotta go."

"I'm comin' for you, Tommy." The car door slammed shut, and Nash charged. But the driver floored it, racing forward. Nash dove into a snowdrift to avoid getting hit. The big SUV churned up slush and ice as it made a big U-turn around the pool. Nash got to his feet and chased after it, getting off a couple of low shots at its rear tires before it reached the street and careened into traffic.

"Son of a… Teresa!" He reversed course and ran back to the truck.

The keys! Hell, Teresa had them. He banged on the glass with the butt of his gun. He could hot-wire the thing if he could get inside. He struck it again, desperate to get to her.

The sirens were on top of him now. Red-and-blue lights flashed off the glass.

"Police! Drop your weapon!"

He smashed the glass and the window shattered.

"Drop it!"

Nash raised his hands. "I'm a federal agent. A woman's been kidnapped."

But the blue suit wasn't listening. All he saw was the

gun in Nash's hand. The shotgun on the ground. The wrecked car with the bloodied driver and passenger.

"On your knees," the older cop ordered.

What was he supposed to do? Shoot two real cops?

With a nod that he was complying, Nash went down to his knees on the cold asphalt and set the gun on the ground beside him.

"These two are dead, Paulie." The younger cop moved away from the wrecked SUV.

Nash glanced over at the car, recognizing the faces. Maybe a little intel would convince them to let him go. "The vics are Santiago Vargas and Davey Gallion. They're a cartel lieutenant and enforcer. Look 'em up. They both have warrants."

"Yeah, and who are you? The tooth fairy?"

"I'm a federal agent. I've worked undercover on a task force to nail these guys. My badge is in the room." The black cop picked up the shotgun and went inside while the older one tucked away Nash's sidearm and pulled his arms behind his back to handcuff him. Although it hurt like hell to bend his arm that way, it hurt worse knowing Teresa had been taken hostage. "An accomplice of theirs just kidnapped an innocent woman. You have to let me go."

The younger cop returned with his go bag. "Hell, Paulie. He's got a whole arsenal of firearms in here."

The cop named Paulie dragged Nash to his feet. "You sure you're not some kind of enforcer, too?"

He pushed Nash toward the squad car. "Look inside the bag. My badge is in there. I'm a federal agent."

"Okay, tooth fairy. We'll look."

They put him in the back of the squad car until the younger cop had cleared the motel room and Paulie had called dispatch for the M.E. and backup. By then Teresa, and any chance of catching Tommy before he took her to Graciela, was gone.

Chapter Thirteen

"Sorry about the makeshift accommodations, Agent Nash." The young police officer, DeShawn Britt, knocked on the door of the third-floor interview room to bring him a cup of coffee and apologize. "We had a tornado blow through here this past summer. It took out a good chunk of the building and we're still repairing—"

"I know." The tight quarters and the one-way mirror didn't bother Nash, other than it didn't leave him much room to pace. There wasn't an officer he'd met yet in KCPD's Fourth Precinct offices who hadn't told him some chapter about the storm that had hit downtown Kansas City. He didn't wish that kind of hardship on anyone. But right now he didn't care if a blizzard hit the city. It wasn't going to stop him from doing what he needed to do. "I've already been waiting half an hour and time is critical. It's imperative that I talk to—"

The interview room door opened, and a short muscular detective with black hair and a fitted black fatigue sweater stepped in. Nash had seen him only once before, a brief glimpse of his profile in Teresa's apartment. But the man was on duty now. And judging by the unrevealing expression on his face and the hardware he wore holstered beneath each arm, Detective AJ Rodriguez was serious business.

"I hear you're looking for me." Nash could believe that more than one suspect had quaked in his boots in this room as the veteran detective walked in, followed by a big bruiser of a blond cop. AJ dismissed the uniformed officer and nodded toward the other man. "My partner, Josh Taylor."

"Good to meet you, Nash." Josh stepped forward to shake his hand while AJ moved to the opposite side of the interview table and crossed his arms over the badge that hung around his neck. Josh noticed the sizing up, too, and laughed. "Good luck."

Nash might have stood a head taller than Teresa's brother, but he had to respect that the guy could take him. Especially if he had blondie here to back him up.

Nah. AJ Rodriguez looked tough enough to take him all on his own. Nash pulled up to his full height, ready to stand his ground.

"You kidnapped my sister?" AJ accused.

"I needed a nurse. She saved my life."

"And now you got her kidnapped by a drug cartel?"

"Once she made contact with my office and alerted the mole to where I was hiding, I knew they'd use her to get to me. She was safer with me than out there on her own, unprotected."

"They're using her, all right." AJ fisted his hands on top of the table and leaned forward. "Is this how the DEA runs their undercover ops?"

Nash hadn't expected this conversation to go smoothly. But he didn't have time to soothe egos or earn Brownie points with Teresa's family. "I'm not going to try to explain how I'm worthy of your sister. I'm not. And I'm not going to explain how desperate and dangerous life gets when an undercover op blows up in your face. If you're the vet Teresa claims, you already know that." Nash mir-rored AJ's position at the table. "I need your help."

AJ and Detective Taylor listened while Nash gave them a sit rep on Tommy Delvecchio, the Gracielas and the price on his head.

"Puente will have the DEA there. But he's more in-terested in rounding up Graciela's men and getting me out of there." Nash looked big brother straight in the eye, sending a message between men, not cops. "You and I have the same goal."

AJ nodded. "To save Teresa."

"I have a plan. Will you help?"

"Josh, you working tonight?"

The blond cop grinned. "I'm always on the job when you are, buddy. I've got time for a little backup."

Nash nodded his appreciation. Neither man had to like him or trust him, but he was counting on them to care about Teresa. "I promised her she'd be home safe to her family by Christmas. That's one promise I intend to keep. I'll do whatever it takes to make that happen."

Josh excused himself from the room and got on the phone to call for some of the support they'd need. Talk-ing cop to cop now, Nash pulled his black book from his pocket and tossed it onto the table.

AJ picked it up and thumbed through the pages of notes while Nash explained. "I want you to give that to my boss, Jesse Puente. His number's in the front. It spells out who the mole is in our office. If I can't take Tommy Delvecchio out when I go to that warehouse, I need you to give that to him."

"All right." AJ stuffed the book into the back pocket of his jeans. "Let's do it."

Nash pulled out his phone and punched in the num-ber that had been repeated so often on Angel Sanchez's phone. The same number had been found in Santiago Vargas's phone, as well. He placed it on speaker mode and set the phone on the table.

As expected, Tommy Delvecchio picked up. "Nash. Problem with the cops? For a while there, I didn't think they were going to let you make your phone call to me. Your little girlfriend has been a bit of a handful."

That sounded like his girl. *Give 'em trouble, darlin'.* "Put her on. I need to know she's okay."

"Of course." There was a scuffle of movement, and then a soft, familiar voice.

"Charlie?"

"I'm coming to get you, Peewee."

Instead of crying or begging for help or even saying *I love you* again, she shouted into the phone as it was being taken away. "I counted eight men, including your friend. Two outside and—"

Bless her brave heart.

Nash couldn't be prouder. Or more afraid. He was going to kill Tommy if one hair on her beautiful head had been hurt.

Tommy was back on the phone. "Señor Graciela is anxious to see you. While he's pleased you took care of Señor Vargas for him, you're still a blot on the family pride." He gave Nash the address of a warehouse and AJ nodded, indicating he knew its location. "Shall I assume you're on your way?"

"Yeah. I'm ready to make the trade."

Nash disconnected the call and put away the phone.

But AJ stopped him before he could reach the door. "Are you in love with my sister?"

"Yes."

He thought AJ would need some time to process that admission. Nash was damn sure he wasn't the man AJ would choose for his baby sister. He even thought, as the overprotective big brother, he might want to take a swing at Nash. AJ would make a hell of a poker player because right now he wasn't giving away a thing.

The detective simply nodded at Nash and opened the door. "Let's go get her."

"WELCOME, NASH." TOMMY DELVECCHIO was grinning like the Cheshire cat as he locked a pair of handcuffs around Nash's wrists. Nash clenched his fists together in front of him, testing the strength of the steel restraints while Julian Sanchez patted him down and took both his Smith & Wesson and the gun strapped to his ankle and set them on the rusted tire rack beside the door.

Nash could see his breath in the cold air of the run-down warehouse near the Missouri River that looked a lot like that chop shop where he'd been wounded. Tommy must have scouted out both locations when he'd set up that ambush and faked his death. Tommy might have been a lying scumbag cheat, but in a lot of ways, he was predictable.

Maybe Nash could use that predictability to his advantage. "Nice digs, Tommy. So this is what your dealings with the Gracielas have bought you?"

"Actually, it's bought me a nice place down on Isla Tenebrosa. No extradition to the U.S. from there. And now that I'm officially dead, I'm going to start a new life and enjoy the payoff." Tommy shrugged. "This is just a business meeting, fulfilling the last of my obligation to Señor Graciela."

"No wires, but he's wearing a vest," Julian reported. "Do you want me to take it off him?"

Tommy picked up the two guns, sliding one into each coat pocket. "No. Let him enjoy the illusion of having a chance at surviving. A bullet to the head will kill him as surely as one to the heart."

"Where is she?" Nash wanted eyes on Teresa, to see for himself that she hadn't been harmed and to try to somehow communicate his crazy idea for a plan where they could both get out of here alive.

"Now, now. You've forced me to be very patient. You can do the same. There's a certain procedure that needs to be followed." Tommy nodded to Julian to shove Nash into step ahead of him before following them into the warehouse's main storage area.

It was a cavernous room with a second-story loft running along the east and west walls. He saw two more armed guards up there, one on each side, watching out the windows. There wasn't much cover in the abandoned space, just a few stacks of pallets and empty crates and one rust bucket of a forklift off to one side.

But the old desk in the middle of the concrete floor was the most important spot in the room.

"Nash?" Teresa stood up from the chair beside the desk.

"Sit down." Berto Graciela sat in the chair behind the desk. As soon as he pointed to the man Nash assumed was his bodyguard du jour, the hired gun pushed Teresa back in her seat.

She instantly shrugged her shoulder away from the goon's big hand. Her wrists were tied in front of her, the hood of her turquoise coat billowed around her shoulders, and several strands of hair had worked loose from her ponytail and fell around her face. Nash met her gaze with the shadow of a grin. Good. He wasn't surprised to see she'd put up a bit of a fight, but he was glad it hadn't been enough to get herself hurt.

"We need to stop meeting like this, Peewee." Nash

raised his fists in front of him and jerked at the handcuffs. Her dark eyes widened, sensing he was trying to communicate a message. *That's it, darlin'. Figure it out. Play along with me. I'll keep you safe.*

"Here, Nash." Tommy walked past him to the desk, setting the two guns and the keys to the handcuffs on the corner of the desk. Teresa's gaze drifted over to the bounty Tommy had taken from him.

But Nash's gaze had settled on a more imminent threat. Tommy drew back his coat and pulled a knife from his belt. "Tommy!"

Nash lurched forward. Julian Sanchez caught him by his bum arm and jerked him back into place. The pain that blossomed in his shoulder was nothing compared to the fear of seeing Tommy open that knife and lean over Teresa. But Tommy lifted Teresa's hands from the desktop and sliced through the rope that bound her. He straightened and tossed the bindings at Nash's feet. "A gesture of trust."

"You think I'm ever going to trust you again?"

Tommy took Teresa by the arm and pulled her up beside him. "This is the deal we made. Her life for yours."

"Nash, no," Teresa wailed. She dropped her face into her hands. Was she coughing? Or crying?

Wait. Teresa Rodriguez crying? What was going on here? The woman Nash knew was more likely to elbow Tommy in the gut than break down in tears.

But whatever game she was playing, Nash was the only one who seemed to realize her behavior was off. Was this some kind of reply to his silent message about her brother and a boatload of reinforcements from KCPD and the DEA taking out the two guards outside and lying in wait for his signal to storm the building and rescue her?

"This is all very touching." Tommy jerked Teresa's

hands away from her face and pulled her to one side. "I'm glad you made a friend here in Kansas City. But Señor Graciela would like to say a few words to you before we complete the transaction."

Berto Graciela rose from his chair behind the desk. The scalp beneath his thinning gray hair was pink from the cold. But there was nothing vulnerable about his dark eyes and grim expression. He straightened the scarf at his neck and strolled around the table to face Nash. "You made me lose face in my own organization. You and your men were undermining me at every turn."

Nash glared down at the shorter man. "Just doing our job."

Graciela nodded at Julian Sanchez, and the enforcer delivered a kick to the back of Nash's legs, driving him down to his knees. He grunted as the concrete jarred through his body. Teresa's soft gasp of concern was real this time. Nash lifted his gaze to hers and warned her to stay put. It wasn't as if he hadn't survived worse punishment.

Now that Berto held the superior position, he held out his hand toward his bodyguard. The man pulled a gun from his belt and placed it in his boss's hand. Berto slipped a bullet into the firing chamber and pointed the gun at Nash's head. "I had to put a stop to it."

Nash refused to flinch. AJ was waiting for his signal, but he needed to know the truth first. For Torres and Richter. For Teresa. For her sister Emilia and all the lives Tommy's treachery had endangered. "So you recruited Tommy Delvecchio. He told you who our agents were so you could kill them. Then he staged his own death so the DEA would never know he was the traitor."

Berto nodded. "I lost millions of dollars because of you. The people who worked for me lost faith in my leadership. I want to end your miserable life right now, but your death will serve me better if I take you home and kill you in front of my men. Then everyone will know that I am the rightful chief of the Graciela organization."

Nash looked away from the barrel of Berto's gun and glared at Tommy. "We were your family."

Tommy shrugged. "Yes, well, Señor Graciela paid me an obscene amount of money to become a part of his."

"Captain Puente had no idea you were a traitor."

"No one did." Tommy seemed to enjoy confessing his sins almost as much as Nash needed to hear them. "But I couldn't finish the job I was hired to do, because you wouldn't die."

Nash spared a loving glance for Teresa before lifting his gaze to Berto Graciela. "All right. Let's do this. I know you're a man of your word, even if Agent Delvecchio isn't. You put a hit out on me, not her. Let her go and I'll come with you without a fight."

Berto nodded to his bodyguard, and the man went to get Teresa. But Tommy, the weaselly scumbag, wouldn't let go. "She's just the bait. You can't really let her go. She's seen our faces and knows our names. Her brother's a cop."

The older man turned, clearly disgusted with having his word challenged. "If she is a problem for you, Mr. Delvecchio, you take care of it. She is of no concern to me."

"Fine. We'll let her go." He checked his watch. "Your plane is ready at the airport. We need to get going anyway."

Interesting. So Tommy was willing to be responsible for several good men's deaths as long as he didn't have to pull the trigger himself. Nash could work that kind of cowardice into his plan.

Tommy shoved Teresa into the bodyguard's chest, and the man started dragging her toward the front exit. But Teresa had never been one to simply go quietly along. "Wait. I want to say goodbye to him first."

The bodyguard looked to Berto. Berto nodded. He lowered his gun as the bodyguard released Teresa and she ran to him. "Somehow it makes me feel better to know that someone will mourn your passing, Señor Nash. Just remember, you are the cause of her suffering."

Nash swore he heard Teresa mutter, "Oh, shut up." She helped him to his feet and tucked herself inside the loop of his bound arms. Her hands reached up to cup either side of his jaw and angle his face down to hers. "I love you, Charlie Nash. If you get out of this alive, you come back to me. You owe me."

He looked down at her with all the love he possessed. "I know, darlin'. I'm good for it. I promise. You are the bravest woman I know."

He met her halfway when she pulled his face down to hers to share one last beautiful kiss. She thrust her tongue into his mouth. And something more. That sneaky little witch. It wasn't necessary, but she'd just made his job a lot easier.

Nash's teeth clamped down on the hard metal of the key she'd swiped from the corner of the desk.

He pushed the key into the pocket of his cheek and pulled away. "I love you, Teresa."

Then the bodyguard was pulling her away. Tommy followed them toward the door. Berto nodded to Julian to stand back. As soon as Sanchez released him, Berto lowered the gun and pulled the trigger.

"Nash!" Teresa cried, breaking away from her captor.

The bullet ripped straight through Nash's thigh, collapsing him to the floor. "Now I feel better, and he will be less trouble to us." He handed the gun off to Julian Sanchez. "Bring him."

But that first gunshot was the signal AJ had been waiting for.

A battering ram broke open the front door. "KCPD!" A window shattered overhead. "Drop your weapons! On the ground! Now!"

"Nash!" The moment Teresa reached him, Nash threw his arms around her, dragging her beneath him, shielding her with his vest and body as a dozen of her brother's closest friends stormed the building.

Julian Sanchez and the bodyguard returned fire and were instantly put down. Berto raised his hands over his head and dropped to his knees. Tommy dove behind the desk as several more shots were fired.

"Clear!" The two guards up top had been subdued.

Uniformed officers and detectives swarmed in. Captain Puente and Cruz Moreno went straight to Berto Graciela and put him in handcuffs. While Cruz read Graciela his rights and escorted him out the door, the captain hurried over to Nash and helped him sit up. "You're a hard man to find." He winked at the petite woman clutched to Nash's side. "Good to see you again, Ms. Rodriguez. I trust we can be straightforward with each other now?"

She was scrambling to free herself, but Nash wouldn't allow it. "Yes, sir. Sorry I couldn't tell you everything."

"You were protecting your partner. Protecting the mission."

Nash turned and pressed a kiss to Teresa's temple, thanking her, beaming with pride at Captain Puente's praise.

The captain glanced down at the blood staining Nash's jeans. "How many pieces is this guy in?"

Teresa shook her head. "Too many."

Josh Taylor, the big cop Nash had met only that morning, stood up from behind the desk. "I think this is one of yours, Nash."

Teresa and Captain Puente helped Nash to his feet at the sound of Tommy's wailing. With their help, he limped over to Detective Taylor to find Tommy handcuffed and rolling on the floor, holding his side, bleeding. His frightened expression made him look a lot like the kid Nash had felt so much grief and guilt over only twenty-four hours earlier. "I'm shot," Tommy whined. "I'm shot."

Josh shrugged his big shoulders. "As far as I can tell, it's just a graze across his rib cage."

Holding Teresa beneath his arm, her strength supporting his, Nash shook his head. He had no pity for the traitor he'd finally exposed. He simply looked down on the man who'd sold out Nash and his team and grinned. "I knew you weren't ready to be a field agent. You're not even smart enough to wear your vest."

Puente wasn't in a joking mood as he hauled Tommy to his feet. "You and I are going to do some major debriefing, Mr. Delvecchio. I don't envy your situation. There's not a cop in Texas who's going to be on your side. And I doubt the cartel is going to be thrilled that you didn't finish the job they paid you to do."

"Captain." Tommy was pleading with him as he and Detective Taylor carted him away. "You've got to give me some kind of protection. I can give you intel on the Gracielas. I've got names on at least…"

Just when Nash thought it might all finally be over, AJ Rodriguez sauntered up on noiseless footsteps, holstering one of his guns beneath his left arm. When he reached for Teresa, Nash didn't try to hold on to her.

"Good work, little one." AJ wrapped her up in a tight hug and kissed her cheek. Big brother was almost smiling when he pulled away. "Look at my baby sister bringin' down a drug lord. You said eight men. We've got them all accounted for, all in custody. Ambulances are on the way."

Nash leaned his hip on the edge of the desk, taking the pressure off his throbbing leg. "You boys know how to put on a good show here in K.C. I appreciate the backup."

"I did it for my sister, cowboy. Not you. But I'm grateful you made sure she didn't get hurt." With a grudging respect and a whole lot of gratitude that was completely mutual, AJ reached out to shake Nash's hand. Then he lowered his gaze to the blood oozing down the side of Nash's jeans. "Is your boyfriend okay?"

"My boy—?" Teresa beamed a big smile. She threw her arms around her brother. "Thank you, AJ. I love you."

"I hope you know what you're in for, Nash," AJ warned, smiling at Teresa as Josh Taylor called him away.

Looked as though he might pass muster with Teresa's family after all.

He reached for Teresa as soon as they were alone. But she knelt down in front of him instead, ripping open the bullet hole in his pant leg to inspect his wound. "Looks like a through-and-through. It's not bleeding enough to indicate the bullet nicked an artery. But you still need—"

"To go to the hospital. I know." Enough. Enough distance, enough interruptions, enough waiting to know for certain that she was finally safe. Nash pulled her to her feet and hauled her right up to his chest, claiming that beautiful mouth in a kiss.

Endless moments later, she pulled away, smiling. "Seriously, Nash? You need to stop getting shot. You should just ask me out on a date."

Epilogue

December 25

DEA agent Charles Nash stepped off the third-floor elevator at Kansas City's Truman Medical Center and strode down the hallway. Well, he moved with as much purpose as a man with healing bullet wounds to his shoulder and both legs could.

He'd been back in Houston for a few days, writing up reports, attending his friends' funerals, making some big decisions. He'd even done a little Christmas shopping.

He was a Texas boy, born and raised, but his heart was here in Missouri. So he'd booked an early-morning flight to KCI. Now he was here with a bag of gifts in his hand and a transfer request to the Kansas City office of the DEA in his pocket.

He didn't have to be a cop to figure out where the party was. He followed the sounds of Christmas music and laughter to the common room of the children's ward. He unbuttoned his heavy coat, pulled off his new black Stetson and inhaled a steadying breath before stepping into the brightly lit room.

He saw Teresa first, dressed in light green hospital scrubs with a red-and-green holiday scrub jacket. She sat at a table near the Christmas tree with Laila Alvarez and two other young patients, playing some kind of board game that involved lots of laughter.

When Teresa saw him in the doorway and stood, the din in the room suddenly quieted. That awkward moment of being the uninvited guest showing up at the party sent a shiver of nerves down Nash's spine.

But the moment passed the instant Teresa smiled at him.

Suddenly, he wasn't the outsider who'd brought danger and death to their city. He was a friend. He was welcome.

Emilia Rodriguez-Grant toddled over to give him a hug. "Merry Christmas, Nash. There's plenty of food and punch. Make yourself at home."

He met her husband, Justin Grant, and their son, Joey. He met other sisters and husbands and nieces and nephews. Josh Taylor and his wife and two daughters welcomed him. And then AJ Rodriguez walked up to him with his wife and sons.

AJ shook his hand. "Merry Christmas, Nash."

"Merry Christmas, AJ."

And while he appreciated the offers to take his coat and bring him cookies, Nash was here for just one reason. Well, two.

He'd never played Santa Claus before, but he had a bag of gifts he was eager to deliver. He crossed the room to the game table and knelt down beside Laila Alvarez's wheelchair. He pulled the big box from the top of his bag and set it on her lap. "I told you I owed you one for hiding me in your room that day. I'm a man who repays his debts and keeps his promises." Her soft brown eyes were wide with anticipation. "Open it."

The little girl made quick work of the bow and tissue paper inside. "Mom! Dad! It's a cowboy hat." Nash took the smaller version of the hat he'd worn and placed it over the girl's knit cap. She pushed herself up out of her wheelchair and fell against Nash, wrapping her frail arms around his neck. "Thank you, Mr. Nash."

"You're welcome, darlin'." He carefully set her back in her chair and stood, turning to Teresa. He tried not to let the sheen of tears shining in her eyes get to him. "I brought some other gifts. To replace the ones that got damaged in your apartment. I didn't know what you had. There's some stuff for boys and girls both in here."

When the children in the room hurried to the tree to open the new gifts, Teresa finally moved around the table. She slid her arms beneath his coat and wound them around his waist, leaning against his chest. "You didn't have to do that."

"Yeah, I did." Nash pressed a kiss to the crown of her hair and hugged her right back. "Merry Christmas."

"Merry Christmas, Charlie."

He had one more gift from the jewelry store tucked away in his pocket for Teresa. But he'd wait until later, when they were alone, before he'd ask if she'd accept it.

Right now there were too many children and family members and friends around, all enjoying the celebration.

"These are the best presents ever." Proudly wearing her new hat, Laila spun her chair around. "Did you get what you wanted for Christmas, Teresa?"

Teresa leaned back against Nash's arms, tilted her face up to his and smiled. "I did."

* * * * *

"Trust me, I've had a lot of practice resisting you."

Rayanne blinked and stared up at him. "Excuse me?"

Blue was surprised that she was surprised.

"You think all that time we worked on those cases together that my mind was solely on the job? I've been attracted to you since day one."

For just a heartbeat, she looked a little pleased about that. Then she shook her head. "You don't remember all that, remember?"

"Oh, I remember some things."

Things that caused him to stray into the stupid realm again, because he brushed a kiss on her cheek. Thank goodness it was only her cheek, because he could have sworn he saw little lightning bolts zing through her eyes.

She let go of him so fast that he had no choice but to sit back on the bed or he would have fallen. "Blue, this can't happen again."

He nodded. "I know."

And he did.

Didn't he?

RUSTLING UP TROUBLE

BY
DELORES FOSSEN

Published in Great Britain 2014
by Mills & Boon, an imprint of Harlequin (UK) Limited,
Eton House, 18-24 Paradise Road, Richmond, Surrey, TW9 1SR

© 2014 Delores Fossen

ISBN: 978-0-263-91376-7

46-1114

Harlequin (UK) Limited's policy is to use papers that are natural, renewable and recyclable products and made from wood grown in sustainable forests. The logging and manufacturing processes conform to the legal environmental regulations of the country of origin.

Printed and bound in Spain
by CPI, Barcelona

USA TODAY bestselling author **Delores Fossen** has sold over fifty novels with millions of copies of her books in print worldwide. She's received the Booksellers' Best Award and the RT Reviewers' Choice Award, and was a finalist for a prestigious RITA® Award. In addition, she's had nearly a hundred short stories and articles published in national magazines. You can contact the author through her webpage at www.dfossen.net.

Chapter One

Deputy Rayanne McKinnon's breath stalled in her throat, and she did a double take. No, her eyes hadn't deceived her.

She was looking at a dead man.

At least, he was supposed to be dead.

But dead men didn't move, and this one was definitely doing that.

He was crouched behind a big pile of rocks. And he had his attention trained on the back fence that coiled around the pasture of her family's ranch. It was that particular fence and a tripped security sensor that'd caused Rayanne to ride out and have a look. She'd figured a cow had gotten out.

She darn sure hadn't expected to find *him*.

Even though he was a good twenty yards away and had his face partially concealed with a low-slung white Stetson, Rayanne had no trouble recognizing him.

Blue McCurdy.

Just the sight of his ink-black hair, rangy body and chiseled face sent her stomach churning. An invisible meaty fist clamped around her heart, squeezing and choking until her chest was throbbing like a toothache.

The memories came. All bad.

Well, mostly bad, anyway.

Rayanne pushed aside the ones that were good, including the little tug of relief at seeing Blue alive.

She cursed both her reaction and the man himself. Blue was the last person on God's green earth she expected or wanted to see, and yet here he was on McKinnon land.

The question was, why?

This couldn't be about the baby.

Could it?

Rayanne opened her mouth to shout out that *why* as to the alive part and remind him that he was trespassing. But a sound stopped her cold. The soft rumble of some kind of engine, and it was moving along the fence line.

Blue reached beneath his leather vest and pulled a gun from the back waist of his jeans.

That got her heart thumping, and not in a "relieved you're alive" sort of way. Rayanne drew her Colt, too, and stepped behind a live oak. As a deputy sheriff, she'd had more than her share of experience in dealing with bad guys.

Blue McCurdy included.

If he was up to something shady, and it was pretty clear that he was, then Blue had brought trouble practically to her doorstep. That was another *why,* and Rayanne hoped she got answers soon.

The engine sounds stopped, and Blue adjusted his gun. Whoever was out there had put him on edge. He certainly wasn't jumping out from those rocks to greet anyone.

Mercy.

If this was trouble worse than Blue himself, then things were going to be *bad*.

She wanted to watch for a few more seconds to try to figure out what was going on here, but just in case things went from bad to worse, she'd have to fire off a text to someone who could respond from the ranch house. There wasn't good enough phone reception in this part of the property for a call, but a text would usually go through. She'd learned that during the three months she'd been back here at Sweetwater Ranch while awaiting her mother's murder trial.

That put the clamp on her heart again, and she cursed it, too.

Blasted feelings!

Why the heck did they have to keep messing with her head and every other part of her? It had to be the pregnancy hormones, because she'd never felt this moody and whiny before.

Rayanne thankfully didn't have time to dwell on that, because she saw the movement in the trees behind the fence. Blue must have seen it, too, because he ducked lower.

Waiting.

Not hiding.

It was a subtle enough difference for Rayanne to ready her Colt. She didn't want Blue dead before he could explain to her all those *whys* that kept racking up.

Including why he'd left her naked in bed nearly five months ago.

Rayanne cursed him again and cursed herself for allowing any man to get that close to her. It wouldn't happen again, and as soon as she found out what Blue wanted, she'd send him on his way.

Or maybe arrest him.

Another flicker of movement, and this time she got a glimpse of a man dressed in dark clothes. Tall, marine-like build. Definitely not a friendly sort.

That got her tugging her phone from the back pocket of her jeans, and she sent a quick text to her stepbrother, FBI agent Seth Calder, to request some backup. Hopefully, he was still at the ranch and hadn't left for work yet, so he could get there in a hurry.

"McCurdy?" someone shouted.

But Blue didn't answer.

The shouter yelled Blue's surname again, and this time Rayanne got more than a glimpse. She saw his face and picked through the features to see if she knew him.

She didn't.

But apparently Blue knew the guy well enough to hide from him.

"We know you're here," the man added. "And we're not leaving until someone dies."

That felt like a punch to her chest. Yes, she was a cop, but that didn't mean she enjoyed diving into gunfights, especially now that she had someone else to consider.

Her unborn baby.

Plus, she wasn't exactly keen on taking a huge risk like this to save a man whom she hated.

"Damn you, Blue," she mumbled, and debated if she should identify herself. It might get the gunman running.

Or not.

It was just as likely to get him to start shooting. Because it was clear this guy wasn't a cop out to arrest Blue. Cops didn't make threats like that.

Not good cops, anyway.

She glanced back at the paint gelding that she'd ridden in on. He was grazing on some pasture grass and would maybe stay put. Rayanne didn't want him in the middle of, well, whatever the heck this was.

Keeping her gun ready, she crouched down and hurried behind another tree. Then another. Moving closer to a dry spring bed that was deep enough to give her some cover. It was also closer to Blue. When she slipped behind a third tree, Blue snapped his head in her direction.

Their eyes met.

Rayanne's narrowed.

His eyes widened.

Blue didn't seem any happier to see her than she was to see him, and using just his left hand, he made a sharp palm-down gesture that Rayanne had no trouble interpreting.

Stay put.

Something he darn sure didn't do.

She could have sworn that her presence changed whatever plan Blue had had in mind, because he appeared to curse, and then he maneuvered toward the end of the line of boulders. Away from her. And closer to the big guy who'd warned him that someone was going to die.

At the rate he was going, that someone would be Blue.

She saw the man's hand snake out. Gun clutched and aimed. He fired right into those boulders where he'd no doubt heard Blue moving around. The bullet smacked into the stone, making a sharp zinging sound, and it was quickly followed by another shot.

Another gunman, too.

No. Not this. If all Hades was going to break loose, why not wait until she had backup?

The shooter's partner ducked out from cover just a few yards from Blue and pulled the trigger. That one clipped the boulder at just the right angle to send some rock chips flying right at Blue. Rayanne got just a glimpse of the blood from the nicks those rocks caused before more shots came.

Sweet heaven. She couldn't just stand by and let this happen. Rayanne scrambled into the dry spring bed, keeping as low as she could, but she lifted her head just enough so she could take aim at the marine-sized guy.

She fired.

And missed, but it got his attention, all right.

Blue's, too.

He cursed at her. "Get down!" Blue yelled.

Rayanne had no choice but to do just that when the gunman sent a shot her way. *Too close.* Ditto for the one he aimed at Blue.

She fired back but didn't wait to see if she'd hit one of them. Then she scrambled down the spring bed, making her way to the boulders that Blue was using for cover.

"What part of *get down* didn't you understand?" Blue snarled.

No greeting, no explanation as to why he was on her family's ranch with gunmen after him.

Just that barked question.

Thankfully, his attention didn't go in the direction of her stomach, because it wasn't a good time to have to explain the small baby bump that she had hopefully hidden enough with her bulky jacket.

"I'm the one with a badge," Rayanne snarled back. "So if anyone should be staying down, it's you. Plus, you lost your right to give me any kind of advice when you disappeared without so much as a word."

Yeah, the timing for those words sucked, but Rayanne couldn't stop herself. Blue had crushed her, and it was hard to fight back all those emotions.

"You want to save your girl, McCurdy?" the man yelled. "Then both of you put down your guns and come with us so we can talk."

Rayanne clamped her hand over Blue's arm in case he intended to fall for that. Clearly these fools didn't have talking in mind. But Blue didn't move. He only glanced down at where she had hold of him. His long-sleeve black shirt was between her hand and his skin, but she could have sworn she felt every inch of him.

Every inch.

And she cursed her body's reaction again, along with jerking back her hand. Definitely not the time for those memories to rear their ugly, hot little heads.

"Time's up, McCurdy," the man added. "Come out now or you die."

The last word of that threat had barely left his mouth when the shots started again. This time it was Blue who did the clamping. He took her by the shoulder and pushed her to the ground. Her mouth landed right in the dirt and blades of grass that hadn't already been stomped down.

Rayanne didn't stay down, though. She wasn't sure why Blue was suddenly playing cowboy-in-shining-armor, but she wasn't having any part of it.

"Please tell me these bad guys are really bad," she said, levering herself up just enough to get off a shot. "Bad as in worse than you and that this isn't some botched attempt to arrest you."

His gaze cut to her, and those gunmetal-blue eyes narrowed. "No one's as bad as I am."

He paused as if waiting for her to agree or disagree. She didn't do either, but a comment like that definitely fell into the agreement category. Of course, she'd known Blue was a bad boy before she landed in bed with him, so it shouldn't have surprised her that he'd continued his bad-boy ways.

"If you're asking if they're the law," he added, "they aren't."

Rayanne almost pressed him for more about why they were after him, but it'd have to wait. The directions of the shots changed, and it wasn't a good change, either. The two gunmen appeared to be moving away from each other and closing in on Blue and her.

Blue glanced at her again. "You take the one on the right. I'll get the one on the left."

Just on principle, she hated taking orders from Blue, but it was a decent plan considering their position. Rayanne waited, listened, and when she thought she had a good pinpoint on the shooter, she leaned out and fired. Beside her, Blue did the same.

Rayanne heard the two sounds almost simultaneously. The thud of the bullet and a groan of pain. But it wasn't her shot that'd caused those sounds.

It was Blue's.

He'd hit his target, but judging from the way the bullets kept coming, she'd missed hers.

The man who'd done all the shouting started to curse, and she tried to follow the sound of his ripe profanity. It was hard to tell where he was as he darted through the woods toward his partner, who was either injured or dead. Rayanne was hoping it was the latter because she didn't want to battle a riled, injured would-be killer.

She leaned out from the rocks again, aiming her gun at the sound of the movement and the footsteps. But another shot came their way.

Mercy.

Not from one of the two gunmen but from another direction. To their far left.

Rayanne pivoted toward the newcomer and fired. This

time she didn't miss, but again she couldn't tell if the man was just injured or dead, because the shots from the other gunmen drowned out any telltale sounds.

But there was no mistaking one sound.

Even over the blasts and her own heartbeat crashing in her ears, she heard—and felt—one of those bullets. It didn't slam into her.

It hit Blue.

And it didn't just hit him. It tore off a chunk of rock that smacked against his left temple. She knew the exact second of impact from both the bullet and the rock. Blue groaned in pain.

And Rayanne could only watch as he collapsed against her.

She didn't look at him. Was too afraid of what she might see. Besides, she had to deal with the person who'd fired that shot.

The anger slammed into her, along with the fear she had for the baby. She tried to shut out all thoughts when she took aim. However, she didn't get a chance to fire. That was because the moron stopped shooting and started running.

Escaping.

Rayanne nearly bolted after him, but then she looked down at Blue. Unconscious. He was breathing, sucking in shallow breaths, and there wasn't a drop of color in Blue's face.

But there was color everywhere else. Lots of it.

From his blood spilling onto her.

Chapter Two

Blue heard the voices and opened his eyes.

Big mistake. The light stabbed through his head like razors, and a very unmanly sounding groan clawed its way through his parched throat.

That stopped the voices.

He heard movement. People shuffling around, and despite the pain, he reached for his gun.

Not there.

Even though it was hard to think, he figured this couldn't be good. Unarmed and in god-awful pain. He hoped he didn't have to fight his way out of there, because judging from the way he felt, he'd already had his butt kicked bad.

Blue had another go at opening his eyes. This time he took things slower and cracked just one eyelid so he could have a look. There was an elderly man with salt-and-pepper hair looming over him. No gun, either, but he was sporting a very concerned expression.

"I'm Dr. Wilbert Howland," the man said. "I did your surgery."

It took Blue a moment to process that. Surgery likely meant a hospital, so he glanced around.

Yep.

He was in bed, flat on his back, surrounded by sterile white walls and an antiseptic smell.

"Surgery?" Blue repeated. He tried to pick through the images and sounds that spun like an F5 tornado through his head.

"You were shot," the doctor provided. "And you have a concussion."

With the help of the ache in his left shoulder nudging him, Blue remembered getting shot and being smacked in the head with a piece of flying rock. Hard to forget the blistering pain from those two things. He also remembered the gunmen.

Three of them.

That gave him a jolt of concern. "Where are the guys who shot me?"

"Two are dead. The other one's missing."

Blue groaned again. "The missing one will come for me." At least Blue thought he would.

"You're safe here. And you're going to be fine," the doc assured him. "The bullet didn't hit anything vital, but you did lose a lot of blood because it took a while to get an ambulance out there to you."

No memory of an ambulance. Zero. No memory of how much time had passed, either. Definitely something he should be able to recall.

"Where are my clothes?" he asked, glancing down at the hospital gown.

"Bagged. I'll have someone bring them to you if the sheriff doesn't need them for processing."

Right. Because the clothes might be needed for an investigation. "I want the Stetson and the vest. They're my good-luck charms," he added.

The doc gave him a funny look. No doubt because he was in the hospital. But he was also alive.

That meant the good-luck charms had worked again.

The doctor leaned closer and waved a little penlight in front of Blue's eyes. More pain. Heck, breathing made it worse, too.

"If it hadn't been for Rayanne," the doctor said, "you might have bled out. She added pressure to your wound to slow down the blood flow."

"Rayanne," Blue managed to say, and he got a glimpse of her peering over the doctor's shoulder.

The relief was instant, and Blue released the breath he didn't even know he'd been holding.

Yeah, it was her, all right.

She had her ginger-brown hair pulled into her usual ponytail, though strands had slipped out and were dangling around her face and shoulders. When she stepped to the doctor's side, he saw the blood on the front of her buckskin-colored jacket.

"You're hurt." Blue tried to sit up, but the doctor stopped that.

Rayanne shook her head. "That's not my blood. It's yours."

More relief. It was bad enough that he'd been shot, but it would have been much worse if the bullet had gone into Rayanne instead.

But why did she look so, well, riled at him?

This wasn't the first time they'd gotten shot at together. As an ATF agent, he had worked on a few cases with her when the investigations had landed in her jurisdiction. So why was she eyeing him now as if she wanted to rip off his aching head?

And the questions just kept coming.

Why had he been shot, and where the heck was he? He knew the hospital part, but he'd been in several hospitals in San Antonio, his hometown, and this wasn't one of them.

"Why'd those men want you dead?" Rayanne asked. "Why aren't *you* dead?" she tacked onto that.

Clearly she had some questions of her own.

Blue opened his mouth to get busy answering them and realized he didn't have a clue. "Start from the beginning," he insisted. "I want to know what's going on. Why can't I remember how I got here?"

Rayanne huffed. More eye narrowing, and those gray eyes that at times could take on a warm, sensual glow certainly weren't warm or sensual at the moment. They were like little slabs of ice jabbing at him.

"A sensor alarm went off at the ranch," she finally said, "and when I rode out to check, I found you trying not to draw the attention of three gunmen who drove up on the back side of the fence."

On one level that gave him a serious shot of adrenaline, but on another it was just plain confusing.

Think, Blue.

Not easy to do, but he sorted through some of the fog and remembered going to the ranch that Rayanne's family owned.

Estranged family, he mentally corrected.

Rayanne had told him that she might have to go back to Sweetwater Springs because her mother was possibly going to be arrested for the decades-old murder of an alleged lover, Whitt Braddock.

And that was where Blue's memories came to a grinding halt.

"Why were the gunmen there?" he asked. "And why are you so mad?"

Her next huff was considerably louder. "Could you give us a minute?" Rayanne asked the doc.

Dr. Howland didn't seem exactly comfortable with that, but he eventually nodded. "Only for a minute or two. And go easy on him."

"You want to know why I'm mad?" Rayanne repeated once the doctor had stepped out. "Well, for starters you slept with me almost five months ago and then disappeared without so much as a Post-it note."

Oh, man.

He'd slept with her?

Blue remembered the attraction between them. Felt it blood-deep even now. But he'd always fought falling into bed with her because he had a strict rule about not having sex with coworkers.

Blue shook his head. "I don't remember."

And that was saying something. Rayanne wasn't exactly forgettable, and sex with her should have stuck in his mind like permanent glue.

"I have amnesia?" he asked. That was sadly the best-case scenario here. The worst would be some kind of permanent brain damage.

She lifted her shoulder. "You'd have to ask the doctor about that."

And he would, the second the man came back. For now, though, he needed as much info as possible. "What happened after I disappeared?"

Rayanne studied him, the way a cop would study a suspect she thought was lying through his teeth. "I got word that you were dead. I can't think of any good reason you'd let me believe that other than you really did want me out of your life."

Oh, mercy.

It felt as if twin heavyweights had slugged each side of his jaw at the same time. Blue couldn't speak. Heck, he couldn't even catch his breath. Yeah, he was pretty much the love-'em-and-leave-'em sort, but there was no way he'd do something like that to Rayanne.

Would he?

"I looked for you when you left," she continued, "but I got a message from your foster brother saying you were dead. That you'd been killed in Mexico."

There was a massive amount of fog in his head, but he could sort through enough to remember some things.

"I don't have a brother, either a real one or a foster," he insisted. "And I sure as hell didn't die in Mexico. I'm right here." Blue reached for her, but she stepped back as if he'd tried to tase her.

Before Blue could get out of bed and do something to convince her that he wasn't the bad guy here, the door flew open. Blue reached for his gun again. Cursed when it wasn't where it belonged.

However, Rayanne pulled her Colt from her shoulder holster.

False alarm. It was Dr. Howland, but he wasn't alone.

The sandy-haired, linebacker-sized guy who came through the door spared her and then her gun a glance as he flashed his badge and made a beeline for Blue. Thankfully, this man wasn't a blurry memory.

It was Blue's boss, Agent Caleb Wiggs, from the Bureau of Alcohol, Tobacco, Firearms and Explosives—ATF.

At least, Caleb had been his boss five months ago.

With everything else going on, Blue figured he could be wrong about that, too.

Rayanne seemed to know him, as well, and judging from her scowl, Caleb wasn't on her list of friends, either. She reholstered the Colt as if she'd declared war on it, but she watched him with those cop's eyes.

"You all right, Blue?" Caleb asked. He set a bag on the foot of the bed.

No way could Blue answer yes to that question. It might garner him a lightning bolt for such a big lie. "What's going on?"

Caleb didn't answer, but he looked at Rayanne and the doctor. "I need to talk to Agent McCurdy in private."

"Agent McCurdy?" Rayanne questioned. She huffed. "Don't you mean former agent?"

That got Blue's complete attention. Great day in the morning. Along with his mind and gun, had he managed to lose his badge, too?

"I mean *agent*." And Caleb didn't sound any friendlier than Rayanne. "Blue still works for me."

"Wait a minute," Blue said, trying to figure this out. It didn't help that his shoulder started clamoring for more pain meds. "What's the date?"

"October 6," the doctor provided. "And I hope everyone remembers that I just dug a bullet out of my patient here. He needs some peace and quiet so he can recover."

"And he'll get it," Caleb insisted. "I've already made arrangements to have him moved." He tipped his head to the bag. "Figured you could use a change of clothes for the drive to another hospital. One where I can make sure you have some security."

"He's not going anywhere, not until I get some answers first," Rayanne insisted right back.

That started a staring match between his boss and the deputy he'd apparently crossed lines with. Big ones.

All four of them volleyed glances at each other. "I'll give you a few more minutes," the doctor finally said. "After that my patient *will* get some rest."

Dr. Howland shot Caleb and Rayanne a warning glance that only an experienced doctor in charge could have managed, and he walked out.

Even with the doc's latest exit, Caleb didn't answer right away, and when he finally did open his mouth, he looked at Rayanne, not Blue.

"I can't wrap all of this up in a neat little package for you," Caleb started. "I honestly don't know why Blue disappeared."

"You said it was because he had ties to criminals," Rayanne reminded him.

Oh, man. And Blue just kept mentally repeating that.

"He did have criminal ties." Caleb's gaze finally came to Blue's. "If you've got an explanation about that, I'd like to hear it, because you didn't just disappear five months ago. You walked away from your job at the Justice Department, and the only reason you're still on payroll is because I've covered your butt and put you on a leave of absence."

Hell. This just kept getting worse. Not the leave-of-absence part but the reason Caleb had been forced to do something like that for him.

Criminal ties?

No way. He didn't need his memory to know that.

"The doc must have given me some meds that messed with my head." A head that Blue now shook. "Because the last thing I remember was finishing up a case with Rayanne. After that, it's just bits and pieces that don't make sense. Why did I leave? And why did I come to the McKinnon ranch today with gunmen after me?"

"That's what I'd like to know," Rayanne mumbled, but then she waved off any answer he might give. "My brother Seth got IDs on the two dead guys. The bodies are being examined now, and there's a CSI team searching the woods for evidence."

Seth, an FBI agent. Blue had never met him, but he'd heard Rayanne mention him.

"The dead men's names are Leland Chadwell and Brian Kipp," Rayanne continued, and she watched his face. Maybe to see if there was any sign of recognition.

There wasn't.

Blue had to shake his head again. "Who are they?"

"They're hired thugs," Caleb provided, "and, among other criminal sorts, they often work for Rex Gandy."

Now, that was a name that rang bells the size of Texas.

Could this mess possibly get any crazier?

Gandy wasn't just a thug—he was a rich one and had all kinds of nasty ties to gunrunners, money launderers and drug traffickers. As an ATF agent, Blue had dealt with Gandy on several occasions but always when he'd been undercover, and Blue had never been able to find evidence to arrest the piece of dirt.

"Gandy hired these men to come after me," Blue said like gospel. "Why?"

Caleb gave him an odd look, as if the question had come out of left field. "You don't know?"

Since it seemed the answer was clear to both Caleb and Rayanne, Blue went with the obvious answer. "Because Gandy's riled that I keep investigating him." But he investigated a lot of people, and that didn't spur an attack to kill. "Why come after me now?"

Again, he got that look. Obviously, he was missing something here.

"I've arranged to have Gandy brought in for an interview," Caleb added.

That was a good start, but Blue wanted a whole lot more. "You plan to answer my question about why Gandy would want me dead now?"

Caleb shrugged. "I figure it's connected to whatever the heck you've been doing for the past five months, and I don't have any details about that." He mumbled something that Blue didn't catch and scrubbed his hand over the back of his neck. "I need to talk to Dr. Howland and see how long this memory problem of yours is going to last."

Caleb added some really bad profanity and made a swift exit. Only then did Blue see the cop outside his door. Local, no uniform, but he had a badge clipped to his belt and was wearing a sidearm.

That didn't do much to ease the already twisted knot in Blue's gut.

Of course, a cop-bodyguard was only partially responsible for that. The main reason for the knot was the woman standing beside his bed and glaring at him.

"All of this is true?" he came out and asked.

She nodded. Her jaw muscles stirred. And she studied him. "Is this memory thing an act?"

"No." He couldn't say it fast enough. "I have no reason to fake memory loss."

He hoped.

Though he knew it would hurt, Blue lifted his head off the pillow and levered himself up. It wasn't pretty, and he did a lot of wobbling to get to a sitting position.

"What the heck do you think you're doing?" Rayanne snarled, and she reached out to take him by the arms.

Probably to force him back down. But being flat on his back wasn't much of a bargaining position, and if he hoped to get answers from her and not smart-mouthed comebacks, he needed to try to soothe some things with Rayanne.

If that was possible.

She continued to protest, even called him a bad name, but Blue got his feet off the bed. He also reached for the metal pole that held his IV so he could use it for support.

That, however, ended a lot faster than he'd planned.

Everything started to spin, and the dark spots winking in and out prevented him from seeing much. Or keeping his balance. He would have pitched forward if Rayanne hadn't caught him.

"Don't make this worse than it already is," Rayanne snapped.

She put her hand on his back to steady him. Bare skin on bare skin.

The hospital gown hardly qualified as a garment with one side completely off his bandaged shoulder. Judging from the drafts he felt on various parts of his body, Rayanne probably got an eyeful.

Of course, it apparently wasn't something she hadn't already seen, since according to her they'd slept together five months ago.

"Will saying I'm sorry help?" he mumbled, and because he had no choice, he ditched the bargaining-position idea and lay back down.

"Nothing will help. As soon as you're back on your feet, I want you out of Sweetwater Springs and miles and miles away from McKinnon land. Got that?"

Oh, yeah. It was crystal clear.

It didn't matter that he didn't know why he'd done the things he had, but he'd screwed up. Maybe soon Blue would remember everything that he might be trying to forget.

Her phone rang, the sound shooting through the room. And his head. Rayanne fished the phone from her pocket, looked at the screen and then moved to the other side of the room to take the call. It occurred to him then that she might be involved with someone.

Five months was a long time.

And this someone might be calling to make sure she was okay.

Blue felt the twinge of jealousy that throbbed right along with the pain in various parts of his body, and he wished he could just wake up from this crazy nightmare that he was having.

"No, he doesn't remember," she said to whoever had called. She turned to look back at him, but her coat shifted to the side.

Just enough for Blue to see the stomach bulge beneath her clothes.

Oh, man.

It felt as if someone had sucked the air right out of his lungs. He didn't need his memory to understand what that meant.

Rayanne was pregnant.

Chapter Three

Rayanne heard the low groan that Blue made, and she whirled around, expecting to see some evidence that the pain had gotten significantly worse.

It wasn't pain, though, that made him groan.

His mouth was partly open, his attention fastened to her stomach, and she knew the reason for his reaction. He'd clearly noticed that she was pregnant.

Now it was her turn to groan. She hadn't intended for him to see the bump and had thought it was hidden well enough. Apparently not. It was getting harder and harder to hide it these days.

"Hold on a sec," she said to her brother Seth, who was waiting on the other end of the line with what no doubt was important info.

Probably not as important as this, though.

"Is that my baby?" Blue came right out and asked.

He'd put one and one together pretty darn fast for a man with supposed memory issues and a concussion.

Rayanne considered lying, only because she didn't want to deal with the truth right now, but if there was any trace of the real Blue left in his banged-up head, he wouldn't let go of this.

Plus, she was fed up with this whole lying mess from

Blue. It'd be like the pot calling the kettle black if she started telling whoppers, too.

"Yes, the baby's yours," she said, holding her hand over the phone so Seth couldn't hear.

Her brother already knew, of course, but she hadn't shared the news with a lot of people, only her doctor, mother and siblings. Not the estranged ones, either: Cooper, Colt and Tucker. Nor her *father,* Roy. Though she was certain that they, too, had noticed her growing belly.

Blue didn't exactly take the news well. He sucked in a quick breath, nearly choking on it. Rayanne wanted to blast him for his reaction, but the truth was, she'd been stunned, as well, when she'd seen that little plus sign on the home pregnancy test. She'd done her own share of quick breaths and head shakes.

"For the record, this is my baby, and you just happened to be the one who fathered it." She might have added more of a warning, something along the lines that Blue had zero claim to this child or any other part of her life, but she heard Seth calling out to her from over the phone.

"Can this wait a second?" Rayanne snarled to her brother.

"No," Seth snarled right back. "I'm sending you a photo of something you need to see. And this isn't a suggestion—it's an order. Stay away from McCurdy. His boss is on the way there."

With that, he hung up before she could tell him that Blue's boss had already arrived. The quick hang-up also left her to wonder what the heck else had gone wrong now.

"When are you due?" Blue asked.

Rayanne hated to give him any details whatsoever, but

it seemed a little petty to withhold something he would figure out, anyway. "In four months."

Exactly nine months to the day since Blue and she had lost their minds and landed in bed. A big mistake, obviously one he hadn't been able to handle, because he'd walked out on her—literally. She'd woken up to find him gone. No note on her pillow. No phone calls. No contact of any kind.

Until now, that is.

"Four months," he repeated, sounding like a man on the verge of losing it.

She ignored him for the time being when there was a little dinging sound from her phone to indicate she had a text. Rayanne looked at it.

And looked again.

Her shoulders tightened even more, and she stared at the liar in the bed.

"What kind of sick game are you playing, huh?" she demanded from Blue.

"No game," he assured her. "What's going on? What's got you so upset now?"

"*This* has got me upset." She shoved the phone right in his face, but judging from the way he squinted, his eyes were still too blurry to see the small print.

"Why, Blue?" she practically yelled.

It was loud enough to get the doctor and Caleb running back into the room, but Rayanne didn't budge even when Caleb tried to push her out of the way.

"He owes me an answer," Rayanne said through clenched teeth, and she showed the text to Caleb.

"Where'd you find that?" Caleb asked.

She kept her glare on Blue. "It was in his shirt pocket. The one that the medics cut off him when they put him in the ambulance. They gave it to Seth so he could process it for possible evidence."

"What is it?" Blue demanded.

"It's a hit order," Caleb finally said. Rayanne was glad he'd answered the question, because she might have choked on the words.

Blue shook his head. "Who was supposed to die?"

Rayanne's glare got worse. "Me."

She let that hang in the air for several long moments. "And the reason you were at the ranch today was because someone hired *you* to kill me."

"Not a chance. I wouldn't have agreed to do a hit on you," Blue insisted. His intense gaze swung to Caleb. "What do you know about this?"

Caleb lifted his hands, huffed. "Nothing. But then, you've been off the radar for five months, remember? I have no idea what you've been working on or who you've been working with."

And that said it all.

Maybe this was some kind of unauthorized undercover work, but it didn't matter. Whatever Blue had gotten involved in, he'd brought the danger to her and the baby. Her family, too, since her sister, brothers and father were all living on the grounds of the ranch.

The doctor checked the clock on the wall. "Those couple of minutes have long been up. Mr. McCurdy just had a bullet dug out of him and lost too much blood. He needs rest."

"I don't want to rest." Blue sat up again. Tried to stand again, too, but this time it was Caleb who stopped him. "I want to find out what's going on."

"I'll do that." Caleb's voice didn't exactly soften, but he helped Blue back onto the bed.

Not lying down.

Blue would have no part of that. Instead he sat on the edge of the mattress. "You really think I'd try to kill you?" Blue asked her.

Rayanne could feel the veins start to pulse in her head. "I don't know what to think when it comes to you."

It was impossible to keep the emotion out of that little outburst. The anger. The worry. And yes, the embarrassment. She wasn't the sort of woman who dropped into bed with a man. Any man. But especially a work partner.

Yet she had.

Once and only once had she broken that rule and slept with Blue.

And look where that'd gotten her.

Nearly killed, pregnant and she had a coat smeared with her ex-lover's blood. An ex who couldn't remember diddly-squat, including the little fact that he could have fathered her child.

However, Blue apparently did remember how to be pissed off, because his nostrils flared. "I wouldn't have killed you," he repeated.

His voice was no longer weak. Those words had a bite to them. Maybe because she'd insulted him with the accusation.

Tough.

Because it could be more than an accusation. It could be the truth.

"Then why'd you have the hit order?" she pressed.

"Those minutes are over," Dr. Howland growled.

They all ignored him, but Blue shook his head, looked at the doctor. "How long before my brain gets straight?"

"Probably a lot longer if you don't get the rest you need." He huffed. "Look, I don't know if the memory loss is from the concussion, the bleeding or the emotional trauma of being in the middle of a gunfight. The only thing I know is that most people make a complete recovery. But they do that by resting and recuperating, not by getting in a shouting match with visitors who shouldn't even be here."

"It wouldn't be from emotional trauma," Caleb volunteered, once again ignoring the doctor. "Blue's been in the middle of plenty of gunfights." He, too, checked the time. "I'll make some calls and speed up the arrangements to get you out of here."

"Is moving him a good idea?" Rayanne asked, bringing their attention back to her. It probably sounded as if she was concerned about his health.

Okay, she was.

But not in a "welcome home, lover" kind of way. She didn't want a move to delay the return of those memories, because she had to know what the devil was going on.

Dr. Howland opened his mouth to speak, but Caleb beat him to the punch. "I'm moving him. Blue's a federal agent, and he needs to be debriefed."

That got her attention fast. "Debriefed about what?" Because that was one of those fancy fed words that usually meant an agent was involved in something classified or deep undercover.

Caleb shot her a glare that could have withered spring grass. "This isn't your concern, Rayanne."

"To heck it's not." She lifted her phone screen in case he'd forgotten what was on there. "Someone hired him to kill me."

"And we'll get to the bottom of this. Not you. *We*," Caleb repeated, tapping the shiny gold ATF badge on his belt. "I'll be back to move him," he added to no one in particular, and he left the room again.

"Your turn to leave," the doctor insisted, looking directly at her.

Rayanne started to do just that. After all, she could do her own investigating from the Sweetwater Springs sheriff's office. She wasn't a deputy there. Her job was one county over, where she was on a leave of absence. But since her brother Cooper was the sheriff and since the shooting had happened on the ranch, she figured Cooper would be more than willing to give her some space to work.

Because something beyond the obvious wasn't right here.

"I need to speak to Rayanne alone," Blue said.

She combed through every bit of his expression but couldn't tell if he was remembering something or if this was yet some other ploy. It didn't matter. If he had anything to tell her, she wanted to hear it. Because if he did indeed confess to being a hit man, she was going to arrest his butt. And she didn't care if this was a federal case or not.

Of course, if he confessed to something like that, jurisdiction was the least of her worries.

The doctor released a long, slow breath. "At least stay in bed when you talk," he demanded.

Dr. Howland added a warning glance to both of them and then went into the hall. Caleb was out there, his phone pressed to his ear. No doubt making those arrangements to move Blue to another hospital.

The moment the doctor shut the door, Blue got up again, and this time it was a slightly less wobbly attempt.

He took hold of the IV pole with his right hand and started walking.

"Don't," he mumbled as if he expected her to object.

She didn't. But Rayanne did drop back a step when those wobbly steps brought him her way. And not just her way but directly in front of her. She resisted the urge to back up some more and held her ground. No gaze dodging. No fidgeting. She put on her lawman's face and watched as he did the same.

For a second or two, anyway.

"I need to do something," he said.

That was all the warning she got before he reached out, slid his hand around the back of her neck and put his mouth on hers.

Rayanne gasped, but the sound got trapped between their lips, and Blue ignored it. He kept on kissing her. Kept on moving his mouth over hers as if he had a right to do that.

Just kept on stirring heat that should have been stone cold.

It wasn't.

And that riled her to the core.

Damn him for bringing all the heat and the memories flooding back. She'd buried Blue five months ago. Not just him, either, but that one hot night they'd shared. Rayanne intended for that to stay dead and buried.

She would have knocked him senseless, but apparently he already was. She didn't shove him away, not with all his injuries, but Rayanne slapped her palm on his stomach and then backed up.

"What the heck are you doing?" she snapped. And thank goodness it sounded gruff and not breathless.

Somewhat of a miracle since her breath was indeed a little thin.

"Still think I'd try to kill you?" Blue asked.

The cocky voice had returned in spades. Cocky demeanor, too. Blue was a pro at that in part because of his hot cowboy looks. Sadly, he was the best-looking man she'd ever met, and her stupid body wasn't going to let her forget that.

Rayanne managed to hang on to her glare. "You kissed me to convince me that you don't want me dead?"

He lifted his shoulder. The one that'd been shot. And he winced enough to wipe that cocky look off his face. "In part. I was hoping it'd make me remember."

"Did it?"

That prompted him to run those sizzling gray eyes over her face and then lower. To her breasts. Then lower still. She didn't know how he managed it, but a once-over like that from Blue felt like foreplay despite her pregnant belly.

"No," he finally said. "But trust me, I'm pretty sure every part of me but my brain remembers you."

Oh.

That felt like foreplay, too, and since that was the last thing she wanted, she did step back. She'd already had a big dose of Blue, and she wasn't sure she could survive another round with him.

Best to think about the other mess. The one that involved those gunmen, living and dead. "Why'd the shooting happen? Give me something to go on. *Anything* to go on," she added when he just stared at her.

Blue kept staring. "The last solid memory I have is the evening when we finished up that case over in Appaloosa Pass."

She knew exactly which evening he meant. Rayanne had gone over the detail dozens of times. "The investigation had gone wrong. An innocent bystander was killed."

He studied her. "We were upset."

Oh, yeah. Rayanne had never broken down before. Not in front of anyone, anyway. But she had that night, and she'd ended up in Blue's arms.

And with him in her bed.

He cleared his throat as if he'd filled in the blanks of his memory with some spicy details. "Afterward, did I say anything?" Blue asked. "Call anyone?"

"No, but someone called you. You said it was your good friend and fellow agent Woody Janson. You didn't put the call on speaker, but I heard him say he wanted you to meet him in a diner in San Antonio." Rayanne paused. "The guy sounded like he was in some kind of trouble."

His head snapped up. "So Woody might know what happened. I need to call him." Blue was already moving toward the landline on the metal table next to his bed, but Rayanne snagged his wrist to stop him.

"Woody's missing," she explained. "He has been since you left. I searched for him, but I stopped when your foster brother called to tell me you were dead. Or according to you, the man pretending to be your foster brother."

"He was definitely pretending. I'm an only child, and I had no siblings when I was placed in foster care. Did you run the number of the caller?"

She had to shake her head. Rayanne had no intention of telling him that she'd kind of fallen apart after hearing he was dead. Investigating the caller had been the last thing on her mind.

It wasn't now.

Once she had this other issue of the hit resolved, she'd

look into a fake foster brother making an equally fake death notification.

She made the mistake of looking at Blue. Her eyes meeting his. And that punch came, one that brought the memories flooding back again. For a few bad seconds, anyway. Thankfully, her phone rang, giving her mind something better to do than remember intimate things she should forget.

"Seth," she answered after seeing her stepbrother's name on the screen. "I need some good news."

"Sorry. Won't get it from me. How's Blue?" But it sounded more like something he should say rather than something he wanted to know. It was one of the reasons she loved Seth. He wasn't a natural-born hugger, but if he thought it'd help her, he'd do hugs.

And walk through fire for her.

"Blue's alive," he said, obviously able to hear Seth's question. Blue grumbled something else that she didn't catch, and he shuffled his way back to the bed, dragging the IV pole along with him.

The back of his gown was wide open, giving her a much-too-good view of his naked butt, which on a scale of one to ten was a forty-six. Rayanne did some grumbling of her own and looked away.

"What's the not-so-good news, then?" Rayanne asked Seth.

"Just got off the phone with Rex Gandy. And no, he didn't confess to hiring those gunmen who attacked Blue and you. In fact, he claims he hasn't seen them in months."

That seemed to be going around. "Please tell me you're still bringing him in for questioning."

"Yes and no. Gandy will be coming in, but I can't question him. The ATF has called dibs on this."

Rayanne tried not to groan too loud. She hadn't expected to be allowed to do the questioning, but she'd wanted Seth in on the interview. Or a second choice would have been her brother Cooper. They weren't exactly on the same side when it came to their mother's trial, but Cooper was a decent sheriff. And better yet, both Seth and he would have told her exactly what Gandy had or hadn't said.

But the ATF was a different matter.

"I'm guessing Caleb Wiggs will run the interview?" she asked.

"I'm sure he'd like that, but Gandy's already objecting."

"Why? They have some kind of history together?"

"Gandy won't say. He just told me I'd be a bloomin' fool to trust Caleb. And before you ask me, I'm already on it. I'll check out the connection between the two men and see if there's any reason for me not to trust a fellow Justice Department agent."

Good. Because she'd already been blindsided enough and didn't want to go another round with a man she couldn't trust. "If you can, go ahead and run another check on Blue's missing friend, Woody Janson."

Seth stayed quiet a moment. "You think he has something to do with this?"

"I don't know what to think," Rayanne admitted.

She heard Seth's heavy sigh. "Does Blue know about the baby?"

"He knows."

"And what the heck is he going to do about it?" Seth snapped.

"Absolutely nothing, because I'm not going to let him do anything."

Again, it seemed as if Blue had filled in the blanks about the conversation, because he glared at her in a stubborn way that only he and a mule could have managed.

"Hold a sec," Seth suddenly said, and the line went silent. Probably because he'd had to take another call.

Maybe one that would give them good news.

Any news, she amended.

She watched as Blue fumbled to get back in the bed. Another view of his backside. But it didn't hold her attention, because she saw the sweat pop out on his forehead, and he was clenching his teeth.

Clearly in pain.

Rayanne reached for the door to see if Doc Howland was still hanging around so he could give Blue another dose of meds. But reaching for the door was as far as she got.

"We have a problem," Seth blurted out when he came back on the line. "You have your gun?"

That didn't help steady her nerves, and they were already on edge just hearing the tone of Seth's voice.

"Yes. Why?" Rayanne asked her brother.

"Because I just got a call. A guy matching the description of the missing gunman was spotted on the traffic camera just a block from the hospital. He's not alone, and he's headed your way."

Chapter Four

Before Rayanne even said a word, Blue knew something else had gone wrong.

He didn't waste his energy on another groan or more profanity. He'd already been doing way too much of that, and he was already figuring this wasn't something a groan or cursing could fix.

"The guy who tried to kill you is less than a block away from the parking lot," she explained, helping him from the bed. "Backup's on the way, but it might not get here in time."

Yeah, he'd been right about that something gone wrong.

What he needed was a gun so he could try to protect Rayanne. And the baby. Of course, she wouldn't exactly appreciate any efforts from him to protect her, but she was going to get those efforts whether she wanted them or not.

Well, maybe.

His third attempt to stand wasn't any easier than his first two had been. Blue had to fight to push away the pain, but he finally got to his feet. In the same motion, he yanked the IV needle from his arm.

"What do you think you're doing?" Rayanne snarled.

"We're getting out of here. I figured that was pretty obvious."

Judging from the way her eyes widened, then narrowed, that wasn't so obvious after all, and it clearly wasn't the solution she'd had in mind. "We can hide in the bathroom."

"Bullets can go through the door, and I'd rather not be trapped in a small room with someone gunning for me."

Even if he couldn't remember who exactly wanted him dead or why. But he seriously doubted these thugs were coming here to fill in his memory gaps or have a conversation with him. Whatever he'd done to rile them, it was serious enough for them to send out a death squad. A squad that, according to the hit order, he was supposedly a part of.

He wasn't.

He hoped.

Even without the memories to prove it, Blue knew in his gut there was no way he would kill Rayanne. Agreeing to do it and making someone else believe it, however, was a different story. He could have done that for some reason that he hoped like the devil would become clear to him soon.

"My brother will be here in a few minutes," she reminded him. "And there's a deputy outside."

That was a start, but it wasn't nearly enough to fight off hired guns. "Stay away from the door," Blue warned Rayanne when she headed in that direction.

Blue rifled through the bag that Caleb had brought him, and he located some jeans, a shirt and boots. No badge or gun. But he did drag on the clothes so he could ditch the drafty gown. Every move he made was a painful effort.

"You got a backup weapon?" he asked, stepping in front of her.

A gesture that caused her to scowl and mumble something that didn't sound pleasant. "No. I only carry backup when I'm on the job."

Not good. But at least he had her weapon. Something he would have to convince her to hand over to him. Of course, that was only part of the convincing he'd have to do.

"You took a huge risk saving me earlier," he reminded her, dropping his gaze to her stomach, "and I won't let you take another one."

"It wasn't a risk."

But she stopped, knowing that there was no way she could convince him otherwise. Heck, she could no doubt still hear the sounds of the bullets flying around her. Yeah, it'd been a huge risk.

"I had no idea three gunmen would be out there when I rode out to the pasture," she added, "and I certainly didn't take the risk for you. I took it because I wasn't in a position to do anything else. If I'd tried to get out of there, one of them would have spotted me and tried to gun me down."

Fair enough. Too bad the fairness couldn't continue, because Blue snatched her gun, and before the protesting gasp could even leave her mouth, he eased open the door. The lanky dark-haired deputy was indeed still there, and he was on the phone.

"I'm Deputy Reed Caldwell," he said, his gaze snapping toward them. He shoved the phone back in his pocket. "There are three of them, and they're in the parking lot."

Man, they had gotten there even faster than he'd thought. Rayanne and he probably had only a minute or two at most because in a town the size of Sweetwater Springs, the exact location of his hospital room likely wasn't much of a secret.

"How much backup's on the way?" Blue asked the deputy at the exact moment that Rayanne asked a version of the same. They were both still lawmen to the core, and whether Rayanne liked it or not, they were also on the same side.

For this, anyway.

"The sheriff and another deputy," Reed answered. "Both are Rayanne's brothers, and they're about five minutes out."

Good news about her brothers coming so fast. Blood kin meant they'd no doubt fight hard to make sure Rayanne stayed safe. Not so good news about the five minutes, though. That was more than enough time for the armed goons to get inside and do plenty of damage.

Blue glanced around and spotted exits at both ends of the corridor, which was lined with doors to patients' rooms on each side. He considered having Reed duck inside one of the rooms with Rayanne.

Any one of them but his own.

However, if the gunmen managed to pick the right door or if they just started randomly shooting, Rayanne could be hit or worse. Innocent bystanders could be, too. Right now he was a bullet magnet, but he wasn't sure he trusted this deputy who he didn't even know to be the one to protect Rayanne.

"Which exit is closest to the parking lot where those gunmen are?" Blue asked.

Reed pointed to the one to his left. Blue got all three of them moving in the opposite direction, and he hoped he could get Rayanne out of the hall before trouble arrived.

"You sure you're well enough to be doing this?" the deputy asked.

"No, he's not," Rayanne answered for him.

She was right. He wasn't well enough. Not well enough to fight off gunmen, anyway, but the pain zapping through him wouldn't stop him from getting Rayanne to safety.

Blue heard some sounds. Shrieks and shouts of people panicking. Someone had no doubt spotted the gunmen, and those sounds were far too close for comfort. He dropped back so that he'd be between the gunmen and Rayanne. He also kicked up the pace a notch, racing toward the exit.

"I'm sorry," he mumbled to Rayanne. He didn't have any experience with pregnant women, but he figured it wasn't a good thing to make her run like this. Of course, the stress wasn't good, either.

"Don't do anything that will make me regret this any more than I already do," she snapped.

That was Blue's intention. To do no more harm. Then once he had her safely tucked away, he could figure out who these morons were and what they wanted.

He could also deal with the baby then.

Just thinking about it now clouded his head. The pain did, too. And a clouded head was a good way to get them killed. He needed to think straight and be able to react.

They got to the exit just as Blue heard another unwelcome sound. Footsteps.

Not the ordinary variety, either.

These were the footsteps of someone flat-out running, and they seemed to be headed straight toward them.

Blue took out the *seemed* when he spotted one of them. There was no seeming about it. They were coming for them.

The first was big, bulky, mean looking.

And armed to the hilt with a gun in his hand and two others in holsters.

He looked a lot like the other two guys who came running in behind him.

Blue practically pushed Rayanne to the exit when the deputy opened the door. They raced with her.

Not a second too soon.

A shot cracked through the air.

Blue bit back the profanity when the bullet tore through a chunk of the doorjamb. Getting shot at twice in one day sure wasn't how he'd wanted this to play out.

"Hurry," Blue told Rayanne.

He shut the door. No lock. And the exit led them to a large covered area where vehicles dropped off patients. It was way too open for comfort, and Blue hoped there weren't any gunmen lurking outside waiting for them.

"My truck's this way," Reed said.

Blue hoped "this way" was close, because the armed idiots wouldn't be far behind. They ran, a lot faster than Blue's body wanted to run, and while they were mid-stride, the deputy took out his keypad and used it to open a silver truck.

"Stay ahead of me," Blue warned Rayanne. She didn't argue, thank goodness, and she held her hand protectively over her belly.

The moment they made it to the truck, Blue threw open the door and pushed Rayanne inside. Reed and he quickly followed, but Reed had barely managed to get the engine started when the gunmen bolted from the exit.

The three pivoted around, looking for them, and it didn't take them long to spot the truck. The goon in the lead took aim.

Fired.

Just as Reed peeled out of the parking lot.

The deputy thankfully didn't waste any time getting them the heck out of there. Blue spun in the seat, ready to return fire. Well, as ready as he could be considering he was dizzy as all get-out.

But he didn't have a shot, anyway.

It was too big a risk that he might hit someone other than the snake who'd just tried to kill him—again.

Reed practically flew out of the parking lot, and Blue heard and saw the cruiser then. Rayanne's brothers, no doubt. Maybe they'd be able to catch these dirt wads so that Blue could question them. Or beat them senseless for this stunt they'd just pulled.

"I don't think they're following us," Reed said, his attention volleying between the road and the parking lot. He reholstered his gun and took out his phone. Probably to call his boss, the sheriff, to let him know what was going on.

"Please tell me this jogged your memory," Rayanne mumbled through clenched teeth.

Blue had to shake his head. Man, that hurt, too.

However, his vision wasn't so blurry now that he couldn't see how pale Rayanne was. And that her hands were trembling. He'd worked with her on several cases and had never seen her like this.

But then, he'd never seen her pregnant, either.

It still wasn't a good time to think about it. Not with

those gunmen so close. However, Blue just couldn't shove it aside.

"You must hate me," Blue said, keeping watch around them in case those goons surfaced.

Her gaze whipped toward him, her eyes narrowed more than just a bit. "You're right about that. I do."

He wanted to think she was exaggerating, but he doubted she was. After all, he'd just endangered her life twice in a very short period of time. Then there was that part about sleeping with her and then running out on her without so much as a *thank you, ma'am*.

"I'll get to the bottom of this," Blue assured her, but judging from another of Rayanne's huffs, it was no reassurance at all. Of course, she didn't have a lot of reasons to trust him.

So Blue went in a different direction. One that he hoped would be common ground for them. "I need a truce, only until this mess in my head settles down, and I can figure out what's going on."

She certainly didn't agree.

He looked at her stomach again. "And I need you to be checked out by the doctor. All that running couldn't have been good for you and the baby."

"The running wasn't a problem. The doctor said I could keep up my workouts." Her mouth tightened as if she'd told him more than she meant to.

Still, it didn't matter. He'd call the doc first chance he got and have Rayanne checked out, because that hadn't been just a workout session.

"I'm not the one who needs to see the doctor," she mumbled, and she threw down the visor so Blue could get a glimpse at himself in the vanity mirror.

He was pale, beads of sweat dotted his face, and he

didn't look like an ATF agent ready to take down some killers. He looked like a man who'd just had surgery.

"I'm okay," he lied.

He probably wasn't even 50 percent yet, but he didn't have the luxury of recovering when there were gunmen out there who wanted to make his injuries even worse than they already were.

"I filled Cooper in," Reed said when he finished his call. "He's the sheriff and Rayanne's brother," he added to Blue. "Cooper wants us to wait at the sheriff's office while he and the others go after those men."

It was a good plan. Well, a safe one, anyway, for Rayanne. Blue hoped her brother would be able to catch them, but if the men hadn't followed Reed, then they'd probably already hightailed it out of town so they could regroup.

And come after him again.

Reed pulled his truck into the parking lot of the sheriff's office, and even though Blue didn't see anyone suspicious lurking around the building, he got Rayanne inside as quickly as possible. However, with the exception of a woman working at the front desk, the place seemed deserted, and that put him on edge again.

"We need to lock up," Blue told the deputy.

But Reed was already doing that. He obviously knew that they were vulnerable to another attack. Rayanne knew it, too, because she snatched her gun from him. At first he thought she'd done that just because she was upset that he'd taken it from her, but Blue realized he was wobbling.

Ah, heck.

"You need to sit down," Rayanne snapped, and she slid her arm around his waist, leading him into one of the offices. Sheriff Cooper McKinnon's nameplate was on the wall next to the door.

Disgusted with himself, Blue shook his head. "I should be the one protecting and taking care of you."

That earned him a predictable eye roll from her. "I'm pregnant, not incompetent."

Rayanne practically dumped him into a chair, then shut the door. Locked it, too, before she went to the window to make a cop's sweeping glance of the parking lot. No doubt checking to make sure those gunmen weren't lurking around out there.

Blue intended to do the same, but first he needed a gun. Since they were in the sheriff's office, he figured it wouldn't be hard to find one of those, and he started his search in the desk drawers.

Thankfully, the drawers were within reach, which meant he didn't have to stand up just yet. He really needed a moment or two to catch his breath and try to settle the tornado going on in his head.

Blue finally located a Smith & Wesson. Some extra ammo, too, which he crammed into his jeans pocket before he joined her at the window. He'd barely had time to get in place when there was a sharp knock at the door.

"We got another problem," Reed announced.

Rayanne hurried to the door, threw it open, and yeah, Blue could tell from the deputy's expression that something else had gone wrong.

Reed shook his head. "I don't know what you and Blue started, but all hell's breaking loose at the ranch. We need to get out there *now* because someone's trying to kidnap your sister."

Chapter Five

Rayanne had braced herself for more bad news, but she'd expected Reed to say that the gunmen had been spotted near her family's ranch. She darn sure hadn't expected to hear that someone had gone after Rosalie.

Someone who obviously had a death wish.

Rayanne wouldn't just stand by while someone hurt her twin sister.

"Let's go," Blue insisted.

Good thing, too. Her feet and mind had frozen in place, and it was the touch of Blue's hand on her arm that got her moving.

Rayanne's stomach was already churning. Her shoulders were still burning from tensing them so much, but she ran toward the back exit of the sheriff's office. Well, she started running, anyway, but like before, Blue played cowboy-bodyguard and positioned himself in front of her.

"I would suggest you stay here…" Blue mumbled. He didn't finish that.

Didn't have to.

Because there was no way she would stay put with Rosalie in danger. Of course, the trick would be to save her sister while not putting herself right back in the path of bullets. It was still a fairly new mind-set for her, but she had to think of the baby.

"What happened?" Rayanne asked Reed the moment they were inside the truck and on their way.

"A feed-delivery truck arrived, and your dad noticed something funny about the men."

"Roy," she automatically corrected. It'd been a while since she'd called him Dad, not since she'd been a kid, but Rayanne hated that she had even brought it up at a time like this. "Funny?" she questioned.

"Yeah. They weren't the usual guys who make the delivery. Your... Roy asked them to show some ID, and that's when they pulled guns on him. They demanded that he take them to Rosalie, and they said she'd be fine, as long as Blue and you cooperated, that is."

"Cooperated with what?" Blue and she asked in unison.

Reed shook his head. "They didn't get a chance to say. A ranch hand saw what was going on, and he got his gun. They exchanged a couple of shots, and the men started running toward the back pasture. The ranch hand and some others went after them."

Oh, mercy.

Rayanne's imagination was much too vivid, and she could see the whole thing playing out in her head. If any of her lawmen brothers had been there at the ranch, it would have made her breathe a little easier, but they were all in town looking for the men who'd come after Blue and her.

Maybe that'd all been a diversion.

So these jerks could kidnap Rosalie.

Her sister was a nurse and didn't even know Blue, but if there was even a shred of truth in what the men had told Roy, then they would have taken Rosalie hostage to manipulate Blue and her in some way.

"Was anyone hurt?" Rayanne asked, holding her breath.

"No. But Roy said it was a close call."

Like the one that Blue, Reed and she had just had at the hospital. Rayanne was getting sick and tired of the danger.

"You'd better get your memory back soon," she mumbled to Blue. "And hurry," Rayanne added to Reed, though the deputy was already doing just that.

It seemed to take an eternity, but the McKinnon ranch finally came into view. Rayanne didn't see any signs of chaos in the pastures. The horses were grazing as usual. But when Reed reached the house, she spotted the four ranch hands on the porch.

The men were all armed, standing guard.

Reed had barely brought the truck to a stop when she barreled out and raced toward the house. However, Rayanne had managed only a few steps when the front door opened, and her sister and Roy peered out. They both frantically motioned for her to get inside.

There was no sign of the gunmen, but it was obvious the danger hadn't passed. The goons wouldn't need Rosalie if they had Blue and her in their sights, and that was the reason Rayanne went back and helped Blue up the steps.

"Get inside," Blue snarled at her.

Again, he was doing that protector thing, and it set her teeth on edge. Of course, anything he did at this point would cause the same reaction.

"I'm sorry," Rayanne said when Rosalie's gaze met

hers. Her voice was all breath and clogged with way too much emotion.

"You have nothing to be sorry about," Rosalie scolded her, and pulled Blue and her into the foyer. "We're fine. Dad stopped them before they could get in the house."

Dad.

That was a different way of putting her teeth on edge. Rosalie had obviously gotten past the fact that twenty-three years ago, when Rayanne and she had been barely six, their parents had split over rumors that their mother had had an affair and then killed her lover.

Rayanne hadn't.

She was sure their mother was innocent of murdering her alleged lover, Whitt Braddock, but still Roy had sent her packing. Rosalie and her, too. Well, he hadn't done anything to stop their mother from taking them, anyway, despite having kept custody of his sons.

Rayanne didn't intend to let go of that old grudge anytime soon. Nor the grudge she was holding against Whitt's grown kids, his widow and even his elderly father for pressing for her mother's arrest.

Still, for now, she mumbled a thanks to Roy for protecting Rosalie.

"You must be Blue McCurdy," Rosalie said. "And you obviously need to sit down."

Rayanne still had her arm looped around him, but her sister took one look at Blue's face and lent him an arm, too. Together they led him toward the family room just off the foyer. Rosalie not only made sure he sat on the sofa, she began to examine the surgical wound beneath the bandage.

Only then did Rayanne see the blood seeping through

the bandage. It wasn't much but enough for her to suspect he'd popped a stitch or two.

"Blue McCurdy," Roy repeated.

Unlike Rosalie, he had no friendly, nurturing tone in
his voice. Probably because he'd heard about Blue dumping her. Not from Rayanne, but Rosalie and he had no
doubt had a few chats.

Roy and her mother, too.

He was apparently visiting her mother in jail, where
she was awaiting trial. In the grand scheme of things,
it was petty to think of it now, but seeing Roy always
brought out the pettiness in her.

Roy kept staring at Blue. Nope, it was a glare. He
likely felt the need to defend his daughter.

Well, she didn't want that from him, either.

What was it with these unwanted men in her life doing
unwanted things? But that question vanished when Rosalie eased back Blue's bandage, and Rayanne got a glimpse
of the angry-looking wound beneath.

"I'll get the first-aid kit," Rosalie said. "Some pain
meds, too, and once the danger's passed, you'll need to
go back to the hospital."

"No hospital and no pain meds," Blue insisted. "I need
a clear head in case those men return."

"No sense arguing with him," Rayanne said to her
sister. "He's hardheaded and won't listen even when he
should."

"Like someone else I know," Rosalie mumbled, and
headed out of the room.

The corner of Blue's mouth lifted. Enough of a smile
for Rayanne's body to give her another punch of something else she didn't want. A reminder that his smile had
always had her hormonal number.

Heck, who was she kidding?

Pretty much all of him could heat her up, but those days were long gone.

She hoped.

"I'll keep watch at the door," Roy said when Rayanne sank down on the sofa next to Blue, but he paused, glanced at her belly and looked on the verge of asking how she was. However, he must have realized it wasn't a good time to play daddy because he walked away.

"He's worried about you," Blue mumbled. "*I'm* worried about you?"

"I'm not the one who's been shot and is bleeding." And Rayanne had another look at the wound. Yep, he'd popped a stitch, all right.

"I'll be fine."

"Right. You can tell that lie to my sister, and she might believe it. I see otherwise."

That darn smile of his threatened to return. "Worried about me?"

Rayanne huffed a lot louder than necessary to show her disapproval. "Worried that I won't get you out of my life soon enough." She winced, paused. "I'm also worried that you won't get your memory back and be able to tell me why all of this is happening," she amended.

His gaze met hers, and the muscles in his jaw started to stir. "I haven't had time to give it a lot of thought, but there's only one reason I would have left you like that. And it would have been to protect you."

"Don't you think I know that?" she blurted out before she realized she was even going to say it.

Good grief.

It wasn't the time for *this* conversation, one that involved admitting that Blue had been a decent man. However, since she'd jumped off this particular cliff, Rayanne just kept going.

"Knowing that doesn't help. In fact, it only makes it worse. I'm a cop, Blue. I can take care of myself. You had a choice. Crush me or put me in danger. Trust me, I would have preferred the danger."

"Crush you?" he challenged.

Mercy, she hated that she had ever admitted something like that to him. Blue already had enough power over her with these blasted feelings that she still had for him.

Well, those feelings could take a hike, because she didn't want another dose of Blue.

Too bad her body had other ideas.

She still had the taste of him in her mouth. Literally. From the test kiss he'd laid on her at the hospital. To jog his memory, he'd said. It'd done a lot more than that.

It'd jogged hers.

And it had reminded Rayanne of why she'd landed in bed with him in the first place.

"What's going on in your head?" Blue asked in that deep Texas drawl that did pretty much the same thing to her body as his kiss had done.

Rayanne didn't even bother to scold her hormones, because it was clear that her body wasn't listening to a single warning she was doling out to it.

"If you were trying to protect me," she said, forcing her mind back on what it should be on, these blasted attacks, "then the questions are who's responsible and why?"

Blue didn't jump to answer, but he shook his head. "I don't know." He paused. "If I'd known you were pregnant—"

"Don't," she warned him.

"Don't shut me out of this," he warned her right back. "You've had weeks to come to terms with it, but I've only had an hour or so."

"Trust me, it'll take more than a few weeks to come to terms with it."

"You're not happy about the baby?" Blue came out and asked her.

"I didn't say that. I *am* happy." Scared out of her mind, too, but Rayanne kept that part to herself. She'd never admit that to him. To anyone. She already felt vulnerable enough without adding more to the mix.

"I'm sorry," he said, but didn't clarify exactly what he was apologizing for this time. Nor did Rayanne have time to ask, because her sister hurried back into the room.

Rosalie had not only the first-aid kit but a pan of water. "I called the doctor," she said, and got busy cleaning the wound. "After we're sure these would-be kidnappers are gone, he's coming out to check on you."

Good. Especially since Rayanne figured she stood no chance of talking Blue into returning to the hospital.

"Were you two talking about the baby?" Rosalie asked, volleying her attention between them and Blue's wound.

"No," Rayanne said at the same time that Blue answered, "Yes."

Rosalie made a sympathetic little hmm-ing sound, one that made Rayanne mentally curse herself. Rosalie's own newborn daughter had been stolen from the hospital only hours after she'd been born, and Rosalie would no doubt give up her life to get her baby back.

And here Rayanne was, not jumping for joy at the idea of motherhood.

Not on the outside, anyway, but Rayanne knew the bottom line here. She hadn't planned on this baby, hadn't planned on a baby, period, but she already loved this unborn hormone-generating machine with all her heart. And she would do anything to protect it.

Rayanne was so focused on that thought that she jumped a little when her phone buzzed. *Get a grip.*

"It's your boss," she told Blue when she saw Caleb's name on the screen. Blue took it from her and put the call on speaker.

"Caleb," Blue answered.

"Where the hell are you?" Caleb snapped.

"Someplace safe, I hope," he said. "Please tell me something else hasn't gone wrong."

"Wish I could say that, but I just had a conversation with a criminal informant. A reliable one." Caleb paused. Cursed. "Blue, you'd better get some rest. I've fought it and lost, and the department's given me no choice."

Blue did some cursing of his own. "What the heck are you talking about?"

Caleb cleared his throat. "I mean I'm going to have to arrest you."

Chapter Six

Blue glanced at the bottle of pills that Dr. Howland had left for him. When the doc had examined him about twelve hours earlier, he'd insisted that Blue take one every four hours to manage the pain. He hadn't and had somehow made it through the night in the guest room at the McKinnon ranch.

But Blue was certainly eyeing that bottle now.

The pain was a dull throb in his shoulder and head. Had been since he'd woken up in that hospital bed. And while Blue figured those little pills would take the edge off, they might also dull him enough so that he couldn't think his way out of this situation that was now his life.

Not a simple situation, either.

This one had plenty of layers.

One of those layers gave a sharp knock on the door and opened it before he could even issue the standard *come in*. Rayanne stepped inside, her gaze swinging from him to the pill bottle.

Then to his bare chest.

It was the second time in just as many days that she'd caught him shirtless. At least he had on jeans this time and not some butt-baring hospital gown. Hard to look like a man who could protect her while half-naked.

Blue considered reaching for his shirt, but Rayanne walked closer, a plastic bag looped over her wrist and a cup of coffee in each hand. "Thought it'd help with the headache," she said, and thrust one of the cups in his direction.

He darn sure didn't refuse it. His head might be a tangled heap of memories, but his body was screaming for caffeine. One sip, and he figured this just might be the cure for what ailed him.

Part of what ailed him, anyway.

Too bad he couldn't cure the rest of it with a few sips of strong coffee.

Rayanne dropped the plastic bag on the bed. "Your 'good-luck charms,'" she mumbled.

Blue glanced inside and saw that it was indeed his Stetson and his brown leather vest. Both had a few new scuffs, but he was glad to have them back. "Thanks."

"Thank the sheriff when you see him. He brought them when he finished his shift."

Which meant the CSIs likely hadn't found any trace or fibers that could help with the investigation. The possibility of that had been a long shot, anyway, but Blue had held out hope that there would be something to give them a lead.

"You never did say why the vest and hat were lucky," she commented. "Or maybe you don't remember?" Rayanne added with yet more skepticism. She clearly still didn't believe he had memory loss.

"I remember," he said under his breath. "It's a long story. I'll tell you about it sometime." Maybe.

Probably not, he amended, since he'd never told anyone. Some doors were best left closed.

Rayanne made a sound that could have meant anything, maybe even a twinge of hurt that he hadn't bared his soul. If she knew the story behind it, she'd thank him, since she didn't deal any better with emotional baggage than Blue did. Or at least she hadn't before the pregnancy.

"Rosalie will be up soon to check your bandage," she continued. "Since you refused to go back to the hospital, Dr. Howland wants her to call him if there's been any change in your condition. Is there a change?" she quickly tacked on to her update.

"Not with the memory. The pain's manageable." That last part was a downright lie, but if he said it enough, it might actually start to happen. Besides, Rayanne had enough to deal with without worrying that he was going to keel over.

Taking some long sips of coffee from her own cup, Rayanne sank down on the foot of his bed. Not too close to him, though. But it was close enough for him to notice that she wasn't drinking coffee but rather chocolate milk.

She looked tired and amazing all at the same time. She was wearing her usual jeans and a plain tan shirt that hugged her body just enough for him to see another layer to this complex situation.

The baby bump.

"We're not going to discuss that now," she said, obviously following his gaze. "Or that," she added when his wandering eyes landed on her mouth.

Blue couldn't help it. He smiled. Even with the danger breathing down their proverbial necks, Rayanne could do that to him.

Sadly, his smile seemed to only rile her even more.

"Caleb already called earlier this morning," she informed him.

Ah, so that was the source of this particular riling.

Well, it must have been darn early, because it was barely eight o'clock now.

"And?" Blue asked when she didn't continue.

"He'll be here in about an hour, and yes, he still says he'll arrest you, that he doesn't have a choice. The powers that be believe you're a dirty agent."

Not exactly a surprise. Before he'd finally had to collapse in bed, Blue had spent a few hours trying to sort out why a criminal informant had claimed Blue was on the payroll of criminal kingpin Rex Gandy. He wasn't any closer to learning the truth than he had been last night, but he'd need to learn it soon if he hoped to stop Caleb from hauling him into custody.

"If Caleb's superiors are taking the word of this CI," Rayanne continued, "then they must have some kind of proof to go along with it."

Blue felt as if she'd slugged him. "We're back to you thinking I'm a criminal?"

She lifted her shoulder. "I think the CI might think that. Probably because you gave him a reason to believe it. Like maybe some kind of deep-cover investigation that you didn't bother to tell anyone about. Something that would make you look like a criminal."

Blue couldn't dismiss that, but without details and proof, he didn't have a way to clear his name. "Whatever it is, it obviously involves you."

Rayanne stared into her cup of milk. Nodded. "Let's play this through and see if it jogs anything in your memory. Five months ago something happened, something big enough and dangerous enough for you to start this investigation that's brought you here. We'd just finished that case in Appaloosa Pass, so maybe it's connected to that?"

It was his turn to nod. "If so, then it's linked to Gandy because we arrested one of his so-called lieutenants."

It'd been a solid arrest, too. His team and Rayanne had found not just a stash of illegal weapons but plenty of paperwork and even a witness who could put the lieutenant away for life.

Except the guy's life hadn't lasted that long.

He'd gotten into a fight during lockup and had been killed by another prisoner. Yet something else Blue needed to investigate. Had the lieutenant been killed in a jail fight or had he been targeted for a kill because of things he could have told the Justice Department?

Things about his boss, Rex Gandy.

Blue paused, thought about that some more. "So maybe this is a simple case of revenge. Gandy wanted to get back at us for the arrest or even the death of his thug cohort, and he set me up to make it look like I'm a criminal."

Rayanne made a sound to indicate she agreed with that. "One who'd accept a contract to kill me."

Yeah, and that was where their theory fell plenty short. "Gandy must have known that I wouldn't kill the woman carrying my baby."

"He probably didn't know I was pregnant." She gave him a quick glance. "I haven't told anyone other than family, and I've been trying to keep it hidden."

Blue had several questions about that but decided to go for the obvious one. "Why?"

Another shrug. "I just wasn't ready to deal with the questions yet."

Yeah, because questions about the baby meant questions about him, too. Not that he needed it, but it was yet more proof of how much he'd hurt her.

And how much she detested him for hurting her.

Heck, he detested himself, too, and the only thing that would make this better was for him to learn why he'd walked out on her in the first place. Even if he'd had doubts about sleeping with her, he wasn't the sort to go slinking out on a walk of shame. And he especially wouldn't have done that to Rayanne.

Rayanne's gaze came to Blue's, and this time it wasn't for just a glimpse. Their eyes met, held. "Swear to me that this memory thing isn't an act."

The woman certainly knew how to keep him on his toes. "Why in the name of heaven would I fake that?"

"So that you can keep the details of whatever you're involved in to yourself," she readily answered, which meant she'd thought this through.

He huffed, cursed. "There's no reason for me to do that." Blue pointed to the bandage on his shoulder. "This bullet could have hit you. Trust me, I want to remember anything and everything about the idiots who put you in danger."

And he intended to stop it.

That stopping started with his figuring out how to get Caleb off his back. Then he needed to find their attackers and force them to talk. The first was doable.

Maybe.

The second would likely take some solid detective work and a hefty dose of divine intervention.

Blue forced himself to get up. He was moving a little easier now, and the caffeine had indeed helped with his throbbing head, but he required more than moving just a little easier. He needed a break in this case, and he needed it yesterday.

"I'll make some more calls," he explained. Maybe to

some other CIs who could perhaps explain what the heck he'd been doing for the past five months. Someone out there had to know. He doubted he'd been living in a hole in the ground all this time.

Rayanne took her phone from her pocket and handed it to him. He reached for it, wobbled just a little, and lightning fast, Rayanne set her cup on the floor and came off the bed to take hold of him.

Just like that, he was in her arms. Well, almost. She slid her arm around his waist, putting them side to side with a whole lot of touching. His body didn't seem to understand that this was just part of her nursing duties.

"Best not to get any more head injuries," she mumbled. "And if you smile, I might hurt you."

Oh, he smiled, all right, because he was obviously losing it. The proof of that was the stupid stirring in his body, especially one part of him that thought he might get lucky. He wasn't in any shape to get lucky, even if Rayanne had been willing.

And she clearly wasn't.

"Just resist the temptation," she snarled.

He wasn't sure if they were talking about his smile or something else. "Trust me, I've had a lot of practice resisting you."

She blinked, stared up at him. "Excuse me?"

Blue was surprised that she was surprised.

"You think all that time we worked on those cases together that my mind was solely on the job? It wasn't," he assured her before she could respond, though it looked as if she was too thunderstruck to say much of anything. "I've been attracted to you since day one."

For just a heartbeat, she looked a little pleased about

that, but then Rayanne shook her head. "How can you remember that?"

"Oh, I remember some things."

Things that caused him to stray into the stupid realm again, because he brushed a kiss on her cheek. Thank goodness it was only her cheek, because he could have sworn he saw little lightning bolts zing through her eyes.

She let go of him so fast that he had no choice but to sit back on the bed or he would have fallen. "Blue, this can't happen again."

He nodded. "I know."

And he did.

Didn't he?

Well, his brain knew that it was a dumb thing to do, but his brain and other parts of him hadn't exactly made some good decisions lately.

Cursing that and himself, he put Rayanne's phone on the nightstand, took the clean shirt that Rosalie had left for him and put it on, trying not to wince or make some other sound to prove he'd lied about the pain. However, before he could even button up and start those calls, her phone rang, and he saw Caleb's name on the screen.

Blue hit the speaker button so he could talk while he finished dressing. "Still plan on arresting me?"

"The criminal informant won't back down. He's pressing for the charges against you, and he added more than his sworn testimony to the table." Caleb paused. "He's got proof."

That brought Rayanne to her feet, and she moved closer to the phone. "You'd trust so-called proof from a criminal informant over the word of one of your agents?"

"I would if the agent can't vouch for what he's been doing for the past five months." Caleb paused again. "The

CI has photos of Blue meeting with a guy named Burrell Parker. He's a low-life arms dealer, and we're almost positive that he's the one who arranged for the hit on you."

Blue didn't have to think long and hard about that. "Maybe I was meeting with this guy Parker because I got wind of the hit and was trying to stop it."

"Maybe, but you took money from him. The CI got a picture of that, too. And before you say anything, yeah, it smacks of a setup, but I can't just dismiss it. I need to bring you in and try to clear all of this up."

Blue had a different notion about that. "I'd rather not be behind bars while you're clearing up things that affect me and the people around me. I need to help."

"Then help by telling me why you met with Parker," Caleb fired back.

"I don't know." And he cursed himself again. This blasted concussion was beyond an inconvenience. "But I'm guessing Parker works for Rex Gandy like those thugs who tried to kill Rayanne and me yesterday?"

"No," Caleb argued. "Well, if he does, there's no obvious proof or connection with Gandy, but Parker had a connection with someone else we know. Your former partner and friend, Woody Janson."

Of all the things Blue had expected Caleb to say, that wasn't one of them.

"Woody's missing," he reminded his boss. Or at least, that was what Rayanne had told him.

"Yeah, missing under suspicious circumstances. You remember he phoned you right before you, too, disappeared under that same cloud of suspicion. What I need to know is what you two discussed that night."

Blue tried again to pick through that whirl of thoughts in his aching head and came up blank. "I don't know."

"I don't, either," Rayanne volunteered, "but I'm pretty sure that Woody called because he was in some kind of trouble. What about the CI? Did he say where Woody was?"

"Like the two of you, he claims he doesn't know, but Woody's in a couple of those pictures of Blue meeting with Parker when the hit on Rayanne was arranged."

Again, Blue hadn't seen that coming, and he wished he could force the memories to come. But the more he pushed, the worse the pain got.

"We need to find Woody," Rayanne mumbled.

"*I* need to find him," Blue corrected. To get some answers about that meeting that had put him in hot water. "It's too risky for you to be involved in this."

A burst of air left her mouth, and it was most definitely not a laugh. "I'm already involved. There's a hit order out on me, and just because you didn't fill it, that doesn't mean it'll go away."

"She's right," Caleb said. "But the question is, why was the hit ordered on her in the first place?"

Blue had already gotten a headache over that question, too, and it'd been the very thing on his mind when he'd fallen asleep the night before. "Someone must have thought I told her something she shouldn't know. Maybe something about this thug Parker. And that means I want to talk to him."

"I'm already working on getting him in for questioning, but you won't have any part of that. Rayanne, either. Look, I'm trying to buy you some time, Blue, but I've got people breathing down my neck. They want you brought in now."

Blue hated to play the pain card here, but it wasn't a total act. "What if I'm still under care of a doctor? I had a bullet dug out of my shoulder just yesterday, and I'm thinking the last thing the doctor would want is for me to be hauled off to jail."

Where he wouldn't be able to work on clearing his name. Or where he wouldn't be able to protect Rayanne. Something she wasn't going to like, but Blue didn't plan to give her a say in the matter.

Caleb didn't jump to agree, so Blue continued bargaining with him. "Give me forty-eight hours."

Now Caleb reacted. He cursed again. "Please tell me you don't want that time so you can interfere with an active investigation where you clearly have a conflict of interest?"

Now it was Blue who didn't jump to answer. "You want the truth?"

"No," Caleb said. Then he groaned. "Don't do anything that'll make me regret this, and I'll see what I can do about getting you those twenty-four hours."

"I asked for forty-eight."

But Blue was talking to himself because Caleb had already hung up.

Blue stared at the phone a moment and considered calling his boss back to push for more time. However, he had more important things to do. Like arrange for some extra protection for Rayanne and her sister since these bozos had already tried to use Rosalie to get to them.

"How much are you going to fight me on this?" Blue came out and asked Rayanne.

She stared at him, put her hands on her hips. "Probably a lot. Why? What do you *think* you're planning to do?"

Oh, yes. She'd fight him, all right. "I want Rosalie and you to move to a safe house."

"And you?" Rayanne tipped her head to his bandage.

"Of the three of us, you're the one who's least capable of fighting off bad guys."

"You're wrong. I've got plenty of incentive to fight off anyone who comes after you." Now he did some head tipping. To her stomach.

She groaned. "I knew this would happen, but I want it to stop. You left, and I learned how to get along without you. It stays that way, got that?"

Blue would have assured her that she was wrong and that he didn't intend to agree to her *got that?* but there was some movement in the open doorway. He looked up, expecting to see Rosalie with the supplies to change his bandage, but it was her brother Colt.

"You two need to table this discussion," Colt said, not exactly in a friendly tone, either, "because someone just drove up. He says his name is Rex Gandy."

"Gandy's here?" Rayanne blurted out, already hurrying to the window.

Blue hurried, too. Well, as much as he could, and even though it earned him a huff, he stepped in front of Rayanne. He had no trouble spotting the man leaning against the white Cadillac that was parked in the drive at the front of the house. Bulky build, salt-white hair and a chunky cigar clamped between his teeth.

Yeah, it was Gandy, all right.

If the man was nervous about walking into the lion's den, he sure didn't show it. He appeared to be lounging, his legs stretched out in front of him, not paying any attention to the two ranch hands.

Both had guns trained on the man.

As if he knew he was being watched, Gandy looked up, his gaze sliding across the windows. The sliding stopped when his attention landed on Blue.

He smiled.

It was even more motivation for Blue to get Rayanne moved to a safe house. He didn't want men like Gandy being able to get this close to her. Heck, a hundred miles was too close for this snake.

"What does he want?" Blue asked Colt.

"Says he wants to talk to you."

Blue kept his stare fixed on the man. "Did he give any reason why I'd *want* to talk to him?"

"Yeah. Gandy says he's here to help you. In fact, he claims he's got exactly what you need to clear your name."

That got Blue's attention, but he was betting that Gandy hadn't shared what he had with Colt.

If Gandy had anything at all, that is.

This could be some kind of ploy to draw them out into the open.

"You want to talk to him or not?" Colt asked.

Blue nodded and grabbed his vest and Stetson. "But not here. Let's haul him down to the sheriff's office and see what this piece of slime has to say."

Chapter Seven

Twenty-four hours.

With everything so crazy around them, that was what Rayanne's mind kept going back to—the very short deadline that Caleb had doled out to Blue. The minutes were just ticking away, and if Caleb followed through on his threat to arrest Blue, then he would soon be hauled off to jail.

Blue had done plenty of things to rile her.

And crush her.

However, she hadn't seen a shred of proof, not proof that she'd believe, anyway, that he'd intended to carry out the hit on her.

Now they were on this too-tight time limit, and despite how she felt about the scumbag waiting in the interview room of the sheriff's office, if Rex Gandy could clear any of this up, then she would welcome anything he could give them.

Not because Blue was the father of her child.

No.

It was because the sooner they got all of this cleared up, the sooner Blue could leave. Again. And the sooner her life could get back to the seminormal it'd been before he'd reappeared in her life.

Rayanne moved out of the doorway of the deputy's office where Blue was finishing up some phone calls, and she went across the hall to the observation room. Blue hadn't wanted her to be involved when he talked to Gandy. Rayanne hadn't exactly wanted that, either, but she also didn't want to be sheltered like a damsel in distress.

Even if that label did sort of fit her these days.

She wanted to have an active part in identifying the men who'd taken shots at Blue and her, and that part started right here with Gandy.

"You're scowling," she heard someone say, and she looked up to see Seth standing in the doorway of the observation room.

Seth was the lone black suit in a sea of jeans, cowboy boots and rodeo buckles. Mr. FBI with the star-quarterback looks. And even though she didn't like that he'd no doubt put aside plenty of work to be here, she was thankful he'd done that for her. She was even more thankful there was no need to tell him that.

Saying thanks wasn't her strong suit.

Hearing it wasn't Seth's.

Her brother walked closer, until he was shoulder to shoulder with her, and he looked through the two-way mirror at Gandy, who was seated at the table.

Not alone.

Gandy had two lawyers flanking him, both dressed in cowboy duds like their boss. Both looking as much like snake-oil salesmen as he did.

"When's the last time you combed your hair?" Seth asked, glancing at her.

Rayanne frowned. "When's the last time you had a busted lip, because you're working on one."

It was a customary sister-brother exchange, no doubt something Seth had started to get her mind off her troubles—both Blue and the ones on the other side of the glass. However, Rayanne ran her hand over her hair and shoved some of the strands back into her ponytail.

Fixing herself up a little had nothing to do with Blue, she assured herself, and she was almost certain she believed it.

"How are you?" Seth asked.

He didn't look at her stomach, but Rayanne knew what he meant. "I'm taking my prenatal vitamins," she settled for saying. "Drinking my milk and eating right."

"Dodging bullets, too, from what I hear." He paused. "I agree with Blue. You need to go to a safe house."

Great. Now they were ganging up on her. "When did you talk to Blue?"

"Last night after the doctor left the ranch." It was Seth's turn to scowl. "I told Blue if he hurts you again, that I'd kill him."

Oh, man. "You what? You had no right—"

"It's a brother's right." He leaned in, dropped a kiss on her cheek. "But I gotta tell you, I don't think he's got any plans to hurt you. And I don't believe for one minute that he was at the ranch to carry through on a hit. I think he was there to save you."

Because she was riled at Seth's threat, she wanted to snarl and argue, but she couldn't. Not about that, anyway.

"I don't need you to fight my battles," she grumbled.

"No, but I do enjoy seeing you riled, so I'll try it more often." With that brotherly jab, Seth strolled away, and it was only after he was out of the doorway that she saw Blue standing there.

"Everything okay?" Blue asked, eyeing Seth with

slightly narrowed, cautious eyes. The way a man would eye a coiled diamondback rattler.

"Far from it. Apparently, Seth wants to play the part of my personal protector, too." She paused, reined in her temper. "He threatened to kill you, but you know he wouldn't do that, right?"

Blue lifted his shoulder, winced a little. Something he'd been doing not only on the ride over but since they'd arrived. She made a mental note to call the doctor and have him check those stitches again.

"Seth's your brother," Blue said. "He doesn't want you hurt."

That didn't excuse Seth's Neanderthal approach to interfering in his kid sister's life, and she hoped her huff conveyed not only that but the end of this particular conversation.

"Are you ready to go in there and find out what Gandy claims he has?" she asked. She stared at the bruise on his head. It was a nasty purple color today and went from his hairline to the edge of his eyebrow. "Or have you come to your senses and are willing to let the sheriff or one of the deputies do their jobs and deal with this jerk?"

"No. I haven't come to my senses." And Blue added one of those half smiles that Rayanne wished she could wipe off his face.

Or at least share with him.

She was too worried to smile about anything, and she hated that scum like Gandy could hold Blue's badge in the palm of his sweaty hand.

"I just talked to Burrell Parker," Blue said, glancing down at the notepad he was holding.

Rayanne pulled in her breath. She had known he was

on the phone, but she hadn't guessed he was talking to the very man who might have ordered a hit on her. "And?"

"And he denied everything."

She shook her head. "But there are photos of you meeting with him."

"Parker says those are pictures of me threatening to blow his head off because I wouldn't give him information about my missing partner, Woody Janson."

Rayanne took a moment to process that. It made sense. From everything she'd read about him, Parker was dealing in illegal arms, and it was the sort of thing Blue and his former partner would have investigated.

"You don't remember talking to Parker about Woody?" she asked.

"No, but the ATF had already accessed Woody's phone records. The calls end the same time he disappeared, but prior to that, Woody apparently had several conversations with Parker. I don't know about what."

"But before the concussion, you would have known about the conversations," she finished for him. "And you would have most certainly asked Parker about them."

He nodded. "I did ask him, and Parker says he has no idea what happened to Woody but that Gandy might know."

Rayanne huffed. Of course he would say that. Parker and Gandy were rivals in the gun business, and he'd say or do anything not only to take suspicion off himself but also to set up Gandy.

However, that didn't mean Parker was lying.

"Caleb's bringing Parker in for questioning," Blue continued. "He might be able to get something from Parker that we can use."

Something to help clear Blue's name and end the danger. Rayanne welcomed that with open arms.

Blowing out a long breath, she raked her hand through her hair, only to remember that she'd just fixed it. Sort of. She made another attempt to fix it.

"Ironic that when I woke up yesterday morning, I thought the worst thing I'd have to deal with was my mother's upcoming murder trial," she mumbled.

And while that was horrible, it still paled in comparison to the danger all of this could pose to the baby. Her mother still stood a strong chance of being found not guilty. At least to Rayanne's way of thinking, anyway. But the threat to the baby was immediate, and there didn't seem to be a reprieve in sight.

"I promise, I'll fix this," Blue said. It was a promise he likely couldn't keep, but for some stupid reason, Rayanne latched on to it.

However, she didn't latch on to him.

When he moved closer as if he might give her a hug or something, she stepped back. Best to keep not just physical distance between them but some emotional space, as well. Her hormones were still playing tricks on her, and her body might think a hug from Blue was a whole lot more.

And it couldn't be.

Blue mumbled something about wishing him luck, and he walked out. A moment later Rayanne watched as he walked into the interview room with Gandy.

When his attention landed on Blue, Gandy chuckled, his gut wobbling. He hooked his thumbs behind the grapefruit-sized rodeo buckle and leaned back in the chair.

"Somebody messed you up bad, didn't they, boy?"

Gandy said. "Bruised up your pretty face, and if I'm not mistaken, that's a bandage beneath your shirt. Hurt much?"

"Yeah," Blue readily admitted, doling out a dose of the same cocky tone that Gandy was using. "And I'm thinking that the somebody who did this to me might be you."

If Gandy was alarmed by that accusation, he didn't show it. He dismissed it with the flick of his hand. "I got better things to do than take shots at a rogue gun agent and his deputy girlfriend."

Well, at least Gandy hadn't said *pregnant* girlfriend, but that didn't mean he didn't know. And if he knew, he could somehow use her and the baby to get to Blue.

If this was all some kind of cat-and-mouse game to do just that.

"You said you had proof to clear my name," Blue reminded him, dropping down in the chair on the opposite side of the table from Gandy and his legal entourage.

"What, no small talk?" Gandy joked.

"We could stretch this out. I could also find a reason to arrest you. Any reason."

That got Gandy's lawyers whispering to him, but the man waved them off and leaned forward, propping his elbows on the table. "I don't want to get involved in this." For the first time since this conversation had started, Gandy seemed serious.

"You're the one who came to the McKinnon ranch looking for me," Blue reminded him. "You've involved yourself in this already."

"Yeah, but only so I could make sure I don't get blamed for the bullet that somebody put in you yesterday."

Blue met the man's stare with one of his own. "It was your hired thugs who attacked me."

Gandy quickly shook his head. "They haven't worked for me in a while. Not for Parker, either. Let's just say that trio of idiots was freelancing."

"Who hired them?" Blue pressed. "And you'd better not say it was me."

"No, it wasn't you." He reached for his jacket pocket but stopped when Blue pulled his gun. "You're a mite touchy, aren't you? I've already been frisked, and I'm not packing heat. This bulge around my waist is just from too many rare T-bones and plenty of beer."

The joking tone was back, but Gandy still waited until Blue had given him a go-ahead nod before he took out the small padded envelope and tossed it on the table between them.

"What's that?" Blue studied it, but he didn't touch it.

"It's surveillance images of your meeting with Parker. The very one that your boss has pictures of."

Blue lifted the edge of the envelope and Rayanne caught a glimpse of the flash drive inside.

"How'd you get this?" Blue asked, taking the question right out of her mouth.

Gandy flexed his eyebrows. "I like to keep my eyes on my competition. Now, you likely can't use that as evidence, because it wasn't exactly obtained with Parker's permission, but if you listen to it, you'll hear that it clears your name."

"Listen to it?" Blue repeated.

Gandy grinned. "It has audio, and it's real clear, too. Your boss can hear you threaten Parker if he doesn't man up about your missing agent friend. Of course, that's just a summary of the threat. You used a lot more words and some very creative profanity."

So Parker had been telling the truth. Gandy, too.

About this, anyway.

If that surveillance flash drive was what Gandy said it was, then it would indeed stop Blue from being arrested.

Gandy's attention stayed fixed on the nasty bruise on Blue's head. "You do remember this conversation with Parker, right?"

"Sure," Blue lied, and that came easily, too.

Of course, he'd had a lot of practice with deception during his deep-cover assignments. However, it did make him wonder if in that whirl of memories, his deep-cover lies were getting mixed up with the truth. Not good. They needed him to be able to sort through this and help identify the person who'd hired those thugs.

"So why help me?" Blue asked Gandy. It was yet something else that Rayanne wanted to know, too.

Gandy didn't jump to answer, and he eased back into his chair. "Because this is gonna turn into a big stinkin' mess, and I don't want to be part of it." The man's gaze went to the mirror. "I'm guessing your girl's there, watching."

"My *girl* is none of your business," Blue snapped.

"Yeah, she is. Well, she is in that whatever I'm about to take out of the other pocket pertains more to her than to you."

That brought Blue to his feet. "What the heck are you talking about now?"

Gandy took that something out of his pocket. A photo. And as with the flash drive, he slid it Blue's way. "You won't recognize the fellow in the photo, but your girl will."

Rayanne knew Blue wasn't going to like this, but she hurried straight toward the interview room and threw open the door. She got the exact reaction that she expected.

Blue scowled at her, mumbled something and stepped in front of her.

Gandy just grinned that stupid grin and slid the photo in her direction. Despite Blue being in her way, Rayanne got a good look at it by peering over his shoulder.

It was a grainy shot probably taken from a long-range lens. Two men seated at a booth in what appeared to be a café. Her attention first went to the man on the left.

And her stomach tensed.

It was one of the men who'd tried to kill them. He was dead now, lying in the city morgue, but it still sent an ice-cold chill through her to see that face.

That chill got worse when she saw the other man in the photo.

"No," she heard herself mumble, and despite Blue's maneuvering to stop her, she got around him and picked up the picture for a closer look.

"You know that man?" Blue asked her.

Rayanne nodded, didn't trust her voice to say more right away.

"That's Wendell Braddock," Gandy explained for her. "He's the father of the man who Rayanne's mother is accused of murdering."

Blue cursed and stepped in front of her again. "Please tell me you got that picture from the surveillance flash drive and that it has audio to go along with it," he said to Gandy.

Gandy shook his head. "Afraid not on that one. But from what I heard, your girl here is smart. A deputy sheriff and all. Shouldn't take much for her to come up with a reason why Wendell Braddock would be talking to a hired gun and why the Braddock patriarch wants her dead and buried."

No. It didn't take Rayanne long at all.

Wendell was an old man, in his mid-eighties, but he was rich, the owner of not just a successful ranch but several equally successful companies.

And he hated her and her family.

Rayanne was well aware of that hatred, not just from Wendell but from the entire Braddock clan. Still, it was a shock to see the man in that photo maybe cutting a deal with someone he was hiring to murder her.

"Must be hard," Gandy went on, speaking to Rayanne. "Your mother in jail, and Wendell's grandson holding the keys to her cell."

Blue shot her a questioning glance, and she nodded. "My mother's at the county jail in the town of Clay Ridge, and Aiden Braddock is the county sheriff."

Gandy smiled. "Aiden's daddy is Whitt, the man Jewell's accused of murdering, and his granddaddy is Wendell. A bit of a tangled mess, huh?"

Blue shook his head. "Why the heck was that allowed to happen?"

"Because Mom couldn't be held here in Sweetwater Springs, where her son Cooper is the sheriff," Rayanne explained. "The alternative was to have her sent to another county, and she didn't want that, because she didn't want to be that far from the ranch."

It was something that still didn't sit right with Rayanne. That being close was nice for visits, but it had come at a high price, with her mother being in the custody of a man who no doubt hated her. It was on a long list of things that troubled her about her mother's situation.

Including this latest development—that photo of Wendell.

"This explains why those men tried to kidnap Rosalie," she mumbled to Blue. "So Wendell could get revenge against my mother."

"It *could* mean that, or not," Blue argued. "Remember, a photo made it look as if I was meeting with someone to set up a hit. Without audio to go along with that, we have no idea what that meeting was about. Heck, it could have been just to set up Wendell so it takes our attention off the real person behind this."

Blue shot a cold, accusing look at Gandy.

It was a reasonable argument, especially since Gandy had been the one to give them the photo, but now it was Rayanne who shook her head. "I have to talk to Wendell."

Of course, Blue stopped her from bolting out of the room. Probably because she looked a little crazy and ready to do something totally stupid—like confront Wendell at gunpoint and demand the truth.

Blue first grabbed the surveillance flash drive that Gandy had given them, then took her by the arm and led her out into the hall. Another good idea, since this wasn't a conversation that she wanted to have in front of Gandy. He was practically gloating and clearly enjoyed being the bearer of bad news.

About this, anyway.

Maybe Gandy had been the one to set all of this up after all. If so, it was working. Wendell was now at the top of her suspect list. However, that didn't mean she would erase Gandy from that list anytime soon.

"This could be exactly what Wendell wants you to do," Blue said the moment that he had the interview room door shut. "If you go after him half-cocked, he can have you arrested. Heck, he could have all of us arrested, since you know we'd stand up for you."

Yes, she did know that.

And Rayanne cursed that and everything else she could think of to curse. "Wendell wants to punish my mother by hurting Rosalie and me."

Blue took her by the shoulders and forced her to look him in the eyes. "If that's really his plan, then don't give him the chance to do that. We'll find the third surviving gunman, and we'll get him to talk. If Wendell hired him, then we'll prove it."

She hated that he could be so darn logical at a time when she just wanted to grab Wendell or Gandy by their collars and force them to talk. Considering that Blue was sporting an injury that one of them had perhaps given him, he no doubt wanted the same thing.

"Everything okay?" Cooper asked.

Rayanne had been so caught up in her anger and the conversation with Blue that she hadn't even heard him come up behind them.

"You need to bring Wendell Braddock in for questioning," she said, handing the photo to Cooper.

As she'd done, he studied it a moment before the muscles tightened in his jaw. "Yeah, I'll bring him in." Cooper looked up from the photo, his attention going back to Blue. "You finished with Gandy?"

Blue nodded. "He had this flash drive that proves I'm innocent. I need to get a copy of it to my boss ASAP so he can kill the arrest warrant."

"I can do that for you, if you like," Cooper offered. "I can also finish up the interview and ask the Rangers to help us keep an eye on Gandy, if you want to go ahead and take Rayanne to the hospital."

"The hospital?" she snapped.

Cooper checked over his shoulder as if making sure that no one was within earshot. No one was. "Doc Howland called and said you never showed up for an ultra-sound that he said he told you that he wanted to do after the shooting incident."

Rayanne released the breath she'd sucked in. For a moment, one horrifying moment, she'd thought Cooper was going to say there was something wrong with the baby.

"I figured I could have the ultrasound after things settled down," Rayanne said. "Besides, I'm feeling fine."

Cooper gave her a flat look. "You might deliver that baby before things 'settle down.'"

Not exactly a comforting thought, because it was the truth.

"Go to the hospital," Cooper insisted, and he turned his attention back to Blue. "You're not looking too steady on your feet, either. Wouldn't hurt for you to at least have another checkup."

He was right—Blue didn't look too steady. It was a generous offer for Cooper to tie up loose ends for them, especially considering he had to have a ton to do in order to wrap up the paperwork on the attacks.

And given the fact that he was barely on speaking terms with her.

However, she'd always heard that her estranged brother was a decent sheriff, so maybe this was all about doing his job and had nothing to do with family or favors.

"Thanks," Blue said, handing him the flash drive.

Cooper's attention slid back to her again. "You won't go after Wendell," he said, and it wasn't a suggestion. He was sounding more and more like the sheriff that he was.

Or a very stubborn brother.

She already had one of those. Didn't need another one.

"She won't go after him," Blue answered.

Rayanne huffed. "I'm standing right here. I can speak for myself."

Both of them stared at her so long that the stares turned to glares. "All right," she mumbled. "I won't go after Wendell." Not today, anyway. "But if he's behind this—"

"Then I'll arrest him," Cooper assured her. "Just because we're not on the same side when it comes to Jewell, that doesn't mean I won't do my job."

She nodded, eventually, and mumbled a thanks.

"One of the deputies is at the hospital, tying up some loose ends," Cooper added. "If you run into any trouble there, he'll be able to respond."

Rayanne felt obligated to issue another thanks. A first. She wasn't accustomed to doling out multiple thanks to someone who disliked her mother as much as she loved her, but this was far from normal.

Blue got her moving toward the back exit, and once again he played the part of the supercop by getting in front of her and taking the first look out into the parking lot. He took his time checking things out, too, and after some long moments, he hurriedly ushered them into her truck. He got behind the wheel, of course, even though she was in better driving shape than he was.

"You should have told me that the doctor wanted to do an ultrasound," Blue mumbled.

Rayanne braced herself for a lecture, and she was ready to lecture him right back. After all, Blue had refused to go back to the hospital despite the fact he was only twenty-four hours out of surgery.

"Would you mind if I go to the ultrasound with you?" he added, driving out of the parking lot.

Oh, so no lecture. But it was something that still

caused a rise in her emotions. Viewing an ultrasound together seemed like something a couple would do.

And they weren't a couple.

But there was another angle to this. Rayanne really didn't want to see the doctor alone. She'd never thought of herself as a scaredy-cat, and she honestly believed all was well with the baby.

Or maybe that was just what she needed to believe.

Still, she could get news that would be impossible to take. News that was too painful even to consider, that there might indeed be something wrong.

"You can be there for the ultrasound," she finally said. "But this doesn't mean anything."

Blue made that little sound of amusement. "Sure it does. It means everything. Thanks."

Maybe he didn't realize how much that rankled her. Okay, he probably did. Blue could usually manage to get a rise out of her.

And surprise her.

"I figured you'd be running for the hills by now," she mumbled. "I'm sure having a baby wasn't on your to-do list."

He glanced at her stomach but didn't get a chance to confirm or deny what she'd just tossed at him, because her phone rang.

"Cooper," she said after looking at the screen. Something had better not have gone wrong with Gandy. Rayanne pressed the button to put the call on speaker.

"Get out of your truck now!" Cooper shouted. "I just got a call that there's a bomb in it."

Chapter Eight

Blue slammed on the brakes, drew his gun and reached for Rayanne to pull her from the truck.

But then he stopped.

Not easy to come to a standstill, because he was fighting his instincts to run like the devil and get Rayanne to safety. It was the same for Rayanne. She already had a death grip on her gun and had latched on to the door handle.

"This could be a trick to get us out in the open," Blue reminded Cooper, though he figured the sheriff had already thought of that. "How credible is the call?"

"No way of knowing." Cooper cursed. "The name and number were blocked. Do what your gut tells you, and I'll get someone over there to help you ASAP."

"We're on Main Street," Rayanne told him. "Between the hardware and the antiques stores."

She looked at Blue, her eyes wide and her breath already gusting. Obviously, Rayanne was waiting for him to go with his gut.

"We're getting out now," Blue insisted. "Keep watch around us."

He would definitely do the same, and even though he

was going with that whole gut-trust thing, Blue hoped this wasn't a huge mistake.

After he made sure no one was lying in wait to attack them, he threw open the truck door and pulled Rayanne out on the driver's side.

Oh, man.

There was a closed sign on the hardware store. He sure hadn't seen that when he'd stopped, but with Rayanne in tow, he ran toward a small newspaper office next door. Not his number-one choice of places to take cover since the front of the building was literally a wall of glass, but it beat going back into the street.

Maybe.

Perhaps it was the pain roaring through him, but he was getting plenty of mixed signals. One critical one, though. This didn't feel like a ruse.

It felt like yet another attempt to kill them.

"Get down!" he shouted to some men who were chatting just up the block. "Stay away from the truck!"

Hopefully, they'd listen and maybe it'd be enough to keep them and any other innocent bystanders out of harm's way. While he hoped, he added that this could just be a bad prank by kids with too much time on their hands.

Blue got Rayanne inside the office, and he pulled her to the floor next to the reception desk. No one was seated there, but it didn't take long before he heard footsteps running from the back. He levered up, took aim.

And got a shriek from the forty-something brunette woman who bolted toward them.

"Bomb threat," he warned her, and that got her running back up the hall. Good. Maybe she'd stay put.

Or not.

She kept going, straight out the back door. Blue hoped

there wasn't someone out there waiting, but at least the woman wasn't near the possible bomb.

Blue intended to get Rayanne away from the windows, as well, and back into one of the offices, but he had another look outside to make sure they wouldn't be gunned down the moment they stood.

And he saw something that caused the skin to crawl on the back of his neck.

There was a man on the opposite side of the street. He had on a nondescript brown delivery uniform and was standing by the side door of the antiques store. The guy was nondescript, too.

Well, except for the matching brown cap.

The man had it slung low so that it concealed part of his face. Again, it might be nothing, but Blue wasn't exactly in a trusting kind of mood.

"You recognize him?" Blue asked Rayanne.

She lifted her head just long enough to get a glimpse before Blue pushed her back down. "No. But I don't know many locals. Is he armed?"

"Could be. He has several boxes on a trolley, and they're blocking a good portion of his body." What the guy wasn't doing was looking their way.

That still didn't mean he wasn't a hired killer. He could just be watching to see what was going on.

"Come on," Blue insisted. "I need to get you away from this glass."

Rayanne didn't argue, but she also didn't have time to move before her phone rang.

Blue glanced at Cooper's name on the screen again. "We're in the newspaper office," he said the moment that Rayanne hit the answer button. "Please tell me this is all a hoax."

"Still trying to determine that," Cooper answered. "The bomb squad's on their way. Stay put until then."

He would, but he also kept his attention on the delivery man while he got Rayanne moving away from the window. Blue made sure she stayed low, and he kept himself in front of her in case this situation went from bad to worse.

"You're grunting," Rayanne whispered. "How bad is the pain?"

At the moment he hardly felt it, but Blue was sure it would hit him again when this was over. For now, he only wanted Rayanne safe.

They made it to the edge of the desk when Blue saw the delivery guy move. Not a slow, easy gesture, either. The man turned, leaving the boxes on the trolley, and he ran toward the back of the antiques store. Blue threw himself over Rayanne.

And not a second too soon.

The blast came.

It was deafening. A thundering ball of fire that hurled flames and debris in every direction, and it shook the entire building.

Including Rayanne and him.

This definitely hadn't been a ruse. That explosion was the real deal. The wall of glass shattered, and both the shards and the pieces of the truck slammed through what was left of the front of the office building.

Blue was instantly punched and pelted, but he forced himself to stay put. For several moments, anyway. Once he thought it might be the end of the flying debris, he got Rayanne moving into the hall so he could put some distance between her and anything else that might be about to come their way.

"That man could be coming," she said, her voice as shaky as the rest of her.

Yeah, and that was why he had to get her to safety.

Blue moved them up the hall to one of the offices, and he shoved Rayanne inside. She tried to pull him inside the room with her, but he stayed put.

And he took aim in case the killer was right on the heels of that explosion.

Still no sign of the delivery man, but it was chaos out there now. People shouting. Sirens blaring. Blue caught glimpses of people scattering to get away from those flames and a possible second explosion. Not that there'd been any indication of two bombs, but he wouldn't put it past the person who had orchestrated all of this.

Rayanne's phone rang again, and a moment later he heard her answer, "Cooper, we're okay. We're still in the newspaper office." She paused, punched the end-call button. "He says to wait here, that he's on the way."

Waiting sucked, but Blue knew it could have been a lot worse. If someone hadn't phoned in that bomb threat, then Rayanne and he would have been inside the truck when it turned into a fireball.

But who'd made that call to warn him?

Since the bomb hadn't been a hoax, maybe that meant someone close to the attacker didn't agree with this plan to kill Rayanne and him. Or maybe the explosion was meant for another reason. Perhaps just to torment and scare them.

If so, it'd worked.

Blue was scared, not for himself but for the hard-headed woman crouched next to him. Rayanne wasn't the backing-down sort, and she would try to go after this goon and get hurt. Or worse.

That took him right back to the theory that someone could be doing this to force Rayanne and him into what could end up being a failed attempt at some vigilante justice. Still, that didn't tell Blue who would do this or why.

"You're sure that Stetson and vest are lucky?" she grumbled.

Blue nearly laughed, *nearly*. Rayanne probably hadn't asked that to ease the tension, but it did just a little.

"We're still alive," he reminded her.

"Yeah, but if one more bad thing happens to us, I'm stripping them off you."

Again, she'd eased the tension, and embarrassed herself a little when she no doubt realized how that sounded. Blue could have dug himself a really big hole if he'd invited her to strip off his clothes anytime, anywhere. And that was an invitation he really wouldn't mind extending to her.

Rayanne's phone rang again, and this time she put it on speaker. "Colt's at the back door of the newspaper office," Cooper said. "He's got a truck that I want you and Blue to use to get to the ranch. I don't think it's a good idea for you to be in the middle of this."

Blue agreed, but his ATF training kicked in. "You might need help catching whoever did this."

"Yeah, but the best help you can give me now is to get my sister out of there."

Rayanne made a small sound. Not quite a huff but close enough. Probably because she was still at odds with Cooper and didn't appreciate him calling her *sister*. Or maybe she just didn't like being treated like a pregnant woman instead of a deputy sheriff.

Tough.

She was pregnant.

"I'll get her home," Blue assured Cooper. "Colt's cleared that back area?"

"As best he could. Just be careful."

Oh, Blue would.

They raced toward the back door, and the moment Blue eased it open and looked outside, he spotted Colt. The deputy had his gun ready, and he handed Blue the keys.

"The ranch hands know you're coming," Colt assured him. "They'll help you secure the place."

It wasn't as good as having armed, nonpregnant peace officers, but at least the ranch hands would be armed. Blue got her inside the truck, and he headed out.

He didn't have to remind Rayanne to keep watch. She did. She also kept her left hand positioned over her stomach. Not that he needed it, but it was yet another reminder of just how high the stakes were.

Thankfully, there weren't a lot of cars on the road leading out of town, and no one followed when he took the turn toward the ranch.

"I'm calling Seth," Rayanne said, still keeping watch. "I want him to make sure your boss gets that recording. The last thing we need right now is for him to arrest you."

She was right, but it surprised him that she'd remember to do something like this on the heels of the explosion.

"Gandy gave us a surveillance flash drive that clears Blue," Rayanne said when her brother answered. "I know you and Cooper can't stand the sight of each other, but you need to pick up the flash drive from the sheriff's office and get it to Agent Caleb Wiggs. We gave it to Cooper, but clearly he's got enough on his hands right now."

"Good day to you, too," Seth grumbled. "Are you all right?"

"What do you think? Someone just blew up my truck."

"I heard, and I'm repeating my question—are you all right?"

"I've been better," Rayanne said on a weary sigh. "Just please get the flash drive to Blue's boss."

"That explosion's given you a one-track mind, sis. Okay, I'll get the flash drive from Cooper—you'll owe me big-time for that—and I'll personally deliver it to Caleb Wiggs. In return, I want a favor from Blue."

"I'm listening," Blue said.

"Take care of my sister."

The look she shot Blue let him know that she wasn't happy about needing a babysitter, but then the look softened, and a sigh left her mouth. Maybe she'd resigned herself to the fact that Blue was going to be around a lot longer than she'd wanted him to be.

Blue thanked Seth, ended the call and took the final turn to the ranch. There were no vehicles on the road, but there was a black truck parked at the end of the cattle gate.

"What the heck?" Rayanne mumbled, moving to the edge of the seat.

Blue wanted to know the same thing.

There was a man and a woman standing outside the truck, and they darn sure weren't alone. There were four ranch hands standing between the couple and the road, and each hand had a gun pointed at their visitors.

Blue slowed to a crawl, but he got close enough to get a better look at the man. At first he thought it was Gandy making a return visit.

But it wasn't Gandy.

This man had his arms folded over his chest, clearly waiting.

"Is that who I think it is?" Blue asked.

"Yes." Rayanne pulled in a hard breath. "It's Wendell Braddock."

Chapter Nine

Even on a good day, Rayanne wouldn't have offered Wendell a friendly greeting, and today certainly didn't qualify as good. Well, other than the fact that Blue and she had managed to survive yet another attack and were still alive, but the sound of that blast was too fresh in her ears to play nice with a man who might want her dead.

Might.

Of course, Gandy could have made it look as if Wendell was the bad guy. Gandy had certainly had enough practice doing bad-guy stuff. It didn't mean Rayanne intended to trust Wendell or any other member of the Braddock clan.

"I'll handle this," Blue insisted. "Wait here." He brought the truck to a stop and would have bolted out if Rayanne hadn't taken him by the wrist.

She was about to tell him that he was in no shape to battle anyone. However, she had to reassess that when she studied his face. Blue probably was still in pain and weak from the surgery, but he sure didn't look it.

"You look mad enough to rip off Wendell's head," she warned him. "If he's behind these attacks, I wouldn't mind you doing that, but if he's not, it'll be hard for him to give us any answers if you beat him senseless."

Blue didn't jump to agree with her. He sat there for a moment, obviously trying to rein in his temper. The sound of the explosion was no doubt too fresh in his head, as well.

He finally nodded, got out and then shot her a scowl when she followed him. Rayanne slid across the seat and got out on the driver's side so that she'd be next to Blue.

"A little bird told me about the trouble you've been having lately," Wendell greeted. He looked and sounded about as friendly to them as Rayanne felt about him. "Also heard that you might be looking to pin that trouble on me."

"I'd love to do that," Rayanne greeted right back. "Why? Are you here to confess?"

"He most certainly is not," the woman next to him said. "What he should do is go home and let his lawyers deal with this."

Wendell smiled, not exactly in a happy way but more like a man who was trying to placate the woman. "This is my assistant, Ruby-Lee Evans."

"I'm his nurse," she crisply corrected. "And I'm his friend. He had a bad spell with his heart just last week and he's not thinking straight. He shouldn't be putting himself through this kind of stress."

Rayanne didn't know the dynamics of what was going on here, but Wendell was a widower, so it was possible Ruby-Lee was more than just an assistant, nurse and friend.

"I'm not gonna last much longer," Wendell added, his gaze shifting back to Rayanne. "But it'd better be long enough for me to see your murdering mother get what she deserves. And what she deserves is a needle in her arm."

Rayanne had expected that attitude. Heck, half the

town felt the same way. But it cut her to the core that her mother could actually be convicted and given the death penalty for a crime that Rayanne was certain she hadn't committed. Of course, the Braddocks were equally certain that she had.

"Is that what the attacks on Rayanne are about?" Blue asked. "You're trying to give Jewell McKinnon what you think she deserves?"

For several moments, Wendell didn't say or do anything, but then he shook his head. "I'd love nothing more than to see that witch Jewell suffer by losing a kid or two. Then she'd know what it was like for me to lose Whitt. But, no, I didn't put a hit on Rayanne."

"You're sure about that?" Rayanne pressed. "Because a little bird told me that you'd met with the very man who tried to kill Blue and me. That same little bird said there was proof—a photograph."

"I meet with a lot of people," Wendell answered. "But I don't meet with hired killers. I don't have so much as a parking ticket, much less contact with felons."

"Are you saying the photo was doctored?" Rayanne snapped.

"I'm saying if I met with somebody like that, then I wouldn't have known who he really was. Somebody's setting me up."

Blue huffed. "And who would do that to a kindly old man like you?"

Wendell shrugged, obviously not offended by his sarcasm. "Rex Gandy. I heard he wasn't happy when he found out you were an undercover ATF agent who'd been digging into his business and that Rayanne here helped you out with that digging."

"His *illegal arms* business," Rayanne corrected in case

Wendell didn't know just how dirty Gandy was. However, she was betting that Wendell did know. The man seemed to be well-informed about all of this.

"Why would Gandy come after Blue and me now?" she came out and asked. Maybe, just maybe, she'd get a truthful answer.

"I don't know for sure, but if I had to venture a guess, I'd say it's because he figured out that Agent McCurdy here was alive and well. Or maybe I should say alive and dirty." Wendell smiled again. "It doesn't bother you, girl, that your man was hired to kill you?"

"A lot of things bother me," she settled for saying.

It concerned her more that Wendell had details that he had likely gotten from Gandy. She didn't want these two snakes teaming up against Blue and her.

But maybe they already had.

Blue and she exchanged glances, and she saw in his eyes that he'd come to that same conclusion. If so, it was an unholy alliance with plenty of money and just as much motive. Both men could want revenge against Blue and her.

"So why are you here?" Blue asked Wendell. "To warn us about Gandy?" He didn't wait for the man to answer. "Because we already knew he was a dirtbag. The question is, are you a dirtbag, too?"

That clearly didn't please Ruby-Lee. She mumbled something about leaving and tried to get Wendell back in his truck. The man shook off her grip.

"I'm a still-grieving father who lost his son because of her mother." Wendell tipped his head to Rayanne. "I don't care what happens to either of you, but I want my name kept out of this. I don't want Rayanne or you or her badge-wearing brothers to try to muddy the waters of her mother's trial by saying I tried to kill you."

And it would indeed muddy the waters.

So much so that her mother's attorney could ask for not just a change of venue but perhaps a mistrial since it'd been the Braddocks who'd pushed for Jewell's arrest. So Wendell had a good reason to have his name not associated with any harm that might come Rayanne and her siblings' way.

Still, that didn't mean Wendell was innocent.

"Maybe you believe you can have your cake and eat it, too," Rayanne suggested. "You could get revenge against Jewell by killing one of her kids and then placing the blame on somebody else."

Wendell certainly didn't deny it with words, but that sent a flash of anger through his eyes. "You're barking up the wrong tree, little girl. Keep doing it, and you might just get hurt."

Wendell turned, and Ruby-Lee and he got back in his truck. Rayanne wanted to grab him, haul him to the sheriff's office and force him to say more.

But he wouldn't.

Wendell would just hide behind his lawyers and claim the McKinnons were harassing him. What she needed was proof, even if that proof cleared Wendell's name.

"You need to be looking at Gandy," Wendell said, speaking through the rolled-down window. "Or somebody else," he added, and he looked straight at Blue.

Because her arm was right against Blue's, she felt his muscles stiffen. "I'm not behind these attacks, so you'd better not mean me by that *somebody else*."

Wendell shook his head. "Just repeating more little-bird talk. I figure once your head heals, you could remember all sorts of things that a certain person might not want you to remember."

"What person?" Blue snapped. "You?"

Wendell smiled a syrupy-sweet smile that no one could have mistaken as genuine. "No, Caleb Wiggs, your boss."

BLUE MADE THE CALL to Caleb the moment he got Rayanne inside the ranch house. But he cursed when his call went straight to voice mail. He wanted answers *now,* but obviously he was going to have to wait. Blue left a message to phone him back ASAP, and that wait had better not be too long.

"Stating the obvious here," Rayanne said, "but Wendell could be lying."

Yeah, Blue knew that, but until he heard that from Caleb, it wouldn't sit easy in his mind. Why the heck would a man like Wendell even sling an accusation like that when he must have known that Blue could easily find out he was lying?

Well, he could if Caleb would answer his bloomin' phone.

"Have there been any hints that Caleb's dirty?" Rayanne asked.

"None." But he had to shake his head. "I don't remember any."

So why did he have this nagging feeling that there was something to remember? Something caught in that whirl of details still inside his head? Blue hated to have doubts, but they came. Man, did they.

"Sit," Rayanne insisted, practically putting him onto the sofa in the family room. For a moment he thought she'd done that because he looked ready to explode, but she eased his vest and shirt off his injured shoulder and checked the bandage.

"I'm fine." Blue nearly pulled away from her but then quickly figured out that he liked Rayanne fussing over him. Even if she was scowling when she did it.

"At least you didn't pop your stitches this time." Rayanne put his clothes back in place, and in the process her fingers brushed over the left side of his leather vest. She pulled her hand away, but she looked at the spot where she'd likely felt the slight indentations caused by pinholes.

They were still there after all these years.

"I don't remember you ever wearing your badge on this vest," she pointed out.

"No." And because he didn't want her to move away from him, he said something that he hoped would make her stay. "But there was a badge on it a long time ago. My dad's."

Well, she didn't move. Probably because he'd never before mentioned his father to her. Come to think of it, he hadn't mentioned him to anyone since he was a kid. It was part of that baggage that he'd always sworn he wouldn't discuss.

"He was a cop?" she asked.

Blue nodded. "A small-town deputy sheriff."

Like Rayanne. That tightened his gut a bit because he wanted things to turn out a lot better for her than they had for his dad.

She opened her mouth, met his gaze for just a second, and with just that glance, he could practically see the wheels turning in her troubled head. Rayanne was still trying to keep him at arm's length, but a personal conversation like this had a way of pulling a person closer, not pushing him away. She knew that as well as Blue did.

"It's none of my business," she said. Rayanne would have gotten up, too, if Blue hadn't taken her hand.

"Maybe not, but since that's my baby you're carrying, if anybody's got a right to know, it's you."

That didn't help the scowl, but she didn't knock his hand away. "We agreed we weren't going to talk about this yet."

Not really. She'd laid down the law, and he'd had too many other things on his mind—like keeping her alive—to argue with her. Blue didn't want to argue with her now, but with Rayanne this close to him, those memories were starting to stir again.

The kiss in the hospital.

And before that, before that rock had crashed into his head, there'd been some scalding-hot looks between Rayanne and him. They'd both had enough sense not to act on that heat, because work and sex rarely mixed.

Well, except for the one night.

Blue figured it'd been a pretty good mix.

He reached out and slid a strand of hair off her cheek and back in the direction of her ponytail. "I wish I could remember sleeping with you."

"I wish you'd quit talking about it," she fired back.

Yeah, that was his Rayanne. She could get testy if you weren't on her side, and she probably wasn't sure if she could fully trust him yet.

She could.

But that kind of trust had to be earned, and it wouldn't help matters if the heat got all mixed up in this again.

"I might just kick you six ways to Sunday if you try to kiss me again," she warned him.

"It'd be worth it," he mumbled.

That put some more annoyance in her eyes, but she stayed put as if steeling herself to weather a mighty storm.

Blue eased his hand onto her shoulder, then to the back of her head. He slipped his fingers in her hair and gave Rayanne a chance to settle and go still. He also kept an eye on her knee. She wouldn't actually try to hurt him— well, maybe not, anyway—but he didn't want her using that knee to try to get her point across.

Besides, he already knew this was a mistake.

The mistake went full-blown when he touched his mouth to hers. He felt the jolt just as he had in the hospital. Felt the heat, too.

She shook her head, maybe trying to clear it, but she didn't back away. Instead Rayanne cursed him.

Then kissed him right back.

Another jolt. It was a nice one that slipped through his body and settled right behind the zipper of his jeans. He kept things gentle. At first. But with each movement of their mouths, each shift of the pressure, the heat went from a simmer to a full flame.

"You taste good," he whispered against her mouth.

"You taste bad," she answered.

He pulled back, met her eye to eye. His eyebrow rose a fraction.

"You always were the bad boy," Rayanne explained. "And I don't want you to taste good. Or smell good. Or feel good." She cursed him again and gave his hand a slight squeeze before she looked away. "But you do, and that makes you bad."

Sadly, he knew exactly what she meant. Did that stop him?

No.

"This would be so much easier if I didn't remember

the attraction," he told her. "I could focus just on making sure you and the baby are safe. Yeah, I know," he added before Rayanne could dole out another warning about that. "A conversation about the baby's off-limits."

She stood, her back to him now. "Once your memory returns, then you'll know more of how you feel about what happened between us."

Okay, now he was confused. "Are we talking about sex?"

Rayanne didn't jump to answer, but after several long moments, she nodded. "Sure."

Which was probably female code for *you idiot, we're not talking about sex.*

Blue stood, fully intending to admit his idiocy—embrace it, even—and insist on the heart-to-heart that Rayanne clearly wanted to avoid. However, his phone rang before he could even get the conversation started. Huffing, he glanced at the screen, figuring it was Caleb ready to give Blue some much-needed answers.

But *Unknown Caller* popped up on the screen.

He hit the answer button and put the call on speaker. "Agent McCurdy," he answered.

"Blue," the man said. His voice was a husky whisper, mostly breath. "This is Woody Janson."

Woody, his missing friend and former partner at the ATF. "Where are you?"

"Someplace safe. I can't say the same for you, Blue. You're in deep trouble. Rayanne, too."

"Yeah, someone's trying to kill us. What do you know about that?"

"Everything," Woody answered. "God, Blue. I'm so sorry."

Chapter Ten

Rayanne held her breath, hoping that Woody would just blurt out everything he knew. Not only about the attacks but also about why Blue had gone missing in the first place. However, Woody didn't.

"I have to go," Woody said instead. "But we need to meet right away."

Of course he would say that, and Blue shook his head before the man even finished. "I'm not leaving Rayanne, and I don't want to take her off the ranch. Just tell me what you know."

"I can't get into it all over the phone. Someone might be listening. I'll send you a text with a meeting place and time." With that, Woody hung up.

Blue cursed, groaned and tried to call the man back, but he didn't get an answer. However, he did get a text within just a few seconds. One that obviously confused him, because he held up the screen for her to see the address.

Now she groaned. "It's a house on the ranch, about a quarter of a mile from here. It used to belong to my grandfather, but when he passed away, he left it to my brother Tucker. He lives there now."

Blue stayed quiet a moment, obviously giving that

some thought. "He's the one who's a Texas Ranger. You think he knows Woody?"

"Maybe, but Tucker's not there and hasn't been for a couple of days. He and his fiancée are in San Antonio trying to expedite the paperwork for the twin babies they're adopting."

Just to be sure that Tucker hadn't returned, Rayanne tried to call his house phone but as expected, she got no answer. "When does Woody want to meet?"

"In thirty minutes."

So soon. Rayanne heard the concern in his voice, the same concern flashing in her head like a neon sign. Danger. But was the danger worth learning what Woody might know?

Everything, the man had said.

"Can we really afford not to hear what he knows?" Rayanne asked.

Again, he started shaking his head. "I'm not putting you in danger again."

"Maybe the danger's already right here. You heard what he said about you and me not being in a safe place. If there's something going on, I want to know what it is so we can stop it."

"Yeah," he mumbled, but he didn't sound convinced.

"You could text him back and tell him to come here instead."

More head shaking. "I don't want him inside."

"Then we'll talk to him on the back porch with the ranch hands standing guard. If he tries to bring anyone else with him, we'll know and nix the meeting."

Still he didn't jump to agree, but his jaw was flexing. "You won't be with me while I talk with him."

Because she wanted to hear what Woody had to say,

Rayanne considered arguing, but she felt a strange flutter in her stomach. Like butterflies flapping their wings. The timing was certainly odd—and a little eerie, too—but she was certain this was the baby.

A first, though the doctor had said she would feel "quickening" around twenty weeks, and that was exactly how far along she was.

Blue practically jumped to his feet. "Are you okay?"

"I'm fine. The baby just moved, that's all."

Her words were meant to assure him that she wasn't in pain or anything, but those little flutters were one of the most important things that she'd ever experienced.

Blue pressed his hand on her stomach, but the fluttering stopped. She wasn't sure who seemed more disappointed about that—him or her. Rayanne hadn't expected to want to share this with anyone, including Blue, but she found herself wanting to do just that.

"The text," she reminded him, stepping back so that his hand was no longer on her stomach.

Yes, it was a special moment, but distractions like that could get them killed, or at least prevent them from getting the information to put an end to the danger.

Blue glanced down at her stomach, then the phone, and after mumbling something, he sent the text to Woody switching the location to the back porch. The moment that Blue got a confirmation text back from the man, Rayanne called one of the top ranch hands, Arlene, and told her about their visitor who'd be arriving shortly. She asked Arlene to make arrangements for some security.

And for Woody to be frisked for weapons.

It might be overkill, but after everything that'd happened, Rayanne wasn't taking any chances.

"Is it possible to sneak up on the house from the back?" Blue asked the moment she was done.

"Maybe," she had to admit. "There are acres of pasture, some with trees and rocks like the place where those other men attacked us."

That got his jaw muscles working again. "You *will* stay inside." He waited until she nodded. Waited even longer until she actually said "Yes" before they started toward the back of the house.

They'd made it only a few steps when Blue's phone rang, and Rayanne held her breath while he checked the screen. She hoped Woody hadn't already changed his mind about this meeting. Hoped even more that nothing else had gone wrong.

"It's Clifford Hale, Caleb's boss," Blue said, and he hit the speaker button. "Agent McCurdy."

"Blue," the man said, his voice all business. "Where the hell is Caleb?"

"I don't know. I was about to ask you the same thing. He's not answering his phone or returning my calls. What's going on?"

"Well, it's not good, and he needs to come in and answer some questions."

Blue huffed. "Questions about me?"

"Yes, and his possible involvement with one of the suspects in your shooting. Rex Gandy."

Gandy again. She hated how his name kept popping up, and she nearly blurted out some questions for Hale, but Rayanne figured those questions would be better coming from Blue, one of Hale's fellow agents.

"Possible involvement?" Blue repeated. "You got any evidence?"

"I got squat, other than a questionable tip from an

equally questionable criminal informant who wants to be paid and could be yapping his trap just for the money."

"Is it the same one who claimed I'd been hired as a hit man?" Blue pressed.

Hale hesitated, probably because he was trying to figure out how much to tell him. "Yeah, the same one. But I'm sure Caleb could clear all of this up if he'd just get his butt back in here and start talking."

Rayanne hoped that was true. Not just for Caleb but for Blue and Woody, as well.

She waited to see if Blue was going to mention the meeting with Woody, but he saw her eyeing him and must have guessed what she had on her mind, because he shook his head.

"Speaking of clearing things up," Blue said to Hale, "I'm not guilty of trying to kill Rayanne McKinnon. There's a lot of crazy stuff going on—"

"I know," Hale interrupted. "I just got off the phone with Sheriff Cooper McKinnon, and he filled me in. Don't worry. He's working on it and so are the FBI and the ATF. Me included. The pictures and flash drive that Gandy gave him have already been sent to the lab for analysis—"

"That's a start," Blue interrupted right back, "but I got a visit earlier from a man in one of those photos, Wendell Braddock. He implied that Caleb's dirty and wants me dead because of something I might remember once I recover from this concussion. Is any part of that true?"

Rayanne didn't like the long silence that followed.

No. Not this. There were already too many people they couldn't trust without adding lawmen to the mix.

"Like I said, I'm working on it. If Caleb contacts you, have him call me immediately. And if he doesn't, I want his badge. *Tell him*." With that barked order, Hale ended the call, leaving Blue and her staring at each other.

It sickened her to think of Caleb as a suspect, especially after the way he'd acted in the hospital. All concerned about Blue's well-being. But just minutes after that concern, the gunmen had shown up to attack them.

Was it possible that Caleb had orchestrated that?

"Well, I guess this means I won't be arrested," Blue mumbled, sliding his phone into his pocket.

That was something at least, but they needed a lot more things to go right. Like getting information that actually made sense.

"How would Wendell have found out about all of this?" she asked.

Blue shook his head. "Maybe from Gandy? I doubt they're friends, but Gandy could have just called him. Unless there's a leak in the sheriff's office?"

"Not likely. Cooper might be pigheaded and blind when it comes to our mother's innocence, but he runs a tight department. He wouldn't have anyone working for him that he didn't trust." She paused, thought about it. "But Gandy would have almost certainly called Wendell if he thought Wendell could make our lives more difficult."

Or put them in more danger.

"If Gandy's behind the failed attacks, then maybe he thought he'd be able to spur Wendell into killing us," Blue suggested.

Her pulse was already thick and throbbing, and Blue's words didn't help steady it any. As a deputy, she was accustomed to people wanting to harm her, but that was only while they were in the commission of a crime. This was, well, more personal, and because of the baby, the stakes were higher than they'd ever been.

"Your visitor's here," Arlene called out from the back of the house.

When Blue and Rayanne made it to the door, they found the woman standing guard there. Rayanne also spotted the tall, lanky man making his way along the side of the house. Not alone. There were two armed ranch hands trailing along behind him.

Blue gave her one last reminder to stay put, and he walked out onto the porch, which stretched across the back of the house. Rayanne stayed at the glass-front door and watched the man come up the steps. She'd never seen Woody before, but she didn't have to know the man to see the fear in his eyes and the vigilance in his body language.

Woody wasn't any more comfortable with this visit than they were.

"How'd you get here?" Blue came right out and asked.

Woody hitched his thumb in the direction of the road. "I hid my car behind some trees and walked. I don't think anyone followed me, but if someone gets close to my car, I'll get an alert on my phone."

A phone that he had clutched in his hand like a weapon. One of the ranch hands was holding a Glock, no doubt Woody's, probably taken when he searched him.

Woody looked at the bruise on Blue's head and cursed. "How close did you come to getting killed?"

"Close," Blue readily answered. "And because of this lump on my head, I've got some gaps in my memory. You said you knew *everything,* so start from the beginning. Tell me what happened that put Rayanne and me into this mess."

Woody pulled in a long breath, cast an uneasy glance around him. A cop's glance. "Five months ago I was deep undercover in a militia group, and I overheard a conversation between two thugs who said that they'd been hired to stop you."

"Stop me why?" Blue immediately asked.

Woody shook his head. "They were vague about it, but I gathered that you'd gotten too close in an investigation."

"Gandy," Rayanne mumbled.

Woody looked over Blue's shoulder at her and nodded. "That was my guess, too. But these men hadn't been hired to kill Blue. They were going to kidnap both of you and then torture Rayanne until Blue agreed to fix the investigation."

Rayanne eased her hand to the doorjamb to steady herself. She hated such a wimpy reaction, but it wasn't every day that she heard of plans to torture her.

"Why go after me to get to Blue?" she asked.

"They'd been watching him and knew that you two had spent the night together. I guess they figured you meant a lot to Blue." Woody's attention shifted back to Blue. "I sneaked away from the group as soon as I could and called you."

"A conversation that I only vaguely remember," Blue said. "What'd you tell me?"

"That you were both in danger and that if you hurried, you might have time to catch these guys before they got close enough to carry out their plan. I gave you their location, and you said you would arrange for someone to guard Rayanne before you left and went after them."

Blue looked back at her, probably to see how she was handling all of this. She tried to look strong, but Rayanne was certain she failed miserably. He'd left to try to save her.

And it had worked.

Well, until now, that is.

"While I was on the phone with you," Woody continued, "I realized someone was listening in on our conversation. It was one of the members of the militia group that I'd infiltrated. I hung up, and he took a shot at me. I barely managed to get out of there, and I went on the run."

Well, that explained Woody's disappearance. In part, anyway.

"Why not run to the ATF?" Blue asked him.

"Because those two thugs had personal info about you. The kind of info they could only get from classified files at the Justice Department. I figured there was a mole in the ATF, and I wanted to do some investigating before I went waltzing into a trap that could get me killed."

Judging from the way Woody kept looking around, he still thought being killed was a possibility. It was. He was in danger just by being around them.

"I haven't found proof of a mole," Woody continued a moment later, "but I've heard bad buzz about Caleb."

Blue nodded. "So have I. Is he dirty, or is someone setting him up like they did me?"

Woody lifted his shoulder. "Some guns recently surfaced that you had confiscated in a raid earlier this year. Well, according to your report, you had. Caleb claims he didn't know anything about it, and he has no idea how the guns got back in the hands of some drug runners. Since you were presumed dead, you weren't around to answer questions about it."

"I did confiscate weapons," Blue verified. He touched his fingers to his head as if trying to draw out the details.

"I told you about them, and my report would have gone directly to Caleb. It's possible he didn't read it. Or remember it. But it was a big cache."

"Is that why Caleb's under investigation?" Rayanne asked Woody. "Because of those weapons?"

"That's part of it, but the buzz also points to something else." Again, Woody's attention landed on her. "There's a criminal informant, Lennie Sunderland, who's clamoring that Caleb wants you both dead because now that Blue's back, he could have told you about those missing weapons."

Well, they finally had a name to the rather chatty CI who was slinging accusations right and left. "Blue didn't tell me anything about weapons."

"You're positive?" Woody pressed.

While nothing about this visit had exactly made her comfortable, that put her on full alert. Because Woody could be the person behind the attacks, and hiding the chain-of-custody trail on those weapons could be his motive. Of course, the others—Wendell, Gandy and maybe even Caleb—apparently had motives, too.

Caleb could be trying to cover up his own crime.

"I'm positive Blue didn't tell me," Rayanne assured the man, and she remembered every detail of the night that'd changed her life in both good and bad ways.

"Why'd I fake my death?" Blue asked Woody.

"I don't know for sure. In fact, I thought you really were dead. But in light of everything that's happened, I can guess that when you didn't catch the men hired to kidnap and kill you and Rayanne, you thought *dying* was the best way to keep her safe. And it worked until someone found out you were alive."

Blue cursed. "I shouldn't have come here. I brought the killers to her."

That wasn't easy to hear, either, and Rayanne reminded herself that there had to be more to it than that.

"I don't think you had a choice but to come here," Woody insisted. "Someone found out you were alive, and I'm sure it didn't take long for word to spread to the wrong people." Woody paused. "God, I'm so sorry, Blue, but I might be the reason word got out."

Even though she couldn't see Blue's face, she saw the change in his body language. "What do you mean?" he asked.

Woody wearily shook his head. "I was looking for a way to eliminate the militia so that I wouldn't have to stay in hiding. I needed access to some information through some of our old contacts, and I used one of your aliases."

Rayanne's stomach knotted. She'd worked with the ATF enough to know that while in deep cover, agents sometimes used not only identities but code words set up by the criminals. Code words that told the thugs and gunrunners they could trust this person. When Woody used Blue's alias and code words, then those thugs would have believed it was Blue himself using them.

"I honestly thought you were dead," Woody repeated.

Blue groaned and looked back at her, and in his eyes, she could see the apology. An unnecessary one and one he didn't get a chance to voice aloud, because Woody's phone beeped.

The man hadn't exactly been at ease during any part of this visit, but the small sound put him on alert.

"Someone's near my car," Woody mumbled, his attention zooming to his phone screen. "I have it rigged with security cameras." He pressed some buttons, and Blue moved closer to have a look, as well.

Both Woody and Blue cursed.

"You recognize him?" Woody asked.

"Yeah." Blue took the phone and held it up for her to see the man prowling around the car. He was armed with a rifle with a long-range scope, and there was another gun tucked in a shoulder holster.

"That's the hired gun who came to the ranch yesterday to kill us. He's the one who escaped." Rayanne tried not to shudder. "Where exactly are you parked?"

"Too close. By your brother's house."

Oh, mercy. He was right. That was too close. Especially since the gunman had that rifle. He was already in range of the ranch house.

"Get Rayanne away from the doors and windows," Woody told Blue. "And no one's to follow me. Too dangerous." He snatched his Glock from the ranch hand and bolted off the porch.

Woody hit the ground running.

Chapter Eleven

Blue was thankful for everything Woody had just told him, but he hoped they hadn't gotten that information at a sky-high price—another attack.

"Set the security alarm," he told Rayanne.

His gun was already drawn, and Blue locked up. He did the same to the front door, and then Rayanne and he raced upstairs to the guest room where he'd been staying.

There were still plenty of windows in the room, but he didn't want her downstairs in case the thug tried to break in and started shooting. This way, the guy would have to make it up the stairs to have a chance of getting to her.

Blue would stop him before that happened.

"Stay down," he warned her. "And call one of your brothers for backup."

While Rayanne made the call, Blue hurried to the window that would give him the best vantage point to see if the assassin was coming after them. Well, it would if the guy came to the house and took a direct route to get there. It was possible that he'd try to sneak closer to the ranch house some other way.

"Colt's already on the way. Arlene called him." Rayanne sank down onto the floor, her back against the door. "Do you see Woody and the other man?"

"No. I don't even see his car." Of course, Woody had mentioned that he'd parked near some trees, so the vehicle could possibly be hidden.

"You believe everything Woody said?" Rayanne asked a moment later.

Blue had already given that some thought during their conversation. "I can't think of a reason he'd lie...unless he's the one trying to kill us."

She made a sound of agreement. "He could have said those things about Caleb to make him look guilty. Of course, Caleb's own behavior doesn't help matters, since he's not around to defend himself."

No, it didn't help, and that was even more reason for Blue to find Caleb and talk to him. However, he didn't want to do that by putting Rayanne at further risk.

While he kept watch, he tried to force the memories to come. And some did. Fragments of his conversations with Woody. Some images of him leaving Rayanne asleep in bed after they'd made love. Even a few bits and pieces of him going after those men who'd planned to kidnap and kill Rayanne and him.

Nothing in those fragments led him to believe the man was lying.

"You faked your death to save me," Rayanne said almost in a whisper. "I need to thank you for that."

She still didn't sound pleased that he'd taken such measures to protect her, but Blue wasn't about to apologize for it. It'd kept her alive.

The baby, too.

And because he'd done such a good job of faking his death, it had prompted Woody to use an identity that had ultimately gotten the wrong person's attention.

But who was the wrong person?

"I'm remembering some stuff," he told her.

Rayanne stayed quiet a moment. "*Stuff* about us?"

"Some."

"Some?" she repeated in a mumble, and then added a little *hmmp* sound. "You've been on the run for nearly five months, and it's possible you've gotten involved with someone else."

Ah, so that was the reason for her mumble of disapproval. "No memories of that, and I suspect getting involved with another woman was the last thing on my mind."

Especially after he'd been with Rayanne.

That thought didn't exactly please him. He didn't need his full memory to know that he wasn't the sort for a permanent relationship, but that had to change now. The baby made this permanent, and while that wouldn't please Rayanne, Blue didn't want an out when it came to his child.

His phone rang, and without taking his attention from the window, he hit the button to put the call on speaker. Blue had hoped it was an update from Woody, saying he'd caught the assassin, but it wasn't Woody's voice that poured through the room.

"This is Wendell Braddock," the caller said. "Did I call at a bad time?"

Blue couldn't tell if the man's dripping sarcasm was directed at their current situation or just at this whole mess in general.

"I'm busy," Blue snapped. "What'd you want?"

"Just heard about that photo of me that you got from Gandy. It was altered. I didn't meet with any hit man, but someone obviously wanted to make it look as if I did."

Blue wouldn't believe that until he heard it from the

lab or Rayanne's brother, but it did make him wonder. "How'd you find out so fast?"

"I have connections here and there," Wendell readily admitted.

That definitely didn't ease Blue's doubts about the man. Plus, the timing of the call was suspicious, and Wendell could have made it just to distract him.

"Somebody doctored that picture so we'd be at each other's throats," Wendell went on. "That way, he'll have a better shot at killing you."

"Yeah, yeah."

Blue had already figured out that potential angle, and he hit the end-call button, hanging up on him. It'd likely rile a man who was already riled, but it was better than Blue losing focus with a call that could wait.

Even if there was nothing to see.

Not Woody and not that hired killer.

But in the distance he heard a siren. Colt. Maybe if Woody needed help, Colt would get to him in time. Blue hated that he couldn't be out there himself, but he wasn't about to leave Rayanne unprotected.

Blue held his breath and tried to listen over the sound of his own pulse.

Had he heard some kind of popping sound?

Maybe.

But if so, it definitely wasn't a gunshot. Not a regular one, anyway, but it was possible a shot had been fired from a gun fitted with a silencer. Or maybe it was just his imagination galloping out of control.

He was so focused on trying to figure out what it was that the next sound nearly caused him to jump out of his skin. Hardly a manly reaction.

The ringing echoed through the room. Not Blue's

phone but Rayanne's, and he figured it was Wendell calling to whine about Blue having hung up on him.

But it wasn't.

"It's my mother," she said, and she let the call keep ringing until it went to voice mail. "If I talk to her now, she'll hear the concern in my voice, and it'll cause her to worry."

That must have been a big no-no for Rayanne since her mother had to be calling from the county jail, where she was being held without bond. Prisoners didn't get to make personal calls whenever it suited them, and this was probably the only call of the day or maybe even the week that Jewell would be granted.

The siren came closer, and Blue spotted Colt pulling to a stop near the white house where Woody had said he'd parked. Despite the fact there were now two ranch hands in place to give him backup, Colt didn't get out right away. Several moments later Blue's phone dinged.

No sign of Woody or the hired gun, Colt texted.

Heck. That wasn't what Blue wanted to hear. He wanted the assassin arrested and locked away so he couldn't attack again. It also would have been nice to question Woody some more, too.

A car's here, Colt added. I'll look around.

Blue relayed the texts to Rayanne and continued to keep watch.

From the corner of his eye, he saw Rayanne push the voice-mail button on her phone, and even though the sound was obviously turned down, Blue still heard her mother.

"I'm sorry you didn't answer, Rayanne." Jewell's voice was soft. Soothing, even. "I just wanted to check and see how you were. Are you taking care of yourself?"

Blue got another flash of memories. Of Rayanne in the back pasture when she came to his aid. And when she'd put her own life in danger.

No, she hadn't been taking care of herself.

She'd saved him.

"Your sister visited me this morning," Jewell went on. "She brought Seth with her. They wouldn't admit it, but I could tell he was there to protect her. Rosalie said Blue had come back and was staying at the ranch…."

Well, that would have been an interesting conversation. Since Jewell didn't know the reason he'd walked out on her daughter and now had put both Rosalie and her in danger, Jewell was likely one upset mama.

"Soon maybe you can tell me how you feel about Blue's return," Jewell continued. "*Or not.* I doubt you'll want to talk about him, but here's some motherly advice. Forgiveness is good for the soul and the heart. I love you, Rayanne. We'll talk soon."

So, not a riled mama protecting her baby girl. Blue expected Rayanne to dismiss that "motherly advice" in some way, but instead he heard a sound that he darn sure hadn't expected to hear.

"You're crying?" he asked when he heard the distinctive sniffs.

Blue glanced at her again and saw her quickly wipe away the tears. "It's hormones. They've got my emotions out of whack."

Because Blue considered himself a smart man, he didn't challenge that, though he wished he could go to Rayanne and pull her into his arms. He'd known her a couple of years now and had never seen her close to crying. Maybe hormones had something to do with it, but he figured the main reason was the stress over her mother's situation.

And their own.

"There are only four people I'd take a bullet for," Rayanne added in a mumble, "and my mother's one of them."

"Who are the other three?" he automatically asked. Why, he didn't know. Wait, yeah, he did. He wanted to hear Rayanne say who exactly was important to her.

She paused so long that he wasn't sure she'd actually answer. "Rosalie, Seth and now the baby."

"Wait." Now it was his turn to pause. "I've heard you say that before. Before I left, I mean, and before you were pregnant. You didn't say the baby then—"

"Because I had no idea that I was pregnant when you left." She stood, and after another glimpse of her expression, Blue knew that she expected this conversation to end.

It didn't end, though.

Rayanne tilted her head to the side. "Just how much of your memory are you getting back, anyway?"

"Some things." And some of those things he wouldn't share with her. No reason for her to relive the shooting here at the ranch when her memories were no doubt way too fresh. "It's nowhere near complete. More like flashes of images, sounds…scents."

Her eyebrow rose. "Scents?"

"Of you mostly and that night we were together before I left. You smelled like cinnamon."

She looked away, and Blue figured that was a good time to get his attention firmly back on the window.

"I'd had a cinnamon latte," she confirmed. "You remember our conversation?" Rayanne added that last part tentatively, like a woman walking on eggshells.

Again, he remembered only parts of the chat they'd had, and Blue pressed himself for more, hoping his brain would cooperate. However, before that could happen, his phone rang, and he saw Colt's name on the screen. Blue put the call on speaker, hoping this wasn't another dose of bad news.

"Still no sign of either of them," Colt explained. "You're sure Woody was headed this way when he left the ranch house?"

"Not positive. He could have gone elsewhere. I lost sight of him for about five minutes or so while I was getting Rayanne to safety."

"So she's okay, then," Colt said, sounding very much like a brother.

"Yeah," Blue verified. For now. He needed to keep it that way.

"Well, Woody's car is empty and completely clean inside," Colt continued a moment later. "From the looks of it, the steering wheel and gear stick have been wiped down. Nothing in the glove compartment. There's not even a scrap of paper or debris on the floor. I phoned in the license plate, and it's bogus."

Probably because Woody hadn't wanted the vehicle traced to him. He was an ATF agent, after all, and knew the tricks to staying hidden.

"Then how did the assassin find Woody?" Blue asked, more to himself than Colt.

"Hard to say. The ranch hands and I are following the tracks now, and it appears the gunman came in from the main road. Probably walked here, because I don't see evidence of a second vehicle. That could mean he had Woody under surveillance."

Yeah, or else the guy had managed to put a tracking

device on the car. But the assassin didn't need a track-ing device or surveillance for that. If Jewell knew about Blue being at the ranch with Rayanne, then it was likely all over town.

So maybe the gunman was solely after Woody this time instead of Rayanne and him?

"Wait," Colt said, grabbing Blue's complete attention.

"What is it?"

Then Colt cursed. "I found something. *Blood*. And lots of it."

Chapter Twelve

Blood.

Considering her queasy stomach, it wasn't a good thing to keep thinking about, but Rayanne couldn't get it off her mind.

Blood that Colt had found near the car parked by Tucker's house. Fresh blood that indicated a fresh, possibly fatal wound despite the fact that so far they had found no body, and no one had shown up at E.R.s in the area sporting a wound that could have produced that amount of blood.

It'd cost her a good night's sleep, and she figured it would continue to cost her until she learned if the blood belonged to Woody or the assassin who'd tried to kill Blue and her. She was praying it was the assassin, but if it was, then why hadn't Woody contacted them?

Or maybe the blood was from both men, the result of an attack that left them both injured. They could have both managed to escape. Maybe they were in hiding and tending their wounds. She hadn't heard any gunshots, but that didn't mean the men hadn't used other weapons.

Woody could be out there somewhere, bleeding.

Dying, even.

With that unpleasant thought repeating in her head,

Rayanne gave up on another attempt to sleep, threw back the covers and got up. She caught a glimpse of herself in the chrome base of the lamp on her nightstand. Even with her reflection distorted, the lack of sleep was evident all over her face.

She checked her phone again, something she'd been doing throughout the night, hoping that by some miracle she'd somehow missed a call with an update on the investigation. An update to tell her that everything was okay. Bad guys had been caught. The danger had passed.

No missed calls, though.

The sun had just come up, the light spearing through the edges of the curtains, and outside, she heard sounds of the ranch hands, their day already beginning. Normally, she'd be starting it right along with them. Doing whatever needed to be done.

Riding fence.

Checking on the new foals.

Anything to stay busy and keep her mind off her mother's upcoming trial and her daily contact with a father and brothers who resented her being there. And she kept busy to keep her mind off Blue.

Of course, she was no longer grieving his death in between the bouts of cursing him for walking out on her.

No.

With Blue under the same roof, she was cursing him for a different reason.

He'd disappeared to save her. Then he had returned to save her. And he just kept on trying to save her. As if she needed a cowboy hero in a leather vest to do that.

Okay, it was nice to have one, especially when that protection included the baby.

However, her vest-wearing hero only added to her

worries, too. She couldn't risk that kind of hurt again, no matter how many times Blue saved her. She couldn't go back to that dark place that she'd barely managed to claw her way out of five months ago.

"Relationships," she mumbled like profanity.

Well, at least one relationship hadn't kept her up all night. Thanks to Seth's prodding, Rosalie would be leaving for a safe house soon. Of course, Seth's prodding hadn't worked on Rayanne. She had no intention of dropping the investigation and going into hiding.

Blue wouldn't, either.

And that was another reason for her to stay put. He would never admit it to her, but he was nowhere near 100 percent, and that bum shoulder could get him killed the hard way.

The sound of hurried footsteps in the hall got her jumping to her feet. Rayanne braced herself for a knock. And for more bad news. But no knock. The door flew open, and a naked Blue came rushing in.

Well, he was nearly naked, anyway.

She'd noticed the naked parts first. His bare chest. Bare feet. In fact, the only clothing he had on was his jeans, and they weren't even fully zipped.

Rayanne hated that she noticed he was commando.

Heck, she wasn't faring much better in the clothing department, and Blue noticed, too. She was wearing just a T-shirt that didn't cover much, especially since there was more of her to cover these days.

"What's wrong now?" she asked because it had to be something bad for him to come rushing in here half-dressed.

Rayanne braced herself for news that the assassin had

been spotted near, or in, the house. But that was when she realized that Blue didn't even have his gun.

Blue shook his head as if to clear it, and he tore his attention from the T-shirt that barely covered her bottom. He bolted toward her and hauled her into his arms.

"I got my memory back." His words rushed together, the excitement and breath in his voice. "When I woke up, it was just there."

"All of it?" she asked.

"I think so. Go ahead, test me on something. *Anything.*"

Sadly, the thing that came to mind first and foremost was the part about them landing in bed. Since he was half-naked and totally happy and she was in his arms, it was best to go with something much safer.

"How about the conversations you had with Woody right before you faked your death? Do your memories mesh with what Woody told us?" she asked.

He nodded, pulled back, and his grip melted off her. That question also melted some of the giddiness in his eyes. "Yeah, and that means Woody probably risked his life coming here and telling us everything he knew."

"Probably?" she questioned.

"I have no idea what's been going on with Woody for the past five months. Yes, he came here to give us that information, but we can't completely trust his motives."

Blue was right and still doing everything to protect her. Even if it meant not trusting an agent he'd once trusted with his life. After all, Woody could be trying to cover up his involvement in those guns that had made it back into the wrong hands.

"So where were you all these months?" Rayanne risked asking.

And it was a risk.

Because he might tell her a truth that she wasn't ready to hear. Just in case, Rayanne turned away so he wouldn't be able to see her face. He'd already seen her cry in the past twenty-four hours, and that was more than enough. Best not to let him see any pain that this might bring to the surface.

"After I left and faked my death, I kept you under surveillance," he said after taking a deep breath. "I had to make sure Gandy or whoever was behind the kidnapping-hit order didn't go after you."

Strange. She'd felt his presence but had dismissed it because of her sheer anger at his hasty, unexplained departure.

"I never saw you," she settled for saying.

"That must mean I'm pretty good at my job." He added that carefully, as if he sensed something was wrong. It was. This conversation was scaring the heck out of her.

"What'd you do then?" she pressed.

"I kept investigating. Kept looking for answers. Then three days ago I heard from a criminal informant that someone was hiring for a hit on you."

Even though she already knew that, it was still hard to hear. Even harder to feel it. Had the person who'd ordered the hit known she was pregnant? If so, that made him a special kind of monster.

"I didn't know that Woody had essentially blown my fake-death cover," Blue continued a moment later, "so I posed as a triggerman willing to do the hit on you. I came here to the ranch to warn you, but those men caught up with me before I could do that."

Yes, and now the burning question was, who had hired those men?

If they could just catch the remaining assassin, alive, then he might be willing to cut a plea deal, give them answers and put an end to this. Of course, if Woody or Caleb had been the one to hire him, he would be even more hesitant to speak to anyone in law enforcement.

"I know what's bothering you," Blue tossed out there like a gauntlet. "The wording might not be exact, but you said once I got my memory back, then I'd know more of how I felt about what happened between us."

Rayanne pulled in her breath and was glad she wasn't facing him.

"That night, after we made love, you said you'd take a bullet for me," Blue reminded her.

Really? Of all the things that had gone on, why had he remembered that?

"I was caught up in the moment," she insisted. Rayanne no longer had any idea if that was even the truth. "I figured that's why you left the way you did."

"What?" Blue stepped in front of her.

No more hiding her face, so Rayanne tried to hide any hurt that might be there.

"What else was I to think?" She shrugged. "Even though it was just a slip of the tongue, I'd never said anything like that to anyone but family, and then you up and disappeared. I thought you got spooked because maybe you believed I was looking for a commitment."

Blue just stared at her as if she'd sprouted an extra eyeball.

Rayanne threw her hands in the air. "Look, I don't have a lot of experience with relationships, okay? I'm not exactly a warm, open person."

"But you are."

That hung in the air for several moments before he

huffed and continued. "All of this tough-girl stuff is just a wall you put up because it crushed you when your father didn't fight for you to stay at the ranch. He sent you and your sister packing, but he kept his sons. That cut you to the core."

She hated that Blue was right.

Hated even more that he could see through her so easily.

That wall was the only thing that'd allowed her to survive, and she couldn't tear it down yet.

Not even for Blue.

"Whatever," Rayanne mumbled, and she silently cursed the tears she felt threatening. "I just want you to know that I'm taking back that bullet remark. I didn't mean it."

His hands went on his hips. "You're sure?"

"Of course."

Either she hadn't said it with enough conviction or else he flat-out didn't believe her.

"Good," he said. "I don't want you taking any bullets for me."

All right. That went along with the hero stuff and watching over that he'd been doing. But she figured he knew that taking a bullet was just another version of the *L* word. And it was a word that didn't apply here.

She hoped.

Blue wasn't a man to play around with. Beneath those hot cowboy looks was a dark agent who likely had as much fear of the word as she did.

"Are you wearing panties under that T-shirt?" he asked.

Of all the things she'd expected him to say next, that wasn't one of them. Though she had noticed that his gaze kept drifting in that direction. Just as hers kept going to that open flap in his jeans.

"Yes," she snapped. Barely there panties but still panties nonetheless.

He made a slight sound of disappointment, went to the door, shut it and then came back her way.

"I'm going to tell you something," Blue said. "And then I'm going to kiss you."

Again, he'd managed to surprise her. And fire up some heat inside her. This conversation was certainly going in a strange direction.

Rayanne dropped back a step, and her gaze automatically went to his bare chest and unzipped jeans. There was a thin line of dark hair that arrowed down from his navel right to the part that his zipper barely covered.

That part of him and the threat of a kiss had her going all warm and golden.

Exactly what she didn't need.

"You think kissing me is a smart thing to do?" she asked, and kept her gaze on that zipper so he'd know exactly what she meant. Talk about playing with fire.

"No, I think it'll be a really stupid thing to do, but I'm doing it, anyway. And I promise it won't go any further than kissing. After…"

But he stopped, shook his head, and then without even getting into the *telling her something,* Blue pulled her to him and kissed her.

Oh, mercy.

She'd never gotten a bad kiss from Blue, but this one immediately hit all the right buttons. The firm pressure of his mouth on hers.

His taste. His scent.

The way he hooked his arm around her and drew her close. Closer.

Until she was plastered right against him.

All the memories came flooding back to her, too. The ones she'd tried to push aside of just how good, and hot, Blue could make her feel.

Even when it wasn't a good idea for her to be feeling these things.

There was the whole issue of him being nearly naked. Her blasted hormone issues, too. Plus the investigation they should be doing.

But did any of those things stop her?

Nope.

Rayanne just stood there and took everything he was giving her, and it didn't take her body long to start wrestling to bring him even closer, to deepen the kiss even more.

To make sure this mistake was one worth making.

She felt herself moving and realized that Blue was maneuvering them toward the wall. Her back landed against the smooth, cool surface, and even though he stayed gentle, the hunger she could feel inside herself was the exact opposite of gentle.

Rayanne ached for him.

Ached to have him take her the way he had that night five months ago.

And Blue didn't disappoint.

"Just kisses," he repeated.

He moved those kisses to her neck. Right to the spot that he knew would make her melt. And it did. Rayanne couldn't stop the sound of pleasure that escaped from her mouth.

That sound must have been like an invitation to Blue.

That and the fact that she wasn't doing a darn thing to stop this. She certainly didn't stop him when Blue caught on to the bottom of her T-shirt and shoved it up.

"You weren't lying about the panties," he mumbled, his mouth now against her breasts. He slid his hands into the back of the panties, to her bottom, inching down the panties in the same motion.

"You said just kisses," she reminded him.

"Yeah, but I didn't limit them to your mouth."

With that, he dropped to his knees and gave her a kiss that had Rayanne making more than just a little sound. She had to clamp her teeth over her bottom lip to stop herself from letting the rest of the house know what was going on.

Blue slid her knee on his shoulder—thankfully, the one without the bandage—and he just kept on *kissing*.

Rayanne gave up any thoughts of stopping this and instead anchored herself by sliding one hand against the wall. The other she sank deep into his hair.

It didn't take much before she felt her body clench. Before the ripples started and turned to a full-blown earthquake. The pleasure swooshed through every inch of her, and she would have fallen if Blue hadn't been right there to catch her.

Rayanne was still trying to gather her breath and come back to earth when Blue took hold of her and eased her to a sitting position on the bed.

"No," he said, following the direction of her gaze to the hard bulge behind the partly open zipper of his jeans. "You're not going to do anything about that."

"Why not?" she blurted out. It wasn't a good question, especially since she knew the answer. This wasn't the time for "one good turn deserves another."

"Because it won't stay just a kiss. I'll have you on that bed, and those little lace panties won't be much of a barrier to stopping us."

She was having a hard time remembering why that wouldn't be a good idea. Oh, yes. Because it would be a major distraction. And maybe make his injuries even worse. Blue wasn't in any shape for sex, even if her body was trying to convince her otherwise.

Rayanne shook her head. "Are you in pain?" And now her gaze shifted to his shoulder.

The corner of his mouth lifted. "Not that kind of pain." He finally did something about that flapping zipper. He closed it, not easily, but after some wincing, he got himself fully covered.

Peep show over.

Something she shouldn't have been so disappointed about. But she was.

"Why'd you do that?" she asked.

"I couldn't stop myself. I should apologize, I know, but an *I'm sorry* would be a lie. I'm not sorry, and we didn't get a chance to do that the night we were together."

No, that night had happened in a heated rush. The culmination of weeks of hot smoldering looks and lust-filled thoughts. Well, on her part, anyway. Judging from what'd just gone on between them, it'd been the same for Blue.

"You didn't tell me what you wanted to say," she reminded him. Best to move this conversation from well-placed kisses to something safer.

He stared at her, and his jaw muscles stirred. "It's personal…."

"You're married," she blurted out.

He laughed. It was smoky and thick and brought back some wonderful memories. "No. Not married."

Blue didn't get a chance to tell her what he'd wanted to say, because his phone rang. Rayanne groaned not just because of the interruption but because a call this time of morning couldn't be good news.

"It's Caleb," he said after fishing his phone from his jeans pocket.

Definitely not good news. Except that maybe Blue and she would finally learn what the heck was going on with Caleb.

"Where are you?" Blue demanded the moment he answered and put the call on speaker.

"Look outside. We need to talk."

Chapter Thirteen

"Don't go near that window," Blue warned Rayanne.

He put Caleb on hold and hurried back across the hall to grab the rest of his clothes.

And his gun.

A weapon wasn't something he'd ever thought he would need just to talk to his former boss, but Blue wasn't taking any chances. Especially since he'd already taken a huge one just with the morning *kissing* session with Rayanne.

Talk about the fastest way to lose focus, and this call from Caleb was a gigantic reminder that what Blue should be focusing on was unraveling this dangerous puzzle that could get Rayanne and the baby hurt.

While he kept Caleb on hold, Blue dressed and went to the window. Rayanne did, too, and she took her gun from the nightstand, but she stayed behind him when Blue eased back the curtains and opened the blinds.

Yeah, Caleb was there, all right.

He was standing on the road that led to the house and was surrounded by three armed ranch hands, exactly as they'd been for Wendell's and Woody's visits.

Caleb had his phone sandwiched between his ear and shoulder, and both hands were in the air. A black four-door sedan was parked about twenty yards behind him, and the passenger's-side door was open. He'd likely parked there and walked.

But why?

Maybe because the hands hadn't given him a choice, but if so, then had the hands allowed the man closer to the house? Blue made a mental note to instruct them not to do that again. Caleb, or any of their other suspects, could be dangerous.

"Tell the men to back down," Caleb insisted when Blue took the call off hold.

"Not until I get some answers, and they'd better be good answers, too. I know what's going on with you. By the way, Hale said to give you a message—either come in or give up your badge."

Caleb cursed, and even from a distance, Blue could see the frustration on the man's face. He could also see that Caleb was disheveled, his clothes wrinkled. Definitely not the polished agent who'd visited him in the hospital just two days earlier to move him to a "safer" location.

Or maybe move him so he could kill him.

"I was set up," Caleb immediately volunteered.

That would explain why his former boss was suddenly on the wrong side of the law.

Well, it would explain it if he was telling the truth. Of course, Blue knew a thing or two about being set up since someone had tried to do the same to him with that hit order on Rayanne.

"Tell me about those weapons that I confiscated earlier this year," Blue said to Caleb. "The ones that got back into the wrong hands."

"I will, but I'd rather not talk about that while standing out here in the open at gunpoint. I'm not armed. My gun's on the ground."

It was. Blue could see it next to one of the hands. But that didn't mean Caleb didn't have a backup weapon on him somewhere, and even if one of the hands had frisked him, Caleb knew how to hide a gun.

"We'll stick with this arrangement for now," Blue informed him. "I want to know about those guns and why Hale thinks you might be dirty."

Caleb looked up at the house, and his gaze rifled across the windows until he spotted Blue. The muscles in his face tightened. Blue knew pure anger when he saw it. But why the heck was that anger directed at him?

"Hale thinks I'm dirty," Caleb finally answered, "because like I said, somebody set me up."

Blue's next questions were simple. Maybe Caleb would have simple, believable answers. "Who and how?"

Caleb shook his head and gave a weary sigh. "I don't know who did it, but they used a hacker to get into the Justice Department files and plant info about me." He paused. "I thought it might be you."

Well, that explained the angry face. "Me? Why the hell would I do that?"

"To stop me from arresting you," Caleb snapped.

"You've got no cause to arrest me. And besides, I haven't exactly had time to set anyone up. Someone's been trying to kill me, remember?"

"Yes." That was all Caleb said for several moments. "I remember. Do you?"

Blue debated what exactly to tell him and decided to go with the truth to see how Caleb would react. "I remember *everything.*"

For just a moment he thought he saw a flash of concern in Caleb's eyes, and Blue wished he was closer so he could figure out what it meant.

"Good," Caleb answered, after that unexplained flash. "Then you know I'm not dirty."

"Sorry, the only thing I know is someone's trying to kidnap or kill Rayanne and me, and you're on a short list of suspects."

Now he got more than a flash of a reaction. Caleb cursed. "That's why I wanted this meeting. I put my neck on the line, maybe literally, and I did that so both of us could get answers. Rayanne, too. It's not a good idea for the baby and her to keep dodging bullets."

Rayanne groaned softly. Neither of them had told him about the pregnancy. Of course, now that Rayanne was showing, he could have noticed it or even heard it around town. Still, coming from Caleb, it sounded a little like a threat.

"Do you agree we need to end the danger and clear our names?" Caleb asked.

"My name's cleared." Blue hoped. "And how do you plan to end the danger?"

"For starters, this meeting. I didn't come alone." Caleb tipped his head to his car. "I thought it was time we all sat down and talked."

Oh, Blue didn't like the sound of that. And he really didn't like it when the back doors of Caleb's car opened.

And two men stepped out.

JUDGING FROM BLUE's mumbled profanity, Rayanne figured she wasn't going to be pleased with whomever Caleb had brought with him.

And she wasn't.

When Rayanne looked over Blue's shoulder, she spotted the unholy pair.

Wendell Braddock and Rex Gandy.

Coupled with Caleb, they represented all their suspects, gathered practically right at the doorstep. She hadn't wanted them in the same state with Blue, her and her family, much less this close. The only one missing was Woody, and with the way their luck had been running, he might just get out of that car, too, and confess that all four of them were working to kill Blue and her.

"Stay to the side of the window," Blue told her.

She did, but Rayanne positioned herself so she could still see the men. She wanted to watch their expressions in case they showed any signs of guilt. Of course, in Gandy's case, he was probably a sociopath and therefore too good at hiding what was really going on in his head.

"You shouldn't have brought them here," Blue said, his voice a low, dangerous warning and his attention nailed to Caleb.

"Trust me, I didn't want to do that," Caleb answered, adding yet another surprise to this meeting. He took his phone from his ear and pressed a button, no doubt to put it on speaker so the other men could hear the conversation. "They didn't give me much of a choice."

"I don't see you being held at gunpoint," Rayanne remarked. "That means you had a choice. Plus, Wendell accused you of being a dirty agent, so I have no idea why you'd let him get in your car."

"Wendell's accused people of a lot of things," Gandy volunteered, earning a glare from Wendell.

Strange bedfellows indeed.

"I was on my way out here," Caleb said, "and these two were stopped at the end of the road."

"And when the agent here said he was coming out to visit y'all," Gandy continued, "we decided to all come together and speak our piece at once."

"*You* decided," Caleb corrected. "And you threatened to call my boss and tell him where I was if I didn't cooperate. That's the only reason I let you in the car."

Interesting. Or maybe just a flat-out lie. Rayanne really hoped they weren't all in this together. If they were, then at best it was a tenuous partnership since there wasn't a shred of trust among them.

"You weren't afraid one of these stellar citizens would kill you?" Rayanne asked Caleb.

Caleb eyed them both like a pair of rattlesnakes. "Like I said, I didn't have much of a choice. I came because I need to do something, anything, to save my badge."

Rayanne didn't intend to feel any sympathy for him, at least not until Caleb was totally cleared as a suspect. She seriously doubted that would happen with this meeting.

"And Blue didn't give us a choice, either," Wendell insisted. "You're fueling an investigation and dragging us all into it."

"Because one of you likely hired that trio of killers who came to the ranch," Blue fired back.

Gandy rolled his eyes. "Always trying to get in your jabs, aren't you? And where have those jabs got you so far? Nowhere. You've never uncovered a single piece of evidence that could lead to my arrest."

"The day's not over," Blue mumbled.

Gandy chuckled. "Never liked your methods, Blue, but I gotta say, I always admired your persistence. Except in this case, persistence is causing a whole bunch of cops and such to pester me with questions. I want it stopped."

"Yeah," Wendell agreed. "And that's why we need to

sit down and talk. Caleb here wants to save his badge, but I've got a reputation to salvage. I do business with a lot of important people who wouldn't be happy to learn I'm the subject of an investigation, even if it's a witch hunt."

"It's not a witch hunt. And you're not getting in this house," Blue informed them. "Talking won't help...unless one of you plans to make a full confession."

"Nothing to confess to," Gandy said, and the other two mumbled some form of agreement. "Now, the person you should be looking at is your old pal Woody Janson. I've heard rumblings of some confiscated guns making it back into criminals' hands. Who better to do that than Woody?"

Blue and she just stared at Caleb.

"Blue thinks I'm responsible for that," Caleb volunteered. "And since I haven't had the opportunity to talk to Woody, I can't question him about it. But my money's on him, too."

"Yeah, especially since Woody survived the attack and all," Gandy tossed out there.

That got her attention.

Rayanne moved so she could get a better look at the man. Gandy was gloating, probably because he knew he'd just dropped a bombshell.

Even Caleb and Wendell seemed surprised by Gandy's comment. But it could be fake. She still wasn't sure they were here only to convince Blue to back off an investigation that could save their lives.

"How'd you know that Woody survived?" Rayanne asked.

Gandy lifted his shoulder as if the answer were obvious. "Word gets around fast when a former employee of questionable integrity turns up dead."

Blue and she exchanged a glance. "What would that have to do with Woody?" Blue asked, obviously not volunteering anything about Woody's visit.

"Plenty and you know it," Gandy fired back.

"Why don't you fill me in on the plenty that I know," Blue said, his voice dripping with sarcasm.

Gandy smiled as if he was getting a lot of pleasure from this. "A friend of a friend told me that a guy named Ace Butler turned up in a hospital down in Floresville. Ace had been shot, didn't make it through surgery, but his lawyer showed up and tried to pay the doc to stay quiet about it."

"His lawyer?" Blue questioned.

Gandy shrugged. "Or maybe it was just an acquaintance, but the point is—check out Ace and see if he's the clown who tried to kill you two days ago. And if he was, then I'm figuring he had a little run-in with Woody yesterday."

Blue and she had already seen the photo of the man by Woody's car and knew that he was the same idiot who'd come to the ranch to kill them. There'd also been the blood found near Woody's car, and it was still at the lab for DNA testing. If it proved to be a match to this Ace Butler, then it meant Gandy was telling the truth.

Or at least a partial truth.

But why?

Gandy wasn't the sort to volunteer anything unless it benefited him, and in this case, he was probably hoping that the info would put the blame for the attacks on someone other than himself.

"I'll call Seth," Rayanne whispered to Blue.

While Blue stayed at the window, she stepped to the other side of the room to make the call. She filled her brother in on what Gandy had just told them so he could check out the hospital in Floresville.

"How exactly did you come by all this information?" Blue asked Gandy when Rayanne finished her call.

"I'd rather not say," Gandy answered.

"I'd rather you did," Blue snapped.

Gandy's mouth stretched as if he was about to smile or stall them again.

But he didn't get a chance to do or say anything.

Caleb pivoted, his attention rifling behind them. "Get down!" he shouted.

Just as a shot rang out.

Chapter Fourteen

Blue cursed.

From the moment he'd seen Caleb outside the ranch house, he'd figured that trouble wouldn't be far behind. Too bad he'd been right.

He didn't have to tell Rayanne to get down. She ducked to the side of the window, her gun ready in her hand.

Blue positioned himself on the other side, and he put his phone on the windowsill to free up his hands in case he had to return fire or protect Rayanne.

It might come down to both.

"Who fired the shot?" Rayanne asked.

But Blue had to shake his head. From what he could see, it certainly wasn't any of their "guests" or the three armed ranch hands guarding them. All six men went to the ground, scrambling to take cover in front of and around Caleb's car. Caleb snatched up his gun from the ground, and both Wendell and Gandy drew theirs.

Right before the sound of another shot blasted through the air.

The bullet slammed into the ground right in the spot where one of the ranch hands had just been standing, and again, it hadn't come from any of the six.

It'd come from behind them.

From the woods.

"Who's shooting out there?" Blue heard Roy call out. He didn't sound close but rather on the first floor near the stairs.

"We're not sure yet. Who else is in the house?" Blue asked the man.

"Right now it's just me and the housekeeper, Mary. Colt's already left for work. Rosalie's still at the guest cottage. She was supposed to be leaving for the safe house in an hour or so."

Well, that wouldn't happen until this situation was under control.

"Call Rosalie now. Tell her to take cover," Rayanne insisted. "And Mary and you need to do the same," she added, but it wasn't with the same desperate urgency that she'd given to her twin sister.

Blue heard the fear in Rayanne's voice. Saw it more in her face and body language, and he cursed. She and the baby were right back in danger again, and so far he hadn't been able to do a darn thing to stop these attacks from happening. Now here they were right smack-dab in the middle of another one.

"You should call your brothers Tucker and Cooper," Blue reminded Rayanne. "They might not have left for work yet."

Even though they didn't live in the main house, they both had places nearby and both had children. Of course, if they were home, they'd likely already heard the shots and had taken cover, but Blue wanted to make sure.

She nodded, started making the calls, which seemed to help steady her nerves. Good. Anything to keep her stress level down and get her mind focused on something other than the bullets flying.

"Tucker and his family are still out of town," she relayed. "Cooper's at his place. He's staying put to watch his wife and son, but he's called for backup."

Good. Blue was afraid they might need it. There were a lot of possible targets at the ranch, and he didn't want anyone getting hurt. Or anyone being used to draw out Rayanne and him.

"What the hell's going on?" Caleb asked. "Is it one of the hired hands shooting at us?"

"No." Blue hoped not, anyway. "The shots are probably coming from the woods across the road."

A second later Blue was able to eliminate the *probably* when the next shot rang out.

Yeah, it'd definitely come from the woods.

Blue could pinpoint the general area of the shooter, but he still didn't see anyone. Of course, the guy could be perched behind or even up in some of the live-oak trees, which were still green and thick with leaves.

Another shot.

This one slammed into Caleb's car, pinging off the back bumper, and it was close enough to send the men scrambling again. Gandy reached up, opened the back door and dived inside. Wendell crawled beneath the car and out of sight. The ranch hands hurried to the sides of the porch.

Caleb threw open the driver's-side door, too, but he didn't get in. He used the door for cover and took aim at whoever was shooting at them from the woods. He didn't fire, probably because he knew the shooter was out of range of his Glock. Of course, he might have held fire for another reason.

Because he could be responsible for this entire mess.

Heck, any of the three men out there could be.

Maybe the culprit thought it would take suspicion off himself if he was in the center of an attack like this, but if so, Blue wasn't buying it. So far none of the shots had gone anywhere near their suspects, and that meant any one of them could have orchestrated this.

"Are you just gonna let this go on?" Wendell shouted. Even though the man was no longer near Caleb's phone, Blue heard him loud and clear.

Blue didn't get a chance to answer Wendell, because the next two bullets slammed through the window right next to Blue's head. Glass spewed over the room, and Blue practically threw himself over Rayanne to stop her from being cut or worse.

The pain shot through him, and it took Blue a moment to realize he hadn't been shot again. He'd just knocked his shoulder against the wall. He tried to muffle any sound of pain. Failed. And that brought Rayanne off the floor.

There was fire in her eyes, and she tried to bolt to the window, no doubt so she could try to shoot back.

Blue didn't let that happen.

No way would he allow her to put herself in harm's way, so Blue held on to her and wrestled her back to the floor. That didn't help the pain, but because of the hold he had on her, she wasn't in the line of fire when the next bullet came crashing into the room.

The shot slammed into the floor.

Outside, there were other shots. So many that Blue wondered if there was more than one shooter. Heck, maybe the moron behind this had sent an entire army after them.

"I'm hit!" Blue heard Caleb shout through the gaping holes in the window.

Blue scrambled closer, took a quick look outside and

saw Caleb. His former boss was still behind his car door. He had his gun in his right hand, which was also clamped around his left forearm.

And, yeah, there was blood.

"I'm calling Cooper to make sure he's sending an ambulance," Rayanne mumbled. Though both knew the medics wouldn't come into the middle of a shoot-out.

"I'm coming in," Roy warned them, and several seconds later the door flew open.

"Stay down!" Blue ordered, but Rayanne's father was already doing that.

Roy was practically on the floor, a rifle with a scope in one hand and binoculars in the other, and he crawled his way to them.

"Are you all right?" Roy asked, giving both of them glances.

"We weren't hit," Blue settled for saying, but he still had to take some deep breaths to force back the pain. Mercy, this was not a good time for his injury to rear its ugly head.

"How's Rosalie?" Rayanne asked her father.

"She's okay. I told her to go into the bathroom at the guesthouse and get in the shower. It's got a stone surface, and it's the safest place to be in case a bullet ricochets in her direction."

It was, and with the bullets flying, hopefully Rosalie would stay put until this was over. While he was hoping, Blue added that maybe this attack was just limited to the idiot firing at them.

"Maybe I can help," Roy said. "No need for Rayanne to be in the middle of this." His gaze dropped to her stomach. He didn't mention the baby. Didn't have to.

"I'm fine, *really,*" Rayanne snapped, but she didn't

stop Roy from taking up position at the side of the window where she'd just been.

Roy nodded, and if his daughter's curt assurance hurt his feelings, he sure didn't show it. Probably because he was focused on stopping the danger to her and his unborn grandchild.

"There's an old tree house in one of the live oaks out in those woods," Roy said, peering through the binoculars. "The boys built it there years ago, but if it's still sturdy enough, I'm betting that's where the shooter is."

Roy passed the binoculars to Blue. "Look at the tallest tree and see if you can make out anything."

Blue gave it a try, but he saw only the leaves, not a shooter. However, he did see remnants of a tree house. There was enough of it left that it would have made an excellent hiding place for a sniper attack.

"Since your shoulder's messed up, maybe you'd like for me to try to take him out," Roy offered. "This rifle's got a kick, and it won't feel so good when it hits those stitches."

The man was right about that, but Blue wasn't exactly eager to put Roy right in the middle of this fight. Except he already was since the shooter was firing into the house. Still firing outside, too. Several bullets smacked into Caleb's car and the ground around it.

Roy maneuvered closer to the window but had to quickly duck when another bullet slammed into the room. Obviously, this idiot had them in his sights, but maybe Blue could do something to distract him.

"Grab that chrome lamp," Blue told Rayanne, tipping his head to the nightstand. "Don't come any closer but slide it across the floor toward me."

It took her a moment to get it unplugged, and she used

her foot to get it to him. There was plenty of sunlight now, and he hoped the glare off the chrome would shield Roy from the shooter so Rayanne's father could get off a shot.

Blue looked at Roy, and when the man gave him a nod, Blue moved the lamp onto the windowsill. In the same motion, Roy took aim with the rifle.

And he fired.

The blast was heavy and thick, echoing through Blue's head, and Roy quickly followed it up with another shot. He'd been right about that kick. Both times the impact jerked back Roy's shoulder.

Blue looked through the binoculars and finally spotted something.

Or rather *someone*.

He caught just a glimpse of a man dressed in dark clothes scrambling down from what was left of that tree house.

"Shoot at him again," Blue told Roy.

Roy quickly took aim and sent two more bullets the guy's way. Blue couldn't tell if he hit him or not, but the gunman stopped firing.

It suddenly got so quiet that the only sound came from their heavy breathing and the cool morning air rushing through what was left of the window.

Then the sirens in the distance.

Backup. Maybe an ambulance, too.

Blue had another look with the binoculars, moving the sights from the tree house to the ground below it.

Oh, mercy.

There was the shooter, all right, and he was running. Getting away. And there was nothing Blue could do about it.

His lawman's instinct was to hurry out of the room

and go after him. To catch him and force him to tell them what was going on.

But doing that would mean leaving Rayanne in the house.

Yeah, her father was there, but if there was indeed an army out there ready to attack, Blue wanted to be close to her and not out in the woods chasing down a trigger-man. In fact, this could be yet another ruse to draw him out so that Rayanne would be an easier target.

"He got away?" Rayanne asked, obviously picking up on Blue's body language.

He nodded.

She mumbled some profanity and made a call to tell Cooper that it was safe enough for backup and the ambulance to come closer.

It didn't take long for the sirens to get louder, and Blue glanced down at the yard to check on everyone's locations. And to make sure none of the suspects were about to turn a gun in Blue's direction.

But Blue didn't like what he saw.

Or rather what he didn't see.

Caleb was no longer by the car door, and with the bullets flying, Blue had lost sight of him. There was no sign of Gandy or Wendell, either. Maybe they were still in hiding, but Blue didn't like the knot that tightened in his gut.

Something was wrong.

"Wait here with your dad," Blue told Rayanne.

She was shaking her head before he even got to his feet. "The shooter could come back, or he could still be waiting out there for you."

"I figure he's long gone." And likely regrouping for another attack. That was something Blue kept to himself, though Rayanne probably already knew. "Just please stay put."

Whether she would or not was anyone's guess, but he brushed a kiss on her forehead, hoping it would remind her that he had her best interest at heart. For good measure, he dropped a kiss on her stomach, too.

"You're playing dirty," she grumbled.

"Yeah," he readily admitted. And he kissed her on the mouth, too.

That probably earned him a glare, but Blue didn't take the time to verify it. With his gun still ready and gripped in his hand, he went down the stairs and peered out the sidelight windows.

He still couldn't see anything.

Where the heck were they?

However, when he eased open the front door, he spotted the ranch hands still on the sides of the house, and Cooper was making his way on foot toward them. Cooper's own house was just yards away, and another of the hands, Arlene, was standing guard on his front porch. Probably because Cooper's family was still inside.

"Is everyone okay?" Cooper called out to him.

Blue nodded. "Your dad's upstairs with Rayanne."

Cooper lifted his eyebrow. He didn't say anything, but the surprise was in his eyes, verifying what Blue had already guessed. That Rayanne and her father didn't interact much.

Well, until this morning.

Roy had likely saved their lives. That would create an interaction whether Rayanne liked it or not.

"You look like crap," Cooper said to him. "Are you in pain?"

"Some," Blue admitted. "Not enough to stop me from helping you catch this jerk."

"I'd rather you help by staying put. I don't want anyone getting upstairs to Dad. Or Rayanne," Cooper added, and he shot a glance at the car.

Where he'd last seen their three suspects.

Blue doubted any of them would bolt toward the house, but it wasn't a risk he was willing to take. Rayanne and the baby had already been through enough today, and one of the men could be a killer.

The sirens stopped when an ambulance pulled into the drive. Colt was right behind them in a cruiser. The medics stayed put, but Colt got out, and along with Cooper, they started to converge on Caleb's car.

"Is everyone all right?" Cooper shouted.

If anyone answered, Blue wasn't able to hear them. He could only watch as Cooper and Colt made it to the car. Their guns drawn. Their attention nailed to the interior of the vehicle, probably in case one of their suspects came out shooting.

Colt went to the left side of the car, Cooper the right. Both pivoted, aiming their guns.

And Cooper cursed. He looked up, his gaze meeting Blue's. "He's been shot."

"Who? Caleb?" Blue asked.

Cooper shook his head. "Rex Gandy. And from the looks of it, he's dead."

Chapter Fifteen

Rayanne was afraid if she stood up from the kitchen table, her legs would give way and she'd fall. Hardly what she wanted, considering she felt wimpy enough without doing something to prove it.

This pregnancy had changed everything.

And Blue had, too.

Six months ago she would have taken on that shooter and not batted an eye. Well, she was doing more than eye batting now. It sickened her to think of how close Blue, she and the baby had come to dying again. It sickened her even more to know that the threat likely hadn't been stopped.

Not even with Gandy's death.

Because they still didn't know how the man had died. Or why. Until they learned that, the threat was still just as real and fresh as it had been two days ago when her life had turned on a dime.

"You need to eat," Blue prompted her, pulling his attention from his latest phone call so he could slide the sandwich and glass of milk closer to her.

Rayanne picked up the sandwich, only because Blue, Rosalie and Roy were all giving her concerned looks.

Heck, even Colt seemed worried about her. A first.

Well, a first since she'd returned to the ranch. Once, a million years ago, Colt and she had been close.

They were all in the massive kitchen at the ranch. All of them, except her, contributing in some way to the investigation and crime-scene cleanup. Rosalie had checked Blue's bandage several times and was now helping Mary make sandwiches for everyone. Colt and Blue were making nonstop calls. Roy was going over instructions with Arlene on how to beef up security.

Cooper was no doubt making calls back at his own place, where he could better watch his wife and son. Rayanne couldn't blame him. The latest attack had literally been too close to home, and like Roy, he would need to make his own security arrangements.

"I'm okay," Rayanne insisted when Blue continued to stare at her.

She took a large exaggerated bite from the ham-and-cheese sandwich. It tasted like dust. Probably because her mouth was bone-dry and the last thing her stomach wanted her to do was put food in it. Her mind was numb from the adrenaline that'd come and gone, leaving her exhausted.

Blue finished his call with the Floresville P.D., scrubbed his hand over his face and looked at her again. "After you eat, you should get some rest."

She would have bet the balance of her checking account that he was going to say that. "Ditto. I'm not the one healing from a gunshot wound and a concussion. Now, what did you learn about Ace Butler? Did he really die in the Floresville hospital or not?"

"He died, all right. His prints were in the system, and they're a match to the body. There's no surveillance footage of the person who tried to bribe the doctor to keep it quiet, but the cops are interviewing people who might have seen him."

Rayanne had to fight through the fatigue to process that. "So Gandy was telling the truth."

Interesting. Gandy was dead, so he couldn't tell them why he'd doled out that info to them. Or why he'd given them the photo and audio clip. Rayanne had figured it was so it would make him seem innocent, and in light of his death, maybe he *was* innocent.

About this, anyway.

Now the question was, had Gandy's death been by accident or by design? It might be a while before the CSIs could give them an answer to that since Rayanne wasn't even sure they'd be able to recover the bullet from Gandy's head. Maybe fired by the sniper who'd been in the woods.

Or maybe fired by someone much closer to him.

Wendell, Caleb or even Woody.

"Caleb claims he's fine," Blue went on. Obviously, he'd learned that from his call to the Sweetwater Springs hospital, the one he had made immediately before phoning Floresville.

"'Claims he's fine,'" she repeated, studying Blue's expression while she finished off her glass of milk. "Is that ATF code for something?"

"Maybe." Blue shook his head. "Caleb's only slightly injured. In fact, the doc said it was superficial."

Sweet heaven. "So it could have been self-inflicted," Rayanne concluded. "If so, Caleb could have done that to throw suspicion off himself for the attack. He could have not only set up the attack, he could also have been the one to kill Gandy."

Blue lifted his shoulder, winced a little. That brought

Rayanne to her feet, and thankfully, she didn't wobble too much. Well, it was still enough for Blue to catch on to her arm to steady her, but she caught on to him, too.

"We're a pair," she mumbled.

"A pair who should be getting some rest," Rosalie added. "I'm not speaking as a sister now but as a nurse. Both of you are recovering from a trauma, and staying on your feet will only prolong that."

Rayanne couldn't deny that Blue could do with some rest, but she also knew how mule-headed he'd be about this. So she turned the tables on him and played the baby card. She ran her hand over her belly and gave her sister a nod.

Blue noticed the belly rub right away, and it caused a new level of alarm on his face. That got him moving, and with his arm hooked around her waist, they headed for the stairs.

"I know the drill," Rayanne said on the way up to her room. "You'll tuck me in, try to soothe my nerves and then make an excuse to come back down and work. But just know that I'm not coming up the stairs for me or the baby. We're fine. I'm doing this for you, and that means you're getting some rest."

His eyebrow slid up. "Together?"

Her eyebrow slid up, too, and she remembered the scalding-hot kissing session they'd had that morning. "Together we won't get any rest," she reminded him.

Blue chuckled, brushed a kiss on her forehead and maneuvered her into her room. "We won't if we're apart. I know the drill. You'll stew about this and wrongfully blame yourself for the danger."

"It won't be wrongful," Rayanne mumbled. "I should have figured out a way to stop the attacks. Heck, I should just leave, and at least that way, Rosalie might not be in danger—"

Blue huffed. That was the only warning before he slid his hand around the back of her neck, dragged her closer and kissed her. All in all, it was a darn effective way to shut her up, but it didn't stop the truth from being the truth.

Nor did it stop the heat from trickling through her body.

A simple kiss from Blue could do that, but it was because there was no such thing as a simple kiss from Blue. His mouth and every other part of him could cause her to melt with just a single touch. No other man had ever had that effect on her, and she prayed no other ever would.

"You have a bad habit of kissing me at the worst possible time," she mumbled against his mouth.

He eased back and met her eye to eye. "Yeah, it is a bad time." Blue glanced at the bed. Not in a let's-land-there-now kind of way. But he was no doubt thinking about how to make sure she got that rest.

She was thinking about that. And a lot of other things. Every one of those other things included Blue.

Rayanne shook her head. Opened her mouth. And she realized that what she said—or didn't say—in the next couple of seconds could change everything.

It could bring Blue closer to her.

Or keep him at bay.

The question was, what did she want to do?

She had a quick debate with her body. It didn't give her much of an argument, though. *Figures.* Neither did her heart.

And that created a huge problem for her.

After all the pain, was she willing to take that kind of a risk again?

She was still thinking about that when Blue's mouth came back to hers for another of those white-hot kisses. Then she quit thinking and debating altogether. She did something that she rarely did.

She went with her heart.

Rayanne pulled him to her and kissed him right back.

BLUE KNEW EXACTLY what Rayanne's kiss meant.

And it didn't include something she truly needed—rest.

But he was already well past the logic point here, and besides, this wasn't going to stop no matter what he said or did. There were a lot of things between Rayanne and him, and they weren't based on logic.

Blue could feel her raw need in that kiss. In the way her hand clutched him, pulling him closer and closer. Until they were plastered against each other. Since he knew this would lead them straight to the bed, he reached behind him and locked the door. If he was going to do this, then he didn't want anyone walking in on them.

"Your shoulder," Rayanne reminded him when he took those kisses to her neck.

Yeah, he was probably hurting, but his mind was shutting that out at the possibility of having Rayanne beneath him in that bed. But then he thought of another obstacle that could put this burning heat on pause.

"The pregnancy?" he said.

She huffed, pulled him right back to her. "Pregnant women can and do have sex."

Good. Because that was about the only red light that would have stopped this. That and Rayanne saying no, and it was clear from the way her grip moved from his waist to his butt that she didn't have any plans to say no.

She went after his shirt, fumbling with the buttons until she finally got it open, and her mouth landed against his chest.

Instant heat.

Not that he needed more, but Blue did take a moment to savor the feel of her lips and tongue on his bare skin. Unfortunately, that savoring turned up the urgency a significant notch, and he started to fumble with her clothes. Getting her naked became his top priority.

Her shirt was easy. He pulled it over her head and sent it sailing to the floor. Her bra quickly followed, and Blue got to return the favor of sampling Rayanne's breasts. They were full, perfect and, judging from the needy moan she made, very sensitive.

She plowed her fingers into his hair, pulling his mouth even closer so he could kiss her the way that he wanted. He went lower. To her stomach. But Rayanne pulled him back up toward her mouth.

"If those kisses go lower, we know what'll happen," she said. "This time, I want you with me."

Heck, no way could he turn down that offer. He was hard as granite, and he needed her in the worst kind of way.

She left his shirt and vest on but tackled his zipper next. No kisses. Rayanne just stared at him as the zipper went down, and Blue was able to see the fiery need in her cool gray eyes. He was sure his eyes weren't so cool when she slid her hand inside his boxers and touched him.

Oh, man.

The grunt he made sounded like pain. It wasn't.

Well, not regular pain, anyway.

This was pure pleasure.

And thankfully, Rayanne could tell the difference, because she kept touching him until Blue had no choice but to do something about the powder keg of heat that her touching had created.

Blue unzipped her jeans, which were already low on her hips to make room for her pregnant belly. He shimmied them off her, her lacy panties, too, kissing her along the way, until Rayanne obviously met her own heat threshold.

"Let's do this now," she insisted, the urgency clear in her voice.

He turned, easing her onto the bed while Rayanne continued to work on his jeans. He helped by taking off his boots and shoulder holster, and in the back of his mind, Blue was already working out the logistics of this. He didn't want to crush her and the baby with his weight, and judging from the way she was eyeing the bandage on his shoulder, she didn't want to hurt him.

Blue settled it by pulling her onto his lap. His back landed against the headboard, and Rayanne landed against him.

In all the right places.

With everything aligned just right.

Even though he had all his memories of the other time they were together, Blue still felt the jolt of surprise when he sank into her. She felt even better than he'd remembered, and what he'd remembered had been pretty darn good.

This was perfect. And mind-blowing.

Blue caught on to her hips to get her moving. Not that he had to prompt her much. Rayanne met him, pushing against him harder and faster as he pushed into her.

Still no kisses.

Just that intense eye contact that made this seem even more intimate than it already was.

"I can't last long," she said, like an apology.

But no apology was needed. This couldn't last long. The heat and the intensity just kept driving them.

Harder, faster, deeper.

Rayanne leaned in, positioning her hips, until he felt her body give way. Until he felt her slide right over the edge.

She made a sound, a silky moan of pleasure, but he saw the other emotion in her eyes. The wish that this didn't have to end so soon. Blue had the same wish, but he could only hope this wouldn't be the last time he had her like this.

Now she kissed him. Her mouth closing in over his. And that was all Blue needed to let himself slide right over that edge with her.

Chapter Sixteen

With her body slack from the climax, Rayanne collapsed against Blue, careful not to hurt his shoulder. Even though he didn't seem to be feeling any pain, she didn't want to take the risk of making his injury worse.

Especially since she'd just done that to their situation.

This would complicate things and therefore make things worse. No doubt about it. But she hadn't been able to resist Blue five months ago, and she hadn't had any luck resisting him now. Under normal circumstances, that wouldn't have been such a bad thing, but this was far from normal.

She eased off his lap, dropping onto her back, only to remember she wasn't exactly in buck-naked shape. Rayanne reached to pull the covers over her, but Blue stopped her.

"I'm guessing you're not trying to cover up because you're cold," he mumbled, then lowered his head and kissed her belly. Just like that, it rebuilt the heat that she thought had been quenched.

For at least an hour or two, anyway.

"Not cold," she agreed. "But not sure I feel comfortable with my body being sprawled out in front of you."

"Well, you should. You look amazing." He kissed her

again and gave her one of those melting looks, and Rayanne had to fight not to be seduced all over again.

She pulled the quilt over her and sat up, hoping she wouldn't feel so, well, vulnerable, but that feeling apparently didn't have anything to do with nudity. She still felt it when she looked at Blue.

Who was the true definition of looking amazing.

Rayanne sighed. "It'd be so much easier if you were ugly or if I just hated you."

He chuckled, pulled her back to him so that she was in the crook of his good arm. "It'd be so much easier if we were in love."

She frowned, stared up at him.

"You know what I mean," he went on. "You don't trust people because of your father's abandonment, and I don't love because I don't think I deserve it."

That got her attention. "What do you mean?"

He ran his fingers over the small pinholes on his vest. "When my father was alive, he rarely took off this vest. Even when it needed to be cleaned, he'd wait for it at the dry cleaner's. He called it his good-luck charm."

"So do you," she said.

Blue nodded. "I was always begging him to let me wear it to school to show everyone the badge, and one day he gave in." He paused, swallowed hard. "And that's the day that two methheads gunned him down."

Rayanne shook her head. It crushed her heart to think of the pain Blue must have gone through, even if it had happened all those years ago.

"You do know that wasn't your fault and the vest had nothing to do with it?" she asked.

"I know it here." He tapped his head. "Not so much here, though." Blue tapped his heart.

"Kid logic doesn't have to make sense," he added when her mouth tightened a little. "You keep me at a distance because of your father, but I do the same thing. I'm afraid if I care that much for someone again, then... Well, you get what I mean."

Every word.

But where did that leave them? Unable to trust or risk a commitment.

Where did it leave their baby?

"We'll work it all out," he said as if reading her mind, and dropped another kiss on her mouth just as the landline phone on her nightstand beeped.

Since the beep meant someone in the house was trying to reach her, Rayanne slid over a very naked Blue to answer it.

"It's me," Rosalie said. "Woody Janson called here asking to speak to Blue. I've got him on hold for now, but do you want me to put the call through to your room?"

Obviously, Blue was still close enough to hear, because he answered, "Yes," and took the phone. Rayanne moved right next to him so she could hear what Woody had to say.

"Start explaining," Blue snapped the moment Woody came on the line. "What happened to you after you left the ranch, and why are you calling on this line?"

"Wasn't sure your cell was safe. I still haven't been able to prove Caleb's innocent, and I didn't want to take the risk that he was monitoring your phone with a tap. I figured you wouldn't have let him in the house to do the same to the landlines."

No, they hadn't let Caleb inside. Woody, either. Yet the attacks had still happened.

"Did you kill Ace Butler?" Blue came right out and asked.

"Yeah. He took a shot at me. I returned fire, and I hit him. He escaped in a car he had parked nearby. If what I just found out is true, Ace made his way to the hospital where he died."

"He did," Blue verified. "Gandy's dead, too."

"I heard. I hope you don't think I'm all torn up about either Ace's or Gandy's death. They were scum."

"They were," Blue readily admitted, "but what I want to know is did you have anything to do with the attack that left Gandy dead? Because it could have left Rayanne, her family, the ranch hands and me dead, too."

"No, of course not. I wasn't responsible for that." Woody paused, huffed. "Look, I know I'm not exactly high on the list of people you trust, but I want the same thing that you do. My name completely cleared and the person behind these attacks stopped."

Judging from Blue's narrowed eyes, he had some doubts about Woody's innocence. So did she.

"I found out something else," Woody went on a moment later. "I've spent the last half hour trying to verify it, but no luck so far. Still, I thought you'd want to know what I heard from criminal informants."

"I'm listening," Blue assured him.

"I think someone might try to set an explosive device in or near the county jail."

Oh, mercy. Rayanne's heart skipped a beat. "My mother," she managed to say. She scrambled out of the bed, located her jeans on the floor and took out her phone.

"I want details," Blue demanded from Woody.

"Sorry, I don't have them, but I've been monitoring some taps I have in place on two criminal informants, and they were definitely discussing a bomb. I can't verify if they were doing that to find out if I was listening. In other words, a test. Or if the threat's real."

Rayanne's hands were shaking so hard that it took her several tries to press Seth's number, and her brother answered on the first ring.

"Is Mom all right?" Rayanne immediately asked. Blue ended his call with Woody and hurried to her side. "Is there really a bomb threat at the county jail?"

"I don't want you to panic," Seth answered.

Which, of course, made her want to do just that. "There's really a bomb?"

"Maybe. Someone called in a bomb threat, and Mom and the other nine prisoners are being moved to another part of the building. The bomb squad's on the way."

She could tell Seth was trying to keep his voice calm. For her sake, no doubt. But Rayanne could also hear the fear and the concern.

"I don't trust Sheriff Aiden Braddock," Rayanne said. "If something goes wrong, I figure our mother is the last person he'd bother to protect."

Especially since Jewell was charged with murdering the sheriff's father.

"I'm down in Floresville," Seth explained. "I was trying to get a lead on the person who tried to bribe the doctor. I'm heading to Clay Ridge right now."

Rayanne shook her head. "It'll take nearly two hours for you to get there. That's not soon enough if this is some kind of setup to hurt Mom."

"No," Seth said. "You're not going. Is Blue there?"

"I'm here," Blue verified.

"Even if you have to hog-tie her, don't let her go. I'm calling now to find some agents that I trust to work this." And with that, Seth hung up.

Rayanne didn't waste a second getting to her feet, and she started to get dressed. Blue did, too, but he moved right in front of her, forcing eye contact.

"You heard what your brother said," Blue reminded her. "And I agree. You're not going to that jail."

Everything inside was spinning so fast that it was hard to think. "I have to do something."

"Yeah. You have to wait here. Seth will have a team in place soon."

Maybe not soon enough. "This could be a way of getting back at me. At us," she corrected. "If so, Wendell could be behind it."

Blue nodded, continued to dress. "And it could be a ruse to get you to panic. If it is, Caleb or Woody could be behind it. Both of them have access to criminal informants who could have faked this kind of info."

He was right, and Rayanne forced herself to consider that. Still…

"Finish dressing," Blue said. "Then we'll go downstairs and wait for some news."

Despite Seth's and Blue's orders for her to stay put, Rayanne was still debating what to do when Blue brushed his hand over her stomach. It was one of those reminders that she didn't necessarily want.

But needed.

The deputy sheriff in her wanted to go racing to the jail, but the baby had to come first.

Blue leaned in, kissed her. "We'll talk about that later." He tipped his head to the heap of rumpled covers on the bed.

Yes, the heat between them and their apparent inability to fall in love. However, Rayanne was pretty sure that for her, it was no longer an inability.

She was falling in love with Blue—again.

That made her either stupid…human…or both. She was still debating that, too, when there was a knock at the door, and the knob rattled.

"Rayanne?" Rosalie called out.

"She probably heard about the bomb threat," Blue mumbled, and he opened the door.

Rayanne got ready to give Rosalie the same reassurance that Blue and Seth had just given her. But after one look at her sister's face, Rayanne knew a mere reassurance wasn't going to help. There were tears spilling down Rosalie's cheeks.

"The deputy from Clay Ridge just called," Rosalie said, her words rushing together. "A bomb went off at the jail." She paused, swallowed hard. "Mom's been hurt."

BLUE CURSED. NOT JUST because Jewell had been injured but because he knew there was nothing that could stop Rayanne from going to her.

Still, he tried.

"Wait." He caught on to her and turned back to Rosalie. "How bad are her injuries?"

Rosalie shook her head. "The deputy couldn't say. There's an ambulance on the way to take her and the rest of the wounded inmates to the hospital in Clay Ridge."

"I have to see her," Rayanne said, shaking off Blue's grip. She grabbed her holster and gun from the dresser.

Blue darted out into the hall, cutting her off before she could get far. "You should wait until I've had a chance to make some calls."

"You can do that on the drive over." Rayanne looked up at him, and he saw the tears shimmering in her eyes. "What would you do if it was your father who was hurt? And let's take that one step further. What if your father was hurt, and the people around him hated him enough to let him die?"

Oh, man. He'd been afraid she was going to toss that at him. Because it was a darn good argument. If his dad had been hurt, nothing would have stopped him from going.

That meant since he couldn't talk her out of going to Clay Ridge, Blue had to do anything and everything to keep Rayanne safe.

"Who's here at the ranch?" Blue asked Rosalie, following both women down the stairs.

"Roy and the hands, of course. Colt had to go back into town to work."

Not good. The ranch hands had done well so far, but Blue wanted law enforcement for this. "Call Cooper and see if he can arrange for someone to escort Rayanne and me to the hospital so she can see her mother."

Rosalie gave a shaky nod and made the call while they hurried to the kitchen. Roy was there, buckling up a waist holster. Obviously, he was aware that the explosion and Jewell's injuries could be some kind of trap to draw them out into the open.

"I'm going with you," the man insisted.

"Me, too," Rosalie added the moment she finished her call. "Cooper said Colt and Reed are on their way over to escort us to the hospital."

"We can wait for them at the end of the road," Rayanne mumbled. "And they'd better hurry."

Again, Blue had to step in front of Rayanne to stop

her from bolting out the door. "I need to make sure it's safe enough to go out there."

"I'll do that," Roy insisted.

Damn. He was just as stubborn as his daughter. Blue didn't get a chance to argue with the man, because his phone rang, and he saw Seth's name on the screen.

"I'm guessing all of you are headed to Clay Ridge," Seth said the moment Blue answered.

"Even hog-tying won't stop them."

Seth mumbled some profanity. "I'll see what I can do about getting you some help. It's a forty-five-minute drive, and a lot of bad things can happen along the way." He paused. "Is Rayanne listening?"

"No." And Blue moved slightly away from her because he figured this was something Seth didn't want her to hear.

"I just found out from someone in the ambulance that Mom's injuries could be pretty bad," Seth explained.

"Oh, God," Rayanne said, and Blue knew then that she'd heard her brother after all. She snatched the phone from Blue and put it on speaker.

"How bad?" Rayanne demanded.

It took several seconds for Seth to answer. "She's unconscious, has lost plenty of blood and will likely need surgery. That doesn't mean I want you going off—"

That got Rayanne heading out the door again. She punched the end-call button and tossed him his phone, and all Blue could do was draw his gun to help Roy make sure the yard was clear.

Rayanne opened the door of an SUV that was parked close to the house and would have gotten behind the wheel if Roy hadn't stopped her. "I'll drive," her father insisted. "That way, the two of you can keep watch."

"Me, too," Rosalie said, and that was when Blue realized she'd also grabbed a gun.

"I guess it won't do any good to say just how bad an idea this is," Blue grumbled.

Nope.

No good whatsoever.

The best Blue could do was maneuver Rayanne and Rosalie into the backseat so he could ride shotgun. Rayanne got behind Blue. Rosalie behind her father.

"Both of you stay down," Blue warned them.

Whether they would was anyone's guess, but at least Rosalie slid lower as Roy took off.

"It'll take Colt and Reed at least another ten minutes to get out here," Roy said to no one in particular.

"Drive slow," Blue advised him.

The sooner they met up with the deputies, the better, and Blue wanted to minimize their time on the road without the added protection. Since it was already dark, their attacker might be able to hide somewhere along the way.

"I'll call the Clay Ridge hospital," Rosalie volunteered, "and see if there's an update."

Blue needed to start his own calls. The big one had already been made—Colt and Reed were on the way—but he wanted to know the location of their three suspects. And also how someone had managed to set off a bomb in the county jail. He took out his phone to get started just as Roy brought the SUV to a stop at the end of the road.

"We'll wait for Reed and Colt," Roy said. "As soon as they show, we'll all head out together."

Rayanne opened her mouth, no doubt to protest that, but Roy shot her a look that only a father could have managed. Yeah, Rayanne was hardheaded but Roy made it clear that arguing wasn't going to make him budge.

Blue kept his gun drawn, and he kept watch while he made the first call to Agent Hale at the ATF. The county sheriff had likely already arranged for a CSI team, but Blue wanted to get some federal agents on the scene.

"Headlights," Roy pointed out, and he tipped his head to the vehicle approaching.

"I'll make sure it's Colt and Reed," Rayanne said, taking out her phone again. "And if it is, hit the gas and let's get out of here."

Blue's call to Hale went to voice mail, and he put away his phone, his attention planted on those headlights. He wouldn't breathe easier until he had confirmation from Rayanne that it was backup and not someone else ready to attack them.

"It's them," Rayanne relayed several moments later.

Roy pulled out onto the main road, Colt and Reed right behind them, and as Rayanne had said, her father hit the accelerator.

Just as a fireball exploded right in front of them.

Chapter Seventeen

The blast shook the entire SUV, and it took Rayanne a moment to realize what had happened.

Someone had detonated a bomb.

Roy slammed on the brakes, and despite the fact all of them were wearing seat belts, the jolt threw them forward. She heard Blue make a sharp sound of pain, no doubt because the seat belt had caught his shoulder.

"Back up," Blue practically shouted to Roy. "Get us out of here."

Rayanne saw that Colt was already doing that. His tires screamed against the asphalt, and the cruiser sped backward, giving them enough distance for Roy to do the same.

But he didn't get far.

The second blast came at them like a thunderbolt, tearing through the road in the meager space between the cruiser and their SUV. Blue cursed, reached over the seat and pushed Rosalie and her down.

Rayanne had already drawn her gun, but she got it ready in case she had a chance to fire and stop this monster from setting off another explosive.

Blue had been right. The bombing at the jail had likely been designed to draw them out into the open. And it'd worked. But her mother was hurt. Maybe dying. There was no way she could have stayed put and not gone to the hospital.

Now that decision might cost all of them their lives.

Blue's phone rang, and he hit the speaker button. "Are you all right?" she heard Colt ask.

Blue glanced at each of them. "I think so. You see anyone, anything?"

"Nothing.... Wait, maybe something. Look to the driver's side of the SUV."

Rayanne lifted her head to do just that, but all she could see was a cloud of milky-gray smoke caused by the bombs. She knew there were woods on that side of the road. There were pastures on the side they were on. It would make sense that if their attacker wanted to hide, he would use the woods.

"I don't see anyone," Blue told Colt. "How many and how close?"

"I only got a glimpse of one man, and he ducked behind the trees."

If it was the same guy who'd fired at the house earlier, then he could be carrying a rifle and use it to rip the SUV apart with bullets.

That kicked up her heartbeat a significant notch. They had to do something to get out of there alive.

"How bad's the road?" Roy asked. "Can I drive around the damage?"

"Probably not," Colt answered.

Rayanne groaned. If they couldn't move, then it meant they were trapped just waiting for the next attack. And she figured it wouldn't take long for that next attack to come.

"I'm going to try to use the shoulder to turn around

and get us out of here," Roy said. "You keep an eye on the guy you spotted."

"Will do," Colt assured him.

Roy put the SUV in gear, and while Blue and Rayanne kept watch, he maneuvered the vehicle off the asphalt and onto the narrow dirt shoulder. Thankfully, there'd been no recent rains, or both the shoulder and the ditch would have been a bog. Roy was able to gain enough traction to make some progress in getting them turned around.

"Why hasn't he finished us off?" Blue mumbled.

That caused the skin to crawl on the back of her neck, and it was a question she should have already asked herself. For nearly a minute, their attacker had had them at a standstill, and it would have been the perfect time to kill them. Probably Reed and Colt, too, since they would have tried to stop it.

So why were they all still alive?

"This is a kidnapping," Rayanne said.

Blue nodded.

Just as there was a plinging sound as something hit the front of the SUV. A split second later, there was another one.

"Tear gas," Blue and she said in unison.

They didn't have to wait long for confirmation of that. The wispy gas immediately started to spew from the canisters. Their windows were all closed, but the gas seeped through, and they all started to cough.

"He wants us out of the SUV so he can take us at gunpoint," Blue told Roy.

Yes, and then do heaven-knew-what to them.

If it was Caleb or Woody behind this, then they might want to use Blue and her as pawns in whatever dirty dealings they were into. Or maybe they would use her to force

Blue into helping them cover up the plot that landed those confiscated weapons back into the hands of criminals.

And if it was Wendell, then they could be pawns for a different reason.

To punish her mother.

Of course, this could be Gandy's men, carrying out his wishes from beyond the grave. It didn't matter that Gandy was already dead. He could have set this into motion, knowing that he would finally get his revenge against Blue for his investigation.

Despite the fact he was coughing and wheezing as much as the rest of them, Roy kept maneuvering the SUV. He didn't panic and gun the engine; he inched forward, then back, until he had enough room to get the vehicle around the crater in the road and onto the shoulder.

He hit the accelerator.

"I can't see," Roy said through his coughs.

Neither could Rayanne. The tear gas was burning like fire in her eyes, and she was coughing so hard that she couldn't catch her breath. She prayed this wouldn't do anything to harm the baby.

"Stay on the shoulder as long as you can," Colt warned him. "The road might not be stable."

Roy did. The SUV bobbed over the uneven surface of the grass-and-dirt shoulder, and thanks to the night breeze clearing away some of the smoke, Rayanne got just a glimpse of the massive hole in the road. If Roy had gone into that, they would have been stuck again.

"Keep moving," Colt instructed. "Let's get back to the ranch so we can regroup."

And she could check on her mother. Even now, that was pressing as hard on her as this nightmarish situation. If this monster had managed to kill her mother, then whoever he was, he would pay.

Roy finally maneuvered around the massive hole, and Rayanne spotted Colt's cruiser. For the first time since this ordeal had started, she thought maybe they might finally make it out of there.

But she was wrong.

A bullet crashed into the SUV.

"GET DOWN!" BLUE SHOUTED, mainly to Rayanne.

As a deputy, she no doubt had the instinct to try to return fire, but he didn't want her taking a bullet while trying to protect the rest of them.

Roy hit the gas, but another bullet ripped through the windshield and shattered the safety glass. Mixed with the lingering smoke from the explosives and the tear gas, it made it nearly impossible to see.

Worse, the bullets just kept coming.

Not inside the vehicle, though. Now that the windshield was gone, the shooter was aiming at the tires.

Trying to stop them.

Worse, there wasn't just one shooter. There were likely several of them, and they seemed to be stretched out in the woods, firing nonstop as Roy drove past them. If so, then this was a well-orchestrated attack by someone who was desperate to get their hands on Rayanne and him.

"Get off the road," Blue instructed Roy. "Go through the fence and into the pasture."

Of course, there were no guarantees gunmen weren't waiting there, too, but at least the pasture was wide-open, and Blue had a chance of picking off one of these idiots if they came out of cover.

Blue risked glancing back at Rayanne to make sure she was okay.

She wasn't.

Both she and her sister were pale and shaking, but at least they were alive and unharmed. And thank God, they were actually staying down on the seat as he'd told them to do.

It crushed his heart to think of what this was doing to her and the baby. To Rosalie and Roy, too. He was an agent, had been in the middle of gunfire before, and while that never would be routine, the others had to be terrified.

Heck, Blue was, too.

And later he'd kick himself for allowing things to get this far. If there was a later, that is.

"Hold on," Roy said.

Rayanne's father gave the steering wheel a sharp turn to the left and accelerated even more so they'd clear the ditch. It worked, but it wasn't a smooth landing.

Far from it.

The SUV bolted through the wooden fence and sent a spray of debris right at them and tearing through what was left of the windshield. A thick piece of wood smacked against Blue's arm, and he could have sworn he saw stars. He forced aside the pain, not easy to do, and got ready for another attack.

He didn't have to wait long.

The bullets started again. Nonstop. All of them tearing into the lower part of the SUV. There wouldn't be much of the tires left by now, but he hoped it was enough to get them the heck out of there.

Roy hit the gas again, but the SUV didn't move. The flat tires just spun around in the soft ground. They were stuck. *Again*. Sitting ducks with their attackers closing in on them.

"Colt, I can't move," Roy shouted toward the phone, though he kept trying to get the SUV out of the bog. "Anything you can do?"

"It's too risky for you to come out on the road to get to me. I'm coming closer," Blue heard Colt answer over the thick blasts. "The cruiser's bullet resistant, so I'm going to try and get behind you and push your vehicle to get it moving."

That would put Rayanne's brother and Reed in the direct path of those bullets. Still, it might save Rayanne and the baby from being hit, and right now Blue had to put their safety above all others'. However, he did have to wonder how Roy felt about his youngest son taking the brunt of the danger on his shoulders.

"If I get stuck, too," Colt added, "Cooper and some of the ranch hands are on the way out here. Just hold your positions until we can fight off these idiots."

Blue hoped they wouldn't have to fight much longer. Each bullet fired was a risk that one of them could get hurt or killed.

It didn't take long for Colt to come crashing through the fence. The shots kept coming, but as he'd said he would do, Colt turned the cruiser, lining up the front end of it with the back bumper of the SUV. Blue heard Colt rev his engine and could feel the cruiser pushing against the SUV.

But nothing happened.

Colt tried again. And again. Still nothing.

"Hang on," Colt warned them a split second before he hit his accelerator. The cruiser bashed into them.

The jolt caused Blue's pain to spike again, but it would

have been well worth it if it'd worked. It hadn't. Roy cursed when the SUV still didn't budge.

"I'll pull up beside you," Colt finally said. "I want all of you to climb into the cruiser."

Blue didn't care for the idea of Rayanne being outside for even a second or two, but he couldn't see another way out of this. Cooper and the others wouldn't be able to get close, not with the bullets flying, so escape in the cruiser might be their best bet.

Colt pulled up on the driver's side of the SUV, and he aligned the cruiser's back door with the SUV.

"Go," Roy said, motioning toward Rosalie since she was the nearest to the cruiser.

Rosalie gave a shaky nod, and with a firm grip on her gun, she opened the back door of the cruiser. The moment she was in, she scrambled to the side, motioning for Rayanne to follow her.

Despite the roar of the bullets, Rayanne hesitated. She was no doubt thinking a jolt like that could harm the baby. And it could. But staying put could do the same.

"Just take it as easy as you can," Blue told her.

Her gaze met his, and even in the darkness he could see the raw emotion in her eyes. Emotions that Rayanne rarely allowed anyone to see.

"You'll be right behind me," she said, and it wasn't a question. More like an order.

"I promise."

But the words had no sooner left his mouth than there was a flash of headlights behind them. The driver had on the high beams, and with the wisps of smoke still stirring around, it made it hard for Blue to see.

However, he could make out two men leaning out of the car windows. Both were armed.

And the car was headed across the pasture right toward them.

Chapter Eighteen

Rayanne got only a glimpse of the gunmen before Blue pushed her back down on the seat. It wasn't a second too soon, because the men started firing.

Not from a distance like before.

These shots were deafening, and they were no longer aiming at the tires. These ripped through the roof of the SUV. If the men were trying to scare them, it was working.

At least, it did for a few seconds.

Then the anger slammed through her. These idiots were putting all of them at risk—including the baby—and for what? Rayanne wished she could grab one of them and demand answers.

Since the SUV door was still open, Rayanne could see Rosalie on the backseat of the cruiser. She had a gun, but like her, Rosalie was having to stay down, too, since some of those shots were coming much too close to her.

So far the back windshield of the cruiser was holding, but it might not for long. It was bullet resistant, but eventually enough shots might be able to tear through it.

Roy threw open his door, positioning it so that it was aligned with the cruiser's door. It would give them a little more protection if they jumped to the cruiser. Still, Rayanne was worried about what could be a hard fall and the seconds that she'd be in the open. She and the baby would be a clean target for those bullets.

"Move over," Roy told Rosalie. "Get on the floor."

The moment her sister did that, Roy threw himself onto the backseat. Well, the edge of it, anyway. He was taking a huge risk by not staying behind cover.

And he was doing it for her.

Rayanne realized that when he motioned for her to jump. He was going to catch her while using his body to shield her.

"Do it," Blue said. "Now!"

She wanted to jump. But wanted Blue to be safe, too, and in that split second of hesitation, Rayanne heard a sound she didn't want to hear.

More tear gas came at them, the metal canister bouncing onto the SUV.

Everything seemed to happen at once. Roy reached for her, but the jolt sent him flying back. Not a jolt from the tear gas. This was another explosion, and the blinding white light from it flashed on the side of the SUV.

The blast vibrated through her body, pounding in her ears while the tear gas blistered her eyes. The coughing started again. Not just for her but for all of them.

And that wasn't the worst of their problems.

She figured those gunmen would soon be out of their vehicle and on their way to take them.

Or kill them.

"Go!" she managed to shout out to Colt. "Leave now!"

At least that way, Rosalie would be safe. Colt, Reed and her father, too.

But Colt didn't leave.

Instead he threw the cruiser into reverse and positioned it between their attackers and the SUV.

"I'm getting Rayanne out of here," Blue said to Colt through the phone. And that was the only warning Rayanne got before he took hold of her.

"Come on," Blue said to her in a whisper. He shoved his phone in his pocket, crawled over the seat and maneuvered her out the door.

"Try to stay quiet," Blue added. "They can't see us. And this is our best chance of getting out of here."

Staying quiet was next to impossible because of the coughing, but at least the combined sounds of the engines helped drown it out. Maybe it'd help enough for all of them to get to safety.

Blue didn't lead her toward the cruiser. Instead they headed toward the fence that fronted the ranch road.

"Rosalie," she said in a rough whisper. Rayanne didn't want to leave her sister back there.

"Colt will get her out," Blue promised.

Rayanne prayed that was true. Colt had put himself, Roy and Rosalie in danger to save Blue and her, and she hoped that didn't cost any of them their lives.

"Keep moving," Blue mumbled.

She did. There was no turning back now. Even when the shots started again, Rayanne knew she had no choice but to keep moving.

The fence was a good twenty yards away, but if Blue and she reached it, they'd have decent cover between the fence and the ditch. Plus, they wouldn't be that far from Tucker's house, and they could duck inside until Cooper and the others could make it to them.

Each step was a challenge. Mainly because her legs were shaking, and it felt as if someone had her heart and lungs in a vise. But each step also took them farther away from the tear-gas fog. The coughing faded, and Rayanne focused just on getting to safety.

Behind them the pace of the shots picked up. Not just from one gun, either. It sounded as if several different weapons were being fired. Maybe from Colt and Reed. If so, that could mean they were in the middle of another gunfight.

The moment they reached the fence, Blue hooked his arm around her to hoist her up onto the rungs. As a kid, she'd climbed this fence dozens of times, but it suddenly felt a mile high.

She glanced over her shoulder, hoping to see Colt's cruiser racing away from the tangle of smoke and vehicles. But it wasn't. Worse, those shots were still coming.

"We have to help them," Rayanne insisted.

"I will. Once I get you to safety."

Rayanne was about to argue with that, but a sound stopped her.

Footsteps.

Not coming from behind them but directly in front of them. Both Blue and she automatically took aim in that direction but didn't fire in case it was family or one of the ranch hands.

It wasn't.

"I wouldn't move if I were you," the man said.

It took Rayanne a moment to pick through the darkness and find him. Wearing dark clothes, he looked like a shadow when he glanced out from the side of Tucker's house.

Blue pulled her to the ground and fired at the mystery man, but the guy had already taken cover.

"Like I said, I wouldn't move if I were you," the man

repeated, not leaving the cover of the house. "You're both belly-down on some explosive devices, and if you so much as wiggle your toes, you'll be blown to bits."

BLUE AUTOMATICALLY FROZE.

He hadn't felt anything unusual when he'd dropped to the ground, but that didn't mean a bomb wasn't close enough to do some serious damage.

Of course, this could be yet another part of the ruse to get them to stay put.

If Rayanne and he didn't fight back, then they'd likely be kidnapped or harmed in some way. Because if this clown had wanted them dead, he would have already fired the shots to make that happen.

So what the heck was going on here?

Blue checked over his shoulder to make sure they weren't about to be ambushed from behind.

No one was anywhere near them.

But in the pasture he could see Colt driving the cruiser away from the stuck SUV. Rayanne's brother wasn't coming toward them but rather headed to the back of the pasture, and there were gunmen in pursuit.

Maybe Colt would manage to get Rosalie and the others to safety, but it was obvious Colt had his hands full. And Blue couldn't wait on Cooper and the ranch hands to come to their aid. He had to do something to get Rayanne and the baby to safety, too.

"What should we do?" Rayanne whispered.

Her voice was shaking a little, just enough for him to hear the fear in her voice. However, she had a firm lawman's grip on her gun, and she had it pointed directly at the man behind Tucker's house.

Blue looked around, still didn't spot an explosive, but

the man did have a gun trained on them. If they moved, he might feel compelled to start shooting. What Blue needed to do was figure out a way to defuse this situation or else wait until the guy left cover so he'd have a decent shot.

"What do you want?" Blue demanded from the man.

"Me? I don't want nothing. Well, other than for you to stay right where you are. Pretty soon you'll be somebody else's problem and not mine."

Even though the guy stayed hidden, Blue saw him mumble something and lean in toward his collar. No doubt where he had some kind of communication device.

"Someone else?" Blue repeated.

"The person who hired me to do this, and before you ask, I don't know who he is. Personally, I'd like to keep it that way. Knowing that kind of stuff can make a person a loose end."

Yeah, it could, especially if it was a federal agent trying to cover up his part in a string of felonies.

"Are you the one who took shots at us at the ranch?" Blue asked. He purposely kept his voice low, hoping the idiot would lean out from cover to better hear him.

He didn't.

The man stayed put. "Yeah," he finally answered. "Nothing personal."

"A man died," Blue reminded him.

"Still don't make it personal."

Blue had hoped he would just keep yakking, because it might help him figure out who was behind this. Plus, it might distract him enough for Blue to get off a shot.

"Someone's coming," Rayanne whispered. She tipped her head to the end of the ranch road. No headlights. But there was a dark vehicle creeping its way toward them.

"Cooper, maybe?" Blue asked.

"No. I don't recognize the car."

Now what? Blue didn't figure this was good news for Rayanne and him, since this was likely the "someone else" that the bozo had mentioned earlier.

And that someone else might have a different notion about keeping Rayanne and him alive.

"Stay down," Blue whispered to her.

"What are you planning to do?" Rayanne immediately snapped.

"First I'm going to try to shoot the guy hiding behind the house, and then you'll roll in the ditch so I can try to deal with whoever's in that car."

Even with just the moonlight, he could see the disapproval on her face. "And if there's really an explosive device?"

"That's why I want you to roll into the ditch. I'll cover you as best I can." Which he hoped was enough to keep Rayanne from being hurt.

"We don't have time to debate this," Blue reminded her, and tipped his head to the vehicle that was now only about twenty yards away.

"Y'all better not be thinking about doing anything stupid," the man warned them.

But Blue was already past the point of thinking about it. He took aim.

And fired.

The second the thick blast rang out, Rayanne went toward the ditch.

No explosion, thank God.

Blue held his breath, praying, and he got off another shot before he rolled in front of her. Both his shots missed, but it brought the man out from cover so he could return fire. Blue pulled the trigger again.

This time, he didn't miss.

"Move," Blue told Rayanne. He wanted to put as much distance between them and the approaching vehicle as he could.

But they didn't get far.

They'd made it only a few inches when both the front passenger's- and driver's-side doors opened. Two armed men jumped out, and they pointed their weapons right at Rayanne and him.

"Move and you die," one of the goons said. Both were heavily armed and were wearing bulletproof vests.

"I've heard that before," Blue snarled. "Heard there were explosives beneath us, too. That turned out to be a lie, didn't it?"

A lie Blue wished he'd figured out sooner so he could have maybe gotten Rayanne out of there.

If the man had any reaction to that, he didn't show it. He mumbled something into the grape-sized communicator clipped on his collar. "Drop your weapons, put your hands in the air and get up," he ordered. "Then walk slowly toward the car."

Blue huffed. "And why would we do that? You'll just gun us down."

"My boss doesn't want you dead," he assured them. Coming from him, it was no assurance at all, of course.

"Really?" Blue asked. He adjusted his position so that he was between Rayanne and the gunmen. "Because I'm getting the feeling that death is on the agenda here."

The goon had another mumbled conversation with the person on the other end of the communicator, and he glanced up the road, where there was another car coming toward them. He didn't react by turning his gun in that direction, which meant this wasn't a threat. It could be yet more hired guns.

"We can go ahead and shoot McCurdy," the man said to his partner the moment the second car pulled to a stop.

"No!" Rayanne shouted. And she would have scrambled in front of him if Blue hadn't stopped her.

"Why'd your boss change his mind?" Blue demanded. He got ready for the worst. If the bullets started flying, he'd just have to throw himself over Rayanne and pray that he got off the right shots before these two killed him.

There was more whispered conversation on the communicator. "He says he's getting tired of waiting for Miss McKinnon to cooperate."

"And why should I?" she fired back.

"Because it'll save McCurdy and you'll get to see your mother."

Blue heard her pull in a breath. "My mother?" she mumbled.

"You've got five seconds, Miss McKinnon," the man said, motioning with his gun.

Thank heaven Rayanne didn't make a move, but Blue braced himself for the fight that was about to come.

However, before the five seconds ticked off, the back door of the second car flew open, and someone stepped out.

"Either get in the car now," he growled, "or your mother and both of you die."

Chapter Nineteen

Rayanne glared at the man who'd just threatened them.
Wendell.

He glared right back at her, and she saw the sheer anger on his face that was no doubt mirrored on her own.

"You hurt my mother," Rayanne managed to say. Not easily. It felt as if someone had hold of her throat—her heart, too—making it hard to speak.

Blue tried to step in front of her. Trying to protect her as he'd done over and over again since this nightmare had begun. But Rayanne held her ground. She wanted to hear what this piece of slime had to say, and she wanted to look him in the eyes when he said it.

"What happened to Jewell was an accident," Wendell said as if it excused everything. "I wanted her very much alive and aware of what was going on, but the idiot who set the explosives didn't do a good job. He'll pay for that."

It tightened her throat even more to hear Wendell admit it aloud. It didn't matter that her mother wasn't supposed to have been hurt. She had been.

And Wendell would pay for that.

"The explosives were only meant to draw you out," Wendell added. He sat down on the edge of the backseat. "No one was supposed to have been hurt."

"Well, they were. Your hired gun could have killed the sheriff, your own grandson," Blue pointed out. Like her, he sounded as if he barely had a choke hold on the anger boiling inside him.

Blue's reminder turned Wendell's jaw to iron. "Like I said, he'll pay for his mistake. Just like Jewell will for killing my son."

Wendell glanced around him, no doubt looking for any signs that Cooper, Colt and the others were approaching.

And they would be.

The question was, would they get there in time to stop Wendell from kidnapping Blue and her?

"I know what you're thinking," Wendell said, his mouth bent into a near smile. "That your brothers or daddy will come to the rescue. Well, that's why we're waiting out here. For a little while, anyway."

"You want them dead," she mumbled.

"All of them. And I figure you're a delicious little piece of bait standing out here like this."

Sweet heaven. He was right. Despite the bad blood between Roy, her brothers and her, Roy had already tried to save her once tonight, and he would no doubt try to do it again.

"Killing Roy won't get back at Jewell," she tried.

Wendell lifted his shoulder. "You're wrong about that." He studied her, smiled. "Oh, you didn't know they've been chatting regularly. Ever since your sister's baby was stolen."

"I knew," she lied. "But conversations don't mean anything. After all, we're having one now, and that hardly means we're on friendly terms."

Even in the moonlight, she saw the anger flash in his

eyes. Wendell wanted only to hurt and didn't want to hear logic.

"Disarm them," Wendell snapped to his two goons. "Then get them inside the car."

Rayanne didn't budge and knew that if she got in, neither she nor Blue would be alive much longer.

"You intend to kill us to punish my mother," Rayanne said. She stepped to Blue's side, despite his attempts to stop her, and she slid her hand over her stomach.

She'd never used the baby card, but she would now. She would do whatever it took to survive so that her precious baby could survive, too.

"You really think you can kill a pregnant woman?" she demanded.

Wendell kept tossing her glares while he continued to keep watch around them. He didn't seem to notice the men making their way across the pasture, coming from the direction of the ranch house.

Cooper? Maybe some of the hands. Whoever they were, Rayanne hoped she could distract Wendell long enough for someone to get off a shot and send this monster to his maker.

Of course, it could be more of Wendell's hired guns out there, too, but Rayanne couldn't let her thoughts go there. Blue and she had to survive this for the sake of their baby, and while they were surviving, she had to make sure Wendell didn't take out anyone else to quench his need for revenge.

"I can do whatever it takes to avenge my son's murder," Wendell answered. "Besides, losing a grandchild will make the cut even deeper for Jewell."

And there it was, all spelled out for her. Rayanne

hadn't thought for one minute that she could actually negotiate with Wendell, but now she was sure.

"If you're going to kill us, anyway," she said, "then we might as well die on McKinnon land. You, too. Because I figure Blue and I can get off a shot before your men take us out. One shot's all we'll need to make sure you're dead."

The corner of Wendell's mouth lifted. "You always were a scrappy one. I'm sure Jewell will take it especially hard when she finds out you've been murdered."

"If Jewell lives," Blue tossed out there. "This could all be for no reason. That probably leaves a bitter taste in your mouth, huh?"

The two goons tightened their grips on their weapons, obviously waiting for their boss to give the word to put them in the car. That was when Blue and she would need to make their move. Hopefully by then, whoever was in the pasture would be in place to help them.

Wendell didn't respond to Blue's verbal jab. He just made another sweeping look around. Thank God whoever was in the pasture ducked down just in time. So that probably meant it was friend and not foe.

"For someone so hell-bent on wanting us dead," Blue went on, "you saved us by phoning in that there was a bomb in Rayanne's truck."

"I didn't do that. Ruby-Lee did."

Ruby-Lee, his caretaker, who'd been with Wendell when he'd come to the ranch. "Why would she try to help us?" Rayanne asked.

"Because she's a sap, that's why." The disdain was crystal clear in his voice. "She listened in on conversations she shouldn't have and thought one of my men had set the bomb. She figured I didn't know about it or

I would have done something to stop it. *Right*. She tried to stick her nose where it didn't belong, and now she'll pay for that, too."

If the woman wasn't already dead, she soon would be. That was yet another reason to stop this monster and try to rescue the woman who'd saved them.

"Did you set up Caleb and Woody?" Blue asked. Maybe as a distraction ploy so Wendell wouldn't notice the men in the pasture.

Wendell huffed. "Good grief, what does it matter now?"

Blue glared at him. "You did set them up. How?"

"You can hire hackers, good ones, for a lot less than explosives experts. I figured if I could set up the feds, then maybe I could walk away from this clear. But it's too risky. Once you two are dead, that leaves too many McKinnons who might be able to piece things together."

And not just McKinnons but Seth, too. No way would he drop this without getting to the truth.

"Take them to the hospital," Wendell said to the men. "Finish things there and send me photos."

"Photos?" Rayanne and Blue asked in unison.

"You don't think I'd wait around for your brothers to arrest me, do you?" Wendell didn't wait for an answer. "Not a chance. I'm headed out of the country, where I'll be well out of McKinnon reach. All that's left now is the grieving, and if Jewell lives, she'll be doing plenty of that. Because your deaths are just the start. I'll finish all of you off."

And with that death order, Wendell slammed the car door, and his driver hit the accelerator.

He was getting away.

Rayanne wanted to fire into the car to stop him, but she didn't get a chance.

The hired killers came right at Blue and her.

BLUE DIDN'T FIRE when the armed men charged them. Rayanne was still too close, practically right in the line of fire, and if he pulled the trigger, they almost certainly would, too.

Wendell had already given them orders to kill, so it wasn't much of a stretch to believe they would go ahead and murder Rayanne and him right here.

Or rather, try to kill them.

Blue wasn't going to let that happen.

He jumped in front of Rayanne, using his body to block them from getting to her. Both men rammed into him, one hitting his shoulder and nearly knocking the breath right out of Blue.

That didn't stop him.

Blue bashed one of the men on his head with his gun. It caused him to stagger back. Just enough. Blue was able to get off a shot.

The bullet hit the guy squarely in the chest, and even though he was wearing a Kevlar vest, the impact of the shot dropped him like a stone, and he gasped for breath. The injury wouldn't kill him, but it would incapacitate him enough that he wasn't a threat.

Blue hoped.

He kicked the man's gun from his hand and turned to deflect the other goon when he jumped right at him. Blue's gun was out of position to fire.

But Rayanne's wasn't.

She fired, her shot also going into the second man's

chest. She reached down to disarm the man, who was now groaning and clutching his chest, but a sound stopped her.

It was the cruiser, coming from the other end of the ranch road. Colt had obviously managed to circle around. The moment he pulled the cruiser to a stop, both Reed and he jumped out, training their weapons on the men.

"Wendell's the one behind this," Blue said.

"And he's getting away," Rayanne added, already heading for the hired guns' car, probably because it was blocking the road, and the cruiser wouldn't be able to get past it.

Rosalie and Roy got out of the cruiser, aiming their guns at the men on the ground, too, and Blue had to run to catch up with Rayanne.

"Don't you try to stop me," she warned him, and he could tell from that determined look in her eyes that stopping her wasn't even possible. "You know if Wendell gets away, that the attacks won't stop. He'll just keep hiring people to come after us."

Blue cursed. Because it was true.

"Can you handle this?" Blue asked Reed.

The deputy nodded and motioned toward Cooper and some ranch hands who were making their way toward them. "I've got plenty of backup."

Colt nodded and got behind the wheel. Blue took over at shotgun, and Rayanne jumped into the backseat behind her brother. Colt threw the car into reverse and hit the gas while they buckled up.

"Wendell's on his way to the airport," Blue told Colt. "What's the fastest way there?"

"This way," Colt answered the moment they reached the end of the ranch road and turned right. He spun out onto the highway and put the pedal to the metal.

Blue couldn't see Wendell's car, but then, they'd had a head start.

Colt took out his phone and punched in some numbers. "Call the airport," he told whoever answered.

Blue had never been to the airport but knew it was just a small strip, mainly used for private planes and crop dusting. It was likely that Wendell would be the only "customer" at this time of night.

"No answer at the airport," Colt said a few moments later, and he added some profanity. "Either Wendell's paid them off or he's fixed it so they can't answer."

Which could mean he'd had them killed.

It sickened Blue to think of just how far Wendell would go to get back at Jewell. Heaven knew how many lives he'd ended or put in danger, and two of those lives were in the backseat. Blue caught a glimpse of her in the rear-view mirror.

"Hurry," was all she said when their gazes met.

Colt did.

He took the curvy highway as fast as he could and requested backup and roadblocks. Maybe, just maybe, it'd be enough, because Blue didn't want him and Rayanne to live the rest of their lives looking over their shoulders.

"The turn for the airport's just a half mile up on the left," Rayanne told Blue.

Colt probably had no plans to slow down until the last possible second. However, when he rounded a sharp curve, he had to slam on his brakes.

Because Wendell's car was there.

Smack-dab in the middle of the road.

The cruiser's brakes squealed on the asphalt, and Colt turned the steering wheel to avoid a head-on collision and came to a stop.

But before any of them could even take aim, Wendell's driver fired at them through his already-opened window.

The shots blasted into their car, but thankfully, none of them hit them. Unfortunately, the glass cracked and webbed, making it next to impossible to see.

Not good.

Because Wendell's driver stopped firing and hit the gas, no doubt ready to turn the car around and speed away.

"Not this time," Rayanne mumbled. She leaned out the window on the driver's side.

Blue leaned out on his side.

And they both fired.

Not at the car itself, because it was likely bullet resistant. They aimed for the tires before the driver could move.

It was pitch-dark, hardly the best conditions to stop a killer, but Blue and Rayanne kept firing.

Wendell's driver managed to right the angle of the car, and he hit the accelerator again. Colt went in pursuit with Rayanne and Blue still firing.

Within seconds, both the driver and Colt had the vehicles flying down the road.

"Get back in and put on your seat belt," Blue shouted to Rayanne.

She didn't listen. They both fired shots, each of them slamming into the rear windshield of the car. Blue immediately saw the car fishtail, and almost like a swoosh of breath, it left the road.

And slammed into some trees.

Colt hit his brakes, trying to turn the car around so they would have a better shot if Wendell or his driver came out firing.

But they didn't.

The sound of the blast ripped through Wendell's car. A fireball that thundered through the night.

Blue had a split-second realization that there must have been explosives in the vehicle. Another split second to remember that Rayanne was still leaning out the window.

And the fiery debris came right at them.

Chapter Twenty

Rayanne didn't have time to react, but Blue certainly did. He caught on to her and pulled her back inside the car.

It wasn't a second too soon.

A piece of Wendell's car came flying right at her and skidded off the top of their vehicle.

"Get us out of here!" Blue shouted.

Colt did. He hit the gas, and they sped away just as there was a second blast. The impact shook their own car and blew the rest of Wendell's vehicle to smithereens.

"Explosives," Colt mumbled. "I'm betting Wendell hadn't counted on that happening."

No, but Wendell had obviously been using bombs right and left to get to them. They'd been lucky that Wendell and his goons hadn't succeeded. Well, not with them, anyway.

Her mother was a different story.

"We need to get to the hospital," she insisted.

Thankfully, neither Blue nor Colt argued with her. While he continued to drive, Colt took out his phone to make some calls, and Blue climbed over the seat and dropped down next to her. He pulled her into his arms and then checked her over from head to toe.

"Are you okay?" he asked.

"I wasn't hurt," she settled for saying. "You?"

Blue settled for giving her the same lie.

They'd gotten lucky. None of them had been physically hurt, but her mother had been and maybe others. Wendell hadn't cared how many people he involved in his revenge scheme.

"Wendell's dead," she said. No way could he have survived that. Rayanne hadn't been sure how she would feel about that, but she felt only relief. This way, he couldn't hurt her or her family again.

Unless...

"We need to make sure Wendell didn't somehow make it out of the car before it exploded," she mumbled.

Blue nodded and took out his phone, but Colt said something before Blue could dial.

"Reed's taking the two henchmen to jail," Colt relayed to them after he finished his call. "Cooper's getting a CSI team out to the site of Wendell's explosion."

Good.

Rayanne wouldn't breathe easier until she knew for sure.

"I've got a call into the hospital to get an update on Jewell," Colt continued. "Dad's bringing Rosalie to the hospital, too. They're not far behind us."

It had become second nature for Rayanne to scowl anytime Roy was mentioned, but it was hard to scowl at a man who'd tried to save her life.

Ditto for Blue.

Of course, she'd quit scowling at him about the same time they'd landed in bed together. Later they'd need to talk about that and hopefully figure out where to go from here. For now, though, her priority was her mother.

Colt and Blue continued to make calls, each of them

asking for reports and updates. Rayanne considered making one of her own to try to personally speak to a nurse or a doctor at the Clay Ridge hospital, but part of her was terrified of what she might learn.

Her nerves were raw, right at the surface, and with the adrenaline still rocketing through her, she couldn't take any more bad news tonight.

"That was Agent Hale," Blue explained when he finished another call. "He's looking into the possibility that Wendell hired someone to set up Caleb and Woody with those illegal weapons."

"I don't think it's just a possibility," she said. "I'm pretty sure Wendell was telling the truth. In fact, he was bragging about all the criminal things he'd done.... Oh, God. What about Ruby-Lee? He said he was going to have her killed."

"One of the Clay Ridge deputies is on his way to her place now," Colt volunteered.

Rayanne said a quick prayer for the woman. Ruby-Lee had tried to stop a monster and now might have paid for it with her life.

With every muscle in her body rock hard, she was surprised when she felt the little flutters in her stomach. Except this was slightly more than a flutter.

It felt like a kick.

"What's wrong?" Blue immediately asked. "You gasped."

Had she? Rayanne hadn't even noticed, but she took his hand and placed it on her belly. "The baby."

She hadn't expected Blue to be able to feel it, but it was as if the baby wanted to prove a point.

That he or she was alive and well.

The next thump landed right against Blue's palm.

He laughed. It was laced with nerves and fatigue, but it also made her smile.

"Uh, are you two okay?" Colt asked, eyeing them in the rearview mirror.

"Just parent stuff," Blue answered.

Despite the horrible nightmare they'd just left behind and the one they might still have to face at the hospital, it felt good to share this moment with Blue.

He kissed her.

Until he touched his mouth to hers, she hadn't realized just how much she needed it.

Needed *him*.

Rayanne didn't pull away from him when the kiss ended. She stayed there in his arms.

"You know I'm not going away when this is over, right?" he asked.

There was already too much buzzing through her head for her to try and think that through. Was he talking about moving closer to her, or was this about something else?

"What about your job?" she asked, because that was a lot safer than asking about that "something else."

He pointed to the Clay Ridge city-limits sign that was just ahead. "I can get reassigned here or else to Sweetwater Springs."

So they were talking about distance. Rayanne wasn't sure how she felt about that.

Okay, she was.

Yes, she wanted Blue closer. She wanted him to be a big part of their baby's life. But it terrified her to realize that she wanted more from him.

Blue's hand went to her stomach. "You just gasped again."

"Not because of the baby," she mumbled.

Blue stared at her, obviously waiting for her to explain that, but Rayanne had no idea how to even start.

"I'm in love with you, Blue," she blurted out.

That was it?

The best she could do?

Yes, her head was fuzzy, but judging from Blue's pole-axed look, she should have eased into it better. Or maybe she shouldn't have brought it—

He kissed her, cutting off the rest of that thought. In fact, it cut off a lot of things. Her fears. Doubts.

Common sense.

And for that moment, that one wonderful moment, Rayanne got totally wrapped up in his arms and in his kiss.

"Uh, I hate to interrupt," Colt said, "but we're at the hospital."

Oh, mercy. Yes, she was losing it, but the sight of the hospital brought it all home. Her mother could be inside there dying, and she had to focus on that and not the punch from one of Blue's kisses.

"We'll table the conversation for now," Blue said, still eyeing her with some emotion that she thought might be caution.

They got out of the car, and because the three of them were still on edge, they all put their hands over their weapons. Rayanne was more than a little relieved when she didn't see any need for concern.

Good thing, too, since there was more than enough concern in the waiting room.

The moment they stepped through the doors, a lanky dark-haired man wearing a badge approached them. "I'm Deputy Hawks from the Clay Ridge County sheriff's office."

Of course, she'd expected law enforcement to be there. And it wasn't just the deputy, either. She spotted a county jail guard she recognized from her visits to her mother.

"Is there any update on my mother?" Rayanne immediately asked.

Deputy Hawks shook his head. "She's still in surgery."

He motioned for them to follow him and took them into a smaller, private waiting room just up the hall. "Figured you'd be more comfortable in here."

Blue and Rayanne mumbled a thanks, and Colt stepped to the side of the room when he got another call.

The deputy took a seat near the door. "Sheriff Braddock's on the way to the scene of his grandfather's explosion. After that, he'll assist moving the prisoners to the jail over in Sweetwater Springs."

Good. She had enough on her plate without having to deal with another Braddock tonight. From all accounts, Sheriff Aiden Braddock was an upright peace officer, but she'd had her fill of Wendell and his entire family.

"You should sit," Blue said, and he tried to get her to do that, but her body didn't cooperate. She was suddenly too wired to do anything but pace.

Blue paced with her.

Now that she could actually see him, she looked him over to make sure he wasn't injured.

He was.

There were new scrapes and bruises on his face and hands. Probably on the rest of his body, too. That was when she realized she probably looked just as bad. She pushed her hair from her face, causing Blue to smile.

"You're beautiful," he said as if reading all the doubts in her mind.

She nearly pointed out that it was a lie, but Rayanne found herself smiling. Briefly, anyway. "Thanks."

"So, you're in love with me?" he asked.

Okay, here was where she could say it'd all been a mistake. Something she'd blurted out in the heat of the moment. Then things could go back to the way they were before.

But she didn't want that.

Rayanne nodded. "Sorry. I know that only complicates things."

He squinted one eye, gave her a funny look. "It could, I suppose. Especially if that means you'd add me to the list of people you'd take a bullet for."

It did indeed add him to the list. Except the list was sort of on hold right now because the baby had to come first.

"You won't take a bullet for me," he insisted. "But I appreciate the thought. I'd take a bullet for you, too."

That made her heart soar. And fall. "That list wasn't meant to be a nightmare come true," she insisted. "No more taking bullets."

Maybe that would include no more bullets being fired at them, too.

"No more," Blue mumbled.

Anything else he was about to add to that was cut off when Roy and Rosalie came rushing into the room. Rosalie ran to her, pulled her into her arms.

"Anything yet?" her sister asked.

But Rayanne had to shake her head. She let go of her sister so she could face Roy. There was way too much pain between them for her to pull him into a hug, but she was careful not to issue him her standard glare.

"Thank you," she mumbled. "For everything."

Roy nodded. Blinked hard as if blinking back tears and nodded again. "Glad I was there."

That made Rayanne have to blink hard, too.

Thankfully, Colt gave them a reprieve when he finished his call. "The deputy found Ruby-Lee," he relayed to them. "She was tied up at Wendell's house. Wendell told her his men would be there to take care of her once they finished with Rayanne and Blue."

Thank God those men were now in custody and couldn't harm her. Rayanne made a mental note to call the woman and thank her when this ordeal was over.

And once Blue and she had worked out the possible complications of her *I love you* and the near tears she'd just shed over Roy.

"Cooper got a look inside what was left of Wendell's car," Colt went on. "Two bodies. One of them was definitely Wendell."

So it was really over.

Well, the danger was, anyway.

But the damage to her family might have already been done, and the proof of that stepped into the doorway. Not a doctor but rather a nurse, according to her name tag.

"The doctor will be here in just a few minutes to give you an update," the woman said. "But I wondered if any of you have B-negative blood?"

Oh, God. That sounded serious. "Why?" Rayanne asked.

"It's the patient's type. We're running short, and we usually ask family to donate in situations like this." Her attention landed on Rayanne's stomach. "Can't take a donation from you, though. Nor you," she added, eyeing Blue's injuries.

"I'm O positive, anyway," Blue said.

Rayanne shook her head. "And I'm not B negative. I'm A positive."

Rosalie mumbled the same.

So did Roy.

"I'm B negative," Colt said, stepping ahead of them. He suddenly didn't look too pleased that he and his estranged mother shared the same blood.

Of course, Rayanne was no doubt looking similar about Roy's and her blood connection. It was strange how things worked out like that.

Colt followed the nurse, but he'd been gone only a few seconds when someone else stepped into the doorway.

Seth.

He made it to Rosalie and her in what seemed to be one giant step, and he pulled them both into his arms. "You're both hardheaded for trying to come here." But he brushed kisses on their foreheads and looked at Blue.

"How many thanks do I owe you for watching out for them?" Seth asked.

"None. No thanks necessary. I have my own pretty high stake in all of this." Blue put his hand over Rayanne's stomach. Then eased her back to him. No forehead kiss. He gave her one of his winners right on the mouth.

Seth smiled. Well, sort of. Her brother wasn't actually the smiling sort, but since he wasn't scowling, that was close enough.

Blue tipped his head to Roy. "But we both owe him some thanks. He helped get us out of there. Colt, too."

That caused Seth's usual scowl, but Seth softened—just a little—when he nodded, a gesture that appeared to be a thank-you. Whatever it was, no one had time to dwell on it, because the man in scrubs stepped into the room.

"I'm Dr. Dayton." And with just those few words, he

had everyone's attention. "I did Jewell's surgery to remove some shrapnel from her abdomen. Some of it was deeply embedded, and she lost a lot of blood, but no vital organs were hit. She'll be fine."

Rayanne hadn't even known she was holding her breath until her lungs started to ache. The relief was instant, her breath whooshing out, and she practically collapsed into Blue's waiting arms.

"I need to see her," Rayanne managed to say.

The doctor glanced at all of them. Finally nodded. Just when Rayanne thought she was going to have to get ugly and demand it.

"But keep it short," the doctor warned them, and he motioned for the family to follow him. He led them farther down the hall to the surgical-recovery suites.

Rayanne spotted another guard, a reminder that her mother would be returned to jail as soon as possible. She held her breath again when the doctor opened the door, and she got her first glimpse of her mother.

She was too pale, was Rayanne's first reaction. Too weak looking with all those machines hooked up to her.

But then Jewell opened her eyes and smiled. There was an IV in her arm, but she waggled her fingers, motioning for them to come closer.

They did. All of them. Including Roy. But he stayed back while Rosalie, Seth and she gave their mom gentle kisses on the cheek. The smile lingered on her mouth a little longer until she studied Blue's and Rayanne's fresh injuries.

"Who did this?" Jewell asked, but she turned her attention to Roy for an answer.

"Wendell." And that was all he said. All that needed to

be said. With just the man's name, her mother no doubt knew the motive.

Revenge.

"He's dead," Rayanne added. "He can't hurt us anymore."

Of course, the upcoming murder trial could. But Rayanne pushed that aside. For now, her mother was okay, and that was enough.

"Blue," Jewell said, motioning for him to come closer, too. Her grip seemed as fragile as fine crystal, but she caught on to his hand and pulled him down for a kiss on the cheek. "You'll take good care of Rayanne and my grandbaby."

"I will," Blue said without hesitation. "In fact, I was just about to ask Rayanne to marry me. Figured this was a good time and place to do it."

Rayanne choked on the gulp of air she sucked in. "This is the first I've heard about a proposal."

"Because you've missed a boatload of signals," Seth grumbled. "The guy's in love with you. I'm not sure why, but he is, so my advice is to say yes before the doctor boots us out of here."

"Are you?" Rayanne asked, sounding so stunned that it caused Blue to laugh.

Mercy, she loved that laugh, almost as much as she loved him.

Blue hooked his arm around her waist, pulled her closer. "Of course I'm in love with you. And I love our baby and the life we're going to have together." He paused to kiss her.

Oh, heck. It was one of those mind-scrambling kisses that robbed her of the ability to think. Not good. She figured this was a time when she needed all of her wits.

"Well, I will love our life together if you say yes," Blue amended.

Rayanne nearly glanced at Rosalie, Seth and her mom to see what their reactions were.

But then she realized it didn't matter.

Yes, she wanted them to approve. Wanted them to be happy for her, but she knew in her heart there was only one thing that would make her truly happy.

And he was standing right in front of her.

Rayanne didn't make him wait. "Yes."

Or at least, she got most of the word out before Blue kissed her again. Everything fell into place.

Rayanne pulled back, meeting her mother's gaze. Then she glanced around the rest of the room. This wasn't about rifts, the trial or injuries. It was about one thing.

Family.

Rayanne put her arms around the man she loved and pulled Blue to her for another kiss.

* * * * *

MILLS & BOON®

'Tis the season to be daring...

The perfect books for all your glamorous Christmas needs come complete with gorgeous billionaire bad-boy heroes and are overflowing with champagne!

These fantastic 3-in-1s are must-have reads for all Modern™, Desire™ and Modern Tempted™ fans.

Get your copies today at
www.millsandboon.co.uk/Xmasmod